PERFIDIOUS

DONNA NEWLANDS

To purchase previous books or to contact the author,
please visit:www.doonamoolands.com

Copyright © 2025 Donna Newlands
ISBN: 978-1-923078-76-5

Published by Vivid Publishing
A division of Fontaine Publishing Group
P.O. Box 948, Fremantle
Western Australia 6959
www.vividpublishing.com.au

 A catalogue record for this
book is available from the
National Library of Australia

For Phil and Chantelle.

Loving you both through your health battles
while you fight the good fight.

Acknowledgements

To get this book on your bookshelf, there is a list of people who made it possible.

Thank you to my son, Rhys, for the first readthrough of the manuscript and feedback.

A huge thank you to my very close friend and Editor, Margaret Jenkinson, for her great attention to detail and for questioning *everything*.

Thank you to both of my children, Jaqueline and Rhys, for nitpicking word choices, being my sounding board, bouncing ideas around and setting me straight when required (*extremely rare*).

Thank you to Andrea Morgan, Leading Senior Constable of Victoria Police, for her advice, contributions and explanations of the sequence and chronology of police procedure.

Thank you to Fontaine Publishing Group for getting my book prepped, printed, published and everything in between.

Finaly, thank you to my immediate and extended family, my heroes, for the love and support you continuously show me. You make my world sparkle.

1

Oh Brother

Brian

The shrill sound of the kettle whistle pulls me out of my memories. I was daydreaming, lost in a memory when I was in the tractor with Dad, driving to the north field to fix the broken fence. Dad was whistling a Marty Robbins song; I recognised *The Hanging Tree*. As dad whistled, my memory filled in the lyrics. The sun was high in the sky. I felt warm and happy, as I always did with Dad. After we had finished the fence, we drove back to the shed, then dad opened a cold long neck bottle of beer and poured out two glasses of the ale. I miss dad – he was my best mate, and the only one who didn't shame me after my accident or make fun of me for being slow. Dad and I sometimes went into the city to watch the footy in winter and ate hot pies and had a beer at the pub on the way home. We went to the cricket in summer and ate hot chips. The Boxing Day test was my favourite time spent with dad. Dad was never the same after Mum died. He was always just a little sad. I'm ok that he's gone because he's with Mum now. But I miss him.

As I jiggle the tea bag, I look up and see through the kitchen window. The lace curtains soften the view in which I see David carrying something small, wrapped in a towel. I wonder if it is a dead animal. My brother is broken, and I knew this when he was very young. I knew it when I saw what he did to those little birds. He is smart and clever, but something is wrong with him. He has a sickness. I once saw David drag something on a big tarp out from the underground bunker, the one I'm never allowed to go into, and put it through the tree lopper on the farm. I thought it was a pig from where I was standing at the window because it was far away, and the skin was pink.

David likes to see things hurt. He likes to watch the pain of things he hurts, and it makes him smile in a very odd way. Sometimes he touches himself down there while he hurts the animals.

He hurt Brittany too. She was his girlfriend. I saw him hurt her, but she went away and never came back. She was very kind to me, and she made chocolate chip cookies. I wonder if Brittany ran away or if my brother made her 'go away forever' like the pig. I don't really think it was a pig.

I asked David once what he was putting in the tree lopper, but David said it was just an old shop mannequin and to stop spying. I wasn't spying, I was curious and now I'm worried. I saw that mannequin come out the other side spraying bright red and bloody, so I knew it wasn't a mannequin. It was always too hard to think about, so I stopped being curious and went somewhere else in my head when I heard the tree lopper start up.

My tea is too hot and burns my mouth. I watch the bunker through the tendrils of steam coming off my hot tea in the cold kitchen. David walks across the grass holding the end of a black hose and disappears into the bunker again – he is dressed in big coveralls that look like a spacesuit. I wonder what he is doing. I can hear the air compressor – he's spraying something down there. I put the tea down and decide to quickly run out to look at what is wrapped in the towel. I'm fast and make the journey across the lawn quickly. I can still hear the air compressor which means David is down there. I carefully unwrap the bundle.

2

Disruption of Bliss

Katrina

My alarm brutally yanks me from a blissful slumber, a rare achievement these past weeks. I silence it with a none-too-gentle prod. Jack rolls over and faces the window away from me, taking the sheets and doona with him. The cold air seeps in and curls its tendrils around my exposed right side. Jack's migration across the bed lets loose a noxious gas lethal enough to be considered for chemical warfare. Gagging, I propel out of bed.

I'm dressed and out the door in seven minutes. Fist pump for me. As I lace my runners, I look across the front garden through the foggy haze and can barely make out the neighbour's yard. Checking the temperature on my phone, I am startled that it is a mere 1°C. I have donned fingerless fitness gloves, a precautious security blanket put in place after an awkward spill last autumn on a busy street, witnessed by a host of cars banked at traffic lights. Since that humiliating cock-up, I don't sprint… I jog sensibly, with gloves on.

Out on the street, my shins, arms, and face ache with the cold; my fingernails throb in their nail beds and my eyes ache in their sockets. I know I'll be fine once I start running so I ignore the screaming of my exposed skin and push forward. The gate across the road whines on its hinges in the eerie dawn quiet and I spy our elderly neighbours exit their property for a morning walk, rugged up and hunched against the cold morning air. I hope for non-detection and consider an about face to run up the street in the opposite direction, but Glenda has detected me and yells across the road, offensively loud in the quiet street, "Good morning, Katrina! Aren't you cold?" Well, duh! Get any closer and I won't be responsible if you lose an eye to a nipple. I smile winningly and shrug. This isn't my first time, love. She continues with her early morning jocularity, "We're off to Antarctica. You look like you're off to Bali, ha!" Miles guffaws at his wife's humour. Oh Lordy, older folk think they're so funny. Feeling obliged to join in the jovial exchange, I force a giggle and end the pointless chit-chat, "Ha, that's funny. I'll be warm by the time I get to the end of the street." A little wave, a suppressed eyeroll and a smile that shows all my teeth; I set off at a jogging pace.

The light emitted from the streetlamps is hazy and subdued, lending an eerie ghostly quality to the quiet streets. As I dart across the road between traffic lights, I am almost taken out by a van coasting through the chicanes, camouflaged in the fog, and not sporting headlights in the gloom. I, on the other hand, have on a fluorescent yellow tank top and startle the driver into over-steering through the last chicane and flipping on the missing beams, almost blinding me in the process.

As I run through the park, the fog is thick and obscures everything, leaving the trees and children's play equipment shrouded in muted tones of grey. The streets are quiet this morning and I am mostly alone with my thoughts. I avoid the main running track after last week's unpleasant encounter. On that day, as I was running down the steps to get to the track, an older gent ran up two of the stairs towards me then turned his back, looking left and right up and down the track before turning sideways and whipping out his member, pissing like a racehorse over the rail into the bush below. I was gob-smacked and just stood glaring at him, my face tight and etched in horror as the aroma of hot gum leaves and urine wafted up. He lazily drifted his gaze up to my face and, startled, matched my horror. Unfortunately, he couldn't seem to stem his stream and was trying to turn away from me awkwardly without urinating all over his shoes. I turned and ran back up the stairs, sprinting all the way home. Jack and the kids roared with laughter as I recounted the scene and remarked on my uncanny luck in encountering the weird.

I am already sweating with exertion and creating a mental list of tasks for my Saturday and considering what to cook for dinner tonight. Jack's usual line, "I don't cook, I create" provokes an eye roll. I ease into a comfortable rhythm in time to the beat in my ears and adjust my breathing to sit in this zone for the next forty minutes.

By the time I return home, the birds are noisy, and the fog is burning off to what promises to be a sunny winter day. The heater has been on for a good hour and the house is gloriously warm and welcoming. Jack is sipping coffee at the breakfast bar and making his way through three slices of toast, heavily laden with jam. He is dressed like he's going out, such a handsome man. He greets me without looking up from his phone, "Hey, how was your run?" Squatting to unlace my runners, I reply, "Bloody freezing! Hardly anyone out this morning, though."

Still not making eye contact, Jack's retort is muffled by masticated jammy toast, "That's because everyone else is having a sleep in on a Saturday morning." He finally looks up from his smart phone, "I have to go in to work again today."

Shit! We were supposed to go car hunting today to replace my T-Rex with something from the current epoch. It's hard to keep the disappointment out of my voice, "Really? On a Saturday?"

"Yeah, we're working on something really big for presentation at the meeting on Monday." This is announced like I know what the hell is happening on Monday. I remind him about our planned day to go car shopping. A light bulb moment for Jack, he forgot, "Aw shit, I'm sorry, honey. Can we go next Saturday?" Do I have a bloody choice?

The troops descend the stairs like a heard of elephants and appear in the kitchen fully dressed. Surprised, I query "Why are you all up so early… and on a Saturday?" Lucy delivers an eye roll "We're having breakfast at *Gino's* before we go to the cinema. Remember we're going to the movies? You bought us the tickets!" Oh yes, I forgot. My three kids, despite their age, are all nuts for the Marvel Universe. They load up on snacks and depart in a noisy gust. Jack turns off his phone and puts it on the bench. "I'll brush my teeth and be off. You'll have the house to yourself today. Lucky you!" Yeah, lucky me.

Not ready for a coffee, I put the kettle on and pull out a teacup and toss in the bag. Jack's phone lights up on the bench beside me; I absently glance at it. A message through a social media app has popped up. Before it disappears, I see it's a message from someone called 'Jason' and a little bit of the message shows "Hurry up! I'm naked…"

My eyebrows spike and the blood throbs in my head. My heart thuds in my chest and I wonder what this is. I step away from the bench and listen down the hall. I can still hear Jack's electric toothbrush whining in our ensuite, so I step back and turn the phone on without logging in. The screen lights up and the message is still there. "Hurry up! I'm naked …" and definitely from someone called Jason. Who is Jason and what the hell is the rest of the message? Hurry up, I'm naked-ly running the streets? I'm naked and in the loo with no paper? … I need to read the rest of the message, but I don't want to spy on Jack.

I can hear him returning so I turn on my heel and make great pretence of making my cup of tea. He picks up his phone and out of the corner of my eye I see him glance up at me. I am very busy making my tea… dunk, dunk, dunk-ing the teabag in my cup. My face feels hot and flushed and I have to physically check my breathing. Jack sidles up and slides his arms around my waist, planting a kiss on my cheek. "I'm sorry, honey. I'll make it up to you." I turn around and loop my arms around his neck as I am supposed to; I'm disappointed but I love you, my reaction says. Not *who the hell is Jason and why is he telling you he's naked?* He breaks the intimate moment with a peck on the cheek, even though my mouth is right there, and leaves. Nice.

I retreat into the living room. Like a fresh scab, I pick at the edges of the partial message while I sip my tea. Winnie the Wondercat pads into the room and leaps onto the couch beside me. A complicated grooming technique involving callisthenics and flexibility which only a cat possesses ensues. I decide to distract myself with a word puzzle. I cruise down the stairs to the home office and find our shared tablet and turn it on.

I first click on the social media platform messages and see that Jack is logged on. The message is up as soon as I go in.

Jason: "Hurry up! I'm naked and I want you RIGHT NOW!"

I hold my breath as my head threatens to detonate. My heart rate escalates.

Jack: "Hold on, I'm just leaving. What's with the capitals?"

Jason: "That's me shouting."

Jack: "I told you not to message me. She could have seen it."

My breathing hitches.

Jason: "Sorry. Please be here soon."

Jack: "I'm on my way. I'll be there in 10."

I sag in my seat, devastated, and confused. Who the hell is Jason? Is my husband secretly gay? Wouldn't I know if he was gay? My book club is currently reading a novel about a woman who comes home unexpectedly to find her husband having sex with another man. I don't want to identify with the main character. What the hell is going on?

My hands are shaking, and my heart is thudding in my chest. Scrolling up through a couple of previous messages, most seem mundane and harmless when suddenly I am confronted with a dick-pic. There it is, Jack's member, larger than life, captured in all its turgid glory in a digital picture. Oh God. All the air is sucked out of my lungs, and I wonder how much more I really want to discover today. Dubiously, I scroll a bit further up through the messages, and I see a female nude from the neck to the crotch, splayed legs leaving nothing to the imagination. Clearly, Jason is a female, and she is wearing a pendant I recognise; a tiny forget-me-not flower from her wedding bouquet, captured in resin. The pendant belongs to Anne, Jack's colleague and the wife of his best mate, Shaun. Anne is my close friend too. I feel sick.

The tablet clatters onto the desk and I run for the loo, dry retching several times before I'm rewarded with the bounty. My tea looks very unappetising swirling in the bowl. I tear off some squares of toilet paper and wipe my mouth. I feel hot and sweaty, and my stomach is still roiling. Why oh why had he left himself logged in. I wish I didn't see that.

I don't know how to react to this information. I don't know what to say or do about it, so I go back to the desk, log out of the tablet, and wipe off my fingerprints… I have clearly been watching too much real crime. I put the tablet back in the desk drawer and return to the kitchen upstairs. I feel like I'm having an out-of-body body experience. I can't focus on anything and I'm wandering aimlessly around the house, picking things up and putting them down. This cannot be happening. Why am I not feeling rage or sadness? I'm just numb.

Mechanically, I write up my shopping list and force myself to put the whole thing in my back pocket until I can think of what to do or how to sort it out. I want to feel something other than this shocked numbness. I will not go back and look for more, I will not spy. I will wait for him to tell me.

I need a distraction from this secret Jack is keeping that threatens to ruin my marriage, so I jump into the shower and prepare to distract myself accordingly.

3

Sleeping with the Enemy

Felicity

As I lie awake beside the seething mass of anger to whom I am wed, my cheek smarting and my anxiety blistering, I wonder how I can maintain this charade. His breathing is calm, but I know he's awake and I don't want to poke the bear. I want to cry, but I don't want to encourage another outburst. I must hold it all in until he falls asleep, so I can sneak out of bed, go downstairs and cry in the shower.

Damien doesn't know how to process his feelings, especially remorse, and his only acceptable emotion is anger. I don't even understand how tonight's outburst happened. He walked into the kitchen after work as I was preparing dinner, my eyes smarting from the onion I was cutting. He glared at me and barked, "what are you having a sook about?" startling me.

"I'm cutting up an onion" I replied evenly, pointing the tip of the knife at the offending vegetable sitting innocently on the cutting board.

He jabs a finger violently in my face, "Hey! You don't speak to me like that!" I don't even know what I said. My heart rate escalates as I try to think of a way to quickly defuse his anger.

"Sorry, I didn't mean to sound rude. My eyes are burning."

He looked me up and down like I'm something disgusting, grunted, and stormed past me. It took the entire time he was in the shower to calm myself and get on top of my anxiety.

When he re-entered the kitchen, I had a careful expression of calm serenity fixed to my face. He walked right up to me and kissed me with all the fire and intensity that started our journey all those years ago. I am disgusted that my body betrays me and reacts with desire. He left me breathless, and it is this that feeds his ego. He grabbed himself a beer from the fridge and wandered downstairs to the man cave to watch a television show about flipping houses, going by the dialogue filtering acoustically up the stairs.

* * * * *

He complimented me on dinner as we cleaned the kitchen, side by side; he was the perfect gentleman. He talked about his day, and I answer his questions about mine as elaborately as I could but only mentioning the names of women or men who he knows are fat, ugly, and not a threat. I have a very boring office job and work in the accounts department. Damien is insanely jealous. He loves me, he says, and his jealousy is a sign of just how deep that love is. This is Damien justifying his misplaced anger when someone looks at me, his possession, with appreciation.

I have watched in horror as he smashed up the face of my high school friend. We saw Trent in the car park behind a bar one evening. Trent was happy to see me and gave me a warm embrace. We used to be so close, especially in year twelve. I knew Trent had a crush on me, but he would rather have me as a friend than nothing, so he settled for that. If I had known what my marriage would become, I would have encouraged Trent's gentle love, rather than the abusive marriage I won. It wasn't always like this… but these last couple of years have been hard.

The hug with Trent was only brief but it was affectionate. He turned to shake Damien's hand, but Damien kept his hands in his pockets and glared at Trent with a menacing scowl. Trent was surprised but not after any trouble, so he backed away and said, "Hey dude, didn't mean to cause trouble. See you another time, Liss."

Damien's jaw bunched and a moment later he slammed his fist into Trent's face. Trent stumbled back a few paces and yelled, "Hey, what the fuck man? It was just a hug."

Damien rewarded him with another punch that split his lip and sat him on his backside on hard bitumen. "She's mine!" he growled in Trent's face. He knelt over Trent and launched a volley of blows into Trent's handsome face. I had just about shoved my entire fist into my mouth to stifle the screams, sobs and hysteria building in my chest. I was silently praying for someone to come around the corner to rescue Trent, but nobody came.

Finally, satisfied that he'd got the message across, Damien stood up, unzipped his fly, and urinated on my unconscious friend. Then he zipped himself back up, grabbed my arm and dragged me along with him to the car, which he threw me into violently. That night he called me a whore and clasped his hands around my throat so hard that I blacked out. When I awoke, my head was on his lap and he was sobbing over me, stroking my hair. He thought he'd killed me. As I lay there, my throat aching and my eyes burning, looking into his handsome face contorted in fear and anguish, I wished he had.

I was grateful for the cooler weather as a turtleneck top hid the bruising on my throat. Nothing could hide my eyes. My left eye was vampirical red – a burst blood vessel turning the entire white of my sclera an angry red. The right eye escaped with only the outer half affected. I looked like something straight out of a horror film. My story, that I had food poisoning and had been retching the night before, was believable and brought with it much sympathy. Damien came home with a white gold emerald ring shouldered by two diamonds, trying to make up for his trespass with gifts and bling.

Two days later, I paid Trent a visit to apologise. When he opened the door and saw my eyes, he immediately pulled me into his embrace and whispered, "I'm sorry, Liss." I rested my head into the curve of his neck, this was not on him.

"I considered charging him with assault, but I thought you might pay the price if I did. It looks like you did anyway."

I shrugged at him.

"Liss, you need to leave him. You cannot live like this. Look what I copped for hugging you."

I couldn't take my eyes off his battered face. The dark purple bruising under his eye and the thick scab on his bottom lip. I spoke to the scab, too ashamed to meet his eyes, "I love him, but I'm scared of him Trent. If I leave him, he will find me and he will kill me."

Trent shook his head and looked at his lap. "I would never hurt you like that, never."

I reached for his hand and confirmed, "I know. I'm so sorry Trent, I really am." I kept my hell private.

As I lie here staring at the ceiling, his breathing deepens beside me and the first rumble of a snore echoes in the quiet room. He's still sleeping too lightly for me to surreptitiously escape so I lie, very still, and manage my breathing to calm the anxiety. I wonder if my cheek will bruise. Even though he slapped my face with an open palm, my head bounced off the hard edge of the couch and left me seeing stars. I'm sure there won't be a bruise bad enough that I can't cover it with make-up.

Earlier, after the dishes were washed and dried and the kitchen clean, Damien sat beside me on the couch as I watched an episode of *Doctor Doctor*. I could see him out of the corner of my eye looking at the main character, Hugh Knight, and back at me. I tried to keep my features even.

"Do you like this guy? You think he's hot?" he growled.

I looked at him with big doe eyes, a picture of innocence, "Who are you talking about?"

He points at the television, "this flog!"

"Him? Oh God no! He *is* a flog. But it's a funny show. My favourite character is the Mum, Meryl... she's hilarious." He kept staring at me as I feigned interest in the scene.

"Nah, that's bullshit. You do like him. You probably touch yourself at night when you think of him."

What a preposterous thing to say. My God. So, I glare at him, "No Damien, I don't. He's not even good looking."

After a beat, his voice very low, he whispers, "You know I don't like it when you lie to me, Felicity."

"Damien, I'm not lying. I don't think he's good looking."

Then it happened. His face turned beetroot red, and he shoved me, hard. "Fucking bullshit! Don't lie to me, bitch!" My spine cracked up high and a white-hot pain rose up from my shoulder. Before I could say anything in my defence, his hand reached and slapped my face so hard that it made my eyes burn. My hand rose to my stung cheek, but he pulled it away and slapped the same cheek again in the same spot, even harder, and again, and again. I saw stars and felt faint. I could feel the tears burning my eyes but dare not shed them. I looked at my lap, not daring to make eye contact, cheek burning and heart thudding. Then he pulled me into his embrace and kissed my hair tenderly. Moments later he turned off the television and switched off the lights, dragging me into our bedroom where he proceeded to assert his authority by violently thrusting inside me until he was spent. I'll take photos of this latest violent act tomorrow and add it to the box of documented abuse I have in the lockbox I rent.

As I lay here waiting for him to fall into a deep sleep, I can feel his seed leak out of me onto the sheets. Finally, his snores become rhythmic, and I know he is asleep. I slip from the bed and tiptoe downstairs to the bathroom where I find solace sobbing against the cold tiles of the shower, allowing the jets to wash away my tears and his violence.

4

The Elephant in the Room

Katrina

It's been seven long days since I discovered Jack's little secret. I have been distracted all week because my mind keeps taking me there, even though I don't want to go. I can't sleep at night, and I have headaches all day from the tension in my shoulders. I am mechanical and forge ahead with my routine of running, working at the office and then returning to be the housewife and mother. Then I crawl into bed and pretend to sleep. Hour after agonising hour my brain hurls those images at me and makes me question everything. I don't even know how to broach the situation. I'm scared. I think I'm still in shock... or denial.

I try to maintain some semblance of normal; watching a TV series with Lucy, attending parent/teacher interviews with Mason, discussing a university assignment with Jacob, and I make sure I'm in bed long before Jack retires. Yesterday after school, Mason asked me if I was ok because I was staring listlessly into space while he was talking to me about a week-long excursion into the city that his whole year level is about to embark on. I replied that I was fine and mumbled something about a headache, then snapped back to attention to listen to him, but I don't think my lies are fooling anyone.

Except Jack. Jack is walking around with his head up his arse in La La Land. I look at him and I don't understand how he can come home, peck me on the cheek, and pretend nothing is going on. I love him. I love him so much. I don't want to ask him about this because I want to be wrong.

My eyes look bruised from lack of sleep, and my hair is lank and lacklustre, but Jack doesn't notice. My inner voice starts up an internal monologue I don't want to hear. She points out that we haven't had sex in a while, which I lamely justify with the fact that we've been busy, and we have kids, and we go to bed at different times. She fires back that he doesn't touch me unnecessarily anymore and before I conjure a counter, she screams at me '*HE'S SCREWING SOMEBODY ELSE!*' I mean, it's not like it was when we were young, going at it like rabbits, but we still enjoy sex. She whispers, '*When? When was the last time you engaged in a little bedroom shenanigans?*' I try to calculate the days... weeks, oh wow, it's been over a month. I imagine her arms are crossed, and she is impatiently tapping a toe. Ok, it's been a while I concede in my head. '*Have you got no self-respect? Is this who you have become?*' I don't want to continue to converse with this argumentative bitch.

Jack has just told me he is going into the office again today... the second Saturday in a row. The thought of life without Jack terrifies me. He drifts past me and smells like he's taken a bath in cologne... for her. A white-hot needle pricks the grey matter. I brazenly state, "Whoa, you've gone a bit heavy on the aftershave there. Who is she and where does she live?" Jack turns and stares at me, wide eyed, then laughs way too hard. "You're funny". Yeah, as funny as a jilted wife on the wrong side of the fucking affair. I crimp my eyes at him and kiss him full on the mouth, sidling in to press myself against him. He doesn't get even remotely aroused, and it is soul crushing. Unthwarted, I whisper, "Maybe, since its Saturday, you can be five minutes late and maybe take me into the boudoir and give me a good rogering?"

Jack is wide-eyed again but his phone startles us both as it rings loudly in his hand. It's her. He looks relieved as he answers, "Hi, yep, I'm on my way now. Be there in ten." He rings off and slides his phone into his back pocket, looking awkward. "Sorry, got to go, they're waiting for me." He bends forward at the waist and plants a kiss on the tip of my nose. My heart shudders.

I sit at the kitchen bench in his wake, totally distressed and more than a little heart broken. What does she have that I don't? What does she do that he thinks I won't? The headache kicks up to nauseating. *What are you going to do about this?* The bitch is back. Today is the day I find out what the hell is going on.

I wait for a full hour after Jack's departure. Stopping by *Gino's*, our favourite café, I collect two coffees and a stacked sandwich to share. There is ample parking in the office district early on this Saturday afternoon, so I park on the street and use Jack's spare fob to enter the main entrance doors, walk past the water feature, trickling serenely, climb the stairs to the second floor and stand before the dark office. I ring the buzzer, just in case he is at the office, and they've only used the lights in the boardroom or something. I'm still hoping I'm wrong and that Jack really is working today. I want so badly to be wrong about this, to have misread the messages. The grey matter hurls the explicit pictures to the fore. *There's no explaining those away, is there?* Shut up! Deep breath, then I turn on my phone to find Jack's number, and press 'call'.

Holding my breath, I wait out the ring time. It's going on too long and I realise I have to piece together a message for his message bank. I'm about to abort the call because there's no way my scrambled brain could articulate a message, when Jack answers, out of breath and puffing. Oh God. Oh Shit! My stomach plummets. Oh, Jesus

Christ on a popsicle stick…have I interrupted them screwing?

"Hey, Kat, what's up?" *You're all innocence.*

Trying to keep the quaver out of my voice "Hi hon, oh, why are you out of breath?" *Please don't answer that?*

"I just ran for my phone. I left it on my desk, sorry." *Sure, you did.*

"Oh, er, I thought you were working today." *I'm going to catch you out.*

"I am. I'm at the office now." *You're full of shit.*

"But *I'm* at the office now… and it's dark. All the lights are out." *Screw you, Jack.*

Surprised, in a very high octave "Why are you at the office?" *Gotcha!* Someone hisses "shit" in the background… sounds feminine. It's her.

"Well, I felt sorry for you working on another Saturday, so I brought you coffee and a sandwich." *I hope you feel like a shit.*

Silence. Not even breathing on the other end of the phone. *Caught in the act.* I harden my resolve, I'm angry now. "Hello? Jack, are you there?"

Resigned, "Yeah I'm here." *You're such a shit, Jack.*

"Jack, where is 'here'? What's going on?" *I'm not done yet.*

Big sigh from Jack. "Look, just go on home and I'll meet you there in a bit and I'll explain". *The ruse is up.*

"Jack, is everything alright?" *You're breaking my heart.*

"Just go home, Kat. I'll be along soon." *You are unworthy of me.*

Jack disconnects and my shoulders droop.

Descending the stairs, I sit on the tiled edge of the water feature and sip my coffee, trying to calm my nerves and articulate my thoughts. The gentle trickle of the water feature isn't calming; its white noise frays the edges of my self-control. My bottom lip quivers and hot tears burn my eyes. A tear breaks free and travels down my cheek, unchecked. I'm so sad… so broken by this news. It's not fair; I still love him… I'm still in love with him. He's the love of my life. Why wasn't I enough? Why couldn't he talk to me about us before he sought solace in someone else's arms? Finally, my reaction arrives. Great wracking sobs rock me and reverberate around the empty foyer. The voluble echo of my grief is mournful. I don't want to go home.

I'm not sure that I'm ready for Jack to explain, for my marriage to end and for our lives to take a turn in a different direction. I'm not ready for tomorrow to be so different from today. But I can't hide under the covers from this monster… this one is out in the open now and needs to be slain.

* * * * *

Jack saunters in almost an hour after I've returned. I'm sitting in the living room, curled up in the corner of the couch. A box of tissues, from which I have extracted a healthy number of units, sits beside me; a huge ball of sodden tissues is balled in my hand, evidence of my distraught state. My face is swollen, red and blotchy; probably looks akin to a female baboon's arse in heat.

He sits opposite me on the coffee table and puts his head in his hands. I refuse to speak first; he is the one who has the explaining to do. After a long moment, he looks into my eyes and says he's sorry. "Why did you lie to me?" I ask gently, because I'm hurt, but I won't make this easy for him.

"I don't want to tell you."

What? "You have to tell me… you lied and there has to be a reason for it."

"I don't want to hurt you."

"Too late… I'm already hurt, so out with it. Or do you want me to guess?"

Infuriatingly, he utters, "C'mon Kat, don't make this harder than it already is."

Oh hell no. Now I'm pissed. I am not going to walk on eggshells for this. "Don't make this any harder? And just what is *this*? You mean the affair that you are having and have to admit to? That you have just pissed all over everything that is sacred to me. That you have just thrown away our marriage and everything that it represents? All for what? A romp between the sheets?"

"It isn't like that."

"Oh, well please, enlighten me. How exactly is it?"

"It's love, Kat. I love her."

My eyes bulge. Love? "What about me? You're supposed to love *me*! You *used* to love *me*! What did I do that was so wrong that you went out and found somebody else?"

He looks guilty and moves toward me, "No Kat, you didn't do anything wrong. I just fell in love with somebody else. We love each other." He looks down at his hands. He can't meet my eyes.

"Oh, well that's ok then, as long as it's love."

"I'm sorry Kat, I really am. I didn't want to hurt you, and we didn't mean for this to happen."

Out of the corner of my eye, I see Jacob wander past us on his way to the kitchen. He stops and turns to chat but takes in the scene and quickly pivots to return upstairs.

"Who is it? Is it Anne?"

Jack is incredulous that I have landed on Anne and his eyebrows are almost lost in his hairline. "How did you know it was Anne?"

"Well, I didn't. I had an inkling, and you just confirmed it. Do you think I can't see how you look at her; how she looks at you? She's your best mate's wife…and yes, she's a looker but really Jack? I thought you just had a little crush. At first, in the early days, it made me a little jealous, but I got over it because we're happy. *We were happy!* Anne is my friend. And Shaun is *your* friend. I am an IDIOT! You made a fool out of me". My voice shakes: I sob into the tissue wad.

"I'm so sorry Kat, I really am. We didn't mean for this to happen… it just did."

"How long has it been going on?" God, my crying voice is high and whiny.

"About six months."

"Six bloody months! For the love of God, Jack!"

The thought of this going on right under my nose for half a year is even more devastating. I sob wretchedly into my ball of tissues. Jack is silent. After what feels like an age, I find the strength to pull myself together, hiccupping my grief as I try to reign it in. My face feels swollen and tight. I have to get away from him. I grab the box of tissues and stand; he is forced to look up into my baboon's arse, "Congratulations, Jack. You've made a mockery out of me and our marriage, and you've broken up our little family. We're a statistic now. I hope you're proud of yourself. I hope she was worth it. You know what? You can explain this shit to the kids, I'm out."

With that, I leave the room and retreat to the kitchen to sob my heart out, giving in to the waves of grief as they crash over me. The headache has stepped up to nuclear and threatens to explode.

I hear Jack walk out of the living room and down the hall, fossicking in our room and bathroom, track his footsteps as he darts downstairs to his office, then I hear him return and the front door opens and closes gently; he is gone.

I always believed in the institution of marriage, related it to a house we built together that soon became our home. No amount of emotional scaffolding could hold this marriage together under the weight of betrayal while we try to repair it because Jack doesn't want to repair it. He just walked away from the marriage we built together; let it crumble to the ground. I sit in the empty kitchen among the rubble of 'us' and lament the end of my marriage and all the empty tomorrows that hold no dreams.

I wander back down to our bedroom and see that he has emptied his cupboard, all his drawers and his side of the bathroom. He even took his pillow. There is nothing of Jack left in the house. Just like that, Jack is gone like a smothered candle, and he took my light with him.

5

Vacant Rooms

Katrina

<u>Sunday: Day 1 After Jack Broke Me</u>

I have to tell the kids about Jack's '*hide the sausage*' game with Anne because Jack just up and left and now it's my job. I'm angry at him and I am not kind when I refer to him in my thoughts. I drag myself around the house, trying to find a focus. I decide to go for a run. It is good for me, and I pump the music loud to block the pain of Jack's exit. It's a pretty winter's day; contradictory to the storm in my heart.

When I return, I take a long shower, sob my heart out again at the unfairness of it all and then try to mop up the mess on my face. I quickly dress and catch a glimpse of my face in the mirror. The baboon's arse is in full heat now and my swollen lips look like I've been pumped full of cosmetic injectables.

I go upstairs and summon the offspring. They all emerge from their rooms and react to my baboon arse-face with varying degrees of wary surprise. I tell them we need to have a family meeting in the living room. They look at one and other with wide eyes and parted lips. Descending the stairs, I take a seat in the wing chair and await their arrival, focusing on my breathing. The Queen is seated, and the Court of Shitsville is in session. All three amble in and sit together, united but guarded on the three-seater. Jacob queries, "Where's Dad?" *Probably balls-deep in Anne.*

"Your father has left. He's packed his things and left the house."

A chorus of questions from the three-seater; I hold up a hand to silence them.

They patiently await my explanation. "There's no easy way to tell you this and saying it delicately won't make it any less painful so I'm just going to tell it as it is."

All three of them visibly shrink into the couch. "Your father has been having an affair."

Audible gasps from the three monkeys. Lucy asks "Who with? Anyone we know?"

"Yes, actually, it's Anne."

Jacob stammers, "Our Anne?" I cringe. I always thought of her as 'our Anne' too.

"Yes, the very same. Apparently, it's love." It takes every ounce of self-control not to roll my eyes.

Lucy begins to cry. Mason looks close to tears and Jacob's jaw is set; he is disgusted, and he puts an arm around Lucy in comfort.

Feeling uncharitable towards Jack, but keeping it in check, I continue, "I discovered something was going on last week and his little secret was confirmed yesterday. I don't know where they have gone but I'm sure you will understand that I don't really care right now. I feel very hurt and sad that my marriage is over, through no fault of my own, and that our little family is broken now. I think it is absolutely all right and expected that you will have questions for your father. You can call, text or message him and I'm sure he will be up front and honest with you."

All three look down at their laps so I continue, "At some stage, we will have to talk about what happens going forward and since we're all involved, I'd like you there for that meeting. I cannot afford to the pay this mortgage by myself so of course there will be changes. Having said that, now I'd like to just find my feet. Life goes on. I am not in a great place at the moment but give me time and I'll bounce back. I am here for you, always. Understand that, but I don't really know any more than you do… except that it's been going on for six months or so."

All three heads pop up. Jacob's jaw bulges. He'll be the one to watch. I add some unfelt cheer into my voice, "I think we'll get Thai take-away for dinner. What would you like?"

* * * * *

Monday: Day 2 After Jack Broke Me

I can't sleep. I toss and turn and nurse my pain. I give up on sleep and go for my run earlier than usual. When I make it to the track, it is still way too dark. I should turn around and retrace my steps because it's not safe here on my own in the dark. The lights are few and far between. Through the trees, I see the winking lights of the busy street way up ahead. It's not bright enough but it's better than the dark I'm running in now, so I push forward, faster than my usual pace. I am filled with a sense of foreboding that I can't explain, and the hairs on the back of my neck rise. I decide it's my intuition tapping me on the shoulder, so I kill the music and bolt for the street. A man stumbles out of the thick brush to the right of me and scares the absolute crap out of me. I yelp in surprise and almost clear my own height as I leap in fright. He's probably only urinating - what is it with men pissing on this track - but I'm uneasy. Panic makes me up my pace and Usain Bolt has nothing on me as I sprint for the street ahead. I risk a look over my shoulder but there is nobody behind me. I look forward again just in time to see a grey car parked across half of the path. The engine is running; there is steam jetting out of the exhaust pipe, but no headlights, and the car is empty. What the hell? Maybe it's the dickhead taking a slash in the bush. What kind of idiot parks here across the path? I glance at the number plate trying to memorise it; council should hear about this imbecile. Apart from the fact that it's dangerous, I nearly left my face print in the front side window because the damned thing may as well be wearing commando pants for all the camouflaging. It's a running track and a car should not be across it.

I'm still freaked out, so I run fast all the way home, staying on the well-lit busy streets. I still have a feeling of unease that I can't shake and berate myself for being a baby. It's obviously a lack of sleep messing around with my nerves. That and the fact that my bloody husband has been screwing somebody that I considered a close friend, for six months. If the bitch ever caught fire, I think I'd throw a can of accelerant at her. I'm angry at them both.

After I'm dressed and ready to leave for work, I look up the contact number for the local council, I'll call them on my way to the office, but I cannot remember the numberplate because I have the memory of a squashed apricot. There's an M, a Z and a 3. Bitch chimes in '*a lot of good that will do, Katrina. Why don't you stop being the neighbourhood busy-body and leave it alone?*' I roll my eyes and pause. I am reacting to my own thoughts. I am losing my shit.

I've made Mason's and my lunch and journey upstairs to say goodbye to the kids. Lucy is still snuggled in bed – she has a late class, and Mason is in the shower. I poke my head into Jacob's room and find him sitting fully dressed on his bed. I venture in, "Are you OK honey?"

"Not really. I'm pretty pissed off at Dad." You and me both, mate.

"Yeah, it's not his finest hour."

"I mean, it's disgusting. Shaun is supposed to be Dad's best mate… and Dad's screwing his wife!" I cringe at his harsh words. Jacob continues, "… he's pretty much screwed us all over. What about Daisy and Charlene? They'd be pretty upset too." Jacob refers to Shaun and Anne's two girls. They are like cousins to our three and they're close. "I'm going to message Daisy tonight. Check in on them."

"That's a good idea, Jay. You're in the same boat as they are. I guess I should contact Shaun, but I'm not sure I'm up to it just yet. I feel bad for him. Maybe on the weekend when I've had more time to digest it all. Right, I'm off to work." I lean down and kiss the top of his head, breathing in the smell of my eldest.

I am not ready to tell anyone at the office yet so I try to behave as normally as I can. Nobody makes any comment on the state of my face, and I don't offer any explanations. I've piled on the makeup to cover most of the ugly so perhaps the worst of it has gone unnoticed. I work on autopilot until it's time to return home and make it through another sleepless night.

* * * * *

Tuesday: Day 3 After Jack Broke Me

Out on the streets this morning, my music is loud. Today I stick to the main streets because I got such a fright yesterday when the slasher ran out of the bushes, and I almost got cleaned up by his parked car. I'm still not sleeping – visions of Jack and Anne doing the deed keep flickering on the screen behind my eyes and it is making me sick. I am a zombie. Something is going on at work. There are a lot of closed-door meetings with the big knobs, but I can't read what's happening. Bitch pipes up, *well, for the last six months you couldn't read that your own husband was banging your friend, so don't be too hard on yourself, petal.* Oh, shut up, condescending cow!

John, my manager, walks past my desk and takes in my frown.

"What's up, Katrina? You look pained."

"Oh, I'm just not feeling great today. I have a bad headache and it's making me feel a little ill." This ploy backfires because he takes one look at the baboon's arse and tells me I look a little peaky, sending me home.

When I arrive home, the house is empty and cold. I crawl beneath the covers for a quick nap and sink into a deep sleep. When I wake it is dark, the heater is on, the curtains are drawn, and my door is closed. I can hear the muted sounds of the kids quietly walking around upstairs. I look at the digital display on the clock beside me and almost put my neck out when I jerk upright. It is 9:07pm.

I leap out of bed and race upstairs to apologise to the kids. Lucy tells me it's fine, they didn't want to disturb me, so they let me sleep. They cooked an easy pasta meal and have left mine covered on the kitchen bench.

Well, roll me over and call me shorty.

✳ ✳ ✳ ✳ ✳

Wednesday: Day 4 After Jack Broke Me

I return to the track again today. To my absolute amazement, when I retired at 11pm last night I went straight back into a deep sleep. I feel rested today and the baboon has taken its butt elsewhere.

There's a faint funky smell that I assume is a dead possum somewhere in the bushes. I pass the young Asian girl. I see her most mornings. She always looks so sad, like she doesn't want to be here and is trying to find a reason to stay. I don't know her story, but despair is written all over her young face; it's in the downcast eyes, the downward points of her pretty mouth, the sagging shoulders, the sluggard steps she takes… the mother in me wants to hug her and tell her everything will be ok… but will it? What if she's having trouble at school, or at home? It's none of my business but I feel sad for her and wonder if it's just me reacting to my own pain. *C'mon, Kitty Kat, clean up your own backyard.* I wish this bitch would take her snide comments and piss off.

Jack sent me a message yesterday. He asked if he could come over on the weekend to discuss what we should do going forward. I told him I need some more time. A week is not enough and I'm still not feeling very charitable towards him, so he can accommodate me.

Shaun also sent me a message asking if I was OK. I drafted myriad replies, some of them vitriolic towards his wife and my husband, but all of them were deleted because I can't succinctly answer that question. I ended up just messaging that I'm very hurt and upset but not ready to talk about it yet. I asked how he was going, and he hasn't yet responded. I guess he's feeling the same.

More hushed conversations in hallways and meetings behind closed doors at the office today. Cindy, our receptionist, sidles up and asks what's going on. I tell her I have no clue. Something is definitely in the wind, though. A change is coming.

After work I pop in to visit Mum and Dad and give them the shitty news that Jack has left me for Anne. They are, of course, devastated by this news. They love Jack like he is their own, so I guess they feel betrayed too. Dad's jaw bunches like Jacob's did, he's very angry with Jack for breaking his baby girl's heart. Bully for you, Dad, glad you're on my side. Mum looks like someone stole her last dollar; she feels like she's lost a son and her expression flits between disappointment and sadness. *Fuck you Jack, you're hurting everyone.*

* * * * *

Thursday: Day 5 After Jack Broke Me

On the track, the stench of death assails my olfactories; the dead animal is decomposing at the speed of the continental drift and giving off gasses that would kill a horse at ten paces. I wish it would hurry up and break down already, so I don't have to breathe this stink in. Maybe I should call the council about that. God, I'm starting to sound like one of *those* people. I'll let somebody else call that one in.

The smell escalates to vomit-inducing as I near the thickest foliage lining the path. I increase my speed to get past the stink that is making my stomach roil. My hackles go up again at this same spot. Jesus, what is wrong with me? I run faster lest I offer myself up as a sacrifice to the creepy predator my imagination insists is lurking here.

I see the sad Asian girl up ahead. She doesn't look up as I breeze past. She continues to drag herself along the track. Thoughts of her stay with me all the way home. I hope she's ok.

* * * * *

Friday: Day 6 After Jack Broke Me

I hit the track. I am exhausted because sleep evades me again, but I drag myself out anyway. As I round the bend, the track up ahead is lit with pulsing red and blue lights like a full-blown *Rave* party. There are police vehicles everywhere parked across the track. I run as far as I can and see a cluster of on-lookers. Hazard tape blocks my path so I back track to the steps leading back up to the street and the memory of the old guy with his member flopped out pops into my head and offends me all over again. When I get to the top, I walk over the bridge and peer down through the wire fencing at the scene below. I don't know what's going on. Maybe someone has had a heart attack on the track. I can still smell the decomposing possum and today the stink is ripe. Then I notice the tent surrounding something at the edge of those bushes and my stomach sinks…it's not a possum. They've found someone. Television crews arrive and run towards me on the bridge. I turn and leave the scene. My steps are heavy and halting as I walk home. Today I look like the sad Asian girl on the track. My shoulders sag and my heart is heavy.

After my shower, I turn on the news while I eat breakfast. They have found the body of a toddler on the track; as yet unidentified. A little girl, decomposing in the thick brush. She was discovered by a woman walking her dog this morning. The woman can be seen in the background sobbing.

I push my cereal away; I feel sick. I have been running past this little baby every morning, complaining in my head about the smell. How long has she been there? Days? A week? I feel so awful. I make myself a cup of restorative tea.

Something is pinging deep in my cerebrum; a niggle that won't go away. I frown into my teacup and try to recall it. Lucy jolts me when she breezes into the room.

"Mum, did you hear about the little girl?"

"Yes, it's awful. I have been running past her for days, thinking the smell was a dead possum. I feel just awful."

Another report about the deceased child, urging anyone with information to contact the police. PING! The cerebrum offers up the goods. Oh my God. An audible gasp. Lucy turns to look at me, alarmed.

The thought unravels. The man taking a pee on Monday... the car across the track. Dear God! Could he have been the evil piece of shit who killed her? Was he dumping her tiny body?

"Mum, what is it?" Lucy looks shaken.

"I think I saw something. I think I saw something on Monday. I have to go to the police."

"Mum let me drive you. You're shaking." I accept her offer and grab my bag.

On the way to the police station, I call the office and speak to our receptionist, Cindy, and tell her I will be late in and explain why. She tells me to take my time and if I'm not feeling up to work after the visit to the police station, that I should take the rest of the day off. I know my manager would be ok with that.

Lucy parks in a side street and walks with me to the station.

When I get to the front desk, I tell the constable that I saw someone on the track early Monday morning coming out of the bushes where the child's body was found. The constable excuses himself for a moment and goes behind the front desk to confer with someone. When he returns, another officer has joined him, and I am introduced to a senior constable and led to an interview room.

I take a seat and the leading senior constable, and first constable join me and take a seat opposite. Lucy remains out at reception.

The senior constable makes introductions. I don't catch their names and don't want to ask him to repeat them. He thanks me for coming forward. The first constable is typing my contact details into a computer.

"Mrs Johns, could tell us what you saw on Monday? Take your time."

I babble a little, because I'm nervous, and probably offer up way too much information. "Ok, it was early morning, I'm not sure of the exact time, perhaps around six thirty or six forty-five, but I know it was still dark, because I was thinking that I shouldn't be on the track in that darkness. I was out on my morning run a little earlier than usual, and I could see the street up ahead, even though it wasn't well lit. Then a man came stumbling out of the bushes to my right and startled me. I panicked and ran as fast as I could to get to the road."

The first constable is typing madly. He looks up, "How far along the path did you see this man?"

"About where the tent was this morning. I saw the tent from the top of the bridge. He came out of the thick bushes on my right as I was heading towards the street."

"Can you please describe this man. Give as much detail as you are able."

"Ok, I've been trying to remember him all morning. As I said it was very dark and I couldn't see him very clearly and it was brief, but I did see that he had a light t-shirt on; it looked white, but it was old. He also wore faded blue denim jeans that were a little baggy."

"How tall do you think this man was?"

"I'm not exactly sure because he was bent over and stumbling out of those bushes and coming down a slight rise. I assumed he'd gone in there to pee, er… I mean urinate." My face flames. "I think maybe five foot nine or ten. But I'm not certain."

God I am rambling.

"OK, what else can you remember?"

"He had dark hair, but I can't say how dark. He had a beard. Like a really big beard, a *Ned Kelly* kind of beard, not a *Gandalf.*"

The senior constable looks perplexed. "I'm sorry, not a what beard?"

Oh God, stop rambling like a bloody idiot, "I beg your pardon, I'm nervous. That was a *Lord of the Rings* reference. It was bushier, like *Ned Kelly*, not a wizard-like beard. He gave me a fright, so I ran hard, but I nearly ran into a car, which was parked half-way across the path a little further on, closer to the road. "

Both uniforms mask their surprise, but I can see it in their eyes. I swallow nervously before continuing, "The headlights were off, and it was in the dark shadows of the trees, so I didn't see it until the last minute. It was running, the car was, and I think it was grey or a very dirty white car."

The senior constable's brows lift, "Do you have any idea of the make or model of the car?"

"I am really not good with that kind of thing, but I did notice that the badge on the bonnet, as I skated around it, was three diamonds in the shape of a triangle, if that makes any sense?"

The first constable and senior constable look at each other. The senior constable says in a low tone, "Do you think a Renault?"

The first constable shakes his head, "No, that's one diamond. Maybe a Mitsubishi?"

He types something into his phone and turns it around to show me.

"That's it!" Calm down, Kat.

He types that information in and then looks up at me again, "do you know the model of car?"

I shake my head, "no, but I do think it was a little older, dated, and it was a sedan. The boot lid was open, but there was no light in the boot."

The senior constable looks hopeful, "Did you see inside the boot of the vehicle?"

"No, I'm sorry, I went around the bonnet."

"What about the numberplate. Did you take note of the numberplate on the vehicle?"

"I did look at the numberplate because I was upset that he'd parked across the track, but I don't recall the whole thing because I was freaked out by him surprising me out of the bushes. I just remember that there was a Z, an M, and a number 3 in the plate."

The senior constable and first constable look pleased with this news.

"I'm sorry that I don't remember anything more. That's about it. I didn't really have a good look at him because it was dark and I was frightened, so I hightailed it out of there and ran as fast as I could." Hightailed? What, are you writing a book?

"Thank you for your statement, Mrs Johns. Just a moment and we'll just get you to read through the statement and sign it.

Five minutes later I've read the statement and signed it. The senior constable says, "we will make some enquiries with the homicide squad, and someone will be in contact."

* * * * *

I'm quiet all the way home and Lucy asks twice if I'm ok. How do I answer that? I cannot shake this feeling of dread. I sigh "I'm OK." But I'm not. That poor little girl. My husband the cheat. My friend the whore. A poor little girl who didn't even get a good go at life. My poor heart.

Messaging my manager, I tell him I'll take the day off as he suggested. When we return home, I make a cup of coffee and put the television on. The latest news reports that they think the body belongs to a little girl who went missing over a week ago, but they're waiting for the coroner to confirm her identity. The picture of a beautiful little girl with dark curls and chocolate all around her mouth pops up onto the screen and I remember seeing her story on the news last week before Jack detonated a bomb in my heart. They thought she'd wandered off and there was a search party near the property. Those poor parents. Switching off the TV because I can't take any more of her sweet little face, I drag myself to the bedroom and curl up under the sheets with a book and hope for the feelings of anxiety to peter out. The kids are walking on eggshells. Lucy told them what has happened, and they were full of questions, which I answered as honestly as I could. I still feel sick to my stomach when I think I ran past her every day.

* * * * *

Saturday: Day 7 After Jack Broke Me / Day 1 After Abigail Trenery

The little girl has a name. They have identified her as Abigail Trenery, the same little girl who went missing. My heart breaks for the family.

Late afternoon yesterday, I received a call from the crime squad. Suzie is my contact. She was all business but pleasant enough. I'm not sure how warm and fuzzy I'd be when dealing with homicides all the live long day either. We went over the statement and I promised to call her if I remember anything more.

I try to pull myself out of my funk by baking up a storm of biscuits and slices. My phone rings on the bench beside me. I see a smiling Jack looking at me from my vibrating phone. It takes all my intestinal fortitude not to hurl the phone at the wall. My fingers are gummed with cookie batter. I lick batter off two of them and answer the call; no point putting it off any longer.

"Hi Kat." Oh, like nothing's happened. Like you haven't ripped my heart out and played a round of tennis with it. I choose the higher ground, "Jack."

"Oh, look, I know you said you wanted to wait a little longer but I'm just wondering if I could maybe pop by to see the kids?"

I don't want him in the house or anywhere near me. "Jack, how about I get the kids to organise something direct with you. You can meet at a café for a coffee or something. I'll get them to give you a call."

I don't know what he was expecting but he sounds surprised and… dare I say disappointed. For the love of God, did you think I'd be a quivering mess sobbing on the floor and begging for your return? "Oh, OK."

"I have to go so I'll get them to call. Bye." I end the call. Fuck off, Jack.

I climb the stairs and summon the offspring. "Hey guys, your dad just called. He was hoping he could see you soon. Could you guys please call him and organise that? I don't think he should come to the house so…" I'm not going to rubbish him; he's a great Dad.

They all look at me wide-eyed. Lucy takes charge, "Sure Mum, we'll call him."

I am a bloody saint, restraining myself like that! Returning to the kitchen, I finish the baking, clean up the mess and decide to go for a walk along the track, to see if I can trigger any more memories to help find the arsehole who did this to little Abigail. I stop at a florist on the way and grab a bright bouquet of beautiful flowers to lay at the sight.

As I dubiously approach the place where Abigail was discovered, the place where she lay decomposing for days, I see a cluster of by-standers on the path, talking amongst themselves in hushed tones. There are flowers and stuffed toys, cards, and tiny colourful windmills in a large assemblage, forming a memorial to the innocence stolen here. I move forward and add my flowers to the growing collection of floral tributes, and silently apologise to Abby for this awful sick prick who denied her the basic privilege of every human being; to be allowed to live.

I turn around to leave and see the sad Asian girl, alone and to one side. Today there are tears coursing down her cheeks. I stop walking and make my way towards her, warring within. I decide that I have to ask, I just need to see if she's ok today because I can't walk past another tragedy and do nothing.

I approach her and gently ask if she's ok, bracing for an onslaught of abuse or dismissal. To my absolute horror, she sobs loudly into her hands and drops to a squat on the path. I quickly drop to my knees beside her and hold her sobbing body. I stroke her silken hair and make hushed comforting sounds. Finally, when her sobs subside and she pulls back, I ask if she's ok. She shakes her head. I ask if she can tell me what's wrong and again, she shakes her head. I ask if there is someone, I can call for her? More head shaking. I give her my name and ask hers. She says what sounds like Lee Shoo. I ask if she's in trouble, she just looks at me with those big brown doe eyes, glassy with tears. I ask how I can help but she shakes her head again. She looks into my eyes, and whispers, "thank you," and walks away from me. I don't know what to make of that, but I have to respect that she wants to be left alone.

When I get home, I google her name; it's a common female Chinese name – Li Xiu. At least now I have a name to put with the sad face.

I have an overwhelming desire to just run away from everyone and everything. Too much is happening, and I feel a tightness in my chest. I want the world to just stop for a while so I can catch my breath.

Li Xiu

The lady looks bewildered; she wants to help… but she can't help. I don't want to burden her with my sorrow. I look at the group of people whispering. This is a tragedy. Another little child has been taken before her time. Like Wáng Lěi. I cannot move on from Wáng Lěi's death. He was my shining light and the joy of my life, of all our lives… and he was taken from us too young. I walk this track to get away from the grief that threatens to suffocate me at home, but my heart is so heavy with this misery. Bàba has not returned, Māmā cannot get out of bed and refuses to eat more than a mouthful of yoghurt, and Nǎinai is worried sick; I worry for her. She is too old for this. It is her time to be taken care of.

As I walk past a garden along our street, I am drawn by the display of floral brilliance. Bright yellow daffodils and deep magenta tulips cheerily brighten the garden bed at number thirty-four, and the sight plunges me into despair. I am transported back to the funeral of Wáng Lěi. Māmā had to be wheeled there in a wheel-chair because she didn't have the strength to walk. Her grief was all consuming. She sat, slumped in the mobile chair, dark glasses hiding her swollen, red-rimmed eyes. She numbly endured the service but could not attend the grave. Instead, she sat entombed in the car with all the windows up, her sobs shaking her frail frame as Nǎinai tried to comfort her.

After people started to leave, I climbed out of the car and walked along to Wáng Lěi's grave, stepped gingerly around the huge mound of fresh earth piled upon his grave and knelt beside him, my bright daffodils trembling in my hands. I tried to hold my sadness in, but seeing this mound of raw earth that I knew covered his tiny body inhumed in an impossibly tiny coffin released my pent-up tears. I cried for Māmā, I cried for Nǎinai, I cried bitter tears for Bàba, who could not find it in himself to return for the burial of his only son, and I cried for me. I must walk this earth forevermore knowing that my beautiful brother, our sun, and our moon, will remain forever in the frozen state of a tiny baby. The unfairness of it all makes me wonder why we bother to have children when this kind of tragedy can strike and suck the joy out of all of our lives.

It has only been five weeks but Māmā is dangerously thin, and we are all frozen in our heartache. I know Bàbà doesn't blame Māmā, he did not see the danger in that room either, none of us did, but Māmā blames herself. She placed the cot near the curtains where the cord dangled and enticed Wáng Lěi to play. He was too young to know the consequences of his actions. He played with the cord, somehow circled it around his neck, then sat down and hanged himself. By the time I discovered him in the morning, drawn to the room by the silence when there should have been his adorable non-sensical babble, I was too late. I stood frozen in the doorway, shaking uncontrollably, then cautiously approached his cot with trepidation. His swollen tongue protruding from his blue lips, his blood shot eyes bulging out of his tiny skull and his skin as cold as ice all told of his death long before my screams woke the family. In his rush to get to his broken baby boy, Bàba pulled me from Wáng Lěi and threw me aside. He cried out to Wáng Lěi and lifted his son, unravelled the cord from his tiny neck and I watched in horror as his head fell back, revealing ugly red and purple swollen welts, his unblinking eyes devoid of life. Māmā screamed and screamed... then she slid to the ground and wrapped her arms around herself, rocking. The screams turned into wails; the wails sounded like the mournful song of a whale crying in the sea.

Sometimes I sit in his room, hoping to feel something other than this pain. His pillow still smells like his childish innocence, and I sit in the rocking chair hugging it like it holds his essence, begging him to come back to me so I can feel joy again.

6

The Universe Conspires

Katrina

I wake with a jolt, sweating and breathing hard. I'm trying to remember what terror joined me in my sleep. I think it was about Abigail, baby Abby as she is referred to in the news. I look over at the clock on the bedside table, and it is offensively early; four am. My heart is still thudding and I'm wide awake now. I was dreaming about the man in the bushes; he was clearer in my dream, but I'm not sure if is a figment of my imagination, somehow fabricated and painted there by the dream weaver, or if I'm really seeing him. This awful tragedy that I am somehow linked to is breaking my heart.

Yesterday it was reported that baby Abby had been sexually assaulted, and I can't bear to think on it too much. How horrifying for her parents to know that their precious little girl's last hours were painful, frightening and violently traumatic. It terrifies me that this evil walks amongst us... and I was in a pocket of space on a dark path right near him as he dumped her broken body like it was yesterday's trash.

I toss and turn for a good hour and a half and try to sleep, but I'm just too wired. It's too early to get up and go for a run and I really need at least another hour of sleep to be functional. Finally, I roll onto my back and try some meditation techniques. Starting with relaxing my muscles from the bottom to the top, I quietly talk myself back towards the restful state of sleep. I feel heavy and start to drift when the part of the numberplate from the dirty white car across the tracks pops into my head. My heart is thudding all over again. I quickly get up and run to the kitchen to write it down before it evades me. The second number in the numberplate was a 9… Z-M 39-. Surely that can narrow the search.

I will wait until 8am and then contact Suzie at homicide squad and tell her I've remembered the second number in the number-plate. I make myself a cup of coffee and sit at the breakfast bar, scared witless and hopeful I can help find this sick man.

I hear the key in the front door and Jacob wanders into the kitchen and startles when he sees me sitting in the dark kitchen with my hands wrapped around a mug of coffee, "Hey mum, is every-thing ok? It's just after five thirty in the morning, why are you up?"

"I'm fine, couldn't sleep. You know, I could ask you the same question, but I just heard you come in. Where have you been at this hour?"

Jacob looks sheepish and his cheeks flame, so I raise my eyebrows. "I stayed the night at Amy's house and snuck out before her parents woke up."

"Well, that's a bit naughty!" He grins at me… he's absolutely smitten with his girlfriend and can't hide the fact… and now I know it's gone to the next stage; they're sleeping together. I grin back. Young love is beautiful. Then *she* pipes up, *'Until it becomes boring, and he decides to dip his nib in a prettier ink pot at the office.'*

Ignoring her unwelcome comment, "I have just remembered another number in that numberplate from the car on the tracks so I'm going to call my contact before I go to the office. I wish I could remember the whole thing, but it was dark, and I was frightened."

"That's great, Mum. God, I hope they catch this evil piece of shit!"

"Yeah, me too. So, how did it go with your dad the other day?"

Jacob's expression turns dark, "I didn't have much to say to him. He kept trying to involve me in the conversation, but I don't give a shit. Right now, I hate him."

This is a surprise, "Hon, I know he's had an affair and messed everything up, but he didn't set out to hurt us. It just happened." It's disgusting that I automatically come to his defence.

"Why are *you* defending him? He's a shit and not worthy of your support".

"Don't for one second think I'm supportive of what they've done or how they've gone about it. I'm very hurt, Jacob, very hurt. But he's a good father and has always put you kids first. That hasn't stopped."

"Yeah, except this one time, when he put his dick first!"

Whoa! Where did that come from? *He has a point, Kat.* "Sweetheart, I know you're upset but just give it some time."

Jacob's shoulders droop. "Sorry mum, I shouldn't be talking to you about this."

Shaking my head, "No Jacob, you can talk to me about absolutely anything. I'm not made of china; I won't break. It's ok to be a little upset; I am, but please don't punish him for too long. Just try to be civil if you can."

He nods in understanding, "Now, I'm going for a quick run in the well-lit streets before I get myself together for another day at the office."

* * * * *

Suzie isn't in when I call but she calls back within ten minutes.

"Hi Katrina, how can I help?"

"I remembered another part of that numberplate."

"Ok, just give me a sec…" I can hear her messing around looking for a pen, "right, please continue".

"Um, last week when I reported the man I saw and the car on the track where that little girl was found, I could only remember that the numberplate had a Z an M and a number three in it. This morning, I remembered that there was the number nine as well. It's not much, but I thought it might be a little helpful?"

I can hear her scribbling onto what I assume is a notepad, "every bit helps."

I hope the extra digit narrows down the vehicles for them.

The gentle 'whoosh' of the office door opening brings with it the cool refrigerated air. I have arrived at the office forty-five minutes early. The boardroom door is closed, the lights are on, and I can see shadows behind the frosted glass; it's a full house. What in the heck is going on?

I make a decent dent in my workload. The boardroom door opens and one of the Directors pops out and retrieves something from his office before going back in. As the door opens a second time, I get a glimpse at the solemn faces inside the room and my insides churn.

Cindy enters the office and noisily sets herself up. I look over at her and see her look at the closed boardroom door and then across at me. I shrug my shoulders at her.

It's hard not to imagine something bad is going to happen with all those expressions. I sink myself into being productive until the suction of the Boardroom door makes me look up. The entire contents of the room exits in a noisy clamour, and they all make their way to our individual desks.

John approaches me, "Hi Katrina, could you please save your work and join us in the boardroom?"

I mumble something compliant and feel the blood drain from my face. I turn to see Steven, the Administration Manager, lean over the reception desk and speak quietly with Cindy. Cindy nods and

48

looks over at me, her grave expression matching mine.

We all file into the boardroom and take a seat around the table. The Managers remain standing, making the mood ominous. After the shuffling ends and everyone is quietly waiting in dreaded anticipation, Mr Dobunt, the Managing Director and company owner, a soft-spoken gentleman of a different era, quietly addresses the assembled group, "Good morning, all, and thank you for your time. I'm sure you've noticed some activity of late." A few nods and a quiet chorus of acknowledgement. "We have, in recent weeks, been in talks with Torjetta Enterprises. Last night, all documentation was signed, and the company has been legally transferred to Torjetta. As of five o'clock today, Dobunt Pty Ltd will cease to exist."

There is a collective gasp from his audience. "Torjetta have purchased Dobunt wholly. Unfortunately, for most of you, your employment will cease at five pm this afternoon as Torjetta have only offered employment to three of our management staff. Although it is not legally required, we have prepared a small severance package for those of you who will not be continuing with Torjetta, as acknowledgement from Dobunt of your hard work, and appreciation of your dedication and years of service to our business, in addition to the payment in lieu of notice and any leave owed." He sighs heavily, "Mrs Dobunt has been asking me to take a step back for some time now, to enjoy a simpler life and I have finally decided to heed her request. Thank you, to every one of you, for your loyalty and dedication to Dobunt."

Silence descends. We are all wide-eyed and shocked by this news, which none of us expected. Last week I was thinking 'can it get any worse?' and the universe pondered and then responded, 'challenge accepted'.

We are all supplied with an archive box to pack our belongings. My steps are heavy as I return to my desk and start packing up the last nine years of my nine-to-five life. Cindy is crying at her desk, so I walk over and give her a comforting hug. John pops his head outside his office and asks me for a moment. When I arrive at his office, he closes the door behind me.

"Katrina, I just wanted to take the time to thank you for all you've done for me and this company. I've lost my job too, so I know how daunting this is, but I've had a heads up for at least a fortnight and have managed to secure a position with another firm, which I start next month."

Bully for you, John. He holds out an envelope, "you'll get a bit more because you've been here for nine years, so you'll get your long service leave entitlement, as well as holiday leave owing and the month of pay in lieu of notice. There is also a bonus, which Dobunt want to pay everyone as a thank you."

I'm numb with shock. How the hell am I going to pay for anything anymore? Jack has gone and now so has my income.

He gives me a crooked smile, "If you don't need to rush off, Dobunt is taking us all out for lunch, to try to lighten the mood I guess, but I understand if you're not up for it."

I nod numbly and thank him, then wander back to my desk. Do I want to go out to lunch? My stomach feels crampy, and I think with all the stress of late, I'm going to be rewarded with a runny bum... the hits keep coming!

I trawl through all the emails and files in search of anything personal, which I save to a memory stick before deleting. I empty the recycle bin to make sure everything is gone and then shut down my computer. Cindy sighs heavily so I wander over and ask if she's going to go to the lunch. She says she's thinking about it. Maybe I will go. I think for a moment, then decide, "I think I'll drive my car home and get a lift to the lunch and get a little pickled on the company dime." Cindy thinks this is a great idea and I offer for her to park her car outside my house, and she can come and get it tomorrow. We will catch a taxi to the restaurant.

* * * * *

I enter the house and put the box on the hall stand. Lucy wanders downstairs and is surprised to see me. Cindy follows me inside, "Hi hon. We've all just lost our jobs."

Lucy's jaw drops, "What?"

"Yep, the company has been bought out so I'm dropping this off and then they're all taking us out to a 'farewell' lunch so stuff it, Cindy and I are going to get a great meal and some drinks in at their expense."

"I can drop you both off if you want."

Lucy is a gem. I excuse myself and pop into my room for a moment. I want to see what my severance pay figure is. We have been rewarded with a five-thousand-dollar bonus. Together with the combined long service and holiday leave owing and all other out-standings, there is a five-figure amount on the pay slip. This puts a little spring in my step as I think that might tide me over for a bit until I can find another job.

Lucy drops Cindy and me at the restaurant, and I decide that the deal must have been sweet because the restaurant is quite prestigious and almost everybody from the office is in attendance. The food is superb, and we are spoiled with an endless array of delectable offerings. The prosecco is flowing smoothly, and I think this was a lovely farewell idea. Cindy gets quite pickled on prosecco, and I fear she will have a heck of a headache tomorrow.

As I am helping her out of the restaurant at the end of the afternoon, the door opens and I look up to see Jack and Anne standing before of us, her hand engulfed in his; they look like a beautiful couple in love. I stiffen and swallow hard. I'm not sure how much more my poor heart can take.

Jack stifles his shock and says amiably, "Hi Kat, how are you?" I'm pretty shit thanks, Jack. Anne's face drains of colour, and she takes great interest in her toes.

Cindy looks from Jack to me and back again. She frowns, "aren't you two married?"

Shit! I don't want to be bitchy, so I try for polite, "well we were but… Jack is with Anne now." I see Jack cringe and Anne's shoulders droop further. I don't want a scene.

"I'm OK, Jack. The company has just been sold so today I lost my job."

Jack looks upset and concerned for me, but it isn't pity. I'm grateful for that, "I'm sorry to hear that, Kat."

I try to rise above it all and be civil, "Yeah, me too. Hello Anne."

Anne looks up from her toes with wary surprise. "Hello, Kat."

Jack continues, "Perhaps I can pop over on the weekend and we can discuss things and make sure you're ok to get through the next few months?"

"Um, I'll send you a message," Cindy is still looking between Jack, Anne, and me, and I need to get her out before she starts asking stupid questions. I manage a half decent smile and end this awkward charade, "Well, I'd better get Cindy home."

We leave the restaurant, Cindy says rather loudly, "Kat, why did you let him go. He is so frigging hot!" Jesus Cindy. "I didn't let him go, Jack and Anne have been having an affair for the last six months and I found out about it a couple of weeks ago." Now my heart is broken.

Cindy cries out in horror, "Oh my God, Kat! Oh my God. I'm so sorry. You poor thing. I'm sorry." Then she starts crying. Oh Lord, shut up Cindy!

"It's OK, Cindy." *No, it's not OK, Kitty Kat. No husband, no job… you're a wreck.*

"…and now you've lost your job too," she wails. "aaand, you saw that bad man… Oh Kat, I'm so sorry." Jesus, Cindy, keep it together! When the cab arrives, I pile Cindy into the back seat and climb in after her. We travel to Cindy's house first and I ask the cab driver to wait while I walk her to her door to make sure she gets safely inside. Seamus, her husband, opens the door before we can even get a knock in. I called ahead to give him a heads up that she's a little tipsy. "Hello darling." He leans forward and plants a kiss on her mouth. How sweet. "You OK baby-cake? I'm sorry about your job, honey bunch" Oomph syrupy. *Don't be so cynical... just because you don't have anyone to pour sugar all over you.*

Cindy stumbles forward and sobs into Seamus' chest, "Jack cheated on Kat and now he's with someone else," Oh my God, Cindy! Seamus looks at me, "It's ok, I'm ok. I have to go because the cab is waiting. Take care of her." To the sobbing Cindy "Hon, I'll be in touch. You take care".

I awkwardly run like the clappers to the waiting cab in my high heels, stumbling on the cobbled driveway like a baby goat learning to walk, just trying to get away from this mortifying mess. When the cab arrives home, I practically run inside. Replacing my outfit with a tracksuit, I drop onto the couch in emotional exhaustion. Seeing Jack opened the wound right up again. I miss him; I love him. I still love him, but he is in love with Anne and as much as I want to hate them, it's just not in me. I feel so cheated by life. He was my tomorrow, but he cashed all our tomorrows in and chose Anne instead.

* * * * *

After dinner, when everyone has retired to their rooms, I sit down to watch a little television. A re-run of *Friends* is on, so I make myself a cup of tea and settle in for some light entertainment. A 'breaking news' banners scrolls across the bottom of the screen. Police are talking to a person of interest in relation to the Baby Abby murder investigation.

A feeling of sadness descends and surrounds me like fog as I think of the sick individual who has so much darkness inside him that he could commit such a heinous act of evil upon an innocent little child. My thoughts turn to the parents of baby Abby, and I grieve for them. I'm grateful it wasn't me who discovered her body.

It's a cowardly thought, but I'm not sure I could have taken the discovery and resulting images that would haunt me. I'm already haunted by the knowledge that I saw Mr Evil and his car when he disposed of her body.

As the saying goes, '*things happen in threes*'. Well, it started with Jack and Anne's duplicity and ultimately, their betrayal of our family and hers; somehow getting myself entwined in the Baby Abby murder case; and losing my job at a time when I really need some stability. I just want this catastrophic upheaval to stop. It feels like every time I get knocked to the ground, I find my feet and stand, only to get knocked to the ground again.

Ok, enough of this self pity, I need to get over myself. I decide to change into my pyjamas and pour myself a glass of wine. I log into one of the streaming services we subscribe to and select a good series to sink my teeth into. Lucy wanders downstairs as the program pops onto the TV, which piques her interest, she pours herself a glass of wine and joins me on the couch. We snuggle up under a big blanket amongst the cushions and settle in for some engrossing viewing.

7

My Right to Silence

Brian

They took my car, and my keys and I'm in a small holding cell. They know about the little baby, and they think it was me. My heart hurts for that poor little girl. As soon as I unwrapped the towel, I knew I had to take her. She couldn't go through the woodchipper. Her family should be allowed to bury her. She should go home.

I try not to think of how she looked – that her last hours were filled with pain and fear. I hate David and I don't care that he is my brother; he is evil. But I'm too scared to tell them. I don't know what he has been doing down there but the poor baby barely looked like a baby anymore. I can't escape the pictures of her that flicker behind my eyes.

A sob rips from me and echoes loudly. I can't stop crying for the poor little girl. I wish I didn't unwrap the towel. I wish I didn't know. Someone clears their throat, and I look up to see a police office standing with a man in a suit.

"Brian, this is your public defender."

The man in the suit raises his arm, "Hi, I'm John Lipton, like the tea."

The officer opens my cell and leads both the tea-man and me to a room and closes the door behind him.

"Brian, I am your legal aid representative. Do you understand that you have been charged with the murder of a child?"

I nod at him because I don't trust my voice. I wish dad was here. He would know what to do. But I wouldn't be here if dad was here because the bunker wouldn't be built, and the baby wouldn't be dead.

"Due to the nature of the crime, bail has been refused. Do you understand this, Brian? Do you know what is going to happen?"

I just shrug. I don't know what's happening. But I can't tell them about David.

"We are going to court on Monday to plea to the charge of murder. Are you going to plea guilty or not guilty, Brian?"

Again, I shrug. "I didn't do it, but I can't tell you who did."

"Brian, why can't you say who did this."

"Because I just can't. You don't understand."

"Do you think your life is in danger?"

I look at my lap. "Can I say I'm not guilty and say I know who it did but can't say?"

"This is just a plea hearing – you only need to plead guilty or not guilty. The rest comes later.

"I want to plead not guilty."

"OK. I will see you on Monday."

Tea-man knocks on the door and the officer opens the door and allows him to leave – he takes me back to the dark cell in handcuffs.

I lay in the dark on the small uncomfortable bed with the lumpy pillow and roll over to face the cold concrete wall. I close my eyes and take myself back to that tractor ride across the fields to fix the fence. I wish I could go back there.

I wish I could go back even further when Mum was still alive.

We'd come inside the warm sunny kitchen, walking straight into the yummy aroma of baking. Mum would make a pot of strong tea while we washed up. We'd sit at that laminated old table with the specks of silver on its top and a metal strip around the edge and watch with anticipation as she poured the tea. The knitted tea cosy was an awful orange colour that matched the vinyl chairs. She'd set a plate in front of us with two big freshly baked fluffy scones, still warm from the oven and laden with melting butter, thick jam with giant globs of strawberry and a very big dollop of whipped cream, made from our own cows.

With my eyes closed, I can almost taste those scones and the strong sweet tea. The smell of baking is mingled with freshly mown lawn and takes me to a time when I was happy. I can feel myself drifting off and for the first time in days, I feel at peace.

8

Vic or Perp

Sergeant Daniel Roach sits at his desk resting on his elbows, his fingers in his hair. The evidence inside Brian Porter's vehicle is incriminating. Everything inside that car boot screams guilty of transporting the child's body to the public space where she was dis-covered, but the man just does not fit the bill of murderer. There is a childlike innocence to him that Roach just can't place.

His legal representative came in earlier, but Roach is not sure how far he got with Brian Porter. Brian Porter didn't answer any questions. He wasn't being obnoxious or a smart arse, he just didn't answer. He didn't even look up at the sergeant. He just sat slumped in his seat with his hands in his lap, head bowed, and looking as defeated as a man can look.

Roach wonders if Brian Porter is perhaps the fall guy. He doesn't come across as mentally disabled however, there is some kind of mental simplicity and slowness to him. If anything, he looks broken by the death of the child.

Then again, he could be as guilty as sin and Roach is the idiot here. Their job was to hold him until his hearing to see where it proceeds from there.

This morning as he came down to check the cell, he saw Porter quietly crying. He painted such a sad and lonely figure that Roach felt an almost overwhelming desire to comfort the detainee. He managed to get a grip of his emotions and back away from the cell undetected, but it had set him pondering.

He could not imagine the pain of Abby's parents. Not only that their child had been stolen from them and murdered, but a parent's worst nightmare of violent sexual assault and torture. He usually managed to detach himself from these heinous crimes – the details could mentally mess him up and he regularly attended counselling to keep his mind in check. He needed to keep the cherubic face of his own little girl out of his mind when dealing with these kinds of crimes.

He had a feeling that this abduction would not end well as soon as she was reported missing. Stolen under their noses as they slept in the next room, the cunning way the abductor entered the room silently through a high window and injected her with a small amount of the sedative triazolam, to keep her silent. Trace amounts were found on her little cardigan bundled up with her in the blanket, then they found the needle puncture in her tiny arm. She was only a baby so she could not have wandered off. As soon as the parents woke and found her cot empty, their worst fears were realised.

As the hours ticked on with no sign of her, the state as a whole began to fear the worst. By day nine, they were looking for a body, which was eventually discovered by an older woman walking her dog.

The condition of the child's body was heinous. The fact that the body had been decomposing under a bush for a few days couldn't hide the horrendous wounds inflicted on the poor child. Whoever had done this to her was a sadistic, sick piece of work. The sexual element alone was enough to make the sergeant's stomach turn, let alone the pain inflicted on the rest of her body. Her death was a welcome end to what can only be described as brutal mutilation.

This is what Roach cannot marry with the man in the cell down below.

9

Father, Where Art Thou

Li Xiu

The last memory of my father was the morning we discovered Wáng Lěi. After he cast me aside and unravelled the cord that extinguished Wáng Lěi's light, he screamed his son's name and buried his face in his Wáng Lěi's small still chest. Abruptly, he pulled his face away and gently lay Wáng Lěi in his cot and backed away. Māmā was wailing on the floor, Bàba was backing away in disbelief and Năinai was standing outside the door, peering into the room with eyes as big as saucers and glassy with unshed tears; her fist wrapped in the corner of her apron which was thrust into her mouth to silence her own wails. He turned on his heel, collected his wallet and keys from the ancient apothecary chest by the door, and left the house without another word. He drove away from us, and he didn't look back.

I've called him, but he doesn't answer. I leave long pleading messages, but he doesn't return my calls and he doesn't reply to my text messages. We are all broken from Wáng Lěi's passing, but he has left us all alone when we need him the most.

Nǎinai grows more and more anxious with every passing day. She stands before the living room windows and looks out into the front yard, her apron bunched in her hands, silently willing him to return to us. She struggles to help her daughter-in-law, who she loves like her very own daughter, but she is perplexed by her son's abandonment.

I sometimes see her standing before Wáng Lěi's cot, her arthritic hands on the rail, gnarled twisted knuckles white in her grip. Her mouth is a thin line turned down at the corners, her weathered face gaunt and etched in pain; her silken crepe skin stretched taut over the bones of her face wet with tears.

Yesterday I walked up behind her and put my arms around those stooped, shaking shoulders, buried my face in her soft, white, fine hair, and held her tight to me; giving her permission to yield to her grief and angst. I led her to the kitchen table and pressed her into a chair, placing before her a cup of green tea laced with Baijui, usually reserved for celebration in our home, but today served as a medicinal offering to settle her nerves.

Nǎinai cried for a long time, stooped, and rocking in her chair, sobbing silently into her kerchief. Her sorrow subsided from gasps to whimpers until she sagged in exhaustion. I took Nǎinai's hand and led her to her room, closed her blinds against the harsh afternoon sun, pressed her onto her bed and covered her with a light blanket. Nǎinai slept for twelve hours.

I pilfered a can of tuna from the pantry and forked it into my mouth straight from the tin. We are fast running out of food and money but still, Bàba is silent. I am torn between disappointment that he has abandoned us and a deep hurt that he doesn't care about our plight. Burying myself in my homework, I retired early and hoped for sleep, which finally came at one am, to release me from my waking nightmare.

I'm startled from my reverie by Māmā's nightmare. They usually come in the early hours but today, as I sit at the table eating my breakfast before school, I hear her cry out. Running towards her room, I am joined by Năinai in the hall; her apron brunched in her fists as she follows me into the room. Māmā is sitting up in bed, her hand on her heaving chest, her hair plastered to her sweaty, tear-streaked face. She blinks at me and then remembers Wáng Lěi is gone, and we watch as her face crumples and she sinks back into the bed covers, inconsolable. I sit beside her on the bed, running my fingers through her unwashed hair and wipe the tears from her face. Năinai remains at the door fretting silently and impotent.

10

Moving On

Katrina

Jack arrives at the house and parks outside at the kerb. I can see him through the living room window and wonder if he's bracing himself? As he approaches the door, I watch him reach for his keys before remembering that this is no longer his address and awkwardly shoving them in his pocket. He rings the bell, and the familiar chime plays in stereo as I can hear it both inside and outside the window.

I open the door and he offers a sheepish smile, "I'm not used to ringing the bell," he volunteers.

I try very hard to arrange my features so the vitriolic response firing through my brain doesn't exit my mouth. I'm tired and weary and probably just look like the old hag he traded in for the better model; cementing his resolve that he won that battle.

I stand aside and let him pass before calling up the stairs for the troops to join us. The thunderous sound of their descent down the stairs fills the open void above the stairs as we move to the formal living room. Jack sits in one of the wing chairs, the three kids and I sit bunched together on the lounge; he looks like he's on the outer.

We politely exchange greetings like strangers, but animosity is notably absent. Jack starts the difficult conversation, "So, I guess we need to make some decisions moving forward. For one, what to do about the house?"

I am quick to reply, "Well I can't afford to buy you out, especially now that I've just lost my job, so I guess you either need to buy me out or we need to put the house on the market."

"OK, well I'm not able to buy you out either so I guess we need to put it on the market. I can organise for a couple of realtors to stop by and we will meet them individually and then choose one before we put it on the market. Considering we repainted the entire house inside and out last year and had the floorboards repolished, I guess we just need to minimise the furniture and knick-knacks in the interim to prepare for it. Kat, I am happy for you to keep all the furniture, and we just won't count it in. We'll just split the house fifty-fifty after it sells."

I accidentally sigh because I'm tired and more than a little broken, "OK. We've still got a mortgage, albeit a manageable one, but as I said, I don't have a job".

He ponders this for a moment. "How about I continue to pay for the mortgage and all costs associated with the sale of the house, and I'll keep a record and at settlement, we will take half of those costs out of your share. Is that fair?"

I brighten at that, and Jack looks oddly surprised and sad at the same time. He forces a smile, "Ok, that's great. I'll get it all drawn up legally and pop back next week for you to sign it."

I get up to make a cup of tea and when I return to the room the silence is soul crushing. Lucy and Mason look uncomfortable, but Jacob's face is mutinous. He glares at Jack and utters, "Can I go now?"

He makes to get up out of his seat. Jack puts up a hand to halt him, "If you could please just wait a moment, Jacob, I'd like to talk to you three." Jacob exhibits an eye roll worthy of a petulant teenager and crosses his arms over his chest in irritable rebellion. I'm standing impotently with the tea tray, not sure what to do. I press on and smile at everyone as I deliver the tray and get busy pouring it.

"Look, I just wanted to broach the subject of Anne and me. I… we didn't set out to hurt anyone. We certainly didn't mean to fall in love…" There is an audible sigh from Jacob. Lucy frowns at him, "… it just happened. I understand that you're hurt and angry right now, but I hope that we can move forward from this soon. My love for all of you hasn't changed…."

Jacob interrupts, "you broke our family apart and you broke Mum's heart! You're a selfish arsehole!"

Jack ignores his outburst, I'm sure it's what he expected. "…as I was saying, I love all of you very much. Daisy and Chelsea have warmed a little, although Shaun is still really pissed off. I'll cop that, but I do hope we can move forward soon."

Lucy leaps up and throws her arms around Jack's neck in a welcome embrace, and Mason walks over and rests a hand on his shoulder. Jacob stands too, but he glares at Jack, then at Mason and Lucy, before stalking out of the room.

* * * * *

After Jack departs, I jog up the stairs to have a chat with Jacob. He is on his bed, leaning against the bed head, his arms crossed tightly over his chest and his expression thunderous. Rather than startle him, I knock on the open door to announce myself.

He jerks upright and his head whips around; his mouth a tight line, which softens when he sees me. He was expecting maybe Jack.

"May I come in?"

"Sure," he swings his legs over the edge to make room for me. The bed dips as I sit beside my boy and I snake an arm around his shoulders, "Are you OK, hon?"

His expression flits between anger and sadness.

"Mum, I don't want anything to do with the bastard! He cheated on you; he broke our family apart. I know you asked me to try but… Lucy and Mason might be happy to pander to him but no! I will not condone his disgusting behaviour with acceptance."

Oh boy, "Listen, love, I am so disappointed. Not only that he had an affair, and that it was with his best friend's wife, but also that our little family unit is now fractured. But I've come to terms with it now. It's not like he broke us up just for some sex on the side. It's more than that and I guess under all the hurt and anguish, I understand that bit."

Jacob turns on me, "Mum! Why are you defending him? He ripped your heart out! He broke the golden rule of marriage! We have to sell the house and move now! He has ruined *everything*!"

My hand flutters to my mouth; I'm surprised by his vehemence, "Sweetheart, he didn't do this *to* us. It just happened. Yes, it hurts, and yes, it's disappointing, but let me tell you, there are worse things one human can do to another than fall in love with someone else."

Jacob's face loses colour, like he thinks I've just gone all dark side. I hold up my hands in surrender, "Don't get me wrong, I'm pissed off and very hurt; they shouldn't have gone sneaking around behind my back, but they're still together and I believe, unfortunately for me, that it's love. I guess I just don't have room for anger amongst all the other emotions at the moment. It's not going to bring us back together. Besides that, I wouldn't take him back again anyway because the trust is gone and without trust, you have nothing."

Jacob looks defeated, so I tread gently, "I'm not saying you need to forgive and forget, or that your relationship will ever go back to what it was before this… I'm just saying that perhaps you could cut him some slack. He's still your dad and he loves you very much. That bit hasn't changed."

His arms are across his chest again. Out of habit, my hand massages circles over his shoulders, "Could you perhaps just try to forgive him a little?"

On a sigh, Jacob concedes, "Yeah, I'll try. For you… I'll try *for* you." He's still not giving his father anything.

"And don't be mad at Lucy and Mason, they're just as upset by this whole mess as you are…"

"Well, clearly not!"

"They are, hon, they just don't like the conflict. You know they're both non-confrontational by nature. You've got a lot more spunk in you than they do. That's not a character flaw in either you or them, it's just a difference in personalities. Lucy especially wants this awful uncomfortable energy to dissipate. She's always been 'daddy's little girl' and Mason… well he's just Mason. He's the most easy-going of all my babies. You're my strong and fiery boy and I know that a lot of this anger you feel is on my behalf."

Pulling him into me for a hug, "I'm a big girl, darling, I'll be OK. We'll get through this. And as for having to move, I think it's perfect for a fresh start."

As I make my way down the stairs, I think on how much of a nightmare it is going to be to pack this whole house up and move. Fresh start my arse, it's a pain in my arse.

11

Dinosaur at Large

Katrina

Enough of the sullen indulgence in self-pity. It's time to get off my backside and find another job. I have an appointment lined up at recruitment agency this afternoon, so I have decided to freshen up my curriculum vitae.

I have pretty much kept it up to date so really, apart from a quick read-through and a few small changes, all I have to do is print it and get ready to go. I haven't attended a recruitment agency in at least twenty-five years, having found most of my employment through local advertising for small companies. I am understandably nervous about what I might have to carry out.

* * * * *

After an hour of gruelling tests, I walk away feeling worse than before I started. I can't help but feel like a dinosaur. I had to undertake all manner of tests for computer packages… for functions I haven't performed in literally decades and was dismayed to find I could not recall how to complete a mail merge without surreptitiously looking it up on my phone. I did well with the spreadsheet package, the database software left me pondering whether a refresher course is in order, but alarmingly, as I use so many keyboard shortcuts for a lot of the functions in the word processing package, I really strained the grey matter to think about how to take the long way around those shortcut functions.

After jumping through those hoops, I had to endure a grilling by the smiling consultant, who did not bother to hide her boredom, only to be advised at the end of it all that there aren't any suitable roles available for me anyway. The whole process left me feeling less than enthused about starting a new role as I cursed Dobunt and the universe at large for making this whole process necessary.

Out on the street, it is evident by the wet pavement that it has rained whilst I was in enduring the Spanish inquisition. Flicking through my text messages, I wait for the lights to change at the crossing so I can get to my car, drive home, and forget this wasted experience altogether. Quite a large group of pedestrians has gathered to wait with me and when the lights finally change, the group moves as one across the busy intersection like a flock of sheep. For an insane moment, I consider bleating out loud, 'Baaaah!', but manage to stop myself and stifle a chuckle instead.

There is a small commotion up ahead and people dart around some kind of obstacle. As the crowd moves around the hindrance, I see a woman up ahead has fallen over and landed on the road but instead of helping the woman up, these selfish jackasses are all tsk tsking at the obstruction blocking their path. Squatting down beside her, I offer to help the poor woman up but as she tries to move, she cries out in pain. "OK, don't try to move, I'll call an ambulance."

She hisses breath between clenched teeth and offers, "I slipped on those wet white lines on the road there." I can hear that she is in a lot of pain. As I stand up, the lights change to green and the idiot at the front of the car queue before us leans on his horn… like we've decided to sit in the middle of the intersection for our health. I ignore the idiot and dial triple zero for an ambulance. After another inquisition of sorts, I am assured that the ambulance is on its way. The poor woman's face is pale. The horn blares again and I lose my temper, calling across the intersection like a fishwife, "Oi! Can't you see she's been injured? We're waiting for an ambulance."

He pokes his head out of the open window and bellows, "can you bloody move her onto the footpath at least?" Incredulous, my brain trying to process the idiocy of this driver, I have to actively inject calm into my voice so I don't scream at him like an unhinged lunatic, as I retort, "No, I can't *bloody* move her, she's broken her hip."

He throws his hands up in the air at us like we're just lounging around having a picnic, to purposefully ruin his day. The lights change again, and the newly gathered cluster of pedestrians crosses the road, but not one of them stops to offer help. I am appalled at the selfish prats I share this suburb with. The irate idiot in the car before us, now visibly fuming in his seat, executes a three-point turn, which turns into a thirty-six-point-turn, accelerating dangerously close to us, and screeches away as the lights turn green again. Thankfully the person behind the irate idiot has more sense and doesn't move up; he sees there is a problem and so he waits until the lights change again and calmly performs a U-turn. While the lights are red, all other cars in the queue perform the same turn and thankfully, a kind man offers to help by directing traffic around us until the ambulance arrives.

Meanwhile, I have squatted behind the woman to support her in this uncomfortable position while we wait. She is sweating profusely, tiny droplets gathering on her upper lip and at her temples; her breath laboured, her eyes clenched tightly closed. I wish I could ease her pain.

Mercifully, the ambulance arrives shortly after and following a quick consultation on the road, they believe she has either fractured or broken her hip. While they bustle about getting the gurney ready, she is offered the analgesic pain-relieving drug known as the 'green whistle'. As the Penthrox takes effect, some of the tension leaves her face.

The paramedics take down her details; she gives her name as Beverly Milburn. They advise that they will take her to the hospital, which is nearby, for assessment. The two paramedics turn to me and ask if I'd like to ride along. "Oh no, I'm not actually with her, I was crossing the road and saw that she had fallen, so I offered to help."

The paramedics take my details down and as Beverley is loaded into the ambulance, I am promptly dismissed. I thank the man who helped direct traffic and finally make my way to the car and journey home.

* * * * *

By late afternoon, I've prepared dinner and called the hospital to ask after the patient, Beverley. I am given nothing as I am not a relative, so I make a mental note that I will pop into the hospital tomorrow to check on her.

Sitting down for a spell with a cup of tea, the afternoon news bulletin is loud in my silent house. One of the first headlines is that the 'person of interest' has been detained for further questioning in relation to the death of baby Abby Trenery.

Hearing her name still gives me an uncomfortable pang deep in my stomach. My dreams are peppered with small flickers of activity, taking me back to the day I ran into the bearded man on the track. No doubt, this is my subconscious trying to process the whole event. If this is the guy, I hope they arrest the disgusting predator.

12

To Catch a Fiend and Make a Friend

Katrina

This morning's headline, bannered across the morning news, is that police have placed a man under arrest in relation to the Baby Abby case. The report shows footage of a man led by police; his form bent over with a coat over his head to hide him from the flashing media cameras. His coat slips as he gets into the car, and I can see his beard. My stomach plummets as I realise it is the man I saw on the track. Goosebumps swarm my skin, and I feel light-headed as I plonk myself unceremoniously onto a stool at the kitchen bench.

A reporter faces the camera, a solemn expression etched onto her pretty face. Nobody gets joy out of these awful reports when the depravity of man and the ensuing fall-out is splashed all over our televisions. The familiarity of the track behind her and the usual joyous release of endorphins that benefit my occasion to frequent it is juxtaposed with the discomfort of knowing what happened there.

The reporter continues, "a witness placed the man at the scene in the early hours of Monday August 3rd, emerging from those bushes behind me" she turns momentarily to indicate the thick brush behind her, "… where the body of Abby Trenery was discovered five days later, on August 7th. The man's house has been searched, and a vehicle has been removed from the property and impounded." With a jolt, it dawns on me that I am said witness, and the car is the very one I almost ran into on the track that morning.

Footage of police entering and exiting a rundown weatherboard house with an overgrown garden and broken concrete driveway plays as the reporter delivers the details; the grey paint visibly peeling on the front door, the porch neglected and sagging. Officers are holding brown evidence bags. I wonder what those poor officers have been confronted with inside that dilapidated, ramshackle dwelling. A birds-eye view from a news helicopter shows the vast property with lots of land out back that looks like a small farm. It's overgrown and has been left to ruin.

The news makes me feel sick to my stomach. I imagine those poor, poor parents who have not only lost their child, but the horrendous things that happened to her before she was released into death.

I shake the morbid thoughts away and decide I'll go and see if I can get an update on the woman who fell on the road yesterday, checking the hospital visiting hours as I make my way to the ensuite to let the jets wash away the invisible filth clinging to me after the news report.

* * * * *

I stride to the reception desk with purpose, a large bunch of chrysanthemums in hand and a big smile on my face. The blooms are large and beautiful and, they are sure to brighten the gloomiest of rooms. The receptionist comments on the flowers by way of greeting, "Oh look at those lovely flowers!"

"They are lovely, aren't they? They are for my aunt. She came in last night – I think she hurt her hip after a fall of some sort. Could you please tell me which room Beverly Milburn is in?"

The receptionist taps away and looks up, "Oh yes, Beverley. She is in Ward D on Level one. Just take those blue elevators to level one and then turn left when you exit the lift. Ask at reception for a vase and they'll give you one to take in with you."

"Thank you so much."

The ancient elevator takes an eon to gain one floor, but it gives me time to prepare myself for the second reception encounter. I needn't have worried, I am handed a non distinct, sage green vase and waved in the direction of Beverley's room.

There is a murmur of voices from within, so I gently rap on the door. Beverley is propped on a mountain of pillows and an older gent is holding her hand and stroking her knuckles tenderly. Both look up with blank expectant expressions.

"Hello Beverley, I'm Katrina. It was me who called the ambulance yesterday when you fell."

Beverley's mouth forms the perfect 'o', "Oh hello! My goodness, Katrina, is it? I didn't catch your name, I was rather distracted, and the ambulance driver didn't pass it on to reception, so I didn't know how to find you to thank you."

"Oh no, that's ok. I just popped in to see how you're feeling." I edge towards the bed and point needlessly to the flowers in my hand, "I brought you some flowers to brighten your room."

"Oh, aren't you just a sweetheart." My face pinks in embarrassment. The gent rises and rounds the bed, his hand outstretched in greeting, "Hello Katrina, I'm Kenneth, the husband." Shoving the ugly vase under my arm, I awkwardly shake Kenneth's hand. He looks fondly over at his beloved. "Thank you so much for helping Bev yesterday. That was so thoughtful."

"Of course. There are a lot of people in my suburb who could learn some hard lessons in manners… although there was the nice gentleman who directed traffic around us."

Kenneth offers to take both the vase and the flowers, motions me to the seat he vacated, and heads for the bathroom near the door. Beverly rewards me with a welcoming smile. I like her already.

"Are you ok? I thought you might have broken something; you were in so much pain."

She tries to sit up but winces. Kenneth puts the vase down with a bang and rushes to her side, "Here, let me help you, love."

After much shuffling, grunting, and messing with a control for the bed, she is finally in a more comfortable position, relief evident on her face. Kenneth returns to the flowers as Beverley explains her injury, "I did break something, I broke my jolly hip! I had to have a replacement operation, and you wouldn't believe it, they had me up and walking on it already today. Goodness me but it smarts! The nurse was quite unsympathetic and told me to expect it to be worse tomorrow! She could do with exercising some different facial muscles other than a frown. Awful business. I feel a hundred years old today!"

"But you don't look a day over forty, my love." Kenneth appears behind the large vase of flowers. His face softens when he looks on his wife and I can feel the love emanating off them both. This is what I wanted in my future… but Jack had other ideas.

"How long have you two been together?"

"We're coming up to our 50th Wedding Anniversary, aren't we love?" The tenderness between these two is lovely.

Beverley pins me with a quizzical expression, "I happen to subscribe to the belief that 'everything happens for a reason'. Why did you happen to be in that place, at that time, Katrina?"

"Ha! I had just been at an employment agency discovering that I am, in fact, quite redundant. The company I worked for has recently been bought out, so I lost my job a few weeks ago and I'm looking for work but finding the whole process quite daunting."

Beverly looks at Kenneth and then back at me, "What is it you do, Katrina?"

"My last two roles were *Accounts Officer* although I generally do everything from accounts receivable and payable, payroll, reception, administration… I do it all."

Kenneth grins at Beverley and pats her hand. Beverley turns to me, looking like the cat that got the cream, "Well that's quite a coincidence, our two sons have their own business, a building and construction company, and our clerk left quite suddenly last week to be a full-time carer for her father. We are in the process of putting together an advertisement for someone to come in and do the 'books', as we call it, for three to four days per week. Would you be interested in popping over, after nurse Ratchet lets me out of prison of course, to have a chat about whether it would work for both of us?"

Kenneth tsk tsks, "The nurse is not all that bad, Bev."

"Well, you try having a ball joint hammered into you one night and then being expected to walk on it the very next morning. No sympathy, just impatience and then she told me to 'suck it up, buttercup.'"

Kenneth chortles at Beverley's animated impersonation of the unkind nurse, and it even gets a giggle out of me.

What a surprising turn of events! I am now being propositioned for a job. I respond a little too quickly, "Absolutely! I would love that!"

Kenneth takes my name and contact details and I leave the hospital with a spring in my step and a renewed positive outlook, pondering how things sometimes turn out.

* * * * *

William

Mum looks so small in the hospital bed. I can see she's still in pain, but the nurse was quite firm about her medication. She didn't even crack a smile. No wonder Mum refers to her as nurse Ratched. I'm so grateful to the woman who stopped to help her in the street when she fell… and amazed that she might be the answer to the accounts clerk situation. Thomas came in earlier, and Dad has gone home to grab a change of clothes for mum, vowing to return late afternoon, so it's just Zoe and me in the room, Emilee is bouncing on Zoe's knee while Kaitlyn is off on an errand to find a vase for our bouquet.

A different younger nurse enters and greets us all with a smile. This one seems to have a softer bedside manner, at least. Mum visibly relaxes. She takes mum's blood pressure, "How are you feeling, Beverley?"

Mum's brave expression falters, "I'm in a bit of pain, actually. I don't suppose I can have something to take the edge off the throbbing ache?" Her expression is pleading. The nurse removes the blood pressure cuff and checks the chart at the end of the bed. She frowns, "Of course you can. I'll just go and get you something now." Mum looks at me as the nurse departs, "there must have been a shift change, thank God for that!"

I look up at the television in the top corner, "Do you mind if I turn that up?" Mum shakes her head, but her mouth is pressed in a thin line; she really is struggling with the pain. Reaching over for the remote, I up the volume a little. A *Breaking News* headline fills the screen. The police have arrested the sick piece of shit who killed that little toddler. I look across at Emilee, working her pacifier with her gums and intently playing with the charms on Zoe's necklace. She is the epitome of innocence and, as she is around the same age as the murdered toddler, I wonder how in God's name this arsehole can be so fucked up in his head that he would harm a little baby, let alone sexually assault and kill her.

The nurse returns with mum's medication and a plastic beaker of water with a straw. Mum gratefully takes the pills and swallows them down without hesitation. The nurse looks to the television and closes her eyes, shaking her head is disbelief. "That poor little girl. I wish we had the death penalty in Australia." She quickly covers her mouth, as if shocked that she said the words out loud, "I beg your pardon."

I'm not even shocked, "Oh I agree. What a disgusting excuse for a human." Reaching over to chuck Emilee under the chin, she rewards me with a dribbly grin, pulls the pacifier out of her mouth with a soft 'pop' and speaks gibberish at me. This provokes a laugh from me, echoed by the nurse. Zoe nuzzles Emilee and drops loud, smacking kisses under her chin, rousing an excited squeal and giggle that infects everybody in the room. The news report continues to relay details of the arrest and lists some of the charges, one of which is necrophilia... The nurse beside me draws a horrified breath and my heart faulters and beats in my chest; an indignant rage washes over me. This evil man is not human, he is like a tumour that needs to be removed from society and discarded. You cannot reform that kind of sickness.

Kaitlyn, a welcome distraction, enters with the vase and gets busy filling it in the bathroom and arranging the flowers. When she returns to put the flowers on the beside drawers, she points to the large bouquet of flowers already occupying the space and queries, "Gran, who are these ones from?"

It's only been twenty minutes and it looks as though the meds have started to kick in; Mum doesn't look as tense and the creases between her brows have relaxed. "The girl who helped me yesterday popped in to see how I was doing. She brought that lovely big bunch of Oriental lilies. Isn't the smell just divine?"

"Wow, how thoughtful."

"Hmm, kind of restores your faith in human nature, don't you think?" Mum's smile now looks a bit dreamy. I think she's about to embark on a trip to a magical island populated by unicorns and fairies.

The nurse narrows her eyes, "don't you mean your niece? I thought it was your niece who visited you this morning. I handed her the vase myself."

Mum giggles like a child, "Oops, I dinn't realise she told a liddle wide lie." I frown at her; her smile is broad and euphoric and her words slur, "...thaas okaaaay. she cannnn be my neeeez tooodaaaay." Jesus H Christ, she's positively off her nut. The meds must be some form of narcotic. They've kicked in bloody quick. I look at Kaitlyn and she's silently laughing into her sleeve; Zoe's face is buried in Emilee's jumpsuit, but I can see she's giggling. This is not their regal Gran – she's off her peanut.

The nurse winks at Mum, "your secret is safe with me. Have a lovely evening, Beverley, I'm just about to finish my shift so I'll probably see you tomorrow morning."

Mum startles in slow motion, "Oh shiii, is Nurse Rashettt com-ng bacccccck?"

My eyebrows dart north... she swore and called the other nurse, Nurse Ratched. The nurse hides her mirth, "no, her shift finished an hour ago... and she won't be back until Friday now, so I don't think you'll see her again before you leave."

"Well thank the Lorrrrrd for smol merses. Wha a shaaaaaaame."

I make eye contact with the nurse and I'm about to apologise when she flaps a hand at me as she exits, "your Mum is not the only patient not impressed by her bedside manner – but you didn't hear that from me, sshhh." I make a mental note to call Dad and warn him that Mum is tripping major balls – God knows what's going to pop out of her mouth. I look at mum as she drowsily falls sideways. Kaitlyn leaps up and retrieves the remote from the table and lowers the bed to a horizontal position while I tuck her in. She's drifted off to the land of the dead by the look of her slack face. We gather our things and leave. Mum doesn't even rouse when we peck her on the cheek goodbye, Emilee's peck more akin to a wet suck. The girls giggle all the way to the car.

13

Charity

Li Xiu

We have no food left in the house and the money has run out. Bàba left the house that night and hasn't returned. He doesn't answer my calls and Nai cannot cook air. Māmā is so weak she could barely sit for her spoon of yoghurt this morning, and that ran out also. For the last couple of nights, Năinai has been taking food from the large dumpsters behind the bakery and the greengrocer. She does this under the cover of darkness. She doesn't want to bring shame on our family, but we need to eat.

Nobody knows what to say to me, so they avoid me, even my friends. They eat their lunch elsewhere now so rather than sit alone near the canteen where we used to gather, I sit alone behind the library in the quiet garden with only the birds for company. I don't want them to see that I have no lunch.

My good friend Mase finds me and plonks himself down beside me. He asks where my lunch is. I look at him and shake my head.

He sits beside me and unwraps his sandwich, offering me half. I shake my head no, but he won't be swayed. My stomach grumbles loudly and makes me feel small and humiliated. Mase removes one half of the sandwich and firmly thrusts the other half at me again, brooking no argument. I gratefully accept the offering and force myself to nibble at the edges when I want to indelicately shove it in my mouth. Tears of gratitude fill my eyes. Mase puts an arm around me and pulls me into a firm one-sided embrace. This is my undoing and I sob inconsolably into my hands. Mase removes the nibbled sandwich from my hand, re-wraps it and fully embraces me. I cry into his shirt for a long time, and he lets me, pulling myself together only when the warning bell sounds to herald the end of lunch.

Mase walks with me to the lockers, retrieves his books and then waits while I grab mine, and we walk together to D Block for our English class. He doesn't ask anything of me, or demand explanations and he doesn't shower me with sympathy; there is just a quiet understanding that he can see that I am barely treading water, and he is here to hold me should I go under.

* * * * *

Katrina

This afternoon Mason quietly enters the back door, leans his bag on the floor against the edge of the island bench and sits beside me at the counter. He is home an hour early, ditching during his free period. He looks lost. "What's up, sweetheart?"

He looks down at his hands, his expression forlorn, "Sweetheart, what is it? Has something happened at school?"

After a big sigh, he says, "I have a friend at school who's in a very bad place, and I don't know what to do to help her."

He has my attention, "OK, tell me what's going on with her."

He appears reluctant to share but with a little encouragement, he finally spills, "Her little brother died a couple of months ago in an accident, he was just a toddler, and their whole family seems to be falling apart. Her mum is pretty much bed ridden because she can't eat, her dad has run away because he can't handle the death of his son and her grandmother is struggling to feed them. What can I do to help them, Mum?"

"Can you please bring her home so I can see what she needs help with? Just ask her to come home with you."

Would it be ok if I go back to school now and wait for her after last period, then we can bring her home this afternoon?"

Without hesitation I launch in, "Absolutely. Let me grab my purse and I'll drive you back to school now, so you don't miss her."

* * * * *

We park outside the main gate to the school with ten minutes to spare. Mason climbs out and enters the school grounds to find his friend. I sit back and enjoy the remains of the *eighties-hour* on the radio. I am startled out of my reminiscence when Mason opens the door. Standing beside him is Li Xui, the sad Asian girl from the track. She startles when she sees me, then her face relaxes. "Hello, Li Xui, it's nice to see you again."

Mason is incredulous, "Wait, you two know each other?"

I smile at my boy, "We've met before." Mason scrambles in after Li Xui and we head home.

The first thing I do is make them both a hot chocolate and put a plate of biscuits before them. After a few moments of awkwardness, Li Xui tells her tragic story. My heart is heavy for the burden resting on the shoulders of this poor young girl as she navigates her way through her own grief, made more difficult by the situation at home.

My first priority is to take Li Xui to a supermarket and stock the fridge & pantry at her home. I have no idea what they would usually eat but she does, and she is grateful for the help. It takes about an hour to gather the groceries and get through the check out. Li Xui drops her head in shame as we ring up the total; my arm across her shoulders offers comfort. I whisper that there is no shame in accepting charity… in a time of need it should be welcomed without shame.

As we drive to her home, I explain that I will organise a counsellor to come by the house to talk to her mum and grandmother. "Sweetheart, I'd like to be able to have them speak frankly with your mother in her own language. Could you please tell me, do you speak Mandarin at home or a different dialect?"

Li Xui nods, "we speak Mandarin."

"OK, that's a start. Also, what is your surname?"

Her spine stiffens, "Ying," she says with pride.

"I will also ask the counsellor to speak with you, sweetheart, in either your native tongue or English. Whatever makes you more comfortable. I think you need to speak to someone about how you are feeling."

"I'm ok, I talk with my grandmother. It's my mum I'm worried about."

"We will definitely get your mum some help, but would you mind so much speaking with them yourself?"

"OK."

I wonder if I will be treading on anyone's toes by stepping in like this. "Do you think your grandmother will be ok accepting our help? I don't want to take over, I just want to help."

Li Xui shakes her head, "My father abandoned us; we have no choice."

"OK. We may need to get something signed by an adult to legally organise this. I'm not sure what the laws are."

We draw to a stop at the kerb in front of a neat modern brick home. As we carry the groceries up the stairs to the front porch, the front door opens and an elderly, stooped Asian woman peeps out. She speaks very fast to Li Xiu in a tongue I don't recognise. Li Xiu looks defiant as she rapid fires back in the same tongue. She gently pushes past her grandmother and beckons us to follow. I feel like an intruder, but Mason and I follow her through the entry, past a living area and into a small kitchen. We put all the grocery bags on the kitchen counter. As Mason and I remove the items from the bags, Li Xiu puts them in the pantry and fridge. Poor granny hovers in the corner and looks uncomfortable, but I don't know how to talk to her so when I make eye contact, I smile at her. She doesn't smile back; she looks scared of me and what is happening.

After we've emptied the bags, I begin to fold them neatly as Mason talks quietly with Li Xiu. Someone calls out loudly in the foreign language, desperation in her voice, from a room down the hall. Both Li Xiu and her grandmother still, they look concerned. Mason and I silently wait for something to happen. The person down the hall yells again, intermittently interrupted with sobbing. Li Xiu closes her eyes and a tear escapes and rolls down her cheek unchecked. "She must have heard Mason's voice. She thinks my father has returned. I have to tell her he hasn't."

Mason quickly grabs the remaining empty bags and says to Li Xiu, "Mum and I will let ourselves out. Perhaps you could explain to your mum and grandmother about the counsellor in case we need a signature and so they're not surprised when they come?"

"Please let us know if they don't want this help." I add. She nods, disappears down the hall and leaves us with frightened granny, who has backed herself into the corner, cowering. We head for the front door. As we pass the elderly grandmother, I smile gently and hope she doesn't think I'm a bit touched in the head. Mason looks at her and then bows, which almost makes me whoop with inappropriate laughter. Granny startles at him, but the corners of her mouth turn up a little.

On the short drive home, I ask, "why did you bow?" Mason's face reddens, "I panicked." After a moment, we both burst into laughter. Mason laughs so hard he has tears in his eyes. I consider pulling over until I contain my mirth but we're close to home. I explain to Mason that Li Xiu is the sad Asian girl I used to see on the track. I remember telling him on occasion that I'd seen her and didn't know how to reach out to her. At the time, he told me that I can't fix everyone. Then the Baby Abby tragedy happened and eclipsed everything.

Once back inside the house, I look up Mandarin speaking counselling services in our local area.

* * * * *

Felicity

I've just finished a phone call with Louise. She's organising our annual trip to the Island to her parent's holiday house in a few months. We've all rallied around Katrina after Jack cheated and ruined the marriage. I am looking forward to the escape for the weekend. To be able to relax and not have to measure my words or worry about Damien's mood will be such a treat.

I decide to take myself for a walk.

* * * * *

Nathan

Saxon got us another gig tomorrow. It's a bit last minute but I'm desperate for the extra dosh. My car is in the shop again… fucking lemon. It's such a cool ride but she's been a money pit since I bought her. She's a sleek red V8 Ford XB Falcon GT 351 Coup, chosen because of my love for the original Mad Max movies. Originally, I was going to get her resprayed black, but I just can't let go of the red. Dad's a Holden man and didn't hide his disgust when I rocked up with her, but I can tell he secretly thinks she's beautiful.

The latest breakdown was the last straw. I took it in to the mechanic last week and a different guy greeted me this time. I asked him where the other dude was and he grinned at me, "he's gone, man. He was a dodgy prick!" Maybe this guy will be able to find the issue and fix it once and for all. God, I wish I could do it myself. I told him no more bandaids. I need this car fixed and reliable. He made me rev it a few times and said he's pretty sure it's detonation, whatever the fuck that is. He took in my 'what?' expression and elaborated. "Detonation is when the fuel pre-ignites before the piston reaches the spark ignition." He could have been speaking Spanish for all I understood. I give no shits, just fix it, man. "Sounds expensive."

"Nah man, let me have her for a couple of days and I'll see what she needs. I think I can reset your timing and maybe look at your radiator. We might get away with just another fan. I'll keep the cost as low as I can." He sounds legit, but I have no fucking idea. He runs his hands along her front fender, "She's a beautiful set of wheels". I smile in appreciation.

We're back in the removalist van – it's a great cashy job, so I can put it towards the lemon fund. I miss my ride.

I've decided to stay in tonight, so I'll have a brain tomorrow. I endured some curry from the boys who were off to the pub for Friday night bevvies. I had a few beers while I ate my ham and cheese toasties, but I'm going to hit the pillows and get an early night.

I set the alarm for five am. That's gonna burn.

* * * * *

I wake at one am, busting for a piss. I tiptoe to the bathroom, not wanting to wake Matt, my housemate. Matt Freeburgh is a bit of a weird cat. He's quiet and nerdy and not into anything I'm into. He's not into anything my mates are into either. He's nice enough, just not a real conversationalist. He's a maths tutor. There must be money in it because he's always got cash. Maths is not my strong suit. I'm shit at maths so kudos to him for making it his thing.

As I get halfway down the hall, I can see the weird glow of his computer in the dark. He's sitting in the darkness of the spare room watching something on the screen. His back is to me, and I can see the muscles working in his back. Some chick on the screen is tied to a chair copping punches to the face. I'm about to say something to him when I realise, he's having a wank. Shit! My face flames like it was me who got caught. I dart down the rest of hall to the loo and have to talk my bladder into releasing the bounty. Jeez, what weird porn is he watching? Some weird shit that I don't *want* to know about. Jesus, people are weird.

After I flush, I walk heavily to my room. I don't want him to think I was spying on him. As I pass the spare room, I see the door is closed. Let's just pretend that never happened. How am I supposed to get back to sleep after that weird shit?

14

New Start

Katrina

It is 'moving day' for Jack and Anne, and the kids have gone to help with the move. I'm preparing to go for an interview with Beverley and Kenneth about the office job but first, a nice cup of tea on the quiet back deck, just me and my cheerful avian friends.

According to Lucy, Jack and Anne found a nice two-storey apartment in a quiet suburb near their office (which also means near us). Apparently, Anne's girls are keen to live with them fifty percent of the time but our three have opted to stay with me and visit their dad and Anne.

My phone trills and I run to the kitchen to retrieve it. Lucy's excited voice greets me, "Hi Mum... just wanted to let you know that we've arrived now."

"OK... that's um... well I'm happy for y..." Lucy cuts me off and excited scream whispers into the phone, "Oh my God, the removal guys are here and one of them is freaking HOT!"

A chuckle bubbles in me. "…he just winked at me, and I think I almost died!" This last bit was a squeak.

"Well, you clearly sound alive to me, poppet."

Her excited scream whispering continues, "I played it cool, but he keeps sneaking looks at me. Oh wow… Daisy & Chelsea have just arrived. Gotta go, LOVE YOU!"

Oh, to be young and infatuated at first sight. Go Lucy!

Hopefully Jacob remembers to give Jack and Anne the bottle of red I wrapped this morning. This is me deciding to be a grown up about Jack and Anne. My heart considered wrapping a dead rodent, the cerebral matter overruled the melodramatic centrepiece and good sense prevailed.

* * * * *

Nathan

When we pull to the kerb, I can't help but notice the blonde chick. She is hot. The girl she's with is hot too but the blondie has the most awesome eyes. They're an intense green. She looks my way and rewards me with a smile that shows off her pearly whites. I return the grin and she flushes red then turns and runs inside with her friend. I can see them giggling. I'll take that as a thumbs up. Hopefully by the end of the day, she'll want my number. I wouldn't mind tapping that. I wouldn't mind more than a tap… she's super hot, and probably out of my league but, you never know if you don't give it a go.

This is going to be a great day!

* * * * *

Katrina

As I turn in from the road and snake my way along the driveway, I am already impressed by the grandeur of this property. I'm not sure where to park so I pull up at the door and climb out of my car. I take in the stunning water feature in the middle of the circular drive.

The enormous front door is pillar-box red and stands out like the proverbial dog's bollocks; glass panes adorn the panels either side of the bright door. The said door opens to reveal a standing and mobile Beverley, leaning on a walking cane and grinning broadly at me.

"Good morning, Beverley. Don't you look the picture of health!"

Beverley laughs easily, "Don't be fooled by appearances, love. Come on in."

Immediately upon entry across the parquetry floor, a huge staircase with intricately carved woodwork rises to the second floor. Beverley leads me away from the grand staircase, through the expansive house to a brightly lit conservatory with a curved glass wall, surrounded outside with a lush green garden bed. A series of sunny yellow window seats, peppered with tasselled cushions, follows the curve of the glass wall on the inside. Overstuffed armchairs opposite the window seats complete the circle. A glass dome ceiling washes the entire conservatory in sunshine and invitation.

A squat, chunky, wooden table, already laid with a tea service tray, centres the space. An expensive, understated white china tea pot with matching sugar bowl and creamer jug in delicate duck egg blue trim sit in the centre of the tray. Teacups and saucers and tiny silver teaspoons with an intricate pattern are strategically placed on the saucers. A small platter sporting baked biscuits and slices has me salivating.

Beverley gestures me to take a seat and pours the tea from the perfect tea set. It's only been an hour since I ate breakfast, but I have to try the slice. I add milk to my tea, but Beverley delicately selects a slice of lemon from a small plate and adds it to her tea with a teaspoon of sugar. I feel like her Royal Highness Queen Elizabeth will enter at any moment.

"Beverley, this is a beautiful space."

She looks over her shoulder at the garden outside the wall and smiles. "This is my favourite room in the entire house. This is where I sit to enjoy a cup of tea, to read a book, to unwind after a busy day or to entertain my girlfriends."

She grimaces as she moves in her seat. "Does it still pain you?"

"Not really, just every now and again I get a little pain if I move a certain way. I'm a little surprised at how quickly it mended. The stitches were the most annoying part, to be honest, more so than the actual hip joint."

We talk about current affairs and general chit chat while we sip our tea. The raspberry and coconut slice is all I thought it would be and more. "Where did you get this delicious slice, Beverley?"

"I made that this morning." I nearly choke on my mouthful. I assumed she either bought it at a bakery or café, collected by one of her minions, or her cook produced it. I am ashamed by my assumptions. "It's truly the nicest slice I've ever eaten."

"It was my mother's recipe and she handed it down to me. It's always been a favourite of the boys."

This is a neat little segue into the reason for my visit. We leave the tête-à-tête in the sunny room and Beverley takes me up the grand staircase to the office. This room is neat and orderly. I am thrilled to discover they use the same accounting package I used at Dobunt. There's a copier, filing trays, alphabetised folders and a perfectly run organisation. I already love it and cannot wait to start.

Beverley looks hopeful, "what do you think?"

"I love it! It's perfect. When do you want me to start?"

Beverley looks taken aback, "… don't you even want to discuss an hourly rate?"

"Oops! Yes, I guess we should."

Beverley pulls out the seat and sits, "how does Monday to Thursday, nine to three, at fifty dollars an hour sound?"

Heck, that's more than I was on at Dobunt. I try to hide my surprise and act cool, "Sure, that works for me."

Beverley claps her hands in delight, "That's fantastic! Can you start on Monday, or is that too soon?"

"Monday is perfect. Thank you, Beverley. I'm so excited."

* * * * *

On the way home, I call in to the local bottle shop and collect a bottle of Moët. My children return from a day helping Jack and Anne move into their new home. Lucy is going on and on about the young man from the removalist company, eliciting an eye roll from the boys.

"We had to endure this from both Luce and Daisy. They weren't *that* hot."

Defensive, Lucy quips, "Oh, and you're a good judge of the male form, are you? What with you being completely heterosexual and all?"

Jacob rolls his eyes again. "I'm just saying, they weren't all that."

"Well, from someone who *is* a connoisseur of hot young men, I disagree. They were all that and more… one in particular." She holds up a sticky note with 'Nathan' and a phone number written on it.

Mason slaps a palm to his forehead. "Oh, you didn't!"

Lucy winks at me, "I did. I'm going to give him a call… in a couple of days. I don't want to appear too desperate. He so *cute*." She executes a little happy dance in my kitchen.

I whip out the bottle of chilled bubbles and pour us all a glass, including my underage son, Mason. They all look askance.

"Well, while you lot were out helping dad and Anne move house, and checking out cute guys, I went for a job interview… and I got the job! I start on Monday!"

A loud chorus of cheers from my children and we clink glasses.

Mason takes a deep swig and pulls a face, "Ugh, what is that?"

Lucy narrows her eyes at him, "its Champagne, you uncultured swine!"

I'm so happy I could sing, but I don't want to ruin the moment or make my children's ears bleed. This is cause for celebration and a little win in all the bad shit that has happened lately. It's a reason to smile and the first step on the path y

to my new future.

15

First Steps

Katrina

Within three hours of being in the office, I have emptied the 'in' tray, paid all the outgoing invoices and entered them in the accounting system, worked out the payroll system, created new invoices for clients and filed the paperwork.

My mobile beeps. A text from the real estate agent confirming he has organised a photographer to pop over on Saturday morning to take the photos of the house for the ad in the local rag. To his credit, Jack has organised most of the details. I'm going to miss our house. I think we'll have to rent somewhere until we find the home we want – I don't want to rush into anything too quickly and the kids are with me on that one. They can always crash at Jack and Anne's house if we struggle, and I can stop at Mum & Dad's house. My childhood bedroom is still a bedroom.

For the first time, the phone on my desk rings so I turn off my mobile. Taking a deep breath, I put my professional voice on and answer, "Milburn Construction, this is Katrina speaking,"

There is a pause at the other end, then a richly deep voice falters, "uh, hello Katrina. This is William."

The grey matter feels around up there, comes up with nada. The silence stretches on. Who the hell is William?

"William Milburn... Beverley is my mother."

Oh my God, what an idiot, "Oh William, I'm so sorry. Hello, how are you?" He must think I am a complete dipstick!

"I'm good. How are you settling in?"

"I'm already settled and loving it. This is such an orderly office. Whoever set this up is a very organised person, and I'd like to thank them."

"I set the office up, and you're welcome."

Gosh, his voice has such a deep timbre. The grey matter throws images of handsome movie stars around up there to match the voice.

"Well, you're a very organised man. Thank you for making my job easy."

He chuckles in that deep, throaty tone, "I'm actually after some contact details for an invoice we sent out a couple of months ago."

"Sure, do you want me to follow that up for you?"

Surprised, he stutters, "Er, sure. You don't mind doing that?"

"Not at all, it's part of the job. Tell me who the invoice was for, and I'll follow it up."

He rattles off the details of the invoice, which I note down. "OK, I'll let you know how I go."

"Thank you, Katrina." He pauses as the sound of a large truck roars in the background, and someone calls "Oi Wil!". He comes back to me "I'm sorry Katrina, I've got to go. The cement truck has arrived and it's all hands-on deck."

"No problems. Nice speaking with you William."

"You too. Bye"

My heart is thudding in my chest as he disconnects the call. I find the contact details of the invoice and prepare for battle. To my surprise, I'm greeted with surprised embarrassment and assured of immediate payment.

A half hour later, I see the payment tentatively drop into the bank account.

I compose a text to William, noting his mobile number on the wall above the phone.

Hi William, I called Mark Dunstan about that outstanding invoice. He was a little embarrassed about the mix up. He thought his wife had paid the invoice and she thought he had. Either way, the invoice has been paid and I've seen that it has dropped into the bank account as 'pending'. K

I decide it's time for a quick coffee to have with my lunch, so I dart downstairs to the kitchen. As I pass the conservatory, I see Beverley asleep on the yellow window seat, an open book on her chest; the tassel of the bookmark splayed across her breast. I quieten my steps but the clicking of my kitten heals on the parquetry has woken her. She pops up into the sitting position, completely belying her age, and stifles a yawn.

"Oh, sorry love, I just had a little 'nanna nap', as my boys call them."

I feel awful for waking her from her peaceful slumber in her favourite room, "I'm so sorry I woke you, Beverley. I was just going to make myself a coffee to have with my lunch."

She groans as she gets up off the window seat. "Oh no, that's fine. I just dropped off after reading a bit of my book. Do you mind if I join you?"

"Not at all."

"OK, I'll show you how to use the coffee machine."

* * * * *

Beverley delicately nibbles the cheese and cucumber sandwich she has made herself. I am a little less delicate, almost having to dislocate my jaw and wishing I had a flip-top head to get around this ridiculous roll I made myself this morning.

After some small talk, I ask, "Is there anything you need me to do? I've finished the invoices and all the stuff you asked me to do."

Beverley's eyes widen, "You're already finished all of that?"

I nod. "Well, if you're up for it, perhaps you could familiarise yourself with the superannuation and payroll, which is coming up."

"Absolutely, and that will probably take me up to the end of the day. You mentioned you need me to research some things and investigate costs. I can look into that tomorrow."

My phone buzzes on the table. It is a reply from William.

Wow. That was painless. Thanks.

"It's a message from William," I state to Beverley; I don't want her to think I'm being rude.

"Oh, you've already spoken to the boys then?"

"Not both, just William. He called the office phone, chasing an unpaid invoice." I send him the thumbs-up emoji and put my phone down. After we finish our respective lunches, Beverley excuses herself and says she needs to get onto dinner.

On my way back to the office, I wander into the living room and look at the photos. To my disappointment, no current photos of her boys adorn the walls, just childhood pictures of her boys fishing with a young Kenneth and the first day of primary school. There are some recent pictures of two girls, and a most recent photo of the older girl, now a grown woman, holding a baby. I make a mental note to ask Beverley about them tomorrow.

* * * * *

William

My phone buzzes and an emoji pops up from Katrina. I try not to think about her honeyed voice as the cement pours from the chute into the carefully boxed area that will form the slab foundation for this house.

Thomas, Greg, and I all spread the cement quickly before it goes off or hardens. When the pouring is complete, Greg sees the cement mixer truck off while Thomas and I screed the cement into a smooth surface. It's a warm day and the wind is up so we have to work quickly. My thoughts return to Katrina. I imagine a tall, busty blonde to go with the voice and Percy pops up like a piece of toast. Down boy, jeez. I'll bet she's not hot – people rarely look as hot as you imagine. In fact, she's probably a heifer with a jolly fat face; rosy cheeks and laughs like a chook after laying an egg.

"What are you thinking about?" I look up to see Thomas looking straight at me.

"What? Nothing, why?"

"…because you're just screeding the same spot over and over. Are you worried about something?" My face burns with embarrassment, and I answer a little too abruptly to cover my discomfit, "I'm not thinking about anything. Can't a man be alone with his thoughts anymore?"

Thomas angrily retorts, "Calm down, you flog. I was just asking! No need to bite my bloody head off!"

After glaring at him for a moment, another rude remark on the tip of my tongue, I think better of it, shake my head, and return to the task at hand.

Thomas is shitty and blunt for the rest of the afternoon until I awkwardly apologise for being a jerk, explaining that I was just thinking about someone I had to contact this afternoon. A lame excuse but he buys it, and his attitude lifts a little.

* * * * *

Nathan

Blondie has a name. Lucy turned out to be an awesome chick. Not only is she hot, but she's also good for conversation and weirdly, likes stuff I like. We talked on the phone for almost an hour last night when I finally plucked up the courage to ask her out on a dinner date on Friday. My car should be out of the shop by then. I'll give her a wash and detail and hopefully impress her with my ride.

16

Single Malt Whisky and Honey

Katrina

The 'Open for Inspection' appointments start this Thursday, with the auction scheduled for next month. I'm run ragged with the constant cleaning, but very grateful that I have adult children who can pitch in and help. I haven't even started looking for a place to rent – auctions can be dicey and sometimes they don't sell, so I don't want to be paying rent until I need to.

I've been working at this office for over a month now. I've spoken with Thomas a few times and William almost daily since that first phone encounter. Every time I hear his voice my heart rate escalates. It's deep, rich and velvet smooth like a fine single malt whisky. As much as I want to imagine a movie star to go with the voice, I know he won't be. He's probably five foot four with a balding pate, surrounded by ginger tufts. What do looks matter anyway? Considering I'm only five foot two he'll still be tall to me, and I couldn't care what colour his hair is.

He is funny, quick witted and intelligent; I'm drawn to him. Speaking with him is the highlight of my day and I almost float around the office afterwards. Connecting with someone over the phone is a great way to get to know someone. To be able to connect without the stress of worrying about looks, to just fall in love with a personality, it is refreshing. I can't wait to meet him, and I don't care if he's a short rotund ginger, I like him already.

Beverley has pointed out his daughters, the pictures of the young girls in the living room. They are beautiful; one of them a mother already. I've not had the joy of meeting them yet, but I look forward to the day when all the names are matched with faces.

The next experience I have is the distinct displeasure of speaking with a tall, blonde, streak of pelican shit who rocks up at the door while Beverley is out. I open the door and smile, as per my happy disposition, but I am greeted with a frosty glare from icy blue eyes. She rudely asks who I am, like it's any of her bloody business. Maybe its William's ex? I shelve the catty reply that I could ask the same of her, I am an employee here, and calmly explain that I am the Administration Officer. She flaps a hand and dismisses me with an 'Oh,' and breezes past me uninvited, like she owns the place.

I turn and say firmly to her back, "Beverley is not here."

Spinning on her heel, she narrows her eyes at me, like I'm out of line, and demands in a clipped tone, "Where is she?"

What's it to you, biarch? "I'm not sure, she said she had to pop out to run some errands. May I ask who you are?"

She has the nerve to look me up and down like I was a shady, unsavoury character. I refuse to be intimidated and hold my ground, glaring back.

"I'm Samantha, a family friend. Surely, they've mentioned me?"

Well, someone is conceited, "No, I've never heard your name mentioned. Can I help you with something, or shall I just tell Beverley you called by?" Swinging the door open wide in a *'get the fuck out'* gesture.

"Is William here?" she looks hopeful. Seriously, who is this chick?

"William is working." Dumbarse!

Her glance wanders around the living room, looking for what, I have no idea, then she stiffens and strides like a catwalk model to the front door and says over her shoulder as she exits, "Tell William I popped by."

I don't even benefit her with a response; I just close the heavy door soundly and climb the stairs to the office. As I reach the landing at the top of the stairs, I hear the office phone ringing. I sprint to the office and as I try to turn the corner into the office, my shoes slide out from under me on the parquetry floor and I land heavily on my posterior. My surprised yelp echoes through the empty house like a yodelling ghost at a haunting. "Wahoo-oo-oo-oo!" Thank God nobody is home to see that ridiculous manoeuvre. The phone is still ringing; surely, they'll hang up in a moment. I make it inside the office and yank the phone receiver up and bark, "Milburn Construction," down the receiver, followed by heavy breathing. To my horror, William replies, "Jesus, everything ok?" For the love of God, I close my eyes and compose myself, "Hi William, I'm so sorry. I just had to run up the stairs and slipped over outside the office. I thought I'd missed the call altogether."

"Are you ok?" There is mirth in his voice.

"Well, my pride is a little dented and there will be a nice, purple bruise on my derrière."

He openly laughs, "Did anybody see it?" Oh, you'd like that, wouldn't you?

"No, thank goodness. I'd just closed the door on someone, so I'm pleased she didn't see it."

"Oh, who came to visit?"

"Well, she came to visit you. As if you'd be home in the middle of the day on a Wednesday. Perhaps she doesn't know you're in construction? Said her name was Samantha?"

There's an audible groan down the line. "An ex, perhaps, who just can't let you go?"

"No, *God* no! Look, she's the daughter of Mum's closest friend and engaged to my cousin. We've known her since she was a little girl but boy 'o boy is she persistent."

"She was pretty familiar with the house and very confident she'd have been mentioned."

"Yeah, she's got tickets on herself, that one. She's alright, just a little clingy."

"How does she get along with your girls?"

"Aah, my girls are not fond of Samantha. She was rude to my ex too. She manages to turn a lot of men to water but let's just say that I'm immune to her powers."

Relief washes over me. The stuck-up bitch can go to hell. He changes the subject, and we talk about everything and nothing, as we have been doing for weeks now, and I mentally picture the fat balding ginger to go with the deep voice and get lost in it; I like him very much. I can't wait to meet him.

* * * * *

William

The phone is ringing and ringing and just when I'm about to disconnect, she picks up and yells "Milburn Construction!" down the line, like I've done something wrong.

She explains in that silken voice, dripping in honey she'd just fallen over outside the office. It takes every ounce of restraint not to guffaw down the phone.

This is my favourite time of day. I love speaking with her. She's such a happy little thing. It's like an injection of sunshine in my day. At the mere thought of sunshine injections, my memory throws up Donald Trump talking about injecting sunshine in your veins to get over the pandemic and I'm almost laughing again. Then she tells me Samantha called by. Damn. I wish she'd take the hint. I am just not interested in her. She does nothing for me and given that she behaves like an entitled, spoiled little brat, I'm even less attracted to her. Changing the subject, I want to talk about something that brings the sunshine back in.

Last night, the girls asked when I'm going to get onto a dating website. I told them I'm not interested in meeting anyone via an online hook-up network, and they made exasperated groans. I defensively said, "I don't need a woman. I'm not lonely!" That's a flat out lie, but I want them to let me be. I am a firm believer that when you're supposed to meet someone, it will happen by chance, not because you forced it by going on a dating website. The last thing I need in my life is a bunny boiler to mix things up. Nope, it will happen when it happens.

Frustrated, Kaitlyn added "But all your friends are married or in relationships, Dad. How will you meet anyone if you're just always third-wheeling?"

"Kait, why are you so desperate for me to find a woman? The last two girls I've dated you couldn't stand, and you didn't hide how you felt about them."

"Well, that's because they were both stuck up bitches. Maybe try to find someone who's got a personality and is not all about the genes."

"Harsh!"

In support of her sister, Zoe adds, "Sorry dad, but your taste in women sucks!"

Moments later, tired, and hungry little Emilee cried crankily and drew the attention her way. I bounced my grand daughter on my knee while Kaitlyn heated her dinner and thankfully, we did not return to the conversation.

Katrina draws me back to the now, so I tune in. I love chatting with this funny, vivacious woman who makes me smile without using her wiles, gives me something to look forward to and who just accepts me as the voice at the end of the phone. Usually awkward around the fairer sex, I don't feel anxious or awkward when I speak with her. Conversation flows out of me like I've been emotionally constipated for decades, and the blockage has been released. Katrina regales me with a tale about some old dude urinating in public when she was out for a run. The girl knows how to tell a story and she has me captivated until Thomas stalks up beside me and shouts in my other ear, "Mate, the dirt isn't gonna move itself, is it?!"

I wasn't expecting it and jumped. Calm down, mate! "Yeah, give me a minute. I'll be there in two ticks."

Tom looks at me like I've sworn at him, which elicits a frown. I throw my hands up in a 'what?' gesture. He rolls his eyes and saunters off. Why's he being such a little bitch?

"Sorry Katrina, I'm going to have to go. Thomas is pitching a fit because he needs me to help him with something. Have a great afternoon."

"No worries, Wil. You have a good afternoon too."

That's the first time she has used my shortened name. The way 'Wil' slid off her tongue makes my heartbeat loudly in my chest and blood roar in my ears. Thomas, the bastard!

17

The Heifer and the Ginger

William

Thomas steers the car around the curved driveway, heading towards the front door so I can dash in and grab my wallet. As we pass the living room, I notice the French doors are open and a feminine figure is standing in the open doorway, her arms limp at her sides, her eyes closed and a look of pure bliss on her face, which is angled up to the sun. Her hair gently ruffles in the soft breeze and the skirt of her dress flutters against her tanned legs. Thomas coasts past her and as we pass, the rolling noise of the tyres on the paved driveway breaks her trance and she looks our way as we coast by.

Thomas pulls up at the door and asks "who was that? Do you think it was the woman who's been helping with the office stuff?"

I want very badly for that beautiful figure to be Katrina, but I don't want to be disappointed. "No idea." I mumble and open the door to get out. Thomas cuts the engine and emerges from the other side, his curiosity getting the better of him.

It takes all my self-control to walk into the house rather than run. As I pass through the entrance, I stop in the doorway of the formal living room, and she is still standing there with her back to the doors; the light from the French doors basking her in glorious sunlight. My breath catches in my throat. Thomas brushes past me and walks towards her with an outstretched hand, "Hi, I'm Thomas."

A smile lights up her face as she takes his outstretched hand, "Hi Thomas," I know from the husky voice that it's her, but I wait for confirmation, "…I'm Katrina."

Oh, thank God she's not a heifer in yards of black. Both Thomas and Katrina turn to look at me quizzically. My eyebrows dart north. Holy shit, did I say that out loud?

Katrina says, "I'm sorry, what did you say?"

"What?" Jesus, Mary, and Joseph, I said it out loud. I try to regain my nonchalance, thrusting out my hand, "Hi, I'm William."

She doesn't break eye contact as she takes my hand… and zaps me with an electrical shock. We both jolt after the audible crack between our hands. Laughing nervously, because I'm awkward, she starts giggling, she must be awkward too, and Thomas is just looking at the two of us like we've lost our fucking minds.

"You thought I'd be a heifer?" Oh shit. "I don't know why I said that, sorry." I look at Thomas and he's frowning at me. My face lights up in mortification and I sheepishly shrug my shoulders. She smirks at me, "That's ok. I thought you would be short, fat, and balding… with ginger tufts."

"Whoa, what? That's harsh." An awful guffaw escapes me, and Katrina lets loose a deep throaty chuckle. We're both laughing hard; Thomas is just about giving himself whiplash, looking between the two of us, incredulity written all over his face.

"What the hell are you two on about?"

We both abruptly stop laughing and look at Thomas. Thomas glares at me, "… dude, your wallet?"

"Yep," I snap out of my stupor, "lovely to meet you Katrina, we've got to go."

Thomas looks like a spooked horse, and I feel like an idiot, so I run to the kitchen like the hounds of hell are snapping at my heels, and retrieve my forgotten wallet, then we make a hasty exit.

* * * * *

Katrina

I'm still in awe of William and I can't believe I said that stuff about the bald fat guy. After the door closes behind them, I sneak up to the French doors and watch them as they climb into the car. He's impossibly tall… too tall perhaps? And he's bloody handsome. His eyes are the kind of blue you only see in pictures, and I wonder if he is wearing coloured contacts. My stomach is swarmed with butter-flies as his t-shirt tightens across his back when he reaches for the door handle. I imagine running my hands across his rippling back muscles. Thomas stops briefly beside the driver's side door and looks across at the window. He sees me looking out at them, so I offer a faltering smile and raise a hand in farewell. He nods at me and climbs in the car. I wonder at Thomas' expression. Have the boys just had words? Thomas seemed a little tetchy about the wallet. Maybe they're in a hurry.

I watch the car drive all the way down the long driveway and momentarily lose sight of them as it curves around at the bottom, but it reappears in view before it turns onto the road. I stand there for a while, dreamily thinking about him and imaging all sorts of scenarios before pulling myself together.

As I turn from the doors, I see movement at the top of the stairs and spy Beverley looking down at me over the balustrade. "Was that the boys?"

"Yes, I think they just popped in to grab something."

"So, you finally met them then?"

I try to control my happy smile, "Yes, I can finally put a face to their voices."

Beverley gives me a knowing smile and I don't think I've fooled her with how much I like her son.

* * * * *

William

We are silent in the car for a full five minutes before Thomas breaks the silence "what the hell was that back there?"

My shoulders droop and I sigh. "Sorry, God, how do I explain this?"

Thomas gives me nothing, "we've been speaking almost daily, Katrina and me, on the phone… and I wanted her to be beautiful, to match her voice, but it's never the case, is it? They always turn out to be the worst looking people and I like her so much, that I had convinced myself she'd be hideous, and I'd like her anyway because the person on the other end of the phone was gorgeous in every way imaginable so why should I not like her because doesn't match the image I envisaged?"

"Mate, what the fuck are you talking about? Are you high? You sound 'high as balls' right now."

"No, Tom, I'm not bloody high. I'm trying to explain why I said that."

"So, let me get this straight… you convinced yourself she'd be a big, fat ugly cow so you wouldn't be a shallow arsehole?"

"Well, she did the same thing! Did you hear what she imagined I'd look like? Short and fat… and balding with ginger tufts… hers was way worse than mine."

"You're both off your bloody rockers! I've never heard so much weird shit in such a short span of time!"

"C'mon, surely you've been here before?"

"…and exactly where is 'here'? Pluto? No! I have NEVER been in that weird predicament in my *life!*"

He's pissing me off now, "so you've never spoken with someone regularly on the phone and imagined they'd be really hot and when you finally meet them, they're the opposite of how you imagined… like they've been bashed half to death with the ugly stick?"

He looks disgusted and almost spits the words out, "God, you're a shallow arsehole."

Yeah, that did sound shallow, "don't worry about it. I'm weird, she's weird, we're both weird and I'm fine with that."

"Ok, cool dude." That's his go-to insult, thanks, mate.

"Well, YOU asked… *dude!*" Piss off Thomas, you're a dick.

I fold my arms across my chest like a petulant child because I feel embarrassed, and Tom just made me feel like a shallow prick. He reaches over and turns the radio on, thank God.

After a good five minutes of brooding silence from me, Thomas turns down the radio and I wait for the second barrage… "Sorry, Wil, I didn't mean to be snarky… I just like her, and she clearly likes you, so I got pissed off."

It's my turn to be the spooked horse, "You like her? When did you speak with her?"

"I didn't, I saw her talking to Mum at the hospital when she first did her hip, but I didn't have the nerve to introduce myself and just watched through the window. I stayed outside until she left and then went in… and I thought I'd missed my chance. Then when I saw it was her at the doors when we drove in… I got my hopes up."

"All this time I've been talking with her on the phone, and you never said anything?"

"Well, I didn't know it was her that came to do the office work, until we saw her."

Raking my hands through my hair in frustration, I don't know whether to feel guilty or pissed. I decide on neither.

"I haven't asked her out or anything, Tom. You can ask her out."

"Ah no, mate, I won't be cutting your lunch. You won't get any competition from me."

"Well now I feel shit!"

"Nah, don't feel shit. I get it. I was a dick about it."

"Ah, the infamous '*cool dude*' sarcastic quip."

Thomas grins at me "yeah, that" … and I know we're good again. I wish I could drive back home and have a decent chat with her, face to face. Thomas parks the car, and we walk into the hardware store to collect the order.

18

Betrayed by Blood

Li Xiu

I'm very disappointed in my father. Bàba has just left us with no money and no food, left his family to fend for themselves amid this grief and chaos. Năinai has convinced Māmā to allow the Mandarin speaking psychologist to counsel her. We accepted help from Mason's family for the first session, but we cannot continue to accept charity. The psychologist also spoke with me on that first visit, but I insisted she spend her time with Māmā; she needs this more. The kind woman who came to talk with Māmā told us to see our doctor, who gave us access to a program to provide free help for Māmā, since my father abandoned us. It took some time to organise, and we were on a waiting list for a while but given our circumstances, our doctor pushed very hard, and we were bumped up the queue. She has had three sessions now and Năinai and I can already see the difference.

This morning, Māmā ate breakfast at the kitchen table with

Năinai and me. She still cries in the night in Wáng Lěi's room, but we leave her to her grief; she has lost her child and must walk this earth forever with a piece of her heart missing.

I've found part-time work after school at the local supermarket, which helps pay for food and the bills. Mason also works at the supermarket, so I have a friend there. Mason walks with me to and from the supermarket when our shifts coincide and sometimes, even when they don't. Talking with Mason helps more than talking with the psychologist. I have also spoken with the school counsellor twice, and she gave me some helpful advice for Māmā.

Today the anger and bitterness have taken hold of me. How could Bàba abandon us in our time of need? How could he walk away and leave us alone to deal with Wáng Lěi's death? He doesn't take my calls and twice, he has cut off my call, so I know he sees them. I've left desperate messages for him to come home, told him that Māmā is not good, sent him texts to help us when we ran out of food. He gives me nothing. I'm very disappointed in him so today; I'm going to send him a text message telling him as much. I won't be nice. I'll be disrespectful, but he needs to hear what I have to say.

I begin my text, carefully typing out my long message, and read it twice before I press 'send'.

Dear Bàba. You have abandoned your family and left us to perish. I called and I messaged but you didn't come home or even call. You left us with no food and no money. Năinai had to go through rubbish bins to put food on our table. This is the disgraceful behaviour of rats, but this is what we were reduced to, and we live in shame. We had to rely on charity because we were desperate. I had to get a job to pay the bills. I am sixteen years old, Bàba, and trying to succeed at school. You put this on my shoulders. Năinai has been worried sick about Māmā, who doesn't eat and is barely alive. We all lost Wáng Lěi; we all grieve our beautiful boy. You still have a wife and daughter at home and your mother wrings her hands in worry. How could you put this on all of us? Why are we not worthy of your love and care? I am also your child, and I didn't die. Am I not worthy of your love? I'm disappointed and ashamed to call you father.

My tears plop onto my phone, blurring the message. I don't want to talk with such disrespect to Bàba, but I am desperate to make our family whole again. Māmā needs Bàba to come home, we all do.

Năinai sits beside me on the porch step. She can see I have been crying. She puts her arm around my shoulder and pulls me to her. I cry on her shoulder for a long time while she makes gentle circles on my back. She doesn't say anything, she just offers comfort. Năinai understands my disappointment. She is also disappointed in her son; I see it written all over her face. After a long time, I draw away, "I have to get ready for work. Do you need help to prepare dinner before I go?" She shakes her head no; grateful we have this pitiful income but distressed that the weight of the wellbeing of our family falls on my shoulders.

Tomorrow, I'll take Māmā for a walk around the block in the warm sunshine to get her out of the house and put some colour in her cheeks. Tomorrow is Saturday and I don't have a shift until late afternoon. I'll get up early and finish what is left of my homework and start my study for Monday's test.

After I change into my work uniform, I come back outside to find Năinai still sitting on the step. Her eyes are red and rheumy, she has been crying. I sit beside her and offer her the comfort she gave me just moments ago. Māmā also steps outside, the first time she has set foot over the threshold since the tragedy, and sits on my other side. Māmā leans on my side and tears run down her face and onto my arm. We will get each other through this.

Năinai unfurls her hand, her knuckles gnarled with arthritis. Nestled in her palm is a soft *Peter Rabbit* toy that hung from Wáng Lěi's cot. Māmā reaches for the toy and brings it to her face. She sways against me and silently weeps into the velveteen fabric. This is how Mason finds us when he opens the gate and slowly approaches us.

Māmā and Năinai wave to him, smiling through their tears. They like Mason and all that he stands for. I like Mason too, more than a friend… but I don't tell anyone this. This is my little secret that I hug to myself and share with nobody because I couldn't stand the rejection if he doesn't feel the same. I join Mason on the path. The gate squeaks as he opens it and allows me through before him. We both wave goodbye to Năinai and Māmā and continue down the street to the supermarket.

For the first time in our long friendship, Mason reaches for my hand and holds it in his as we walk on the street. I feel immediately embarrassed, but also elated. I'm sure my cheeks have pinked. My heart thuds deep in my chest and although I can feel his eyes on me, questioning if I am comfortable with this arrangement, I don't meet his eyes… but I don't pull my hand away either. This is my consent. We walk in comfortable silence, enjoying the electricity that travels between us in this simple joy.

19

Courage of a Lion

Katrina

I've finished payroll and send out the invoices. Before leaving for the day, I back up my system and straighten everything on my desk. I haven't spoken with William since that day we met by chance and wonder if he's disappointed in what he saw. I had been speaking with him daily before that and I really felt like we had a connection but the fact that he hasn't called since makes me uncomfortable. I have convinced myself that he's just been busy.

The phone jingles loudly in front of me. I snatch it up and answer, hoping it's not the chatty gent I spoke with earlier who called looking for a quote on a renovation. To my delight, William is on the other end of the line and think '*what a coincidence!*' I'm more than happy to stay back and chat with him. I've missed his calls.

Trying to be cool and not over do it, I try to chill "Well howdy, stranger. I haven't spoken with you for a few days!" *Howdy stranger? Real cool, Katrina!* Aah, the bitch is back.

"Yeah, we've been pretty busy." He sounds flat. I guess he has been avoiding me. Better cut to the chase then and make it as comfortable as I can, "How can I help?"

There is an awkward silence! "Hello, William?"

"Yeah, I'm here. I, ah..." Big sigh. I don't know what to do with this awkward silence, so I wait it out. I hear him draw another breath and then he starts to speak, but his voice is high and cracks like a pubescent boy, "Katr... ugh," he clears his throat and starts again, "Sorry, not sure what happened there. Um, Katrina, I was wondering if you'd like to maybe go out for a meal one night... with me... together?"

Well, there's a surpise! "Sure, I'd like that."

"Really?" Why so incredulous?

"Yeah, really. When were you thinking?" I want to yell that I'm free tonight! Oh, I'd need time to primp myself... and get rid of that single coarse dark chin hair I saw this morning sticking out of my face like an offensive face pube.

"I was thinking maybe Friday night after next?"

"That would be great. What time?" Plenty of time to pluck that strong little bastard out of my face. Better check the lady moustache too.

"I could collect you at, say seven ?"

"OK, that would be great. Do you need me to book somewhere?"

"No, I'll take care of that. Great... see you then."

"OK... I'll speak with you during the week."

"Of course, sure. Bye."

After I hang up, I sit at my desk staring at the phone. My heart beats an excited tattoo in my chest. Maybe I'll treat myself to a little something cute to wear.

* * * * *

William

I sit here panting and grinning like an idiot. She said yes. All that nervous stress and stomach-churning bullshit I put myself through for days, imagining how I'd recover if she said no, feeling like I needed to dig deep and find the courage of a lion to call and ask the question, and it was all for naught.

God, when my voice cracked like a bloody teenager I could have died. I expected the glass in the newly installed windows to shatter, the pitch was so high. I had to wait for Thomas to piss off because I didn't need his audience during that awkward encounter. Thank God I did, imagine if he heard that puberty pitch. He'd be giving me shit for weeks to come.

I told him I'd pack up the last of the site before the weekend, and hung around so long for him to go, I thought I'd probably miss her at the office. He sat in his truck with the engine running, tapping away on his phone. I started to get so anxious I considered throwing a brick at his window. So, I concentrated on packing up the last bits and securing the site until I finally heard his engine roar as he accelerated out of the lot. I could have grown a beard waiting for him to bugger off.

Then I ran to my truck like an athlete and had to calm the fuck down before I punched in the numbers for the office, lest I sound like I'd been engaged in extra curricular activity moments before dialling. My God, I am awkward.

I got myself so worked up and nervous that I sweated like a pig in the cabin of my truck. Now I can smell my armpits and it's offensive even to me. I'm supposed to be meeting Greg at the pub, but I think I'd better pop home for a shower first.

As I pull up at my studio apartment, I spy Samantha's car near the front door. I can see her silhouette inside the vehicle. She looks up and sees me, waving wildly at me. Quickly exiting my truck, I make a run for it, but she leaps out of her car and walks towards me with a big smile on her face, "Well hello, handsome."

Bugger, "Hi Sam, I've just got to have a quick shower before I meet Greg at the pub."

"Oh sure, I'll wait for you."

What? Why? "You don't have to wait – I'll be in and out."

"I was wondering if you could give me a lift and I'll leave my car here – I feel like a few glasses of bubbles today. I'll collect my car tomorrow."

Oh, for fuck's sake. Why the hell did I not just go straight to the bloody pub. I'm pissed off with myself and find it hard to keep my ire out of my tone.

"I didn't know you were coming. I thought it was just the boys." It's not like me to say this sexist shit but she's as persistent as a noxious weed.

She looks momentarily crestfallen, but replaces it with a smile, "I just wanted to surprise my man. I've missed him." Sure, you did. I have no choice but to be polite.

"OK, I'll be out in a minute. Maybe park your car over there." I point to the car port near my apartment and immediately regret my stupidity. Her face lights up like a Christmas tree.

"OK," she chirps, and she executes her best catwalk strut to her car. I continue inside for a quick shower and to curse loudly under the jets at my stupidity in returning here in the first place. I've gone from exhibiting the courage of a lion to becoming the village idiot. What a schmuck!

20

Daddy's Home

Li Xiu

Mason sits close; I can smell his deodorant and I find it comforting. Our heads are together as we work on our homework together. Năinai and Māmā have gone for a walk in the sunshine to get Māmā out of the house. I enjoy the alone time with Mason. His thigh is touching mine, but I won't move away. I like how it feels. His hand brushes mine as he reaches for his pen. His touch feels like electricity shooting through my hand and I stifle the jolt. I look up and straight into his eyes. Holding my breath, I wait for him to look away, but he looks at my mouth. He leans forward and gently touches his lips to mine. My heart beats so hard in my chest I think it's going to explode. His face is inches from mine, and I want him to do it again. I lean forward and touch my lips to his. Mason's face flames, but he leans into my mouth and kisses me properly, the way people kiss in movies. He tastes of the cola we just shared. His mouth is cool and soft; I don't want it to stop.

The front screen door opens, and we jolt apart guiltily. We wait for Năinai and Māmā to come into the kitchen. We have both gone red in the face and I am grinning like an idiot. I sneak a peek at Mason, and he smiles back at me and then guiltily back at the book in front of him. I reach for his hand under the table and my heart goes nuts again.

The footsteps coming down the hall are slow and measured. I look up to see Bàba standing in the doorway. His hair is long and matted, his face unshaven and he looks unkempt. I blink at him, unsure if this is my imagination or if he really is here. Mason looks at Bàba, and then at me. Bàba looks at Mason and then at me. Everybody is looking at me, waiting for my reaction, but I am too shocked to react.

Bàba whispers my name, "Li Xiu".

I stare back at him silently. I can't move, frozen in my seat.

Mason stands abruptly and gathers his things. "I'd better get home."

I can tell he doesn't want to walk past my father, whose body fills the space in the doorway, so he says in a quiet voice, "I'll go through the back", and hastily exits through the glass sliding door beside the kitchen bench. A moment later I hear the latch on the side gate rattle as he lets himself out. I can't tear my eyes away from Bàba.

He whispers my name again, "Li Xiu." I want to cry. I want to sob in relief that he has returned and run to him, but my anger at his desertion stomps all over my fleeting joy and so I don't say anything. To my horror, Bàba sobs my name, "Li Xiu", his voice cracking in desperation to reach me. It sounds so pitiful coming from this man who never cries, never shows emotion. He is the rock of our family, but he's crumbling before me. Bàba falls to his knees and sobs, slumped against the architrave. He sounds so wretched, "Please!" he begs.

I rise from my seat and take a few tentative steps toward him, not sure what to do. He continues to cry with abandon, slumped in the doorway. I quietly walk over and kneel before him. I gently touch his shoulder. I don't know what I expected but he surprises me by placing his hands on the ground in front of my knees, rests his forehead on his hands and begs my forgiveness in that pitiful voice. My heart lets go of the fear and anguish that has been pent up for months, and I place my hands on his quaking shoulders in forgiveness.

I hear the sliding door behind me open, followed by Māmā's scream. She rushes into the room and kneels beside me, screaming Bàba's name. "Bojing, Bojing!"

I stand and get out of the way. Māmā kneels before Bàba, clutching at his hands. He looks up and cries her name, "Chenguang!" He shuffles forward on his knees and pulls her into his embrace and the two of them wail in grief in the doorway.

I look over to see Nǎinai standing in the kitchen, pressed into the corner. The crepe skin on her face is wet with tears. I walk to her with purpose and hold her as she too sobs on my shoulder. I don't sob. I'm all cried out.

While I hold Nǎinai, letting her relief wash over me, I think of Mason and our beautiful kiss. Resting my face on Nǎinai's shoulder, I smile to myself. My world, which was shattered into a million glittering shards this morning, is now temporarily put back together, albeit with craft glue, and I revel in the peace that has settled on me.

21

Dating a Bombshell

Nathan

I'm as nervous as hell as I pull in at the kerb in front of Blondie's house. There's a forthcoming auction sign out front. I wonder where she's moving to.

I picked up the car yesterday and she is driving like a dream. The only lemon about my baby now is the citrus air-freshener sitting in the consol. This mechanic absolutely knows his shit and the other useless dickwad who sucked my wallet dry and did shit-all can get into his douch-canoe and paddle the fuck away. I'm so glad I met this bloke.

I look at my watch and realise I'm about fifteen minutes early. I know how long chicks take to get ready and I don't want to be sitting awkwardly in the lounge room getting grilled by her dad while she finishes her makeup, so I cool my jets in the car for a bit, listening to *Linkin Park* tunes.

Punctuality has been drilled into me by my mum, so I wait until five minutes to seven before I walk up the path to her porch and knock on the front door. My hands are sweating so I wipe them dry on my jeans. Blondie opens the door and greets me with a smile that lights up the whole freakin' street. She steps out and pulls the door shut behind her. A cloud of a soft feminine floral scent surrounds me and kicks my heart rate up.

"Why were you sitting in your car out here?"

Shit, "I was early and didn't want to disturb you while you were getting ready." She makes a cute noise and says, "That's so sweet. I've been ready since six though. I don't wear much make up and I *hate* it when my friends make me wait because they're still trowelling on another layer of orange cement. Ugh."

I look at her and notice that she really doesn't have much makeup on – a little lip gloss and some mascara. How bloody refreshing! Her eyes are a dark grey blue. She's prettier than I remember. Her bottom lip is plump, and I imagine kissing her mouth. My mind goes somewhere disrespectful, so I pull myself together and dart ahead to open the passenger door for her. She looks at me quizzically and I inwardly panic that I'm going to get a lecture about sisters doing shit for themselves. Instead, she smiles sweetly and thanks me before delicately folding herself into my car.

"This is a cool car, Nate. What year?"

"1975. I've been having a lot of trouble with her but only just found out that the last mechanic was ripping me off and not doing a single thing. This new guy just knew straight away what was up and fixed her. I was so happy, I tell you."

As I start her up, the engine roars and crackles as she idles. I look over and notice goose bumps on Lucy's forearms. Oh yeah, she's my kind of girl.

I try to keep the testosterone to a minimum and drive sensibly to the Thai restaurant in a nearby strip of shops.

* * * * *

Our cheap and cheerful meal was delicious. We practically had to be thrown out so the staff could go home. We didn't even realise we were the last ones there until there was sudden silence and I looked around and said, "Oh, oops. I think we'd better get going before they turn us out."

As Lucy stood, I walked to the front of the restaurant and paid for our meal. When I returned, Lucy asked," How much do I owe you?"

"You owe me nothing. Dinner was on me tonight."

As I pulled up to the kerb outside her house, I stopped the car, got out and walked around to open her door. She smiled up at me, "Chivalry is not dead!"

"You can thank my dad for that."

I walked her to the front door. A sensor light came on briefly as she dug around in her bag for the key. When the light went out, she turned to me, and I bent forward and dropped a kiss on her mouth. I drew back straight away because I didn't know what to expect and I didn't want to make it awkward or make her feel crowded, but she surprised me by stepping back into my space and kissing me back. The sensor light blinks on again. Holy shit she can kiss. By the time she pulls away I'm sweaty with my heart ready to explode out of my chest. Other parts of the anatomy also approve.

I grin to hide my embarrassment, "Wanna do this again?"

She smiled back at me, "I sure do. How does next Saturday night work? Do you want to see a movie?"

"Sure, do you have something particular in mind?"

"There's a Mad Max movie marathon showing at that small independent cinema around the corner. It starts next week with the first movie. Are you interested in that?"

My eyes just about bug out of my head and it's all I can do not to scream about her awesomeness in her face. I hope my face isn't doing anything weird. Playing it cool, I nod and say, "that would be great. Text me the details, yeah?"

"Sure. Thanks for tonight, I had a really nice time."

"Me too," she comes back in for another kiss that gives me head spins, lit up on the porch by the sensor light.

Every cell in my body wants to skip back to the car, but I manage to play it cool long enough to get in her and carefully drive away before exhaling.

The cinema she mentioned is right near my rental house. I'll suss if she's up for hanging out at mine after. I should be able to read whether it's too early. I really like her and don't want to scare her off. I'll check with Matt if he's cool for us to use the main living room – he'll probably be spanking the monkey to some *punch'n'judy* porn in the spare anyway. Fuck that guy is weird.

The idiot needs to shut the door – I saw the same weird shit with a different chick going on last night when I popped my head in to say 'hey'. His face lit up like *Times Square*, so all his acne stood out like dog's balls all over his pocked face. Here's an idea dipshit, turn the PC around so I don't accidentally see that shit. Despite stomping around to make my presence known, he still doesn't pick up on it.

Imagine if he turns out to be some serial killer and I've been living with a monster all this time. Shudder.

22

The Date

Katrina

Looking at my watch for the fifth time in a minute, I stop pacing and sit down on the couch. I'm all antsy and need to calm down so I stalk into the kitchen and pour myself a glass of wine. Returning to the living room, I sit quietly. Lucy wanders past and stops at the doorway, "Oh hey mum, are you going out?"

I'm not ready to divulge anything yet, "Yes, I'm going out for dinner with Sonia and Felicity, just the girls."

"Oh, that's good to hear. You need a good night out."

Nodding, "I really do. I've left your dinner on the bench to reheat when you're hungry."

"Thanks, mum, but you didn't need to make dinner for us. We're capable of throwing our own dinner together."

I shrug at her that it was nothing. Lucy continues down the hall to the kitchen. After I drain my glass, I briskly walk to my ensuite to brush my teeth and apply a tinted lip gloss. I spray perfume into the air and walk through it. I want to smell good for him. I return to my bedroom to look in the full-length mirror and wonder if I'm underdressed. Although I'm not wearing denim, I'm still wearing jeans. I like the way my new silky floral top falls over the top of them. I don't like the way my toes feel pinched in the new candy apple stilettos and hope we don't have far to walk from the car to the restaurant because these bloody things will hobble me. The things we do for fashion. I'm a bundle of nervous energy.

My phone buzzes in my pocket and it's William, telling me he's almost here. Quickly turning off the bedroom light, I race to the hall to grab my handbag and yell a goodbye to Lucy in the kitchen, then yell up the stairs to the boys. I pause for a moment at the bottom of the stairs but hear no response. Deaf bastards. Darting back to the kitchen to where Lucy is still standing at the island bench, "Luce, the boys didn't answer, so could you tell them I've gone out for dinner with the girls and their dinner is on the bench? Sonia will be here in a minute, so I'll go out and meet them. Bye." Lucy frowns at me then quirks an eyebrow. I stand on tiptoe and plant a kiss in the middle of her forehead. It leaves a perfect print of my lips in gloss. I don't care, she can be a tri-clops. "Love you, bye," and I race down the hall and out the front door.

I make it to the gate in time to see his headlights approaching. I quickly walk to the edge of the property so anyone in the house looking out the windows won't see the car is not Sonia's. As he pulls up along side me, I grab the door handle and almost rip all my nails off my left hand. Shit! Ouch. I flap my hand like an idiot outside the car until I hear the door locks release. *Rookie mistake, Kat.* Finally, I open the door and climb in. "Hi, William, how are you?" said at a thousand miles an hour. I sound like I've snorted an ounce of smack. *Calm yourself, Kat, or he'll think you're a bunny boiler.* I look over at him. Holy God in heaven, he looks like something out of a magazine. I feel so bloody awkward. I notice he's wearing jeans and relax a little about my ensemble. He dimples at me and my insides dissolve,

"Hi Katrina, you look lovely. I'm sorry if you hurt your hand, I can't release the door locks until the car comes to a complete stop."

"Oh, that's ok. I just wasn't thinking." …and I'm an idiot and shitting myself.

He pulls away from the curb and we head towards to city. He smells amazing and I'm trying hard not to hyperventilate.

* * * * *

William

As I draw close to her house, I spy her standing on the nature strip. Holy shit, she's hot. Her jeans are impossibly tight, like they're painted on. She has a lovely bum. She's curled her hair; it looks soft. Her bright red heels look impossibly high and uncomfortable, but she is walking in them like she was born to. As I'm pulling in, she grabs the door handle and hurts her hand. Bugger! I brake a little too hard so I don't overshoot the mark and can unlock the doors; I pitch forward in my seat. God I'm uncool. As she climbs in, I get a whiff of her soft, perfume; it makes me heady. She greets me with the excited joy I'm getting used to. She's one of those people who is always 'up' and it's a welcome change to the indifference I'm used to. It's contagious. Thank God she's wearing casual clothes; I'd feel like an idiot if she was all dressed up.

* * * * *

Pulling into the underground car park, I find a spot not too far from the elevator and cut the engine. I try to be cool and step out of the driver's side and stride to hers so I can open the door for her. She looks up at me, pleasantly surprised. The echo of the beeping car lock is loud in this underground space and makes her jump. As we walk to the elevator, I throw caution to the wind and reach for her hand. She doesn't resist. My heart pounds in my chest and Percy gives me a wave.

We emerge from the elevator and walk out into the night, hand in hand. The Yarra River twinkles in the lights, as we walk along Southbank Boardwalk. We reach the restaurant and the vacuum of the glass doors opening pulls at us as we enter and wait to be seated. Katrina smiles up at me and my stomach flip flops.

* * * * *

Katrina

The waiter shows us to our table and William reluctantly releases my hand to pull my chair out for me. The waiter stands by impotently until William seats himself, then he fusses about with our serviettes. He hands William the wine list and proceeds to list today's specials, but I am not taking any of it in because I'm floating about inside my head. I am asked if I'd like a drink and I choose a Prosecco, William chooses a beer. The waiter disappears and leave us to our menu choices. Perusing the menu, nothing jumps out at me, but I spy the specials in cursive script on a board behind William. The waiter returns with our beverages and takes our orders; I decide on a prawn pasta. William asks if I'd like salt & pepper calamari for entrée and although this will be too much for me, I agree because I don't want to appear fussy. He chooses the pork belly and the waiter retreats. William's eyes flick up to mine. Hating silence, I'm straight into the twenty questions, "Why did you choose this place? Any particular reason?" He thinks for a moment before answering, "actually, I haven't been out to a restaurant for years. An old school mate of mine is the head chef here, so I thought I'd give it a go, since he's been nagging me to come here, literally for years."

"Ooh, that's cool. Do you cook?"

"I actually enjoy cooking, but it's a weekend thing because I don't get much time with the hours Thomas, and I work." He pauses to take a swig of beer and I see his eyebrows dart north in unexpected appreciation. "What about you? I know you cook but do you enjoy it?"

"Well, I enjoy baking, but I also bake when I'm stressed as I find it therapeutic."

"I'll bet the family love reaping the rewards from those therapy sessions." His eyes crimp at the corners. Lord he's lovely to look at. His eyes are so blue they look unreal, and his long lashes are dark where they join his eyelids, and it looks like he's wearing a fine line of eyeliner… but I think it's just the affect of those lashes. Women would kill for those lashes. I ask the question I've been wondering since I first saw him at the house, "William, are you wearing coloured contacts." He frowns at me then shakes his head, "No, why do I keep getting asked that question?"

"…because your eyes are not a natural shade of blue."

"Well, they are because they're my natural shade of blue."

"Oh, sorry, I was just asking… they're just really blue." *Enough of the Spanish inquisition, Kat.*

"I know, I get that question all the time… and often. I see doubt when I tell them they're not contacts and I can see them looking hard at my eyes, like for the edge of a contact or something. Trust me, they're mine… and before you ask, no I don't wear eyeliner."

This startles a laugh out of me. He narrows his eyes and says, "you were thinking I did, weren't you?"

"No, I'd worked that bit out all by myself." He grins at me. The waiter arrives with crusty artisan bread with an oil and balsamic reduction dipping plate. My hunger dissipates as the delicious appetiser slays it dead. I only eat one small piece, or I won't be able to eat the main meal.

An awkward silence descends and I'm sure he can hear my clicking jaw as I chew the bread, so I fill the silence with conversation. This is my chance to find out about the enigma that is William Milburn.

"How did you and Thomas get to start up your own business?"

"Well, it didn't happen overnight, of course."

"Of course not. Nothing great ever does." He looks at me with surprise.

"Thomas and I both wanted to do a trade, since we were little kids. We love working on the tools and always helped dad around the house when we were lads. I became a builder and Tom became a plumber. Our cousin Greg also works with us, he's an electrician."

"Oh, that's great. I think I've spoken with Greg once on the phone."

"Yeah, he's a good bloke. Anyway, we both started our apprenticeships when we were sixteen years old and after becoming fully qualified, we worked for about a decade in our respective fields with our employers. I wanted more that to just 'work for the man' so undertook a part time course in business management and then asked Thomas if he'd like to start a business together. We both still lived at home and our parents encouraged us to save as much as we could. Rather than buy our first homes, we pooled our funds and created Milburn Construction Company."

"Wow, that's amazing. Is your cousin a part owner?"

"Actually, no. Greg didn't have the funds to join us, so we pay him as a subcontractor. We also have plasterers, bricklayers, painters, roofers, landscape gardeners and a whole host of other subcontractors on our books."

"Yeah, I've noticed."

William comically slaps his forehead, "my God, I forgot you do our accounts and payroll."

"That's ok, I think it's pretty cool."

We are interrupted with the arrival of our shared entrée. I select a small piece of calamari and I'm pleasantly surprised as it almost dissolves on my tongue. The flavour is delicate and I'm grateful he chose the shared entrée. Reaching for another piece, I look up to see him staring at me. "Hey, there." My face reddens. Can he hear my clicking jaw? *Chewing the cud, Kitty Kat?*

He smiles at me. I smile back and heat emanates from, my face. I'm too scared to chew. He breaks the gaze and reaches for another piece.

* * * * *

William

The waiter brings a second round of beverages. Katrina is pretty, her face small and delicate. She is petite in every sense of the word. "How tall are you?"

She grins, "not very. I'm five foot one-ish... or one hundred and fifty-five centimetres, to be exact. I'm too scared to ask how tall you are."

Bloody hell, she's tiny. My brain misfires and shoots 'she's dick height' into my brain. Percy stretches himself; I cross my legs under the table.

"I'm six foot four or one hundred and ninety-three centimetres. Thomas is nearly two meters, he's six foot six."

"Well, that's just ridiculous! I have to have a step in my kitchen to reach the overhead cupboards."

"Ha! I'd hate to climb into a car after you've been driving it." She giggles into her serviette.

"...you'd look like a grasshopper until you move the seat back."

The visual of that makes me laugh. Instantly, I regret it as other diners turn to look at me because of my booming voice. She sees it and giggles again.

The waiter arrives and clears away the remnants of our entrée. A soft hum of conversation continues, and I shrink in my seat. Katrina reaches over and grabs my hand before it slides into my lap. "I'm sorry, that was my fault."

"No, I have a loud voice that gets louder when I laugh. There's no room in this posh restaurant for my voice." I take a sip of water to put out the fire in my face.

"I like your voice. It's deep and *manly*." The last bit is said in a deep baritone, and she stretches her neck and tucks her chin in, her face suddenly pompous.

I choke on the mouthful of water and rudely spit some across the table and plonk my glass down hard. The water shoots up the back of my nose and I'm seconds from disaster as I cover my mouth with the serviette and cough into it. As I'm coughing and spluttering into my serviette, a tight, high-pitched fart is emitted and hurts my arse. She is laughing at me, and I hope to God, she didn't hear it, but more importantly, I hope she doesn't smell it. The waiter arrives with our main meals and as he walks past me and places Katrina's meal in front of her, he takes the smell with him and deposits it around her. She looks up at him and frowns, then gives him a dirty look. She thinks the waiter cracked it before bringing our meals and it's all I can do not to laugh hysterically. She looks at the waiter and then looks at me and makes a face. This is my undoing and I laugh into my napkin like an idiot. Thanking the waiter, I excuse myself for a moment and walk briskly to the bathrooms to release the rest of the noxious gas before it suffocates us both.

When I return to the table and take my seat, I notice her meal is untouched. "Oh, you didn't have to wait for me."

She frowns, "Yes I did, it would be rude to just dig into my meal before you got back."

"Well thanks, I appreciate it."

Her meal is very small. Mine isn't all that big either, the usual for classy restaurants, but it's beautifully presented, and I can't wait to dig in. The crackling looks crispy and I'm almost salivating before I can take my first bite. Across the table from me, Katrina groans in ecstasy. I look up to see her eyes closed. She's the most 'real' woman I've ever met.

* * * * *

After we have finished our meals and the plates have been cleared, the head chef, Vincent, or Vince, as I know him, comes out to our table to say hello. He is as you'd expect a good chef to be, chubby. As the saying goes, '*beware the skinny cook*'. I introduce Katrina and compliment him on the pork. Katrina gushes over her meal and I can see Vince approves. We have a quiet conversation until he has to return to the kitchens. His parting gift is unexpected, "I've taken the liberty of organising your dessert to share, on the house."

"Oh, thanks mate. You didn't have to do that."

"Wil, I've been asking you to come here for years. I want you to come back so this is my treat."

Ten minutes later a platter arrives with a delicious array of desserts, all spectacularly presented, swimming in floods of caramel sauce, scoops of ice cream and two spoons. Katrina smiles at me and takes one of the spoons. She takes a small mouthful and closes her eyes in ecstasy again. She's very demonstrative. I watch her mouth do magical things that wakes Percy from his slumber. Her tongue darts out and licks residual sauce from her bottom lip and I have to look away. Shovelling a mouthful of the chocolate number in my mouth, I am surprised how delicately light it is. Vince has come through with the goods. All too soon, it is time to drive home and end the evening. I don't really want it to end. I hope she enjoyed herself and we can do this again sometime soon. I'm not sure if I'm supposed to kiss her or not. Do I kiss her on the first date? I don't want her to think I'm desperate to get in her pants. Maybe I'll just wait and see what happens. If she doesn't look keen or if there's full silence, I'll just say goodnight. God this is awkward.

* * * * *

Katrina

He pulls the car to the curb and cuts the engine. I am very nervous. We sit in silence for a few minutes then he abruptly ends the date, "I had a great time, Katrina." That's it? No kiss? I smell like a draft horse from hours of sweating over the kiss and I'm not going to get it? I'm glad it's dark in the cabin so he can't see the disappointment on my face. "I had a lovely night, too."

I do the only dignified thing I can do; I reach for the door handle. After molesting the entire door, I whisper, embarrassed, "I can't find the bloody handle!" William chuckles and leans over and locates it in the dark. He tells me to follow his arm to the handle. I run my hand down his forearm, noting the small outline of the vein that kept me salivating through dinner. When I get to his hand, I stop. I don't want to go without a kiss. So, I run my hand back up his forearm, over his bicep, which almost makes me dizzy, like a teenager, then I make out the side of his face in front of me. I whisper his name, "William?" He turns to face me. *Risk it for the biscuit, Kitty Kat.* Throwing caution to the wind, I lean forward and kiss him, then sit back. The ball is in his court now. Nothing. He takes a breath and sighs out. Shit! Then it happens, he leans in and kisses me. His mouth is full and soft and I'm glad there is no light in here so he can't see how red my face is. I feel heady and full of butterflies. The kiss lasts for at least a minute and as he pulls away, I think now is the perfect time to end this first date. I pull back, follow his forearm down to his hand and find the door handle.

"Thanks for a great night, William." I open the door and light floods the inside of the car. His handsome face is still inches from me. His impossibly blue eyes stare into mine. I wait for him to retract to his side of the car, but he doesn't, he puts his hand over mine and closes the door again. After the interior light fades out, he comes in for another kiss but this one is serious. After a couple of minutes of heaven, we both come up for air. Finally, he pulls back, and I open the door and step out of the car. I thank him again and close the door. He waits while I walk up the drive and doesn't pull away from the kerb until I open the door. So, he's not only hot, tall, and spanking, he's a gentleman to boot.

23

The New Girlfriend

Katrina

Finished for the day, I turn off the PC and clear the desk. I hear voices downstairs; I secretly hope it is William. I descend the stairs as quietly as I can. I go in search of Beverley and find her in the conservatory with two young women and a small child, the toddler nestled in Beverley's lap. I recall the photos in the living room. Beverley calls me over to join them. I wander over and Beverley makes the introductions, "Kaitlyn, Zoe, this is Katrina. Katrina, these two beautiful young women before you are William's girls, and this delightful bundle of joy is his grand daughter, Emilee. She looks tenderly at the little girl and smacks a kiss in her tiny neck. Emilee giggles and squirms in Beverley's lap. "Emilee is my first great grandchild. Oh gosh, that makes me sound old, doesn't it."

Beverley does not look aggrieved at being a great grandmother, she looks like she's totally smitten by the little girl. Feeling a little awkward, I reach out and formerly shake their hands. Squatting before Beverley and greet baby Emilee face to face and she rewards me by reaching out and grabbing my nose in her chubby fist and yanking, like its detachable. My eyes water and I emit a small 'oh!'. Kaitlyn and Zoe both leap up in panic, but I've already pulled my head away and planted a smacking kiss on the chubby little hand. Emilee lets out a squeal of delight and the two girls sit back and visibly relax.

"Won't you join us for a cup of tea?" Beverley invites. I don't wish to intrude but I've been wanting to meet the girls for a while, so I accept the offer graciously and pour myself a cup of tea. Beverley retrieves a small, sweet biscuit from the tray and hands it to Emilee to nibble... Emilee didn't get the memo and alarmingly shoves the whole thing in mouth. The silence is broken by all four of us laughing.

"Ah, hello to my favourite ladies!" William bellows. I get such a fright I let out a whoop and almost upset my teacup, my backside lifts of the seat. Emilee starts bouncing excitedly on Beverley's lap.

Hand on her chest, Beverley admonishes, "Oh William, must you be so loud?"

William looks contrite, "Oops, sorry. I didn't mean to frighten anybody." His eyes soften ever so slightly and he almost whispers, "Didn't see you there, Kat."

My cheeks pink and my heart flutters within my rib cage. I smile up at him, "Hi, Wil,"

The girls look at me and my face gets hot. I make a great show of wiping the spilled tea from the saucer with a napkin. When I look up, they are looking at Wil. Wil's face turns puce.

Everybody is looking at everybody and nobody is saying anything. Beverley looks up from wiping Emilee's sticky hands and takes in the four-way awkward stare-fest.

"What's going on?"

"What?" William's face turns positively crimson, and I let out a nervous giggle. Beverley frowns, "William, what are you doing?"

"I'm not doing anything. What?"

I look at the girls and smile, then down into my teacup. My God this is bloody awkward.

"For goodness' sake, William, why are you standing there?"

"What do you mean? I've come in to see my girls." His eyes dart to me and he turns crimson again.

I have to get out of here and put an end to this awkwardness. I throw back the last of my tea and succeed in making a small bit dribble down my chin. I pop the cup and saucer back on the tray and stand suddenly, "Well, I'll be off." I turn to the girls, "It was lovely to meet you both. I hope to see you again."

I turn to Beverley, "Thank you for the tea, Beverley." Emilee looks up at me and gurgles something unintelligible through dribble, shooting her arms up in the air at me to be picked up. I pick her up off Beverley's lap and place her on my hip. I gently bounce her up and down and smile into her cherubic face. Emilee lays her head on my shoulder and pops her thumb in her mouth. I absentmindedly begin swaying from side to side and her eyelids become heavy. Zoe stands and darts forward, "would you like me to take her?".

"Oh, that's ok. Show me where her cot is, and I'll pop her down for you." I offer.

Wil volunteers, "I'll show you." He puts his hand in the small of my back to guide me then remembers himself and whips it away like it's on fire. He darts in front of me, "this way," he beckons, and I follow.

Emilee smells of baby soap and innocence and I drop a small kiss on her silken hair. I'm flooded with memories of my children as babies. He whispers, "Her cot is just over there. Can you see in the dark?"

"I can see it, thank you."

I gently lay Emilee down on her back and she barely flinches. I look up and see Wil smiling down at me. "Hey," he whispers.

"Hey yourself," I whisper back.

He leans forward and plants a soft kiss on my mouth. He deepens the kiss and butterflies take flight. His deodorant and shampoo make for a heady mix for the senses. As we pull apart, he says, "Can I see you again?"

"I'd like that."

He kisses me again and I almost combust. A small movement in the doorway behind him catches my eye. We've been caught kissing, but I didn't see who it was.

"I better go. I'll text you."

He nods and gives me one last peck.

As we emerge from the hall, I collect my bag from beside the seat and say a final goodbye – still giddy from the kiss.

* * * * *

William

I sit down in the seat recently vacated by Katrina. "Any tea left?"

All eyes are on me. "What?" I ask.

"So that's who you've been dating?"

Mum chimes in, "What do you mean?"

I look at the girls and then at mum. I don't want to have this conversation yet. Thomas blusters in like a bull in a china shop. I'm grateful for the loud distraction.

"Hey guys, just saw Katrina leaving." Nobody says a word, he looks between us all. Has something happened?"

Nobody bats an eyelid.

"So, you finally got to meet Katrina?"

Kaitlyn pipes up, "yes, finally… she's lovely."

Thomas grins, "Happy with dad's new girlfriend then?" and winks at them.

Mum is almost surprised right out of her twinset. "Girlfriend? William, are you dating Katrina?"

I squirm under the scrutiny, "we've been out for dinner, yes."

"Why wasn't I told this?"

"Oh, sorry mother, I didn't realise I had to check in my dates with you."

"Well, there's no need to be churlish, William. I only asked. You're very defensive." Mum winks at the girls conspiritually. Oh, for fuck's sake.

The girls giggle and Kaitlyn volunteers, "I like her dad."

I'm sure the tips of my ears are pink, but a warmth spreads inside me. I'm glad they like her because I like her a lot.

I grab a biscuit from the tray and stuff it in my mouth and smile at Zoe. She grins back.

"I like her too, Dad. She's nice."

I look at Mum, "well you know *I* like her William. But don't mess her about, she's an asset to the business."

"Well, now that I have everyone's approval…"

I try to nonchalantly leave the room but realise I'm heading toward the kitchen and have to execute a 360 degree turn and go back past them all to leave through the front door.

* * * * *

Katrina

I return to the house to discover that Lucy has brought her new boyfriend home. Jacob and Mason have already met him, but today is my first meeting. I encourage him to stay for dinner. He's a very nice boy… correction, he's a nice man.

The auction of our house is this Saturday and although I'm still buzzing from my date, I'm a bundle of nerves. We have had huge interest, but you don't know how it will go until auction day.

"How was dinner?"

I smile and stifle a teenage sigh. "It was lovely!"

Nathan politely joins the conversation, "Where did you go?"

"We actually went into the city, to a restaurant in the Southbank area."

Lucy's brows dart up, "Oh, what was the occasion?"

Shit, I was supposed to have gone out with the girls. I try not to embellish too much, "No occasion, we just felt like splashing out a bit." Then I change the subject, "Is everyone ready for next Saturday?"

"What's happening Saturday?" enquires Nathan.

My three children answer in unison, "the auction."

Lucy adds, "didn't you see the giant sign outside?"

Nathan's cheeks flame. "Yes, but I didn't read the details."

Jacob defends Nathan, "of course not, I wouldn't have either!" Both boys glare at Lucy. Lucy holds up her hands in mock defence, "OK, sorry, my bad."

"I'd better get onto that last set of drawers in the downstairs desk. That's the last thing on my list. I've been putting it off."

Lucy volunteers, "if you want to wait until tomorrow, I'll help you and then we can clear out for the final inspections before auction day."

I sag in relief, "That would be awesome!"

I take my wine to my room and decide to read a little before bed. When I close my eyes, I want to pour over every detail of the kiss and relive it all, just a little.

24

Nothing Bewitching about this bitch

Katrina

We've been dating for a couple of months now and still William hasn't made any moves to get me into bed. It's a little weird. I wonder if everything is in working order down south. Maybe there's some need for Viagra. I love his company, but I want to take our relationship to the next level. I'm feeling frustrated.

I'm at the big house helping Beverley set up for the charity event she's hosting tomorrow night. William and Thomas arrive with cartons of alcohol and slip behind the bar to sort it all.

Beverley and I are washing and polishing all the hired wine glasses and flutes. They're covered in fingerprints and dust. Samantha swans in like she owns the place. She struts towards us like she's on a catwalk, which looks weird, and embraces Beverley. "Beverley, how are you? I'm here to help set up." This I have to see. As if she would risk her perfect French polished nails doing anything akin to work.

She notices me, looks me up and down like I'm something the cat has dragged in and says, "you missed a spot", pointing at the glass. I ignore this and cheerily greet her, "Hello Samantha. I haven't missed it, I'm not finished."

She doesn't reply but continues with the icy glare. Rude bitch. I focus on the glass I'm polishing.

"Well, you'd better get a hurry on, there's a lot of glasses."

Samantha turns on her heel and stalks over to William and Thomas at the bar and throws her arms around William's neck. I watch William stiffen and take a step back. Thomas scowls at her.

William, clearly uncomfortable, stutters, "Hi Sam."

She looks in my direction and smiles smugly, like I'm going to get jealous. What a weird unit she is.

"How can I help you, William?"

Thomas barks, "We've got this Sam. You'll just be in the way. Go and help Mum."

Samantha's face pinks and she walks back with less confidence. She starts barking orders at me like she's running the show, telling me where the glasses will be going and how they should be set up. I stand my ground; I won't be ordered around like a servant, "Actually Samantha, we've already worked out how we're going to set the glasses up. You can grab another cloth if you really want to help."

To my absolute shock and horror, she practically bites my head off, "Hey! You don't talk to me like that!" Beverley jerks in surprise at Samantha's vehemence.

I can see William at the bar ready himself to intervene. Calm as a cucumber, I continue, "well, it's just that you said you wanted to help. I was just offering a suggestion. No need to get upset."

Samantha's face is a very unhealthy shade of dark red which makes her blonde hair look positively unnatural and ghostlike. She spits, "You're new here, and you're just a staff member. You would do well to remember that."

Beverley is appalled. "Samantha, please don't talk to Katrina like that. She's not just a staff member, now that she's dating William, Katrina is a part of our family now."

The ice queen looks shocked and horrified. She looks at me with disgust. An unholy expression of pure hatred mars her perfect face and contorts her expression into loathing that is almost tangible.

She manages to pull herself together and says to Beverley with a false smile plastered on her face, "well it looks like you've got it all under control. I'll see you tomorrow, Beverley. Bye William!" she calls over her shoulder.

She walks towards the front door just as Kenneth enters. They chat in the foyer. William wanders over to me. He takes the glass and cloth out of my hand, turns me around and kisses me thoroughly in front of everyone. I'm breathless when we draw apart and a little embarrassed. Beverley smiles at us like we're adorable toddlers. Thomas shouts from the bar, "Get a room, you two!"

I catch a glimpse of Samantha's face at the entrance. If looks could kill, I would be dead.

* * * * *

Samantha

Seeing William canoodling with that awful common bitch makes me sick to my stomach. How desperate must William be to lower himself to her level? She's plain. There is nothing remarkable about her. She is beneath him. Doesn't he know that I love him?

I contain my dignity all the way to the car. I start the engine, put my seatbelt on by rote and carefully drive down the long curving driveway. When I get out onto the main road, I pull into a side street and stop the car.

I'm not sure if I'm hurt, angry or just shocked. My legs are shaking so badly that I look like I'm having a fit. I feel queasy. I have to rectify this awful turn of events straight away… nip it in the bud before it blossoms into anything serious.

I wonder if he's slept with her yet. Has she touched his naked perfection? I don't think so. It's too soon, although you never know. Some older women are just sluts these days. I don't think William would rush in. Oh please, don't let her have slept with him yet.

It should be me he's kissing, me he's making sweet love to, me who dominates his thoughts and dreams.

Who does that bitch think she is? How DARE she lure him into her web. The anger rushes through me like a fever. I grab my scarf from the passenger seat, ball it up and scream into it until my throat aches. I punch at my steering wheel and scream into my scarf pillow again. I'm breathing like I've been jogging. Tears course down my face unchecked… my William has been kissing a worthless maggot. Worse than that, everybody knew except me.

25

70th Birthday Charity Event

Katrina

William and Thomas look very dapper in their three-piece suits. Tonight, they will be part of the wait staff for Beverley's 70th Birthday, for which she has organised a charity event in support of breast cancer for her sister Patricia.

I have chosen to wear a black silk dress with cap sleeves and a sweetheart neckline. The bodice is fitted to the waist, and then falls in feminine handkerchief layers over my hips to just above the knee. A thin layer of delicate lace falls over the skirt with the points falling mid calf. I have coupled this dress with fuchsia satin peep-toe stilettos adorned with soft bows. A single pearl on a silver chain simply dresses my décolletage and silver tear drop earrings decorate my ears. I feel feminine and sexy and on top of my game tonight.

William and I have been dating now for almost nine weeks and he still hasn't made a move to get jiggy between the sheets. I'm starting to wonder if something is wrong with him. I want to get to the next base, but I don't want to seem too eager or desperate so I'm waiting for him to make the first move.

Beverley's friends arrive dressed to the nines. The whole affair is elegant and classy. Hors d'oeuvres are passed around by wait staff, all dressed in black tie attire. William and Thomas work behind the bar, expertly making cocktails and pouring beer, wine, and bubbles. William has already removed his jacket and looks hot as hell in his waistcoat, bowtie, and shirt sleeves. It is all I can do not to swoon. His eyes keep finding me and it is impossible not to get lost in all that blue!

The Ice Queen enters and prances through the room like she belongs there. She is dressed in a skintight electric blue number that looks like a second skin and barely covers her backside. Her shoes are patent leather stilettos in the same colour. Although she is an exceptionally beautiful woman with the longest legs I've ever seen, her outfit is loud and garish and doesn't suit the event. She greets Beverley in a loud and boisterous manner, drawing the attention of everybody in the large space. The men in the room can barely keep their tongues from hanging out of their mouths. She pauses and look me up and down like I am something the cat dragged in, a sneer tugging at her perfect mouth.

I can't help myself, "Hi Samantha, fancy seeing you here." She rudely breezes past without so much as a greeting and beelines for William at the bar. Beverley looks at Samantha as she struts to the bar and frowns, then looks at me. I smile winningly and give her a small wave, her eyes crimp at the corners.

Although Samantha has brought a friend along, a model friend apparently, or so she gushed at Beverley earlier, because 'Greg couldn't make it', she has left the poor man standing in the middle of the room with no introductions. God she's awful. I walk over to him and introduce myself. We chat amicably for a while, and I take two glasses of bubbles from a passing waiter and hand him one. Samantha storms over and interrupts in her brash, self-absorbed manner, "Christopher!" she barks at him. The poor guy jolts and slops a little of the champagne on his suite jacket. He glares at her, "I've been waiting for you over at the bar!" She turns on her heel and storms off. Startled, Christopher looks at me, rolls his eyes and then follows in her wake. Poor guy. I wonder why he panders to her like that. When he catches up to her, she rounds on him and looks like she's giving him a verbal shellacking in hushed tones. Christopher looks over at me and then back at her, shrugging his shoulders like he's not sure what he's done wrong. I don't know what she's doing but I want none of it. I wander over to a group of Beverley's friends and join the chat.

After several hours of talking to the groups, I mosey on over to the bar. Thomas is deep in conversation with a young woman as he shakes her a cocktail. William grins at me as I approach, "you're looking pretty hot tonight, Kat!" He winks at me and makes my pulse skyrocket.

"Why thank you, Milburn, you're looking pretty good yourself."

He flashes me a megawatt smile and I'm drawn to his dimples. Holy cow he is hot. Trying to play it cool, I demand, "pour me a glass of Prosecco, bartender."

He plays along, "coming right up, ma'am."

The beautiful moment is broken by the Ice Queen as she nudges in and demands William's attention. "Hey there handsome, could I please have a Midori Sour?" Startled, William retorts, "sure Sam, as soon as I've finished serving the gorgeous woman beside you her glass of bubs," He dimples at me again. I turn to look her straight in the eye and wink at her, daring her to 'bitch-out' at me. Her glare is glacial, and the smile plastered on her mouth looks foreign. I couldn't give a shit. William hands me my glass and gives me another wink that dissolves my insides. I saunter off to join the throng of people and refuse to look back, even though I know she is still glaring at me. I hope William is looking at my retreating form, that'll piss her off.

Samantha

The alley cat drifts off like the cat that got the cream, swaying her hips in her cheap ugly dress and those awful heels. Ugh. I consider yelling after her, "the nineties called, and they want their dress back!" She clearly didn't look in the mirror; she looks like she spent all of five minutes on her face. There's hardly any makeup on it. The dress makes her arse look huge. I cannot for the life of me see why William is all weak at the knees over her. I need to change that and turn his attentions to me. I wish I could tell him that I have no panties on tonight, that I am here in all my glory, barely covered by this dress and I want him, but I'm not sure he is ready to hear that yet.

I turn back to William, and he rewards me with a smile that makes his dimples pop… but the smile doesn't reach his eyes. My stomach drops in disappointment. After several beats, I smile at him. He raises his eyebrows, "Hi, what was the cocktail again?"

"A Midori sour, please. I'll grab a cab sauv for my friend too."

"Comin' right up." His eyes find the alley cat in the distance, and they soften to a dreamy quality. I want him to look at me like that. He turns to make my cocktail and I am consumed by a rage that feels volcanic. I try to draw Will into conversation while he shakes my cocktail, but he gives me short answers that I can't expand on. I flash him my biggest smile and give him a wink before I grab the beverages to leave the bar. He frowns momentarily and my heart plummets. Why can't he see my beauty? Tears prickle at my eyes but since I spent hours on my makeup, I will not become a humiliated story of tragedy tonight.

I find Christopher deep in conversation with Daddy. Daddy's face lights up when he sees me; I am his little girl and the light of his life, "there you are darling. Ooh, what exotic drink have you got there?" I hand the red to Christopher.

"Hi Daddy. It's not really exotic, it's just a Midori sour." We're joined by Mum.

"Hi Mum."

She greets me cooly, "Hello Samantha. Gosh, don't you think your dress is a little inappropriate for such an occasion? It's black tie." Her eyebrows are arched high in judgement, "what were you thinking?"

Wounded, I try to stifle my hurt, but my retort comes out whiny, "it's not inappropriate. You can't see anything that you shouldn't!"

"Well, I'm reasonably sure that if you were to bend over a fraction at the waist, we would all be rewarded with a glimpse of your underwear."

Christopher blushes and looks away, probably embarrassed for me, getting a dressing down in public. God she can be cold.

I glare at her to let her know that she has upset me, "Well it's lucky that I'm not wearing any."

Shocked, my mother's mouth drops open. Daddy snickers into his wine glass. He loves it when I sass her. She's a controlling witch. Both her and Katrina have ruined my evening. I grab Christopher by the arm and march off, towing him behind me. After a few paces he shakes himself free and growls, "Hey! Stop dragging me all over the place, would you?" Surprised by this uncharacteristic outburst, I stop mid-stride and turn to look at him, wide eyed.

"Oh, not you too! Why is everybody bending over backwards to ruin my night?"

"How am I ruining your night? You're being bossy and I'm not having any of it! What has gotten into you?"

I'm about to burst into tears, so I stride out of the room and into a quiet area to regain my composure. I perch on an overstuffed chair in the conservatory and turn toward the glass windows while I fish through my bag for a tissue. Christopher enters moments later and squats before me and looks into my face earnestly.

"What's going on, Sam?"

I sound like a petulant child as I dab at the corners of my eyes, "I want William to notice me but it's like I'm invisible. He keeps looking at her like *she's* the model."

"Who are you talking about? Who is he looking at?" Christopher looks confused.

"I'm talking about that stupid bitch you were talking to earlier. The one in the ugly dress."

Christopher looks surprised. "Oh, she's nice. I like her dress. What's wrong with her dress?"

I glare at him like my gaze could make his head explode. His eyes widen in surprise before I spit at him, "She's wearing it, that's what's wrong with the dress." I want to slap his face for his betrayal. I hiss at him, "She is the enemy, do you understand me?"

Shocked again, Christopher nods at me like I've become unhinged. I continue unaffected, "I need you to do me a favour, please."

Christopher stammers, "what do you want me to do?"

"I want you to make a pass at her. You know, stand close, whisper in her ear, and really flirt with her. I want you to make William jealous, so he gets angry with her. I want to pour piss all over whatever little sparks are flying between them."

Christopher doesn't look happy with this plan. "What have you got against her? She seems really seems nice. I don't want to be an arse to her."

My mouth purses and it takes a lot of self control not to grab him by the shoulders and shake him until his eyes roll.

"I'm not asking you to be an arse, I want you to hit on her, that's all!"

Christopher almost loses his balance and then his face flames. My legs are slightly apart, and he has seen that I'm not wearing underwear. He stands and glares down at me, "that's not how you win your way into a man's heart, Sam,"

"I don't want to win his heart; I want to get him into bed. His heart will follow later."

"Jesus, Sam, what about Greg?"

Through clenched teeth, I hiss, "what about Greg, Christopher?"

"Well, aren't you dating Greg? And isn't Greg William's cousin?"

My voice has a clear edge to it as I narrow my eyes at him and say in a very cold and menacing tone, "that is my business and not yours. Just go and do what I asked."

Christopher throws his hands up in surrender, "fine, but I draw the line at flirting. I'm not going to be an arse… not for you, not for anybody, ok?"

Throwing him a beatific smile, I grab my cocktail and head back to the collection of fossils in the formal rooms while Christopher finds Katrina and weaves his magic. The fact that William can't keep his eyes off Katrina will work to my advantage. He won't be able to miss Christopher's flirting.

* * * * *

Katrina

The Ice Queen's friend finds me, and we continue our conversation. He is standing exceptionally close to me, like he is conspiritually whispering something in my ear. I stifle the desire to step back and open the gap a little. I'm not sure why he is standing this close, but it feels like something has changed since the last time we chatted. He seems polite, but flirty.

He pilfers two glasses of bubbles from a passing waiter and hands me one. I use the moment to surreptitiously step back when I take the glass from him. To my disappointment, he immediately closes the gap again.

Several people join us and one of Beverley's cards group friends, Charlene, asks if Christopher is my beau. I quickly shake my head and advise that I only met him tonight. Charlene's eyes twinkle at me like something naughty might happen between Christopher and I. Christopher runs with the thread and openly flirts with me in front of everybody. I'm a little out of my depth and wonder what changed with Christopher in the last twenty minutes. Perhaps he's just shooting his shot and I should be better at deflecting said shot with grace. The others move off and we're back to Christopher and me, him standing so close I can smell his aftershave.

I spy Samantha in the distance quickly glancing our way. She strides past us towards the bar and William. I wonder if William knows how obsessed she is with him. Samantha's dress has risen further up by her long leggy stride and has practically become a belt, barely finishing below her perfect bottom. I glimpse a tiny bit of flesh mid-stride and notice with surprise that she is not wearing any underwear and I'm not wholly sure what part of her anatomy I saw in that moment. I glance across and William and he is oblivious to Samantha striding in his direction, instead he is sending daggers Christopher's way. I turn my attention back to Christopher as he leans in to whisper something to me and our mouths almost touch. I jerk back a little in surprise. Christopher's eyes sparkle and slides an arm around my shoulders and smirks at me, "almost snuck a little kiss in then." My face flushes hot. I don't want this attention and try to think of a way to disentangle myself from him without being rude. I hope the formal part of the night, the silent auction, starts soon. I need an excuse to get away from Christopher.

* * * * *

William

What is this guy's deal? He is all over Kat like a rash. I can't believe how close he is standing to her. You couldn't slide a bloody bus ticket between them, he's so close. An unfamiliar wave of jealousy floods me. I want to stalk over there and smack him in the mouth. Why doesn't she step back? I don't want to be possessive, but I can't stand here and let whatever is unfolding over there continue. I look over at Thomas. He's watching the shit-show too. Samantha saunters over to the bar and asks for another cocktail, her voice all breathy. Does she think that's a turn-on? She sounds stupid. I think the prick has just leaned in and kissed her. Nope, this is not going to happen.

I turn to Thomas, "can you cover for me?" Thomas nods and turns his attention to Samantha. As I move around the bar, I notice she has a smug look on her face. I'm not sure what that's about.

Marching over to Katrina and the flog, and gently grab her elbow and whisper as gently as I can, "hey Kat, you got a minute?"

Startled, she looks at my hand on her, and then back up at me, then nods. Steering her towards the French doors, the very same doors I first saw her standing there with her eyes closed and her face turned to the sun. I try to be gentle as I close the doors behind us, but I know I am walking too fast for her, the clip clop of her heels practically running with me.

"William, what's the matter? Are you angry?"

I stop and turn abruptly; she crashes into me. I press her against the trunk of the liquid amber and kiss her hard on the mouth, every part of me pressed against her. Shit, what am I doing? This is bordering on abuse. I let her go suddenly and step back, horrified by my possessive behaviour. "Shit, I'm sorry Kat. I don't know what has gotten into me."

She grabs at me wildly and pulls me in and kisses me back, just as hard. Percy has woken up and makes his presence felt, literally and figuratively. The kiss turns into something that sends white heat through me in all directions and makes my heart pounds like it's fit to burst. When we finally pull apart, we're both breathless.

She looks earnestly into my eyes, her hands on her hips, "William, why won't you sleep with me?"

Where did this come from, "What?"

"This is clearly a reaction to Christopher flirting with me, but you haven't made any moves yourself. It's been nearly nine weeks, and we haven't gone any further than first base. Is something wrong or is there a medical reason? Its ok if there is, we can discuss it."

"What? No. Wait, what do you mean a medical reason? I'm trying to be a gentleman."

"Trying to be a gentleman? You're more monk than gentleman. I'm so ripe I'm just about falling off the tree but still you don't make any advances."

"I didn't want to be pushy."

"Ok, well I'm telling you I want you to take it further. Do you want to take it further?"

"Yes, I want to take it further. I want it so much I could throw you down in the garden beds and take you right here!"

"Well, I don't think that would be a good idea given that we can be seen though those windows." She gestures behind me at the windows. I look over my shoulder and see the Soirée in full swing and Sam's smug face looking out at us. The flog is also looking our way, but he looks crestfallen. Stiff shit, mate.

My hand finds its way into my hair, and I feel flustered. Ushering her away from the windows, we move further down the path in the garden where we can't be seen.

She stands on tiptoe and plants a soft kiss on my mouth. She smiles at me and whispers, "you know I'm staying tonight? I'm in the guest room at the top of the stairs."

My eyebrows dart north, "after everyone leaves, bring a bottle of something and some glasses." She winks at me and makes her way back to the French doors. I have to wait for Percy to deflate before I can follow.

* * * * *

Samantha

Seeing William storm out, dragging her behind him has given me so much pleasure that it brings arousal with it. I am conscious of my nakedness beneath this dress and the heat in my crotch. Christopher joins me and he looks unhappy.

I give him my full attention, "Thank you. That was perfect."

He is unmoved by my declaration. "It wasn't a very nice thing to do, Sam."

I shrug at him. I don't care.

Moving over to the window, I can make them out in the dark. Katrina has her hands on her hips, and they appear to be having an argument. This is perfect. That's all I need, just a small gap big enough to drive a wedge into. William turns and looks through the windows, straight at me. I don't care, I want them to know I see them fighting.

Moments later, Katrina picks her way back through the garden and into the house through the French doors. She heads for the powder room, hopefully to mop up tears.

It is a few minutes before William re-enters through the same doors. He looks flustered as he makes his way to the bar.

I follow William with my eyes then Christopher stands in front of me, blocking my view. His face is set, and he looks miffed.

"Samantha, I'm going home now."

"Ok, bye."

Christopher looks incredulous, "that's it?"

Oh, here we go, "What do you want from me? If you want to leave, leave. Do you need me to stroke your ego before you go?"

"Wow. You're a bitch. Don't call me, Sam."

"Ok, I won't". I dismiss him with the flip of my hand. He turns on his heel and stalks towards the front door. I don't turn to watch him leave, but I can see his reflection in the dark window. He stops on his way to the front door as he passes Katrina. He puts his hand on her shoulder and says something to her and she smiles and nods at him and pats his arm as he takes his leave.

I spin around and glare at him, but he doesn't turn back. Katrina smiles at me as she walks past, her eyes dry.

Beverley takes to the microphone and calls the room to attention to start the formal part of the evening. Everybody moves into the next room to view the items in the silent auction, and I am left here simmering, my good mood ruined. I look over at William and he looks quiet and still a little flustered. Good. Hopefully that will be that, and I will be rid of the alley cat.

26

Bedroom Gymnastics

Katrina

There is a gentle rap on the door. He must have run here; I'm still fully dressed, including heels. As I pull the door towards me, William, carrying a tray with assorted beverages and an array of different glass vessels, grins at me. My heart flutters.

Pulling the door wider to allow him entry, he walks past me and searches for somewhere to place the tray. I point to the bedside table and close the door behind him, turning the lock to ensure our privacy. He offers me a shot-glass of a coffee coloured, creamy liquid and bumps my glass to his, before emptying his shot down his throat. I follow suit and throw it back with a little too much enthusiasm and cop the hit of Baileys at the back of my throat, which almost makes me cough and my eyes bulge in an effort to prevent the fiery liquid from shooting out of my nose. I somehow manage to keep myself nice and swallow hard, but my watering eyes betray me and by the crimping of William's eyes, I know he saw me almost choke.

I spy a tapestry covered footstool at the foot of the bed and retrieve it. Slipping out of my heels, I place the footstool in front of William, climb atop it and find I am almost at eye level with him. This makes for easy access to his delectable mouth. Our kiss is full of storm and fire and ignites desire like a flame to dry kindling. While our mouths are busy, I remove his tie and deftly unbutton his waistcoat and he shrugs out of it, without breaking the kiss. The discarded garments drop to the floor in a whisper. As I slowly unbutton his shirt, I pull away and look into those impossibly blue eyes. I could get lost in those pools of blue, so I let my eyes roam over the magnificent torso revealed. Holy mother of Murgatroyd, he is waaay out of my league. *What a catch, Kitty Kat...check out that washboard. With a bit of luck, he'll having you squealing like a stuck pig before dawn.* I ignore her unwelcome snide remarks.

His body is firm and toned but not bulging like a bull on steroids. Running my hands over the planes of his chest and gentle ripples of his stomach, then back up the flanks of his hard torso, I am suddenly too shy to do this. What was I thinking? If I take my clothes off, my chest is not going to impress him like this, my boobs are going to fall out of the holder and bounce-dangle loosely like tennis balls in stockings and he is going to go limp while I die of humiliation. Panic makes my heart race and I want to run out of the room.

He takes my face in his hands, looks earnestly into my eyes, and asks, "What's the matter?" I shake my head; I don't want my insecurities to ruin what I've been waiting for, for so long. Besides, if I don't take this now, and he does run, I'll never get the chance again. So, I suck it up, shaking my head, "Nothing, I'm just nervous."

He kisses me again and I almost swoon in his arms, heady with desire. I step off the footrest and gently push it behind me with my foot, then loosen his belt and suit pants. They fall to the floor noiselessly and pool at his ankles. I drop a kiss just above his navel and goose bumps swarm his stomach. Slowly, I walk around his almost naked body, trailing my fingers over his lean stomach and slip around behind him. I drop a tiny kiss on his hips, on the two dimples on his back just above his buttocks and continue to circle his magnificent form. When I get to his left side, a long, thick, jagged scar slashes across his left hip and disappears inside his trunks, marring his perfect physique. My breath catches in my throat, and I whisper, "Of course you have a sexy scar."

I look up and lock eyes with him, he's holding his breath and frowns down at me. He probably thinks I'm nuts. "What happened here, Wil?" He looks hopeful, then confused, then his face hardens, and he looks straight ahead. I wonder if it's a sensitive topic. On a sigh, "a childhood accident – I fell and landed on a garden stake. I almost died, apparently." This is delivered deadpan, like he is reciting it by rote or reading it off a page. OK, very sensitive.

"Can I touch it?" He quickly looks down at me again; the frown is back. "Of course, it doesn't hurt."

Gently, I run my fingers along the jagged scar. To my delight, he tightens his abdominal muscles, and the contours deepen. Jesus H Christ, he's built like a Greek God. Who the hell knew all this was hiding underneath his threads? I close my eyes as I read the scar like brail. It feels raised and a little lumpy in spots but at the same time, it feels smooth. Opening my eyes, I lean down and press my mouth to the top silvered edge of the scar. I look up at him and he has a look of incredulity upon his chiselled features. Deepening the kiss, I make my way south, following the jagged line. It is sensual and sexy and thoroughly enlightening. I am almost at the top of his trunks when he unexpectedly pushes me away by the shoulders and holds me at arms length. Surprised, I look up to see his chest heaving and suddenly, I know why he stopped me.

"What's the matter, Wil? Scared you're going to blow the back of my head out!" His eyes widen in surprise, then he throws his head back and laughs. It's a deep, throaty laugh and I have an insane urge to leap back up on the footrest and kiss his bared throat.

William

She's still fully dressed and I'm in just my jocks and socks. This is not how it usually goes. I'm nervous as she makes her way around my body, taking me in like I'm some kind of object of art. I'm embarrassed. I wish I could hide the scar; I don't want it to turn her off and ruin this. Part of me wants to put my pants back on and leave before I see the disgust in her eyes. But she's not Linda, she's Katrina and I hope she can overlook it.

She stops when she reaches it and whispers, "Of course you have a sexy scar," Wait, what? Then she asks what happens and I know it's coming. It's just a fucking scar. So, I move my gaze to the back wall so I can't see the disgust, "a childhood accident – I fell and landed on a garden stake. I almost died, apparently."

She asks if she can touch it. What, why? That's weird. I tell her it's ok, but I still clench everything when her finger touches the top of it. She closes her eyes as she runs her finger down the scar. She doesn't look disgusted. Then, God help me, she kisses the fucking scar. But she doesn't just plant a kiss, she practically makes out with the dip above my hip bone and Percy pops up like a piece of toast. It's a wonder she doesn't get a turkey slap. As her mouth travels south, my forehead and top lip bead with sweat; Percy starts up with a full gymnastics routine it becomes clear that he is going to humiliate me and as the burn begins deep in jocks, I have to yank her away before I disgrace myself.

At first, she looks shocked, then I can almost see the cogs turning and she works out what almost happened. Her eyes darken with desire and a mischievous smirk tugs at the corners of her mouth. Holy shit, this girl is bonkers. I sit heavily on the bed and pull her onto my lap. Her skirt settles around us, but I am conscious of her warm bare thighs either side of mine and Percy is doing push ups in my jocks. I feel hot and sweaty and I'm not sure if it's because all this shit is happening or because I'm stressed about Percy's callisthenics creating a crime scene in my underwear.

She kisses me industriously and I wonder how much longer I can endure standing on the edge like this. I reach for the back of her dress to find the zipper; practically giving her a full back massage in the process because the fucking thing is imbedded somewhere in the dress and requires a qualified detective to locate it. Finally, my fingers find the top tag of the slider and I try to appear cool, and I slowly run it down the meshed teeth until it opens at the back and loosens the front. I pull away as the front billows forwards and slide the straps off her shoulders. She is wearing a pale blue lacy bra that has Percy practically leaping off the cliff. The tops of her breasts bulge over the lace and provide a prominent cleavage. I lean down and kiss the tops of her breasts and feel her shudder in my arms. I close my eyes and list car engine parts in my head, so Percy doesn't get to the finish line. She throws her head back and bares her throat. Planting kisses from under her chin all the way to her ear, I feel her groan deep in her throat, under my lips. *Shit! Carburettor, spark plug, intake valve, piston*…She sways and tightens her thighs around me, pushing her crotch hard against mine, *Oh Lord! Gearbox, Crank, Fly wheel*…

She slides off my lap and drops the dress. She has on matching knickers; my hands become clammy. She lays on the bed and beckons me over. I'm screaming the engine parts inside my head to keep Percy under control but somewhere in the mix, my subconscious has switched to lubrication parts. *CYLINDER HEAD, CAM SHAFT, CRANK SHAFT* and when she whispers my name, I practically shout "drive shaft!" at her. Argh! She suddenly stills on the bed, and I can see the whites of her eyes as she looks at me in shock. Percy deflates and all but disappears and my nuts shrivel and climb north towards my throat. Oh Jesus. "I'm sorry, ah, I was distracting myself with engine parts."

Narrowing her eyes, "You were *what*?" Oh God, she's going to grab her shit and run for the hills. "I'm sorry, er…" My shoulders sag. "… look, I just wasn't going to make it. You're very attractive and in that state of undress, you had me very worked up and, you know, I wasn't going to make it." Why am I speaking like an English professor with a thumb up his arse? She's going to think I'm completely bloody unhinged.

While I am hunched over and looking at my twiddling thumbs and wishing I could drive them into my eye sockets, I feel the bed start to rock. Oh Jesus, she's crying. Could I be any more spastic in the bedroom? She's laying on her back and her hands are over her face so I can't see her expression, but the bed is seriously rocking, like 'earthquake' kind of rocking. I gently touch the back of her wrist and apologise and as she whips her hands away, there are tears all right, all over her face, but she's laughing hysterically. I am perplexed. I don't know if I should be relieved or offended. She takes in my expression and laughs even harder and despite myself, I start laughing too. I don't even know what we're laughing about.

She sits up and finally stops laughing long enough to tell me I'm adorable. What the fuck does that mean? I don't understand the fairer sex. They are such a conundrum.

* * * * *

Katrina

Oh God, he is trailing kisses down my throat towards my ear and I am ready to explode. I need to get to the next base before I go mad, so I climb off, drop the dress, and lay on the bed. As I look at him with my best 'come hither' expression, I hope I look like a sexy woman and not Ursula, the villainous sea witch from *The Little Mermaid*. I murmur his name and he yells "drive shaft!" at a thousand decibels. That jolts me. What the hell? Well, that shocked the desire all the way out of me.

I watch his entire body deflate before me as he mumbles something about distracting himself with engine parts. He's suddenly very formal. What the heck? Then the slurry that is my grey matter sorts it out and I realise he was trying not to lose his cargo in his jocks. Oh, the poor guy. He looks so pitiful. Then I think of him yelling drive shaft and the whole thing becomes impossibly hilarious. I don't want to embarrass him, but I cannot stop laughing and cover my face with both hands, so he doesn't see me go beetroot red and look like a scrunched up newborn mewling baby. He gently touches the back of my wrist and as I remove my hands, my expression is not what he was expecting, and his head turns to the side like a confused Labrador. This makes me laugh harder and then William joins in the laughing too. I finally get in control of my mirth and tell him he's adorable. The Labrador is back but I don't care, he's just gorgeous.

I pull him to me and tell him to think about what's happening in the room, then reach over and turn out the light. I don't want to get distracted and embarrassed by my dangling boobs. What happens next is nothing short of the purest form of pleasure that leaves me tingling everywhere and wholly sated.

I fall asleep in his arms but wake in the early hours overheating. I gently pull away from him and turn to look at his sleeping face. He is an incredibly good-looking man and I hope when tomorrow comes, we won't be awkward and can continue making the wonderful magic that we made last night. His eyes flutter open and I watch his pupils dilate and contract as he focuses on me. He grins at me, rolls me over and pulls me back into his embrace. Judging by the firmness pressed against my backside, we are ready for round two.

27

A Sour Taste

Samantha

I wander into the dining room and head towards the table. The room is flooded with early morning sunshine. Choosing a seat at the end of the table away from the older women, I bask in the warm sun as it flows over me and makes me feel dreamily warm. Beverley sits at the head of the table like a good matriarch. Her sister and friends surround her, one of them my mother; the table seated with rich older women who know how to dress for a classy brunch following an auspicious evening event. I am also of this class and attend the brunch in soft navy pleated culottes, a pale blue cashmere twin set and navy flats. A young niece and a couple of female cousins are also seated near me. They dress in mainstream denim jeans, pedestrian tops, and chunky sandals; class cannot be learned, one must be born into it. However unfortunate their dress sense, I'm glad to be seated at this end with them and not the old biddies. We are the chosen few allowed at the table of the Queen of Kingston House. There's no sign of the trashy, cultureless bitch who has stolen my love. Hopefully she went back to her cave following last night's event and the argument, orchestrated by none other than yours truly. The thought of this pleases me more than I thought possible.

I smell him before I see him. William breezes in and makes a beeline for his mother. She tilts her head to make available her cheek for his polite peck. He adores his mother, as the perfect son should, but he doesn't simper like Greg does to his mother. I suppress an eye roll at the thought of Greg. William's tight tee is stretched over his perfect torso and this sight makes my breath catch in my throat. His navy chinos hug his backside; he is the epitome of the perfect man.

"Good morning, ladies," he cheerily greets the table at large. There is a chorus of greetings and I wait them all out to be sure mine is last and remembered, "Good morning, William." He looks up and his eyes fall on me. I smile at him right up to my eyes; I want him to know I see him standing there. He smiles back, but it is polite and only reaches the corners of his mouth. My heart thuds in my chest. I want him to look at me the way he looks at that stupid, unworthy cow. I am so much more beautiful than she is. I am perfect for him, and I could make him so much happier than she ever could.

Beverley takes the floor because she thinks the world revolves around her. "And what has you so happy this morning?" He has the perfect response, "well what could make me happier than strolling into a room full of beautiful women?" Beverley grins up at her son and he rewards her with a wink. I wish I could be the recipient of that wink. "Flatterer," she rejoins, and rolls her eyes, all the women at the table titter behind their hands. Everyone loves handsome William but none more than me. One day it will be reciprocated, when he finally wakes up and sees me.

The whole moment is ruined by *her* appearance. She has lingered in the house like a dog at a table, hopeful for a titbit. She's making her grand entrance, but I'll not grant her the audience of my eyes. I turn back to look at William, my beloved. He looks up and watches her descend the stairs like she is some kind of beautiful entity. I wish she would fall and land in an ungainly pile at the bottom of the stairs, dripping in her own blood from a broken nose or some such ungraceful injury, but she doesn't. She glides in like she is floating on air, and it makes something inside of me harden in a very unpleasant way. I hope she takes the seat on the other side of the table in the sun, so all her wrinkles will be illuminated, and they can all see her for the troll she is. All the women at the table follow William's gaze and they all sigh, like something beautiful is happening. I want to throw up in a tissue and throw it at her. There's a spring in her step and she smiles at the other end of the table where the ancient beings all greet her, like she's something else. She walks straight up to Beverley and pecks her on the cheek, "Happy Birthday, Beverley." Everybody gasps in surprise, they had all forgotten, and now she has all the admiration because *she* remembered. She hands Beverley a small gift and a card. "I'm sorry I'm late." Beverley looks delighted and takes the gift with reverence, then flaps a dismissive hand; the wholesome Katrina can do no wrong, "Oh honey, we've only just sat down. Would you like a beverage? There's fresh brewed tea in the kitchen or you can have a coffee." I wish they'd take off their rose-coloured glasses. She is *not* all that, Jesus! I can't stand her; it disgusts me that she holds them all in the palm of her hand.

"I'll just pop into the kitchen and grab myself a coffee."

William takes her by the hand and leads her into the kitchen, pulling the door behind them. Beverley unwraps the gift and gushes, "Oh," at the pendent in the box. It looks garish and too busy. I'm sure Beverley will put the ugly thing in a drawer and forget it as soon as she can, but Beverley has class, so she reacts accordingly. After the gushing and obligatory ooh's and aah's finally die out, the pointless chatter continues at the table, but my eyes are on the door. My face is hot because he looks at her like she's perfect. Why can't he see her for what she is? She's common and uncouth and worse than that, she's soiled goods. She's yesterday's news; a 'has been'. He needs someone so much more than her, someone of equal class, someone with poise, grace, good pedigree and who has not already been around the block.

As I'm watching the door, it slowly swings back in a wide arc, and I have the perfect view of them in there. He has her sitting on the kitchen bench, her legs spread wide, and he is standing between her thighs, kissing her like he should be kissing me. Others at the table look towards the door and see the debauchery going on in the kitchen and one of the old biddies puts a hand to her chest and sighs. Disgusting! Beverley turns to see what has caught everyone's attention, then turns back and quips, "two guesses, who can tell me which room Wil spent the night in?" The tittering behind hands takes off around the table like dominoes. All the blood drains from my face. My stomach roils at the thought of her having him like that. My heart is fit to burst out of my rib cage and hot tears burn my eyes. I stand and excuse myself, complaining that I feel a bit heady, and take my leave.

I rush away and make it into the nearest powder room, close the door, sit on the toilet seat and sob into a ball of toilet paper; trying desperately to stifle my anguish. My poor heart. I have imagined kissing him, making love to him, being loved by him for so long. She is unworthy. My agony turns to ire. How fucking dare she. She swans into their lives and whisks him away, right under my nose. The anger helps contain my grief. After ten minutes, there is a gentle rap on the door. "Samantha, are you ok in there?" My mother's voice sounds concerned and then Beverley chimes in, "you took off rather quickly, petal." Forcing cheer into my voice and swallowing my congealing saliva, I answer them, "I'm ok. Sorry, I just don't feel very well. I'll be out in a minute." I'm disgusted to hear my voice quivering. I take a deep breath in to control my emotions before I sob all over again. Silence ensues until I hear Beverley mumble something inaudible to my mother, and they quietly walk away from the door. Mopping the mess on my face, I reapply some make-up and pinch my cheeks to give them colour in the right places. Lining my eyes with dark blue kohl, which makes the cornflower blue of my irises pop, I finish with mascara. My lips are a little swollen from the crying, so I take advantage of the plumping and apply a light liner and add some gloss to benefit my face. Digging in my purse, I locate my small comb and run it through my hair, returning a brilliant, radiating shine. I look at my reflected image and wonder why William can't see my beauty. I have it in spades; everybody says so, the magazine covers I adorn say so. I can walk into a room and make grown men swoon, but not William. William can't see me; he's immune to my beauty, and it hurts in a way that cuts deep and scars. Straightening my spine, I muster my dignity and leave the powder room. Everyone looks up when I approach the table. I smile at them all; I am the embodiment of Nordic beauty, and they can all see it. My calm demeanor suppresses the hurt and pain I feel deep inside after today's betrayal.

"Are you OK, love?" I force a smile at Beverley, it's not her fault a filthy whore swooped in and stole her son from me, "I'll be ok. I think I'll call a cab and go home a little early, Greg will understand."

Beverley is affronted, "you'll do no such thing. William will drop you home." I try to contain my joy at the sudden turn of events. Beverley commands, "William? Could you pop in here, please?" Dutifully, William re-enters the room. "Be a dear and drop Samantha home, will you please? She's not feeling well." William looks at me and hesitates for a moment before agreeing. I look behind Wil and see Katrina, still sitting on the kitchen bench; thankfully she's closed her legs from their natural state. She is staring at me… she has an expression on her face that suggests she thinks I've manipulated this situation. I smile at her winningly and give a little wave, like we're besties. *No Katrina, this was pure chance… it was meant to be.*

Outside on the circular drive, I stand by the passenger door of William's car and wait for him to open it for me like he does for her. He strides past and opens the driver's door. "It's open," he says, as he climbs in and belts up. There is nothing to do but climb in. I barely get the door closed before he takes off down the driveway. I try for polite conversation, my heart thudding at the pure joy of being alone with him in the car, but he won't be lured into anything meaningful. He is polite, of course, too well mannered to be anything else. His aftershave makes me heady. The drive is short and all too soon, he pulls to the curb at the house. Greg's car isn't there, of course, because he's putting on the green with my father. When the car comes to a stop, he turns and looks at me. I smile at him and thank him for dropping me home. Again, he only smiles at me with his mouth; it doesn't reach his eyes. I don't allow the disappointment to show in my face and lean forward so he can kiss my cheek. This is the polite farewell I am expecting but he is reluctant. He makes me feel like a fool leaning in until thankfully, he finally leans in to peck my cheek. I turn my face a little, so it looks like an accident, and the kiss lands at the corner of my mouth and partially makes it on my lips. My heart beats like a drum. I want to kiss him properly, but I dare not. This is not the time to push the boundaries. I pretend to lose my balance and put my hand on his thigh. "Oops," I say, my hand darting to my mouth. The back of my hand brushed something hard against his leg and I wonder if I gave that to him. Maybe making the corner of my mouth was a thrill for him and it is laid bare, strong, and hard straining against his pant leg.

I contain my excitement. There will be a time and a place to make my move. William Milburn will be mine and I will not rest until he is, and until that unworthy bitch is a thing of history, a blight on his past recollections.

* * * * *

William

I wish Samantha would get the fuck out of the car. I just want to get back to Katrina before she leaves. She's sitting in the passenger seat waiting for something. Angling her cheek at me, it becomes clear she wants a peck on the cheek. I wait a beat, consider denying her then think of Greg and decide it's easier to just peck her and get her out of my car. I lean in to do the perfunctory thing and she moves slightly so the peck lands on the corner of her mouth. It takes every ounce of self control to not swipe at my mouth. I know it was deliberate, she is Samantha, after all, but I choose not to let the moment be defined by reacting. She says a surprised "Oops," and falls into me, catching herself with her hand on my thigh, but I can't feel it because she's put her hand on Mum's wrapped birthday gift, which is still in my pocket. So, I only feel the pressure of her weight on the parcel. Her eyes widen and a lascivious expression flits across her face. What was that about? She is a confounding woman and rather creepy. Time to end this charade, "Ok, Sammy, I hope you feel better soon." I smile at her and after what feels like a full five minutes of her looking deep into my eyes, she finally opens the door and climbs out. After she closes the door, I give her a wave and drive off in the haste to make it back in time to kiss Katrina again before she's gone, and I have to wait another week to see her.

On the drive home, I replay last night's sex in my head and have given myself a raging boner by the time I make it home. I sit in the car for a few minutes and wait for Percy to deflate. I can see her car parked ahead so I know she's still here. When I enter the dining room, all eyes are on me. I find Katrina's face and smile. "Any chance I could join you ladies? Or is this strictly a 'women only' breakfast?" Mum looks indignant and chortles, "I wouldn't dream of holding such a sexist event." I pop into the kitchen to pour myself a cup of tea and return to sit beside Katrina. No sooner do I settle into my seat than her hand is on my leg, just above my knee. As I reach for a scone, her hand makes its way up my thigh. My face colours. I take a sip of tea just as her hand makes it to my crotch. The tea catches in my throat and makes me cough. I make a great pretence of putting jam on my scone, followed by a dollop of cream. Katrina lowers her hand; she doesn't want to humiliate me. My mother is watching me with narrowed eyes. I redirect the attention, "what did you get for your birthday, Mum." I launch into a monstrous bite of my laden scone. Her face relaxes and she reaches into her blouse and holds up a delicate sapphire and diamond pendent, dangling from a fine gold chain. "Katrina bought me this gorgeous gift." I move in to see the detail of the pendent. "Oh, well, I guess now would be a good time to give you this, then." I slide the wrapped gift from my pocket and hand it to mum. She fusses with the wrapping, prolonging the joy, and her face lights up with delight when she sees the matching sapphire and diamond tennis bracelet. She squeaks with delight and ask me to put it on her wrist. The sun catches the diamonds, and a Kaleidoscope of colourful lights dance around the white tablecloth. She puts a hand to her mouth as tears flood her eyes. I reach for her hand and squeeze it gently.

As I poke the last piece of scone into my mouth, Tom, and Dad stride in and Tom loudly greets the table. "Good morning, ladies…" then looks at me, "and the thorn." All the ladies laugh heartily at Tom's humour. He kisses Mum on the cheek, "Happy Birthday, Mum," handing her a small gift. Again, she fusses with the wrapping and reveals matching sapphire and diamond earrings. The hand is back at her mouth, the tears back in her eyes. She jumps up and hugs Tom, then walks excitedly to the powder room to attach them to her ears. Everybody at the table is smiling like idiots because we're all caught up in the contagion of her excitement. When she returns, proudly wearing the necklace, the earrings and the bracelet, Dad steps forward places the last of the gifts before her on the table. This one has ribbons and frills, and he delivers it with a soft lingering kiss. For a moment, we are all invisible as the two of them look deep into each other's eyes and hold a silent conversation of love, appreciation, and eternity. They are everything I've ever aspired to in a relationship but have never made the mark. The moment ends and as I look around the table, I see everybody is swept away in the love story that is my parents. Mum pulls on the longest ribbon and all the frills come away to reveal a jewellery gift box. Nestled inside is a glorious two carat solitaire natural sapphire, framed between two glittering heart shaped diamonds, and two smaller diamonds imbedded in the gold band, adorning the blue semi-precious stone. She looks into my father's eyes, and he smiles at her. He takes the ring and slides it onto her gnarled finger. It catches on an arthritic knuckle joint, but only for a moment, before sliding all the way home. He kisses her fingers, and it feels like we're all intruding on their intimate moment.

Tom, uncomfortable with the silence and the mush, plonks himself noisily at the table, dragging the tablecloth with him and causing everything to move suddenly. Teacups rattle in saucers, spoons jingle, a scone topples from the plate onto the tablecloth and the milk jug rocks precariously close to a spill, but Katrina catches it before it topples. He hides his embarrassment by reaching for a scone; his reddened cheeks scream of mortification. After a moment, the table returns to loud conversations. I reach under the table and take Katrina's hand in mine and hold it. She looks at me and smiles softly. Tom ruins the moment, "can you two get a room, already?" Katrina's cheeks pink and Tom yelps when my kick lands squarely in his bony shin; his bum lifting off the seat. "Booooys!" Mum warns, dragging the word out like we're seven and five years old again. He's still a little shit, even at forty-two!

28

Cat Among the Pigeons

Samantha

Seated at a small table at Clique Café, I'm sharing in a mother-daughter lunch. We have a window seat and it's a glorious day, so the windows are open. The sun is pouring through the glass sending coloured silhouette images of our beverages across the white table. I am the object of much attention; an adjacent table hosting an all-male business lunch is full of admiring glances. I am used to it and preen a little.

I've just come from a photoshoot, so my makeup is absolutely brilliant. It was an underwear shoot, so I'm waxed and plucked within and inch of my life, and as I cross my legs under the table, my smooth long legs sliding over one and other and the soft supple-ness of my skin arouses me. Greg will no doubt want to taste every inch of me. That's fine, I will close my eyes and imagine William's mouth devouring the softest, most intimate parts of me. I succeed in making my face flush in my own arousal. I'd better calm my thoughts, or I'll be having a 'when Harry met Sally' moment in the café. It would certainly please the men at the adjacent table.

I look up as a shadow passes by the window and observe the unworthy bitch-troll strolling down the path outside the window, her phone to her ear. Can I not escape her? She is constantly popping up, grossly unwelcome. Mother has excused herself to 'powder her nose' so I quickly collect a menu and hide behind it. I don't want mother to return – like everyone else on the planet, she is wearing rose-coloured glasses and can't see the awful tart's evil, but I can see it. It's dark and surrounds her like a malevolent aura.

As I'm watching her from behind my menu, she stops suddenly and looks at her phone. Then she looks up and her face lights up with elation. She waves like an idiot and runs past the window. Swivelling in my seat, my head is almost out of the window trying to see why she is running when I spy the object of her attention. A tall, strapping, very handsome man running towards her. He holds his arms out and I whip my phone up and catch multiple photos of the two of them as she runs into his embrace. She wraps her arms around his neck and kisses his cheeks multiple times. I am so pleased to be capturing all this disgusting duplicity. Finally, the tables have turned, and I have something solid to sully the reputation of this unworthy whore. I can't contain my joy.

To my horror, they enter the restaurant and wait to be seated. Thankfully, they are directed to the far end of the café, so I don't have to endure a conversation with her, and I can surprise William with this disgusting betrayal before she can manufacture a viable excuse.

She waves like an idiot again at someone out of sight. I see her new beau's back as he shakes hands with whoever she has seen. I want them to sit down and stop making a fuss before Mother returns because she will unwittingly ruin the unveiling of the treachery with her gullibility. Finally, the motion stops, and everything settles in the restaurant. I'm eager to have these photos printed and delivered to William; he needs to know what this whore is up to. He will be so heartbroken by this betrayal, and I'll be there to comfort him. I close my eyes and savour the images of how the comfort will turn into a gentle kiss. The kiss will deepen and before we know it, we will be making magic between the sheets and once he has tasted me, he'll never want the taste of that filthy slut on his lips again.

Mother spoils the daydream when she returns from the powder room. She looks pasty and clammy. "Are you ok?"

"No, Samantha, I don't think I am. I feel very ill. I'm sorry darling, but we shall have to cut this lovely lunch short as I need go home very quickly."

"What's the matter?"

"I'm not sure but if we don't get out of here soon, it's going to become very embarrassing."

I don't require any further prompting. It's like the universe has conspired to make all the chips all fall for my gain. I call over the waiter and advise that we must leave immediately. He nods politely and takes my proffered credit card. By the time we are cloaked and ready to leave, the bill has been settled and we are free to leave.

The table of men look up as I stroll past and all of them stiffen as one and suck in their respective stomachs. I turn and offer them a smile as I leave the restaurant, showing my perfect teeth. *Give the people what they want.* Let them imagine me balancing on their balls tonight, riding them reverse cowboy when they perform duty sex for their dull insignificant others. I physically force the smile from my lips. I am so elated at the prospect of ending the shitty charade between William and the skank, that I could skip, if it wasn't beneath me to do so.

* * * * *

William

I've just returned from my run, and I'm almost at the door when the sound of tyres on the driveway catches my attention. Samantha is pulling into the circular drive. She steps out of her Merc, perfectly put together and the very essence of *Barbie*.

I wish so much that she wouldn't waste her attention on me; I'm not interested. I find it uncomfortable and squirm under her gaze; I wonder how it makes Greg feel. I can't imagine it would please him to see her constantly vying for my attention. Discretion is not her strong suit.

Yes, she is attractive, but she's just not my type. I've seen men fall all over themselves when she is in the room, but I don't get affected by her. I've known Samantha since she was seven. I find her to be cold and calculated and every word that comes out of her mouth is meticulously measured. Everything she does is manipulative and has been since she was a child. I won't let her get under my skin, despite how hard she tries.

She has a very inflated opinion of herself. She talks about her modelling career like she's a *Victoria's Secret* model – she's thirty-two years old and in the modelling world, that's well and truly past it. In her teens and early 20s, she was very successful but even as beautiful as she is, unfortunately models have a shelf life. This doesn't sit well with her, and she continues to sprout the names of magazines she adorned like it was yesterday. In reality it was more than a decade ago. Now, she models for letterbox drop catalogues for local department stores and often shares the page with an oversized model. This grates on her as she thinks the modelling world is 'pleasing and accepting of every body type' whereas Samantha believes only the fortunate ones who can draw on an elite gene pool should be allowed to feature in magazines. I'm not sure if she's a narcissist or just conceited.

Samantha uses her beauty as a weapon; to belittle other women or make them self-conscious and less; and to manipulate men into doing her bidding for her. I don't know why she's singled me out – she's been trying to manipulate me into bed since we were teenagers. I've been married and I've had kids – I don't want to start again and if I did, I wouldn't want to be with someone who can't be told and says "you're wrong" to anyone who has an opinion that differs from hers. She's hard work, that's for sure. Worse than that, she's intelligent and knows just enough about everything to be dangerous.

She approaches and touches my sweaty arm. She doesn't flinch, which in itself is odd because I'm grossly wet with perspiration. I don't like this pedestal she has me on.

"Hello handsome." She saunters up and to my horror, turns her cheek to me. Sweat is dripping off me. "Oh Sammy, I won't touch you, I'm sweaty and gross." Her smile faulters and her expression clouds. I feel like a heel; I don't want to hurt her feelings. "I don't mind," she whispers. I shut that shit down right away, "Ugh, I do. I'm seriously sweaty. I've just got back but I'm not sure anybody is home. Who were you after?"

Her expression is suddenly bright. "You, actually. I wonder if you have a moment."

"Sure, come in." I open the door and grant her entrance. I leave her in the entrance and dart to the linen cupboard to retrieve a towel. I mop the sweat from my face, arms, and neck, then I give her my attention.

"OK, what can I do for you?"

She takes in a big breath. This can't be good, "Wil, look I'm sorry to be the one to tell you this but I think Katrina might be cheating on you." I jerk back as if slapped, no way is Katrina cheating. "I don't think so, Sam. She's not like that."

She's all innocence and doe eyes, "Well I didn't think so either until this afternoon when I saw her with the other man." She hands me an envelope.

"What's this?" I'm feeling shaky and nervous. I don't want to be here in this position again.

"Well, I didn't think you'd believe me if I just told you, so I took a couple of photos to show you I'm not making this up."

My hands shake as I open the envelope. I extract three photographs, all of them of Katrina in the arms of another man. The first one is just their embrace, but the second one has captured Katrina's expression, and she looks very happy to be in his arms. The third one is blurred but she is clearly kissing him. My stomach knots and I have an insane urge to run from the room.

"What are you doing spying on Katrina, Samantha?"

Samantha is horrified, then defensive, "I wasn't spying, I was sitting in the café when Katrina ran past me and into that man's arms. I happened to have my phone out and took photos."

"What do you hope to achieve by showing me these photos."

Her voice hardens, "I didn't do this to you, William, she did."

"We don't know that Katrina has done anything..." I sound like I'm trying to convince myself.

Samantha raises her voice an octave, "with all due respect, William, you didn't see what I saw. She looked like she was really in love with this man. I'm sorry if you don't want to know the truth but here it is right before your eyes."

My shoulders droop. "I'm sorry, Sam. I'm not angry with you. I just don't want to believe it."

"Well believe it, Wil, she's cheating on you. I'm sorry I have to be the one to tell you, but I couldn't stand by and let her break your heart. You need to know the truth."

I am perilously close to tears. "Thanks for dropping those in, Sam. I'm just going to take a shower. You can let yourself out."

I drag myself away and I leave her standing in the entrance as I make my way back out the door to my studio apartment. I am devastated and sick to my stomach. How do I keep getting walked over? I thought for sure that Katrina was different. It felt real but here's proof that she's just like all the others. It took me so long to let someone in again but here I am back to square one.

Samantha

Poor William, he looks completely defeated. My poor darling. This is just the proof I need to show him that she is unworthy. What a whore.

After he goes inside his apartment, I sneak to the door and listen. I gently turn the doorknob; he hasn't locked it. I open it a little wider and peek inside. If he catches me, I'll just say I was worried and checking on him.

I can hear the shower running. I slip inside the door and leave it ajar in case I need to make a quick exit. Tentatively, I approach the bathroom. With my back against the wall, I risk I peek. The shower screen glass is all fogged up, but I can make out William's naked body under the jets. Everything inside me throbs at the sight of his magnificent, sculptured body. I can see his hard buttock clenching.

Both hands are on the back wall of the shower and his head is down. The poor man is probably crying. I wish I could walk in there and comfort him. I imagine how I would seduce him.

I would kiss his tears and his agony away and then I would kiss his wet, hot mouth. He would kiss me back and it would ignite a fire in both of us. Hot, wet kisses, echoing around the ensuite. I'd lick his salty skin and he wouldn't be able to resist my naked supple body. I would awaken a fierce need in him, and our sex would be hard and wet, up against the shower wall. He'd be thrusting his hard tumescence into me, and I'd scream out his name when I climaxed, hard. I know he would take me there because he is perfect in every way.

I have managed to get myself completely aroused imaging myself with William. I turn and head to the front door of Wil's apartment. I gently close the door behind me and make my way to the car. Katrina, walking towards William's apartment, halts in the driveway. She looks perplexed as to why I would be there. Oooh, this is just too perfectly delicious. I hope she thinks we've been having hot saucy sex.

I greet her with my sunny voice, "Hi Katrina, did you have a nice lunch today?"

Confounded, she queries "What? What are you talking about?"

"Oh, I must be mistaken. I thought I saw you today at Clique Café. My bad." Then I stalk with purpose to my car. Heads up, bitch, your ruse is over – the cat's out of the bag and William is as good as mine.

* * * * *

Katrina

What the hell was that about? I wonder why Samantha was leaving Wil's apartment, her quirked eyebrows were suggestive, but I won't fall for that. I wonder how she knows I caught up with Marcus for lunch. Was she spying on me? She's a weird unit, that one.

I knock on Wil's door. I just want one last kiss before I take off with the girls on the weekend away. After a few moments, the door opens. Wil is dressed in only jeans, the top of his trunks peek over his jeans. His stomach is hard and wonderful. His hair is wet, and the smell of his shampoo and deodorant wafts over me. Maybe I'll sneak more than a kiss in. My God, he's a hot. He greets me cooly, "Hello,". This is perplexing.

I give him a wink, "Hiya. Thought I'd pop in for a quick pash before I take off." I step in and stand on tiptoe to peck his soft mouth. Shockingly, he pulls away. What the heck?

"A quick pash? Really?"

"Pardon?" I don't know what is going on. "Why won't you kiss me?"

"Gee, I wonder."

I seriously don't know what is going on or where to go from here. "I just saw Samantha outside."

"Yes, Samantha just paid me a visit."

I wait for him to elaborate but he doesn't. So, I venture, "What's going on, Wil?"

"What's going on? Well, apparently, you're fucking somebody else."

Whoa, where did that come from? "I'm sorry, what did you say?"

"You're seeing two men at the same time. It's called duplicity!"

"No, I'm not! Where is this coming from? I haven't said or done anything that would suggest anything of the sort, so where is this coming from?"

Will purses his lips, "Really Katrina? You're just going to go with lying?"

I'm not going to defend myself a moment longer. I have nothing to answer to. "I am not lying, William. You know how my marriage ended, that's not who I am."

"Well, I would have thought not and yet here is the proof!"

He drops some photos on the hall entrance table. Three photos of me greeting Marcus. And straight away, he has jumped to the conclusion that Marcus is my lover. OK, it does kind of look like we're kissing passionately in the last blurry one but it's a moment after I pulled away from his cheek. Where is the trust? This doubt and suspicion burn like acid, and I am highly offended and upset that I am forced to defend myself.

"Well, if you'd just let me explain…"

"No, I don't think so, Katrina. I think I've seen enough."

How rude. My face is hot. I have done nothing wrong, "So you're just going to assume Samantha is one hundred percent correct and that I am definitely cheating? You don't have the decency to let me explain?"

His face goes red with ire, "I have been down this road too many times, Katrina. I don't deserve this and you of all people should understand that."

I turn on my heel to leave but before I could get through the door, he asks softly behind me, "do you love him?"

I turn back and answer honestly, "yes, very much."

His head drops and his shoulders droop; he looks beaten. Then his face hardens, "You need to leave. Right now!"

I am upset, "without trust, Wil, we have nothing."

He just glares at me. I wonder why he has made this rash accusation with no founding except some photos provided by the super-bitch. I'm boiling mad that he didn't let me explain. He knows what she is like, so this is doubly upsetting. Fine, I'll go away with the girls and give him time to sweat it out over the weekend. I'll return on Sunday after he's had time to calm down and hopefully, he'll allow me to explain it to him. If not, he can go to hell.

As I'm climbing back into my car, my phone slips from my hand and lands onto the driveway facedown. The screen is covered in cracks. Shit. I touch the screen, but it won't work because the LED display is ruined. Sighing dramatically, could this day get any worse? *Don't tempt fate, Kitty Kat.* I yell loudly inside the cabin "Oh fuck off, you!" I've had it with bitches. My God, I'm yelling at my fucking subconscious!

As soon as I start the car, my Bluetooth kicks in so I call Lucy handsfree and tell her I've broken my phone so she won't be able to call me over the weekend while I'm away but if she needs me, she can call or text Louis, Felicity, or Sonja.

"Ok Mum, have a great weekend. Don't worry about your stupid phone – you can fix it when you get back from having a great time with the gals."

After I disconnect, my thoughts return to William. I'm so upset that he accused me of this without letting me explain, that I could cry. Tears prickle my eyes, but I swipe them away angrily. I can't believe he assumed the worst. The first disagreement is always a little heartbreaking – our little bubble has burst. No way I'm going to be swimming in this morbidity... I'm going away with the girls and William can stick his head back up his arse.

Felicity

I hurriedly put my bag in the car and run back in for my handbag when Damien's car pulls up beside mine. I take a long, slow breath before turning to greet him.

"Hi there, handsome. You're home early."

"Did you think you could sneak off without saying goodbye?"

All the colour drains from my face. "That's not what I was doing... I always leave at this time when we go on our 'girl's weekend'.

He breaks into a grin and pulls me into his embrace, "Jesus, calm down, stress-head. I'm just kidding around."

My heart is hammering inside my chest. He pulls away and holds me at arm's-length, "What's going on, honey? You're shaking."

"Oh, am I? It's chilly with that wind." I feign lightness, purposely injecting it and sunshine into my voice. The terror flooding my body needs to be kept in check.

He gives me a wink, "I know something that will warm you up."

My giggle sounds real, masking the deep feeling of dread bubbling within "Oh darling, as wonderful as that would be, I do need to leave now."

"Rubbish, you should always make time for you husband."

He takes my wrist and pulls me in behind him.

Sex is swift and perfunctory. My face is buried in his neck so he can't see my scrunched eyes. He is holding both of my wrists above my head, squeezing them so hard that I hold my breath, so I don't scream. As he reaches his climax, every muscle in his upper body tenses and the pain in my wrists is unbearable. A small squeak escapes me and filters into his ear. He jerks up, all his weight on my wrists; I'm sure they will snap soon. I look up at him doe-eyed, pushing though the excruciating pain to paste a wholesome expression on my face. I'm sweaty with the effort of containing the pain.

Grinning down into my face, he whispers, "I just made you come. I am a God in bed, and you shouldn't forget that."

As he climbs off me, I almost roll into him as the bed dips, He dons his underwear and moves to the bathroom, leaving me alone on the bed. I lay still and find even more pain in the blood rushing through the unpinioned vessels into my hands. My wrists are throbbing, and the ache is resonating in my arms. He knew how much pain he was causing but he did it anyway to remind me of his power, and that I should be very careful to remember this always. How much longer can I endure this torture. I'd leave him if I didn't think he'd find me and kill me.

* * * * *

After I have cleaned myself and put myself back together, I look at the ugly red welts on my wrists and cover them with the long sleeves of a warm knitted jumper.

Damien is sitting at the kitchen bench sipping coffee and reading the paper as I enter the room to retrieve my handbag. I can see the top of my contraceptive pill packet poking out of the pocket of my handbag and almost dive on it to hide it away. If Damien sees that packet and understands what it is, I will not walk away from this house without sustaining some serious punishment and bearing significant marks a lot worse than those on my wrists.

I put every effort into appearing normal and I lean in to kiss him goodbye and poke the packet out of sight.

He kisses me with such passion that something ignites deep in my belly, but he quashes it quickly when he grabs my right wrist and squeezes it with all the strength in his body, his jaw set. Hot searing pain shoots through my arm as I cry out in pain.

"Ow, Damien, you're really hurting me." He uses my wrist to jerk me close and kisses me so hard, that the inside of my mouth tears against my teeth.

In a low, menacing voice he says, "don't you fucking dare look at another man or so help me Felicity, I will kill you both."

He releases my wrist and I stumble backwards. I walk quickly to the door and say as I'm leaving, "I'm going on a girls' weekend, Damien, with GIRLS." His face hardens but I swiftly escape, slam the door closed and run to my car. I start the engine and don't even allow the car to warm up, I just zoom backwards out of the driveway and onto the road of the quiet cul-de-sac. I look towards the house and see his towering bulk filling the doorway, glaring at me with a face like thunder as I accelerate away. I'm sure I will pay for that when I get home, but I have two whole terror free days where I can be myself. I make a mental note to stop being so complacent with my contraceptive pill.

29

Judge & Jury

William

I am utterly devastated by today's revelations. Crushed and feeling very sorry for myself, I'm sitting on the bed, drinking whiskey neat from a tumbler. I want to feel nothing for a while.

There's a hard knock at the door. I think it might be Katrina and I'm torn between wanting to forget the whole thing and telling her to fuck off. I decide on the latter and yank the door open to a surprised Thomas.

He looks wary, "Hey,"

Face like thunder, "Hey yourself."

"Well, someone's in a good mood!"

"Oh, fuck off, Tom, I'm not in the mood for your shit today."

Tom holds up his hands in supplication, "Whoa, dude, I just came by to ask if I can borrow your black belt." He does some kind of weird dance thing, shaking his arse. "I've got a hot date tonight and I forgot mine broke, but I haven't had time to replace it." He stops dicking around and looks at me, "What's got you all shitty?"

I don't want to talk about it yet "Don't worry about it." Shit, he's looking at the photos on the hall stand. "Oh hey, why've you got pics of Marcus?"

I turn around, astounded, "You know this fucker?"

Tom looks taken aback, "Why is he a fucker? I met him today. He's a nice guy."

"Where did you meet him?"

Tom's hands are up and defensive again, "Katrina was having lunch with him at Clique Café. They haven't seen each other in like five months because he lives in Queensland or something. Why are you angry at him?"

"Who the fuck is he?"

"He's her brother."

Oh shit. Oh shit. Oh shit, shit, shit, shit... SHIT!

Tom narrows his eyes, "why do you look like you just shit the bed?"

"Ahhh, shit!"

"...and why do you have photos of him... of them? That's bloody weird, mate."

I panic yell at Tom, "I thought she was having a fling and I just told her to fuck off!"

Tom jerks in surprise, "You *idiot*! Why would she have a fling? She's not like that!"

"Well Samantha came over and was all, "I'm sorry to have to tell you this..." blah, blah and then showed me the pics and they look like... you know."

"Why the *fuck* would you believe a single word Samantha says? You know she's got a hard on for you. She's a crazy bunny-boiler, psycho bitch."

"Well, they look legit!"

"OK, so when Katrina explained it was her brother."

"She didn't explain."

"I can't see why she'd hide it".

"She didn't… I didn't really give her a chance to explain."

"Why the hell not?"

"…I don't know, because I'm an idiot."

"You said it."

"I asked her if she loves him… and she said yes… so I told her to get out."

"Of course, she loves him, he's her fucking brother."

"Well, I didn't know that did I? God I'm an arsehole. What is Samantha up to?"

Thomas offers, "She's a snake, William. How can you not see this?"

Pondering, "you know, the last thing Katrina said was "without trust, we have nothing."

Thomas raises his eyebrows. "I don't think that means its over. Just call her and apologise, Wil. She'll understand."

My elbows are on my knees and my hands are in my hair. How can I have screwed this up so monumentally?

Thomas clears his throat, "I don't want to sound needy but, can I borrow your belt, please? I really do have a date tonight".

The last bit peters out… he doesn't want to rub it in. I go in search of the belt for Tom and wonder how long I should leave it before I call her with my tail between my legs. I don't even know how I'm going to start the conversation. What have I done?

* * * * *

Katrina

We all make it to the holiday house at Phillip Island by late afternoon; I'm the last to arrive. Within an hour we've unpacked and we're making cocktails and share platters of nibbles. The girls and I make this trip every year and have done so for well over a decade – it's our little escape. The holiday house belongs to Louise's family, and

I can see that Shane, her dad, has been down here during the week chopping wood and stocking the fridge with food and beverages for his angel and her friends. Louise is and always will be his little girl. Shane has made sure there is plenty of wood for our fire tonight, all neatly stacked beside the fireplace with kindling in different sizes in a box. He's even set it up for us tonight, so we only need to light the little piece of paper poking out. I'm always delegated the task of starting the fire, as we have a fireplace at home that we light in winter, and of course, our family goes camping every Easter...went camping.

For now, we will nibble from the antipasto platter and enjoy our beverages (and try not to get too pickled before dinner). Later tonight, we'll order woodfired pizzas in from the local pizzeria – this is our tradition on the first night of the weekend away. Tomorrow night, dinner will probably be the local pub and Sunday, after we've tidied the holiday and packed up our cars, we'll enjoy a delicious afternoon tea at our favourite Island café before making the trip home. These weekends are such a wonderful escape for all of us, more so for me this year after the year I've had.

The view from the main living room is extraordinary. The setting sun over the beach has lit the room in brilliant orange light. It's a bit too cool to sit outside on the balcony so we stay in and watch through the massive picture window. Mother Nature has used her most brilliant pallet on today's stunning illustration.

Felicity sidles up and puts her arm around my shoulders. I smile up at her. "Isn't this view just gorgeous?"

"It sure is. I could get used to this."

Felicity is one of the most naturally beautiful women I know. In school she was lanky but by year twelve, she had all the boys panting after her. I don't think she has any idea how beautiful she is. She could have been a model… she still COULD be a model and standing next to her in a bikini on a beach is intimidating. Well, it was. She doesn't seem to go to the beach anymore. I think Damien is a bit jealous. I don't blame him; she draws the attention of everyone in a room as she moves through it. But she has no idea. She is quiet and shy. Louise calls out to Felicity, and she returns to the kitchen.

I want to smell the sea air, so while the girls are busy in the kitchen, I step outside for a moment to hear the breakers. The gentle crashing of the waves as the tide makes its way in is soothing. Further out, the sea looks smooth and undulating under the reflection of her pallet. I tilt my face to the sky to soak in the last of the afternoon sun, closing my eyes in bliss and casting away my fractured thoughts. According to the bureau of meteorology, we're in for a cracker of a storm tonight; hopefully it will be clear by morning so I can take my habitual run on the beach.

I've been looking forward to the weekend away with the girls for such a long time. It's a shame that it has been sullied by whatever drama Samantha caused. Fancy taking photos... bloody stalker. My stomach knots at the thought of William's dismissal. I have to push any thoughts or misgivings about what happened with William away or it will ruin my weekend. A wave of disappointment washes over me that he hasn't called, then I remember that my phone is broken, and I cannot use it, so I left it in my car. He won't call anyway because he knows I'm on the weekend away. It doesn't matter, I guess. I shiver as the sun dips behind a cloud and the wind picks up; the storm is on its way.

Louise gently taps a manicured nail on the window and points to a delicate fluted vessel filled with bubbles, gesturing me inside. I wander back inside to the warmth of the living room. We clink our glasses in a toast and settle in for the first night of our weekend.

* * * * *

William

I'm desperately dialling her number and leaving messages but she's not answering or returning my calls. I've left about eight messages.

The first one was tentative because I didn't really know how to apologise so I just asked her to call me. I left it half an hour then called again, this time saying I hope we can discuss the misunderstanding, trying to downplay my over-reaction. The third time I said I was sorry and admitted that I'd over-reacted and asked if she could possibly forgive me. I thought surely, she'd call me back after that one. The fourth I just said I was sorry again and would give her some space. The rest were just "Hi, me again," messages but I'm probably digging a grave for myself, so I need to stop. I hope she calls me back either tonight or tomorrow. God, I'm an idiot. She's right, without trust we have nothing. I feel sick in my stomach just thinking I may have cocked up the best thing that has happened to me since the birth of my girls.

* * * * *

I hardly slept a wink – tossing and turning and imagining all manner of scenarios. It's ten o'clock Saturday morning and she still hasn't called. I don't know what to do. I will call her one more time and then leave the ball in her court but I'm thinking hard about what I am going to say. Maybe I should write it down.

I wander over to the big house. As I enter the house, I see Tom coming down the stairs. He looks at me, hopeful, "Did you speak to her?" I shake my head and try to keep the misery from reaching my expression.

Mum's pops into the room and her interest is piqued, "speak to who, love?"

I absolutely don't want to get into this with Mum so I kind of blow her off, "Oh, I'm just waiting to hear back from Katrina."

She is *not* satisfied with that and is about to quiz me further when there's a knock at the front door. Tom answers and as the door swings open, Samantha is standing on the doorstep. What the bloody hell is she doing here? Tom rudely greets her, "Oh, if it isn't the troublemaker."

She ignores Tom and looks past him at me, her face all concern. I turn on my heel and stalk from the room – I have no time for her. I blame myself for this mess, but it started with Samantha. I take in Mum's horrified expression as I walk past her and just keep walking. Like a bitch in heat, Samantha runs after me, her stiletto sandals clicking loudly on the parquetry floor. She follows me into the kitchen. I turn around and glare at her as she makes it through the door, "What could you possibly want, Samantha? Haven't you done enough?"

She puts a shaky hand to her chest, "William, why are you upset with me? I didn't do anything wrong."

Like a petulant child, I'm all kinds of messed up, I counter, "Oh, and you're the picture of innocence, are you?"

Her expression becomes bitchy, "don't shoot the messenger, Wil. Someone had to tell you."

Mum has made it into the kitchen, "… tell you what?" she asks, completely befuddled.

Samantha turns to Mum and says, "that Katrina was cheating on Wil."

Mum is having none of that, "Oh my goodness, I don't believe that for a minute."

Samantha is indignant at the mere suggestion she was wrong, "Well believe it. I saw it with my own eyes."

"Definitely not!" Tom barks. "Samantha got it all wrong and has caused all kinds of trouble."

All wide-eyed innocence, Samantha's hand is at her chest again. "Thomas, I wouldn't lie about something as important as this."

"I didn't say you lied, Samantha," he emphasises her name, "I said you got it wrong. I was in that restaurant, and she was with her brother!"

Silence descends on the kitchen. Samantha's spine stiffens and her face hardens. "Well what kind of immoral relationship does she have with her brother? That's disgusting!"

Thomas jerks as if struck, "who were you looking at? She pecked him on the cheek and gave him a hug... like normal siblings. They were having lunch together. I met her brother and had a beer with them. Nothing untoward happened. You've manufactured this whole drama. You have an unhealthy obsession with William... but you're engaged to Greg. That's what is disgusting here."

I put an end to the conversation, "Enough! Samantha, you need to leave please. You have done enough damage."

She stutters and Mum diplomatically deals with her. She gently says to Samantha, "Perhaps you should go, love. Emotions are obviously high here."

She turns to me and spits, "That's because nobody can see through that manipulative *bitch*. You all think she's this wonderful person. She's not. She's common and inbred, and, and *disgusting*. She has wheedled her way into this family and under your skin and you can't see through her. She is not worthy of you, William! I hate her, I bloody *hate* her!" Her face is red and angry, but her eyes are glassy – she looks like she's about to burst into tears.

Mum has her firm voice out and wields it on Samantha like she's a child, "Samantha, that is enough. You do not speak like that about Katrina, not in my house you don't. You need to leave, please."

Her shoulders droop and the corners of her mouth drop; her bottom lip quivers and a tear breaks free and runs down her cheek. Her voice quivers, "I didn't mean to cause trouble. I just didn't want you to get hurt. You mean the world to me, Wil." Somehow, I feel awful, like I've been cruel. Thomas turns away in disgust, he can see through her drama.

Mum softens, "Look love, it's just not a good time now. Perhaps come back another time after all this settles."

She nods bleakly and turns to leave. Thomas is holding the door open for her. She looks up at him as she passes, her expression hurt and vulnerable. Thomas gives no shits and slams the door behind her.

"Thomas, that was unnecessary!" Mum is shocked.

"Tell me you didn't fall for that sob story, Mum. Acting all sad and broken doesn't negate what she just said about Katrina, or the trouble she caused yesterday."

Mum is tapping her toe in exasperation, "Will somebody please tell me what is going on? What happened yesterday?"

Dropping onto a kitchen stool, I tell her what happened yesterday, and I don't leave anything out.

"Oh William, how could you have not let her explain? You know Katrina is better than that! My God, I hope you haven't just ruined your only change at happiness because you have trust issues!"

Cool, so not only have I screwed things up with Katrina, but now Mum is pissed off too. I need this day to bugger off.

* * * * *

Felicity

Louise and Sonja are loudly giggling about something hilarious. Katrina has just walked in from the outside deck and brings the cool evening air in with her. It's a welcome burst of fresh air with the fire making the room in here a little stuffy. She was out there last night too, and I wonder if everything is good in her world. Katrina isn't privy to the joke either, but I suspect their laughter can be attributed more to the consumption of alcohol than whatever the joke was. Katrina rips me from my thoughts, "How are you, Felicity? Everything going well at the office?"

"Yeah, nothing exciting to report. Just gearing up now for end of month, I guess. That's always a manic time."

My wrists are aching, and my glass suddenly feels heavy, so I reach over and put my glass on the coffee table. As I reach out, the cuff of my sleeve rises, and I am mortified to see the dark crimson of the blooming bruises on my wrist. I whip my hand back quickly and rest it in my lap, but I look up in time to see Katrina dart her eyes away and frown.

"How are you, Kat? Still giddy with love?"

Katrina's face flames and a troubled expression flares then disappears behind a façade of a carefully manufactured even expression. I have one of those too, Kat.

"Yes, it's all still wonderful. You forget all the butterflies and joy in the simple things over time. Marriage and kids kind of put a dampener on all the lust." Her face flames again and she looks like a deer in the headlights, "Oh God, Liss, I'm so sorry. I didn't even think…"

"Pah, don't apologise. I've come to terms with not having children. It just isn't on the cards for me. I think Damien wants them more than me."

The thought of bringing a child into our violent household scares me more than any fear I have for myself. I could not subject an innocent child to the violence I have experienced at the hands of Damien. After three painful miscarriages, all of which he blames me for, I became aware that perhaps this was a good thing. As his violence escalated, so did my desire to thwart any possibility of falling pregnant, so I decided to take matters into my own hand and started taking the contraceptive pill.

Damien blames me for our inability to stay pregnant. He says I have faulty genes and 'had better not give him a retard' when I finally do manage to keep one stuck in there. What a stupid man.

He has refused to go down the path of IVF. He says he doesn't want a pickled kid created in a laboratory and raised in a jar; if we can't have one naturally, then he doesn't want one at all. He balked at the mere mention of adoption. "You think I want to spend my hard-earned money on some unwanted piece of trash? Are you fucking stupid, Felicity?" For a terrifying moment I thought he was going to strike me, his rage was so intense. Instead, he raised his voice and dismissed me, "No, Felicity, I DO NOT want to adopt someone else's unwanted fucking kid that should have been a stain on the sheets!"

Louise pulls me from my reverie as she convivially announces, "Time to go, bitches! Dinner awaits."

I feel at peace within. The second day is the best of the long weekend with these girls. The happy snap of my wrists is already in my camera roll in the 'hidden' album. The recent memory has abated, and tomorrow's fear hasn't arrived yet. I can just chill and be happy. I embrace the joy and throw back the last of my wine.

I shout, "C'mon bitches, let's go."

A chorus of 'let's go bitches' reverberates around the room and we finally leave for dinner.

* * * * *

Katrina

We've walked down to the local pub and have started our Saturday night early. I'm already two Proseccos in and probably should slow down a bit or I'll end up getting pickled and tragic.

I'm a little concerned about the bruising I saw on Felicity's wrists. Last year when we were out at a girls' dinner, I saw bruises around her throat to match her bloodshot eyes, but as I was trying to think of a way to delicately enquire, Louise distracted me, and the moment was gone. Now that I've seen those bruises on her wrist, I am convinced that something is going on at home.

We've always thought that she and Damien have the perfect marriage, except that they are missing the children they so desperately want. I don't want to jump to conclusions because I have managed to fall down the stairs and give myself a broken nose and two black eyes when Jacob was a baby and all the kindergarten parents looked at me and then quickly looked away. I tried to explain that I had fallen down the stairs and their expression said, 'a likely story'. So,

I don't want to jump to conclusions, but the way she whipped her hand away and hid it from me, suggests that something untoward is happening.

Louise breaks into my thoughts and wants the low down on Wil and what's been happening. I'm all smiles and sunshine because I don't want to indicate anything upsetting is happening already. I just hope we can work this silly little misunderstanding out when I get back from this weekend.

The conversation turns to Abigail Trenery. The trial won't be until either next year or the year after, but I will be called as a witness because of my part in finding the sick bastard. I think I will attend the entire trial, for Abby. All the disgusting things they did to poor Abigail will come out and I'm not sure I can unhear everything I will learn. I really don't want to dwell on it, and I tell the girls this. They understand and our conversation turns to lighter subjects. We talk about our children, husbands and what's been going on at our collective jobs. Felicity is noticeably quiet.

We decide to take a walk along the foreshore before dinner; our table has been reserved so there is no need to rush back to the pub. We have all taken our shoes off and take long strides in the soft, warm sand, curling our toes and enjoying the sensation of the tiny grains against our unaccustomed winter kept feet. Last night's storm has left detritus and natural debris scattered across the grassy slopes leading down to the sand. People sit on picnic blankets amongst the leaf litter, accosted by marauding and squawking seagulls, hopeful of a chip or morsel of bread, and generally making a nuisance of themselves. Boisterous children match the raucous cacophony making pockets of the lawned area shrill and grating.

Seaweed and flotsam have washed up on the sand resulting in a very messy shoreline smelling strongly of the sea. I can taste the salt when I lick my lips; it is whipped into the air and blown against us in the onshore breeze. The tide is on its way in, so we head for the pier and stroll along the jetty; deciding to take the esplanade on our return trip to the pub.

As we walk up the main street, lined with Golden Cypress trees, the street lined with cars, I finally start to relax and enjoy myself. The sun is warm on my skin, the salty sea air is cleansing and the sounds of young families enjoying their weekend is food for the soul.

I am lost in my thoughts as we walk the Esplanade, thinking of William. A sudden eruption makes us all look at a house as we pass. The top of a double hung sash window is open to allow the cool breeze in. Two miniature shiatsu puff balls are bouncing at the glass: emitting a high pitched, frenzied yapping between the lace curtain and the bay window. A Russian Blue cat, perched atop the open window glares down at the puff balls, tail wagging with controlled disgust, its small triangular face an irritated picture of loathing of the small noisy creatures. A lazy smile creeps across my face but is erased immediately by the noisy rumbling of my stomach. Louise looks at me and grins. She senses something is off.

Felicity strolls beside me and I take the opportunity to gently enquire, "Hey Liss, is everything ok at home? You just seem a little subdued today."

Her eyes suddenly fill with tears, but she shakes her head. I reach for her hand and tuck it in the crook of my elbow and squeeze her fingers gently to let her know that I understand, and that she is not alone.

Dining on pub grub leaves us feeling sated but not overly full. Our walks in the sea air have us mute and weary. The stroll back to the holiday house in the fresh early evening air gives me peace and I feel good. I'll sleep well tonight.

Louise has us in stitches as she regales us with a tale of a 'one night stand with a bogan', as she so delicately termed the experience. The crackling fire lends a soft ambiance to the room, and we have pockets of quiet reflection during the evening. We all decide to get an early night and turn in at the offensively seniors' hour of nine-thirty. Good gracious, imagine!

* * * * *

I am bunking with Felicity this weekend. I leave her alone and don't pry. If she wants to talk to me about anything, she will do so. She may well just want to forget what is happening at home and just enjoy a weekend without the stress.

After my evening ablutions, I return to the room to find Felicity turned to the wall, her back to me. I pick up my novel and decide to read a chapter before I turn in.

One page into the chapter, I hear Felicity sniff. I can't pretend that I didn't hear it. I dart into the bathroom to retrieve the box of tissues and sit on the end of Felicity's bed. I pull a couple of the tissues and hand them to her over her shoulder. She rolls over to face me and I can see that she has been silently crying for a while. I rub her shoulder but don't press her. Manoeuvring herself to sitting position, she rolls up her sleeves and shows me the awful damage to her wrists. I try to mute my horror, but I am so horrified by the state of her wrists that I make a sound.

"Honey, what's going on? Please tell me."

She shakes her head. I promise not to tell anyone but just remind her it would be easier for her if she can at least download to someone.

"Damien is very… jealous. He is insanely jealous. This was to remind me not to look at any men while I'm here."

"Liss, is this a common thing?"

Her eyes drop to her lap, and I detect a barely perceptible nod.

"I know that you love him…"

Her eyes are still on her lap as she nods her head yes, then shakes her head no.

"Honey, you need to leave him."

Her eyes find mine and they are full of desperation, "No, you don't understand. He will find me, and he will kill me. If he can't have me, then nobody can. This is mild compared to sometimes…"

Her voice peters out.

"Sweetheart, how long has this been going on?"

"Pretty much most of our married life. He shoved me once when we were engaged but it was such a random thing, I didn't think anything of it. It's been gradually building for years. A little slap here, and shove there but in the last couple of years, he has become controlling and violent."

"I can't believe this, Liss. This is awful!"

"So now I'm on the pill because I can't bring children into this violent home."

I gently pull her into my embrace and hold her while she sobs. Eventually, the sobs turn to sniffles, and she regains her composure, "it feels so good to be able to just talk to someone about this. Thank you."

"You know, I've wondered before when you had those bloodshot eyes from vomiting…"

"It wasn't vomiting. That night we ran into Trent from school. Trent hugged me hello, so Damien beat him to a pulp and then dragged me home and choked me so hard that I passed out and the blood vessels in my eyes burst. When I woke up, he was crying because he thought he'd killed me."

She holds up her hand and points to the emerald and diamond ring, "this was the apology. He was kind and lovely for two weeks before someone winked at me at the cinema as I was coming out of the bathroom. Clearly it was my fault, so he violently threw the box of popcorn at me in front of everybody in the foyer. They all gasped in horror. He then dragged me home where he punched me so hard in my arm, repeatedly in the same place, that I thought he'd broken my humerus. That bruise covered my whole upper arm from shoulder to elbow and really made moving the shoulder joint painful. I say I am used to it, but the fear is always there. I never know what mood he will be in. He can be in a good mood, but I somehow say the wrong thing and then I know I have to pay for it. There's just a subtle change to his expression and I know I have done it. I don't fight it anymore; I just endure it. I do take pictures to document the abuse though just in case I need to defend myself in court."

The awful horror of the secret Felicity has been harbouring for years makes me feel impotent and useless. I can't contain my own tears.

"What can I do to help you?" I plead.

"There is nothing anybody can do. One day I will get the courage to leave him, but I will have to move to the other side of the world or something. You know what? I'll never feel safe, I'll never stop having to look over my shoulder. This is my bed and I have to lie in it."

"No, you don't, honey. There are places of refuge for you to go and they will help you."

"Kat, you don't know him. He has told me that if I ever leave him, he will find me and he will kill me… and I believe him."

"Liss, just know that you are always welcome at my house – any time of the day or night, I am here for you, always. My house is a safe haven."

Her face crumples and she reach up and hugs me hard and whispers 'thank you' over and over again.

* * * * *

We wake early, having slept like the dead, and have a light breakfast. After packing our things in the car and cleaning up the holiday house, an easy job given we're all a little OCD anyway, and we start our walk back into town for our afternoon tea.

This tradition of the weekend away is my favourite. Light fluffy scones lathered in rich sweet jam sourced locally and decadent whipped cream, complimented with a pot of strong tea. We are uncomfortably full after gorging on this indulgent luxury but the walk back to the house eases our discomfort before we leave for the two-hour drive home.

Although we see each other regularly, this annual weekend away is a wonderful interruption to our ordinary lives and we have come to look forward to them every year. We hug fondly; I hug Felicity extra hard and remind her that I am only a phone call away and if she needs me, I can come and collect her. She nods at me, but I know she won't call, she won't want to involve me in this hell of hers. So, I climb in my car. As I was the last in, my car is the first out; I wave and blow the girls a kiss before backing out of the driveway and starting my trip home. The Bluetooth kicks in and I'm advised that I have thirteen new voice messages... *thirteen*? I look at the cracked screen of my phone; a prismatic array of colours radiates from the shards. The car audio system plays the messages one by one; the first one about forty minutes after I left William's house.

"Hi Katrina, it's William. I wonder if you could please give me a call. Thanks."

Then, another from Wil about an hour later. "Hi, Katrina, me again. I was just hoping we could talk about the misunderstanding earlier today. Um... could you perhaps give me a call?"

Then every forty-five minutes or so a message from William, "Hi Katrina, it's William again. Look, I'm sorry for what happened and for what I said. I completely over-reacted. Please forgive me. Could you please call me?

"Hi, it's me again. I'm sorry, I really am. I understand if you're upset. Could you please call me?" (sigh) "I'll... I'll give you some space."

"Hi, me again. Just hoping you'll call me soon." There's three more like that.

A random message in the middle from someone speaking very quickly in another language. Then a few more from William, all apologising and sounding more and more upset and miserable that I haven't called. The poor guy must think I'm terrible.

Then there's a break and a message from yesterday morning. He sounds desperate, "Hi Katrina. Please could you find it in your heart to forgive me? I'm so, so sorry, and I feel awful that I didn't give you a chance to explain. Please… *please* could you call me?"

Two hours later another one, "Hi Katrina, it's me. Please can you call me? This can't be the end of us… please." His voice cracked at the end of that one. Oh my God, poor William.

And another, "Katrina please, give me a chance to explain. I'm sorry, (a sob)"

Holy shit, he thinks we're over. Another one last night around eleven in the evening. I was already dead to the world while this poor guy is wringing his hands. He must have forgotten I away for the weekend. Shit! He sounds a little drunk and teary, "Hey Katrina, it's me. I really wish you would take one of my calls. I don't want us to end. I want us to move past this. I know I was out of line and a shit but, please don't end us. I made one mistake. It was a big one but surely you can find it in your heart to give me another chance?"

Then the last one is this morning. He has resigned himself to the fact that I'm gone and I'm not coming back because it's been three bloody days since he's heard from me.

"Hi Kat. I just wanted to say that I understand, and I'll stop this bullshit. Again, I'm very sorry for being a jerk and I hope at some stage, later when you're ready, that we have a chat and clear the air. Just so I can have the chance to properly apologise. I understand if you can't do any more of the office stuff. I get it. Take care, Katrina. Be safe."

Oh God. I'm almost crying. I ask my car audio to call him, but the stupid bitch keeps getting it wrong and I'm forced to cancel two calls. I decide that another hour and a half won't matter so I'll just drive to his house and fix it.

It is difficult not to speed all the way. I encounter every red light and refrain from pulling tufts of hair out in exasperation. When I finally turn into the drive from the road, I accidentally do a little burnout and fish tail as I accelerate up the drive. What an idiot. My face flames at my delinquent behaviour caused by my haste and my heart thuds because I got a fright. My tyres screech a little as I pull up too quickly near the front door. I yank open my door, retrieving my broken phone from the dock. I run like the clappers to Wil's studio apartment and bang on the door like a maniac. After no response I bang on the door again. Nothing. I run back to the big house and bang on that door. Beverley opens the door and her expression flits between concern and relief. Without greeting her properly, I ask "Hi Beverley, do you know where William is?" She looks at me… is that disappointment? Don't care, I need to speak to Wil and set this straight.

"Hi Katrina, yes, he's out back. He's been calling you all weekend."

Resigned, I confess in a babble of words, "I know now but my phone broke, and I've been away all weekend, so I didn't get his calls until I got in my car to come home, and they all came through. I had no idea he'd been calling. I really need to see him, Beverley."

She steps aside and looks relieved, "Of course, love."

I run through the house in my sunny dress and strappy sandals, looking for all intents and purposes like I've been living the high life while he's been here drowning in his tears. My heels echo through the quiet house as I race towards the door leading out to the back garden. I can see Wil in the garden seat, his head in his hands. As I round the seat in front of him, he looks up and sees me then to my horror, he drops to his knees and begs for my forgiveness. Oh God, I need to tell him I didn't leave him, "Wil no, Wil listen to me." He wraps his arms around my waist and desperately sobs into my dress, "Please, Katrina, please. I love you." Oh, Jesus H Christ on a popsicle stick, he thinks I mean 'no' to us.

I undo his arms from my waist and slide down into his lap so we're almost on the same level. I take his face in my hands, "William, I'm saying 'no', that you have it wrong. My phone broke," I hold up my shattered phone, "and I didn't get any of your calls. I was away for the weekend with the girls, remember? At Louise's family holiday house?" His expression registers the memory. "I didn't leave you, Wil, and we're not ending. I'm so sorry that you have been going through all of this and thinking I was ignoring you. God, you poor, poor man." He draws a shuddering breath and buries his face in my chest. His breath is hot on my skin. I lift his face and plant a kiss on his swollen mouth. "We're ok, Wil. We're still us."

We stay like this in the garden for a long time until he gets his emotions in check. When he has calmed, I whisper next to his ear, "I love you too." He kisses me and it feels like home. Eventually, I climb off him, so his legs don't drop off from lack of circulation. I look up to the kitchen windows and spy Thomas and Beverley watching us. When we enter, Beverley advises that she's put the kettle on and will make tea; a look passes between Thomas and William as Thomas closes his eyes in a long blink in relief.

We all sit at the table and make small talk and I tell them about my long weekend at The Island. After some polite conversation, I tell them I'm going home to greet my family and unpack my car. We graciously exit and as I stand at my car, I wrap my arms around him. I confess the burnout at the bottom of the drive and the screeching skid when I braked too hard. The deep rumble of his chuckle resonates through his chest. We share a long kiss, before I finally take my leave with a promise that I will return to him tomorrow.

When I return home, the house is practically empty except for Lucy. She's curled up on the couch with Nathan and has already eaten. I can't be bothered cooking for one, so I have a noodle cup instead. Nathan excuses himself to visit the loo and I tell Lucy about what I learned about Felicity and that I'm worried about her. I suggest I might pop over to see her... and I may stay the night. Lucy concedes that it's a great idea and tells me I'm a great friend. I swallow my guilt at lying to my girl and pack an over night bag and return to my man for some much-needed therapeutic reconciliation love.

* * * * *

My knuckles barely rap on the door when it opens to reveal him. He looks exhausted, but so happy to see me. He pulls me through the door and enfolds me in his arms. It feels good to be home again.

He leads me to the couch, and we sit, close. He rises briefly to pour us both a glass of wine and brings the bottle with him. I curl up into his side and we catch an episode of our current favourite series on a streaming service. We watch two episodes before retiring to his bedroom for a slow and steady rumba between the sheets.

30

Caught in the Act

Felicity

I had a moment of panic this morning when I couldn't find my pill packet. After a lot of frantic searching, I had to give up on finding it and dash to the car or I would be late to the office.

The moment I return home, I resume the search. Damien arrives as I was searching in the wardrobe and startles me, "looking for this?"

Damien's bulk fills the doorway, dressed in his khaki uniform and still in his shoes. Caught between his index and middle finger was the missing pill packet. Dread floods my extremities as I try to think of a viable explanation on the fly.

"Damien, I can explain..."

"...Oh, I don't think you need to explain. Who the fuck do you think you are? You think you can make these decisions without discussing it with me?"

"Damien, I just thought I'd skip a few months and give my body a chance to build up whatever is lacking so the next time that baby actually stays."

"Bullshit, Felicity. You are sabotaging any chance I might have of becoming a parent. You are a filthy, selfish fucking bitch! Or are you seeing somebody else?"

"My God, of course not!" His face holds so much rage and I literally shake in fear.

The closed fisted blow to the stomach catches me unaware. As I sink to my knees in the carpeted wardrobe, Damien rips me up into a standing position and just rains open handed slaps down on me. My face, my arms… each one getting harder and bringing tears to my eyes. The hits to my head with his hard palm make a hellish sound and one of them causes a terrible pain inside my ear. He just keeps on hitting and hitting, sending my body this way and that with every blow. I cower to the floor and curl myself into a tight ball to protect myself wherever I can, but this enrages him further and he starts kicking me. I take multiple blows to the back and shoulders but the kicks to my buttocks are particularly brutal; a particularly vicious kick to my coccyx sending pain and spasms up my spine. I hold my breath, so I don't cry out.

It feels like an eon passes before he finally runs out of steam and leaves me, a quivering mess on the wardrobe floor, too scared to even move. The front door slams and the squeal of tyres heralds his departure.

My hatred for him burns in the pit of my stomach. Not a single muscle in my body feels unharmed. It takes a gigantic effort to get myself to the bathroom where I draw a bath. As I wait for the bath to fill, I survey the damage in the mirror. Little scratches on my arms, face and shoulders burn amongst the larger bruises forming. The ringing in my left ear slowly disappears but all sounds seemed to be muffled and muted, like my ear is full of cottonwool. As I turn my head to the side, I notice a trickle of blood coming out of my ear; the bastard burst my eardrum.

The worst damage was sustained on my lower back and backside. Huge welts were already forming and turning into bruises on both backside cheeks, and I can feel bruising around my coccyx. I lowered myself gingerly into the bath and give way to the racking sobs.

When I emerge, there is a message on the answering machine from Sonja. We are all going to drop in to see Katrina later in the evening. I text Sonja to count me in. I want to be anywhere but here, and somewhere deep inside is the knowledge that I will never escape him and there throbs the deep desire to see Damien dead.

* * * * *

Katrina

William and I are going on another date. To quell my excitement, this afternoon I took a quiet stroll around the block. Spring has made all the gardens pop with colour. I stop to admire a rhododendron with an insane explosion of dark pink flowers.

Pale pink blossoms as delicate as crepe paper skitter across the pavement. A dust whirl lifts the fallen petals and scatters them across the neatly manicured lawn, displaying a healthy shade of vivid green blades, now mussed by the unruly presence of the floral detritus.

My fitness tracker buzzes a reminder that I have to get ready for our date, so I hurriedly walk the rest of the way home, my stomach filled with butterflies.

As I'm getting dressed, Lucy comes to the ensuite and leans against the door, asking, "are you going out tonight?"

Trying for blasé, "Yes, the girls and I are going out for dinner."

Frowning at me, "didn't you go out last week?"

Not pleased by the Spanish inquisition, I retort, "Oh, I didn't realise there was a limit on how often I can go out."

Taken aback, Lucy says "No, there's not limit, it's just unusual, that's all."

"Why is it unusual? I've made you all dinner and I enjoy having dinner with the girls."

Lucy puts her hands up in defence, "Hey, I was just asking. You normally tell us when you're going, that's all."

Exasperated, I turn and look her full in the face, "Lucy, I'm going out for dinner tonight with Louise, Felicity and Sonja." Lucy gets her nose out of joint, "fiiiine, sorry I asked," and storms off.

I don't want this discord, so I finish applying my makeup and go in search of her. I find her broodily curled up in the formal living room, pretending to read a book. I sit down beside her,

"I'm sorry I snapped at you. I thought I'd already told you. I won't be out late, I'm just going out for a bite with the girls, that's all."

"It's fine. I was only asking."

God it's hard, "I know and I'm sorry. I'll be home early, don't worry."

"It's just that I thought we were going to make cocktails and watch a movie together tonight."

Shit! I forgot. "Honey, I'm sorry, I completely forgot about that. Can we do that tomorrow night?"

Lucy sniffs and appears appeased, "OK, but don't make any more plans for tomorrow, ok?"

I kiss her cheek and give her a hug, "OK hon, I won't forget. I'm sorry."

She smiles and playfully quips, "it's fine, don't go developing a guilt complex over it."

Crisis avoided.

Wil picks me up at the end of the street. Tonight, he's taking me out to a family favourite restaurant. He said it's cheap and cheerful and it was his favourite place for his childhood birthday night. We share a pizza and some delicious garlic bread.

My phone buzzes on the table and not wanting to be rude, I ignore it. It buzzes again and Will tells me to check my phone. I pick up my phone and there's a text message from Lucy,

'Hi Mum, how is your dinner with the girls going?'

Perplexed, I quickly respond.

'It's going fine. Louise is making us all laugh about some story about an awkward date. I'll fill you in when I get home.'

I watch the little bubble with three dots, waiting for her response. 'Really? How odd.'

I look up at Wil. He takes in my expression, "What's up?"

"Lucy is behaving weirdly."

Wil does his best Billy Idol, "How so?"

Right, he has no context. I explain the exchange this evening when I was getting ready and then my response. "So, you haven't told your kids about us yet?" Wil looks a little disappointed.

"I'm not ready. I'm still enjoying the little secret of us at the moment."

After a moment, I think I'd better call, and I tell William what I'm doing.

Lucy answers straight away. There is laughter in the background, and I can tell she has put me on loudspeaker.

"Hi Lucy, what's going on?"

Lucy gets all cute, "Hi Mum, we're all good. How is your dinner going with the girls?"

"It's going very well thank you."

Lucy asks, "so are all three of the girls with you?"

Something is going on, "Yep, we're all here. Why?"

There is mirth in Lucy's voice, "Well it's just that the girls are actually here." There is a chorus of greetings down the phone.

Shiiiiiiiiit! I cover the phone, "we've been made."

William's face splits with an ear-to-ear grin.

I sigh loudly into the phone. Lucy asks," Who's your hot date, Mum?"

My face flames "Lucy, take me off loudspeaker please."

Lucy's voice comes to me clear. "Lucy, I just wanted to have a little more time before I introduce you. His name is William and we're just enjoying each other's company at the moment."

"Well, Mum, is there any reason that you're not telling us about him."

I look at William and wink, then stand up and pull my seat over so he can hear both sides of the conversation. "Look, I'll bring him home with me tonight but just don't judge him by his appearance, ok?"

William pulls away and frowns. I grin at him cherubically.

Lucy is aghast, "My God, Mum... can he hear you?"

"No, he's gone to the toilet. Look, height, and appearances aren't everything, ok. There is such a thing as a magnificent personality and a presence. He has those things in spades... and he makes me happy."

William stifles a chuckle. After a brief silence, Lucy says, "Jesus Mum, none of us will judge him... even if he's short, fat, bald and ginger."

I remain completely silent. After a few beats, Lucy sucks in air, "Oh my God. Ok, I promise we will not judge. We just want you to be happy, that's all."

"Promise me you won't judge."

"Mum, I promise. I'll word everyone up, so we all react appropriately."

"OK, we'll be there in about half and hour. Make sure my kitchen is clean."

"OK, sure. See you then."

Disconnecting the call, I look at William soberly, then we both burst out laughing.

"You are a wicked, wicked woman... you'll go to hell for this!"

I pick up and chair and return to my side of the table, "Nah, even Jesus has a sense of humour!"

* * * * *

By the time we pull up outside our house, I can see that William is a little nervous. I reach over for his hand and gently kiss his knuckles. He pulls me in for a proper kiss.

I open the front door and beckon William to follow. As we make our way down the hall, all noise in the kitchen ceases as they silently wait for our appearance. I walk in first and all eyes look at me momentarily then move past me to Wil. As soon as he makes it through the door and into the kitchen, everybody in the room laughs. Wil grins, he was in on the joke. I roll my eyes, but I can't suppress my grin.

"William, this is Lucy, Mason, and Jacob, and these are my three girlfriends, Felicity, Sonja, and Louise. Everybody, this is William."

My two sons immediately reach out and shake William's hand and all the girls say hello. I trot off into the butler's pantry to put the kettle on and extract the biscuit tin. I'm grateful I made a batch of butter cookies yesterday and pop them on a plate.

"OK, who wants coffee and who wants tea? Or would you like something alcoholic?"

William and Jacob take a beer, the girls all opt for wine, and only Mason wants a tea.

Lucy and I quickly put a cheese platter together and move everybody to the dining table. William is welcomed into my family and friendship group with open arms. I curse myself for taking so long to introduce him to the most important people in my life.

* * * * *

William

Katrina's family are awesome. I look over at her fussing with wine and my eyes fall on her lovely bottom. I would like very much to be cuddled up and spooning that bottom. I wonder how long it will be before we can have sleepovers.

She walks over and puts a glass of wine before me. As she steps back, she looks up into my eyes and winks; everything south of the navel quivers. She sets her own glass down and sits beside me. Our thighs touch and it's like an electric pulse shoots through me. Her friend Louise keeps looking at me suspiciously. I'm not sure what is going on there, but I am not getting good vibes from that one. The other two are lovely… Sonja has her chin resting on her folded hands and is looking at me dreamily. Better stay clear. Katrina is oblivious to all of it.

She reaches under the table and pats my knee. I can't look at her or my face will betray me. Her kids playfully mock her about being anal and a 'neat freak' and she takes it all in her stride. She has a relaxed relationship with her kids, and I feel at ease.

Lucy makes a noise and sits up in her seat suddenly. "What?" Katrina asks.

"Wait, is this the Wil from work?"

Katrina's face lights up, "Yes."

Lucy nods at Kat and holds up her hand for a high-five "Nice!"

Katrina almost imperceptibly shakes her head and Lucy withdraws her hand and covers the embarrassing move by cutting some cheese to put on a cracker. Katrina's face is still red.

* * * * *

A couple of hours later I bid farewell to Katrina's family and friends. She walks me to the door but before she opens it, she loops her arms around my neck and pulls me in for a thorough kissing. My whole body is on fire and as she presses herself against me, I know she can feel my desire. I practically run out of the door before I embarrass myself.

* * * * *

Katrina

Felicity is quiet and looks almost delicate – something is wrong. I can't ask her about it now, I will have to wait for everybody to leave. She makes eye contact with me and manages a shaky smile. I turn and follow William down the hall to the door.

After seeing William off, breathless from his kiss, I head back to the kitchen and find Louise lurking in the hall. She looks troubled. "What's up Lou?" I wonder if she knows about Felicity.

She ushers me into the living room and closes the door. This feels a bit ominous.

"Kat, do you think William's intensions are honourable?"

Are we in the 19th century? "What do you mean? Where's this coming from?"

"I mean, do you think he's after your money?"

This floors me and I take a moment to respond. "Lou, why do you think he is after my money? It's not like I'm loaded."

"Look I know that, but this house is worth a lot and after you and Jack divorce, you will actually have quite a tidy sum."

"I'm pretty sure he's not after my money, Lou."

"He's very good looking, Kat. I mean, look at him. He's practically a Greek God. He's way out of your league."

I cannot hide my hurt, "Well thank you Lou, that makes me feel just great."

Lou can see that she has hurt my feelings and tries to back pedal, "I don't mean to be awful, I'm not saying you're ugly…"

"…I should think NOT!"

"I'm just saying that he is very good looking, like movie star hot, you know, and you're suburban housewife kind of hot?"

"Wow, not helping yourself here Lou. You're digging a big hole. You should probably stop now."

"I'm not being very articulate. Let me put it another way, if he isn't after your money, then why is he dating you?"

Wow, just wow! "For your information, Louise Jamison, and please note the use of your full name, William is quite well off himself, so he doesn't need my money, but it sure is nice to know what you're thinking."

"Oh Kat, can't you see that I'm trying to protect you? I don't want to see you hurt."

"And yet here you sit, insulting me and telling me he is way out of my league and that he can't possibly be dating me for me."

"That's not what I'm saying, Kat. I'm just saying, it looks a little suspicious."

"Ok Lou, enough, you should probably go now."

"Katrina, you can't possibly be mad at me."

"I can possibly and I am. I've had a tough time since finding out Jack was having an affair and after months and months of misery, I'm happy. I'm disappointed that you can't be happy for me. Nothing gives you the right to burst my bubble."

Louise's face crumples and she buries her face in her hands. She sobs uncontrollably into her hands. I wait for a bit then get up to get some tissues. When I return, she has pulled herself together somewhat.

"I'm sorry Kat, I didn't mean to hurt you. I just want to protect you."

"Well, I don't need your protection. I like Wil and Wil likes me. That's all you need to know. I don't want to talk about this again. If you don't have anything nice to say, then please just don't say anything at all. Now I'm going back to enjoy the rest of my evening. You can either join us or leave."

I leave Louise in my living room and rejoin the happy chatter at my dining table. About ten minutes later, I hear the front door close. Louise has left.

* * * * *

Felicity seeks me out as I exit the bathroom. She pulls me into the living room recently vacated by Louise and turns around, lifts her top, pulls the top of her jeans down. Her back is covered in awful welts and her backside looks unbelievably bad, already mottled with sinister dark bruising. My hands involuntarily cover my mouth in horror.

"Oh God, Liss, what happened?"

She shrugs, like this is nothing big, "he found my pill packet and didn't take the news that I have been controlling the pregnancy situation very well. He burst my eardrum too. He just lost it and hit out. It's going to get a lot worse for me, Kat, so I just want you to hang on to this for me."

She hands me a pink sealed envelope marked *Do Not Open* in her beautiful cursive script. I can feel it contains a letter or note.

"It's just a little insurance policy but I only want you to open it if something happens to me. Even if it looks like an accident. If something happens to me, you need to open the envelope and go to the police, ok?"

"Felicity, how will I live with myself if something happens to you and here I was sitting on this envelope? I want you to get out and get safe now."

"Kat, please don't open it until the worst happens, please? I am hoping that I'll get myself safely out before anything sinister happens but just in case, I don't want him to get away with it."

I don't understand how she can be so flippant about this, but I have not walked in her shoes. Compared to Felicity, I have lived a charmed life. I hope she finds the strength to leave soon.

31

Mini Break

William

Katrina and I lean against the car while we wait for Thomas and Chloe to finish loading up the last few things in their car. We have booked a three-bedroom house in Harrietville, not far from Bright in Victoria's Alpine region, for the long weekend. We've all taken the Monday off before Melbourne Cup Day and we're off on a mini break.

The cool morning air is crisp and our breath wisps in front of us with every word. Although we're rugged up against the chill, by the time we get to our destination, the sun will be high, and the day will be close to twenty-seven degrees. These last few days of spring have provided cool mornings and evenings and days that are the perfect prelude to the coming summer. I remember coming up this way to Falls Creek as a kid in winter, skiing with the family in my youth. Samantha's family owns lodgings and so our two families always took the first week of school holidays up in the snow. Thomas still comes up to snowboard with his mates each year, but these days they stay in accommodation with young people and drink themselves stupid. I got married and had children, so those shenanigans ended for me. Thomas never married, never found the right one… he is Peter Pan; never going to grow up… unless Chloe is the turnkey.

Katrina pulls me from my reverie, "We used to go to Bright in summer during my childhood. It's a tradition that Jack and I continued with our children until a year ago when the kids got too old and didn't want to go anymore. The last trip we took, only Mason wanted to come with us and by the time we got back, he'd realised that it just wasn't the same without his siblings."

"That's a pity; it sounds like you miss it."

She smiles up at me, "I have… so I'm really looking forward to going back there."

Finally, Thomas and Chloe throw the last of their bags into his car and are ready to go. They hold hands on the five-step walk to the car, snatching glimpses of each other constantly; Chloe colouring pink with joy when Thomas winks at her. God help us.

Turning the ignition, the car rumbles to life and I let it idle to warm the engine while I check the bikes are secured to the back. Katrina climbs in the passenger seat ready to go. The quiet hum of my engine is eclipsed by Thomas' V8 as he turns the engine over and gives it a couple of ear-splitting revs that almost creates a shit-stain in my shorts. Within a couple of minutes, both Mum and Dad have opened the front door and peer out at us in their dressing gowns. I turn and scowl at Thomas, still grinning like an idiot at Chloe; revving his engine like a flog has woken them both up and made all the tiptoeing around for the past hour a wasted exercise. His ears pink with embarrassment when he spies them in the doorway, blinking in the morning sun. He gives them a cheery wave to cover his embarrassment…bloody knob.

We wave goodbye to our bleary-eyed parents and quietly roll down the driveway; Thomas' V8 crackling with restraint. Katrina finds a station with music as we accelerate out of the driveway and away from the house… she has to up the volume within a minute to drown out Thomas' Ute, as he opens the throttle and floors it past us. Still a flog. I look at Katrina and see her laughing at my brother's idiotic behaviour. I shake my head and roll my eyes, "Get your hand off it, Thomas. Katrina swiftly plugs her phone in, and her play list pulses out of the speakers. She has excellent taste in music… some songs I haven't heard since the eighties, and they bring back long forgotten memories. The first drumbeats of *Original Sin-INXS* transports me to the lake, hanging with the boys on a lazy Saturday arvo… sinking tinnies and making out with Joanne. She popped my cherry in the back of my souped up '72 Holden LJ Torana GTR-XU1. God, I loved that car. I wish I'd never sold it, but I made up for it with the Holden HQ SS. I still have it to this day, and it's still the infra-red colour it started out as. I'll have to take Katrina out for a spin in it… should probably check she's into muscle cars first. Can't very well call Thomas a flog when it clearly runs in the family.

"Whacha thinking?" Katrina pulls me from my past and look at me expectantly. "This song just takes me back to a different time."

"You were smiling… a girl?"

"Yeah, two of them."

Her eyebrows dart north. I grin at her, "both of my muscle cars were girls… I still have one of them. She's parked in storage, and I take her for a spin every now and again.'

Surprised, she ventures, "When you say muscle cars… do you mean like Thomas'?"

Shit, yes, I'm a flog. "Yes… only I don't rev it like that. Next time I take her out, maybe you could join me."

I barely finish the last word when she blurts, "absolutely!" Cool, she's into that shit!

"Wouldn't have pegged you for a rev-head."

Crinkling her nose, she grins back, "well I'm not really, but my dad is a serious rev-head and in my youth, he dragged us all along to anything with an engine. I discovered that I like super cars and nitro-burning funny cars."

I almost give myself whiplash… "Who are you and what have you done with the woman I've been bedding these past months?"

"Bedd… did you say bedding? Who calls sex 'bedding'? How sixteenth century of you. Next, you'll be referring to me as your wench!" This unexpected conversation produces a loud guffaw from me. We're barely a 1/2 hour into the trip and I'm already laughing.

We had a decent breakfast before we left however Katrina has packed snacks for the three-and-a-half-hour drive. I'm already thinking about those snacks when she reads my mind and reaches behind my seat to retrieve the bag. To my delight, she has made chocolate chip cookies. The first time she made these and brought them to the house, I had tried one, then gone back for another and was embarrassed to admit to both Mum and Dad that I had eaten no less than six of them. She has brought a whole container of them, and I just know that I will make light work of them over the next few hours, whether I'm hungry or not. She opens the lid, and the aroma of the cookies wafts under my nose, "Pass me one of yon treaties, wench." She pauses and looks at me with a face splitting grin; it makes me lightheaded. The music pumps and we drive on, enjoying each other's company. We finally exit the boring Hume highway and head into the beauty of this region.

* * * * *

Katrina

William is devouring the biscuits… where the hell does he put them all? I'm drowsy with the warmth of the sun through the window blanketing me and the steady movement of the car rocking and swaying. We talked through the first couple of hours, mostly about Thomas and Chloe and then the revelations that he owns a muscle car straight out of the '70s. Now we've reached a comfortable silence, Wil's fingers are drumming on the steering wheel, his shoulders dancing to the music. He is very handsome and my heart flutters in anticipation.

We pass another vineyard, which are abundant in this region of Victoria. Perfectly spaced rows of vines, threaded on the catch and cordon wires, trained with heavily burdened arms outstretched like a scarecrow defending fields. The moving scene outside the window is both familiar and nostalgic. Vast rolling hills and deep valleys, verdant with vegetation and broken by deep grooved trenches, are excavated by the passage of fast-moving water after a thorough drenching; the north side is a bald and scarred hillside, pocked with jutting rocks.

Our last trip up here with Mason was greeted with an abundantly green landscape. The unseasonably high rainfall in the months preceding the delayed summer left the countryside green and lush, starkly juxtaposed to the previous summer where months of extreme hot weather had a pernicious effect, baking the earth and desiccating the vegetation, leaving the area parched and tinder dry; a perfect precursor to the conflagrations that tore through. The fierce firestorm that took custody of the arid terrain left the landscape ravaged, blackened, and laid bare, taking with it the natural tenants of the forests and waterways, and forcing an expansive evacuation of thousands of people in the surrounding towns.

The sun glares through the windscreen and bounces off a metal sign, momentarily blinding me. An old forgotten memory, preserved and gathering dust on a shelf in my mind, tumbled to the fore. The brilliant sun, winking on the new metal gate in a blinding arc, glared through the windscreen of my uncle's old Datsun. The smell of the neglected, sun damaged vinyl seats, sagging and split with age, and cracked dash, mingled with the smell of the hot grass and cut hay blowing through the open windows that nearly ruined your shoulder to unwind. My cousin Stacey was at the wheel, driving us around the paddock in the old car. She was only nine years old and could barely reach the pedals but knew the gear shift and worked those pedals like she'd been driving all her life. Another memory flashes in my mind of her snarly neighbour Gemma, who was only a year older than us, trying to join in. Gemma was an awful bitch, and she always seemed to smell of cabbage, so we referred to her as cabbitch. The memory of the 'cabbitch' makes me snort with laughter and subsequently choke on the mouth full of biscuit. Wil pounds my back helpfully, but nothing can stop my eyes from streaming.

We coast through the town of Bright, already packed with holiday makers, and back out the other side, arriving shortly after in Harrietville. We pull up to the quaint weatherboard house and park in the drive behind Thomas' car. Thomas and Chloe have already arrived and moved into the second bedroom, leaving us with the Master and ensuite as per Wil and Thom's agreement. After dumping our bags and the groceries, Wil and I walk through the big old house and out the back door. It's an old home full of character, with a neat and modern interior. The house steps out onto a covered veranda with café blinds and an outdoor patio gas heater for the cooler weather. An alfresco dining area is on the far side of the veranda with an expansive barbeque area on the right, where I'm sure we will do all our cooking.

The yard itself is quite large with a raised bricked platform island in the middle of the grass, sporting a sizeable fire-pit, surrounded by wooden chairs. Wil lifts the lid of the fire-pit, and we see that it is already laid with kindling and wood; a large box of firewood sits beside it. The bottom of the yard is fringed by the river that marks the edge of the property. Wil holds my hand as we look at the beautiful scene before us, the sun high in the sky. The rush of the water over the river stones and the birdsong in the surrounding trees envelop us in the beautiful, melodic song of nature, synonymous with this region. I hug myself with joy at being here in my happy place with Wil.

We return to the house to unpack our things and stock the fridge with beverages for the evening to come. Thomas has pulled some frozen steaks out of the esky, and they sit thawing on the sink. We agree that we will quickly unpack and then drive into Bright and take a stroll through the town… maybe cop a beer at the brewery. Unpacking my case, my fingers touch the soft satin of the black and pink flimsy slip. In the days before our mini break, I ventured into a lingerie store in Melbourne and bought some conservative, but definitely sexy lingerie. I quickly tuck it under some shorts in a drawer to surprise William later tonight. I steal into the ensuite to stash my toiletries and see a claw foot tub in the middle of the tiled floor. This ensuite is the size of my daughter's bedroom. Excitement overcomes me and I execute a little happy dance and let out a little yip of joy. As I spin to exit the room with a huge smile on my face, I almost slam into Wil, who is leaning against the open door watching me make a complete dick of myself. The smile slides from my face as it heats up so hot that I'm sure it will scorch my hair. His lazy grin morphs into something else as he reaches for me and pulls me in for a smooch. The electricity between us could power a rocket. Thomas calls out, "C'mon you two! Time's a wastin'!" and he smothers the embers before they ignite. Wil sticks his head out of the door and yells "Keep yer shirt on!" He takes my hand and pulls me down the hall.

The town of Bright is quaint and holds a cornucopia of memories for me from both my youth and trips with Jack and the kids. I will never tire of its picturesque setting. As we walk down the streets, I recall past stores that have closed in the years gone by as well those that have stood the test of time, stoically resistant to the winds of change that the decades have bestowed.

The Brewery is packed inside and outside as families gather for a lazy lunch, washed down with a pint of craft beer as they overlook the *Ovens* River. We happen upon a table in the sun moments after arrival. A staff member rushes to clear the previous occupants' dishes cluttered in front of us. Couples and young families spill out onto the grassed areas on the banks of the river, picnicking on blankets; some enjoying the warmth of the sun and others are seeking cover in the shade of large trees. Small children nap in covered prams and the parents enjoy a break in duty to enjoy small snatches of peace. The joyous squeals of excited children travel across on the wind from the playground.

The piercing screams of an aggrieved toddler belts out of the open windows, followed by the hushed tones of parents trying to placate the child. I don't miss those days. William and Thomas leave to order our drinks and a light lunch. As soon as they are out of earshot, Chloe gushes, "I'm so excited to be here. This is the best weekend ever!" Although she is in her mid-thirties, she sounds like an excited teen. I rest my chin on my folded hands and smile at her, which she takes as permission to gush like a geyser. "He's so handsome, Katrina. Sometimes I can't breathe. I can't believe he chose me. I think he's the one. I've never felt like this before, never ever!" Oh Lordy.

"I think that's sweet, Chloe. He looks pretty smitten too." Her face pinks all the way up to her hair line. Chloe is quiet and shy and absolutely stunning; tall, girl-next-door kind of pretty, with curves in all the right places. The staff member returns and places bottles of cold iced water and glasses on the table. I pour us all a glass and sip mine, for something to do. Chloe continues, "I've never had a boyfriend before." I almost spit my water across the table at her. "What do you mean? You haven't dated?"

"No, I mean I've never had a boyfriend before. I kissed one guy when I was sixteen and then there was nothing." Holy crap on a Popsicle stick. How is that possible? She's such a stunning woman. She continues, "I went on a couple of dates in my twenties, but it was clear they just wanted to get me into bed. Then I met Thomas at my friend's party, and we just clicked… we went on a date, and he was a complete gentleman. It was clear he wanted more than just sex. He is so gentle and loving," Oh please, don't give me details of your first time.

The boys return to save me. William places a pot of amber ale before me and gives me a wink that makes my insides flutter. The conversation returns to safe ground until the food arrives. They've chosen some food to share… a small wood fired pizza, a bowl of roasted potatoes, some salt & pepper calamari, and an antipasto platter; perfect pickings for a leisurely lunch to wile away the afternoon hours.

After lunch, Wil and I walk along the river while Thomas and Chloe stay at the brewery to enjoy some time alone. Hand in hand we walk past the crowds to a space of quiet serenity. A sign indicates that we are at the beginning of the *Canyon Walk*. We agree to return early tomorrow morning and do this walk. Sitting on the riverbank, I turn to look at Wil and see tiny bright yellow balls of wattle blossom populate the waves of his hair like confetti. A sense of pure bliss washes over me.

The setting sun lights the sky on fire in shades of brilliant burnt orange and catches the ripples on the water surface, unfurling a blanket of diamonds glittering on the wavelets. A single plump duck causes a glitch in the flow, disturbing the natural water path and scattering the diamonds as it hitches a ride amongst the fallen debris and detritus on the gently flowing river.

Back at the house, our evening is relaxing with the boys barbequing the steak while the girls make a simple salad, which we eat on our laps around the fire pit. The evening is cool, calling for long pants and jackets. Thomas and Chloe retire early and going by the giggles carrying across the yard from their window, they're playing hide the sausage between the sheets. Wil and I talk quietly and retire at a sensible hour, vowing to wake early for our walk in the morning. I don't bring the little teddy out tonight – tonight is soft and magical and does not require anything other than our naked bodies.

* * * * *

The cool crisp morning is the perfect setting for a walk in the bush… birds chirping, filtered light peeping through tree branches, the ground and leaves moist with droplets of dew, and the clean aroma of nature as the sun makes its languid ascent into the sky.

Thick, ropey roots and jutting rocks inlaid in the hard earth provide natural steps up the steep incline, and the babble and burble of water cascading over rocks and branches in the stream below provide a soundscape composed of nature's most beautiful instruments. Moss covered logs lay haphazardly strewn along the flowing stream edge; dried, and gnarled silver branches of ancient gums overhang the serpentine river. Wil almost smacks into me when I stop to admire a spider web stretched between branches, glistening with dew and backlit by the rising sun, providing a kaleidoscope of brilliant colour. He slides his arms around my waist and rests his chin on my shoulder as we both immerse ourselves in the sensory indulgence surrounding us. We stop to take photos of each other on the suspension bridge and I fill the camera roll on my phone with a compilation of both nature and us… a truly awesome collection for my reflection.

We return to find Thomas and Chloe waiting with a packed lunch for all of us. We clamour into Thomas' muscle car; William and I in the back seat. Thomas controls his testosterone and doesn't scare the wildlife out the trees by revving the engine. We drive up to Mount Buffalo Chalet and take a stroll through the gardens of the Grand Old Dame, as she is dubbed. There is a short walk that Jacob used to call the 'Middle Earth Walk', some kind of reference to Lord of the Rings, I think. William's long legs easily navigate the boulders and steep steps, while I practically have to execute the vertical splits to mount one of the boulders then fail to successfully ascend the smooth surface and slide down its face and land with a splat on my arse. There is much laughter at my awkwardness as I dust the leaves and dirt from the seat of my pants. We drive further to *Mount Buffalo National Park* and eat our lunch in the warm sun at Lake Buffalo. Chloe has made delicious finger sandwiches which range between delicate cucumber and cheese to exotic salami, grilled peppers, and brie. Thomas produces a bottle of crisp white wine, and we have a wonderful picnic lunch. My phone now contains a lovely assortment of pics of all of us, and our surrounds.

Warmed by the sun, filled up to pussy's bow from our lunch and lulled by the gentle sway of the moving car, I doze on William's shoulder and wake as we pull into the driveway of the rental house. William has also fallen asleep and wakes with me. It takes every ounce of intestinal fortitude just to uncurl myself from this comfortable warm position in Thomas' car.

I decide tonight that I will bring out the sexy lingerie – tonight we will shelve the tango and opt for a full jazz number for our last night before we return to our busy lives. William's response is immediate, and he makes me feel sexy and beautiful all at once.

32

The Conundrum and the Solution

Felicity

Damien has raped me almost daily since he discovered I had been taking the contraceptive pill. He now believes that I have purposely caused the miscarriages, that he WILL impregnate me and that I will NOT take from him what is his God Given Right!

I have endured the nightly assault with a dead eyed stare at the ceiling. I don't participate, I lie there, dead inside and I no longer care if he notices – what's another bruise to add to the bruises already gathered on my tortured body? The inside of my wrists and thighs are constantly red and sore from the nightly rough-handling and assertion of his masculinity, and let's not get started on the damage between my thighs.

Today I am filled with dread. Weeks ago, my breasts felt heavy and sore, and my period was late. I was horrified by my body's betrayal, but I shouldn't worry, I assured myself, I will most likely lose it at week nine like all the others. I didn't tell Damien. I wouldn't give him the smug satisfaction of knowing the nightly rape had yielded a positive pregnancy.

Then week twelve came along and I was still pregnant. Joy turned to terror as I realised that I was going to bring a child into this violence. Today I am attending a 12–14-week ultrasound scan where I will discover the health of the life growing inside of me. The sonographer informs me that I am at week fourteen, the longest I have been able to hold a baby inside of me.

I lay quietly as the sonographer moves the wand device around my abdomen. A weird echoing sound pulses in the room. "That's the baby's heartbeat," she announces with a wide smile.

She smiles at me then moves the device a little further across my stomach. Her eyes widen along with her smile, "Oh! You have two babies. You're having twins!"

Something magical blooms inside my chest and tears flood my eyes. They leak down my cheeks and drop onto the towelling covering the pillow my head rests on.

Finally, I find my voice, "can you tell me the sex? Are they the same?"

"They're not identical, if that's what you're asking. They are fraternal but yes, after I've checked everything is ok, I will check the gender of both babies, but only if you want to know."

I nod and try furiously to keep my emotions in check.

When I leave the clinic, I have the knowledge that I am not only carrying two perfectly healthy children, but I am carrying one of each gender, a pigeon pair my Mum would have called them had she lived to celebrate this with me. How could I be so blessed? How could fate have delivered such a wonderful miracle? Then comes the knowledge that Damien will take them from me. I have to find a way out of this conundrum. I cannot let Damien hurt my babies. I will do anything and everything to protect my children from the violent man I married.

* * * * *

When I pull into the driveway, I am horrified to see that Damien is already home. I don't even make it to the door before he yanks it open and pulls me inside violently.

"Where the fuck have you been?"

"I just went for a check-up, why?"

"Why do you need to go for a check-up? Did you go to get another prescription of the pill? Are you still trying to stop the inevitable?"

"My God, no, Damien, I am not on the pill anymore."

His rage is palpable, "then why aren't you pregnant? What is wrong with you? It's been long enough now that you should have fallen pregnant."

It hasn't occurred to him that he could be the reason I cannot conceive. "Well, that's what I went to the doctor for, to check that everything is ok and in good working order so I could see why it's not happening."

I can see that he is shaking with rage. He is frightening me, and I have more to protect now than myself. I hold up my hands in supplication, "It was just a check up to see if everything is working ok with my body."

"And is it?"

"He ran some tests and I'll get some answers in a day or two." I realise my error. Oh, why couldn't I have said she? Shit!

"He? You went and saw a male doctor? Did he see you down there?"

"What? No, he's just an old man in a white coat, doing his job."

"DID.HE.SEE.YOU.NAKED?" Each word is punctuated by a vicious jab to my shoulder.

I take a step back and feel the pressure of the closed door against my back. I am cornered. "Damien, it wasn't like that."

"So, the answer is YES!" He grabs me by the arm and yanks me to him. His face is so full of rage that it radiates hues of crimson and purple and I can see a giant throbbing vein, bulging vertically in the centre of his forehead, like a fat earthwork lurking beneath the skin. I cannot take my eyes from the giant worm.

He grips both of my upper arms in a vice like grip and begins to shake, screaming at me in an unholy pitch that sounds foreign coming from his mouth. He has become completely mad. He is going to kill me, right here, right now. I think of my precious unborn babies and silently pray for them as the pain intensifies in my arms and neck; something is shaken loose and hits the floor loudly; the sound makes its way into my fractured thoughts. Damien continues to throttle me.

My head whips back and forth brutally and it feels like my neck is going to break and then, he suddenly stops. My head is spinning from the violent shaking and when the dizziness and nausea dissipates, I investigate the face inches from mine, still contorted with rage. There is spittle gathered on his bottom lip. His right eye twitches and half of his face spasms weirdly; the colour drains, and his eyes bulge out of their sockets. The earthworm has gone, slithered off to some other part of his body. Half of his mouth opens and closes, but no sound comes out. I am caught in this surreal moment of time, waiting for something to happen.

An unintelligible noise escapes his mouth along with his breath and he starts making garbled sounds that I cannot decipher. He falls to the floor like he has lost control of all his muscles, and it sounds like a log hitting the wooden floor of the entry. The hot stench of ammonia assails my senses and I realise that he has lost control of his bladder.

I squat in front of him, frantically checking for a pulse, "Damien, what is it? Are you ok?" He makes more of the garbled non-sensical sounds. He is alive. His whole body appears to have turned to fluid and lies in the puddle of flaccid muscle, soaked in his urine.

I reach into my bag for my phone and realise I have left it in the car. In a panic, I run out to the car try to yank the door open, but it is locked. Shit! I run back inside, still panicking, and search through my bag for the keys. They are not in my bag. I look around but cannot see them. I run to the kitchen to see if I can find Damien's phone, but it is not in the kitchen. I run back to where Damien is lying on the floor and scramble over to him; I can see my house key poking out from under his thigh and realise that my keys must have dropped when he was shaking me. His leg is deadweight and heavy, but I manage to extract my keys. Running back out to the car, a high pitched 'bleep' sounds as the car is finally unlocks. I retrieve my phone and dial 000 on the run back inside the house. The emergency operator has to tell me to calm down twice as I babble hysterically about my husband. She advises that an ambulance is on the way, and to lay him on his side so he doesn't choke, and to elevate his head slightly to help blood flow. I run into the living room to retrieve a cushion and return to him. As I try to roll his dead weight onto his right side, his left arm is flailing about trying to grab at me and his eyes are wild and protruding like a spooked horse; he is petrified. I cannot understand what is happening to Damien, but I reassure him that help is coming.

* * * * *

Damien has suffered a severe hemorrhagic left-sided stroke. The entire right side of his body has been affected. Even though he cannot control his right side, his right arm is in plaster as it was fractured with the fall. At the hospital, they gave Damien a full body x-ray, a CT scan, an angiogram, and an MRI scan. Just in case he may be able to regain some movement in the future, care had to be taken to set and knit the bones of his arm correctly, hence the cast. It has been many hours since we arrived at the hospital and I am finally allowed into the room where he rests quietly in the centre of the bed, still listless and groggy from residual effects of the anaesthetic. As I enter his room, his eyes follow my path to the chair beside his bed. Half of his face droops and sags and it is clear, as he grunts, that he cannot speak. Saliva is leaking out of the drooping side of his mouth and despite all he has put me through, I feel a pang of regret for him.

Outside the room, the doctor gave me the grim news that Damien will require full-time care going forward. He advised that Damien will more than likely never walk or talk again, although rehabilitation may help him regain some movement in his right side, and we will either have to place him into a nursing home or have a nurse come to the house daily, and that option would require a whole refit to allow hoists and other paraphernalia to ensure his daily care.

His eyes look defeated, and I see fear in the depths. It is all I can do not to cry in relief. My movements appear jerky and unnatural as I reach for his left hand. He jerks it away from me like my touch burns him. Even now, this broken man is still filled with unmasked hatred for the woman he vowed to love and protect, like I somehow orchestrated this medical emergency.

33

The Ruined Luncheon

Katrina

Beverley has called us all to lunch at the big house to celebrate their Golden Wedding Anniversary. Thomas has brought Chloe along; it's her first introduction to the entire family. Thomas is completely besotted with her, it's sweet. Since our mini break away, we've all four had dinner out a couple of times. I find Chloe easy to converse with and her eyes light up with animation when discussing anything close to her heart; we have thoroughly enjoyed our double dates. Chloe has migrated to Beverley and me, where she feels safe and comfortable.

Also in attendance is most of the extended family. William's daughters Zoe and Kathryn, and her husband Chris, and baby Emilee, bibbed and bouncing on Aunty Zoe's knee. Beverly's sister Patricia, still single at seventy-four and in remission after a battle with breast cancer that ended in a double mastectomy, is busily preparing a salad next to Beverley. Kenneth's siblings are here too, brother Walter and his wife Di, and his sister Barbara, her husband Robert with their sons Kevin and Greg. Greg has just arrived and unfortunately, Samantha the super-bitch was hanging off his arm like a glamorous rag.

As soon as I saw them pull into the drive, my stomach knotted. She is such an awful witch and has created so much strife with her pathetic attempt at chaos and drama when I met Marcus for lunch. Thankfully, William and I have moved past the incident but the fact that she did that in the first place makes me uneasy.

She saunters in with all the confidence in the world and air kisses the space beside Beverley's face, followed by Barbara's. Then she makes a beeline for me, every muscle tenses in preparation. She unleashes a saccharin sweet smile as she approaches and touches my upper arm, all concern and congeniality, "Katrina, I am so sorry if I caused any discord between you and William. That was an innocent mistake, and I apologise. I didn't realise he was your brother, and I thought the worst. Silly me." I stifle the sarcastic laugh that threatens to bubble out of me. I can see straight through her thin veneer. I force my mouth to stretch into a smile of sorts. She drops her arm and puts on a baby voice, dripping with false sincerity and coupled with a look of deep concern "I do hope you can forgive me."

I have no choice but to play along, but I won't roll over that easily, "Oh, don't even think about it, Samantha. It didn't even cause a ripple." Her eyes harden and her expression becomes frosty. I reach over and touch her shoulder as she did mine, "there's nothing to forgive." My smile is sweeter and wider, and I even crimp my eyes to make the gesture as patronising as possible. I can play that game too. Samantha's mouth purses into a tight buttonhole reminiscent of a cat's anus and it is all I can do to stifle my joy. She spins on her heel and stalks to the couch, nestling her backside between Greg and William, then looks directly at me, a smirk on her carefully airbrushed face. This provokes a grin from me, which I couple with a wink. William looks at her and inches across a little bit. Good try, Sammy.

Samantha

We are all gathered in the formal living room, bored senseless with idle chatter before the lunch commences. I am sitting on the three-seater couch beside William, and Greg is on my other side. William moved across a little when I sat down, because he is a polite gentleman, but I've managed to close the gap; my left leg is touching William's, right down the length of our thighs from hip to knee. All nerve endings are firing, and my nipples harden; I get aroused as I drink in the smell of him.

William's daughter Zoe is making stupid unintelligent noises at the baby, Kathryn and Greg's gross, dribbly little sprog-bubble, who is blowing disgusting spit raspberries to the delight of the stupid girl. Its chin is grossly wet and almost makes my stomach heave; I must turn my attention away. I zone in on William and watch his angled jaw move as he speaks with the deep rich baritone that sends shivers down my spine and makes the blood pulse in my veins.

Katrina is on the other side of the room chatting with Beverley, completely unaware of the gentle seduction I have turned on, sub-liminally communicating lust in gentle indistinguishable pulses. The stupid bitch thinks she can play mind games with me; I am the Queen of mind games. *Didn't cause a ripple*, my arse. I know it caused a bloody seismic wave judging by Thomas and William's reactions the following day, but I don't need her to acknowledge it. I took the shine off their happy bubble and cast doubt in William about her faithfulness. I can do it again. I will not stop until William is mine.

William hasn't pulled his leg away so that voices consent... perhaps he is enjoying this gentle seduction. It won't be long, and he will not be able to resist me. My favourite pastime is daydreaming about the moment I finally have him. I wonder how I am going to get him into bed, and what I'm going to do to him first. It certainly won't be anything like the boring vanilla sex she gives him, I'm sure.

I have so much to show him, so much I am willing to do for him, to do to him. It will only take one time, just one moment of weakness to drive a wedge between him and the cow, then when she's out of the picture, I can take my time mapping every inch of his hard body. If he could see me in lingerie, feel what I can do with my mouth and the playground inside my French lace thong, he'd be putty in my hands.

Today I'm going to get the ball started on something else, try a different tact. I'll mess with her head. I'll say things only she can hear and if she tries to tell William or even Beverley the things I say, they won't believe her, of course, because they won't be Samantha things. This will cause more drama, cast doubt and aspersions and it will be the crack I can drive the wedge into. Watch this space, bitch! Game on.

* * * * *

Katrina

Beverley has disappeared into the kitchen to check on lunch. I follow her in and offer to help. She tries to shoo me away, but all components of the meal are concurrently ready to be served and are coalescing into a giant 'to-do' list. She reluctantly accepts my offer of help. I seize the placemats and set the places at the table with the good cutlery.

The formal dining area hosts a huge table that seats twenty and is surrounded by rich, soft cigar leather seats. We will be using almost all those places today. Beverley and Kenneth host this group for Christmas lunch, both in July and December, and the table is well used throughout the year; their love of entertaining and dinner parties is legendary. It is the perfect setting; the table is positioned before the large picture windows looking out over the gorgeous gardens and the whole dining area is full of light and space. Beverley leans in and asks if I could gather everyone to sit at the table.

I return to the formal living room and announce to the room at large that we're about to serve lunch and request that everyone attends the dining area to take a seat. I secretly hope I don't end up near Samantha. I can feel the hatred emanating off her like a dark aura and I am not fooled by today's syrup.

When I arrive back in the kitchen, Beverley asks if I can go into the cabinet in the hall stand to retrieve the silver serving utensils and platter. As I turn to attend to Beverley's request, Samantha chimes, "I'll help you, Katrina." Beverley looks surprised; I don't suppose Samantha offers to help very often; I'm wary of her sudden offer... Samantha doesn't do anything unless she can benefit from it. Add to that, I do not want to be alone with the malevolent bitch, so I try to dissuade her, "That's ok, Sam, I've got it." She bristles at the use of her shortened name; she does not like being called Sam and I know it. She hisses through clenched teeth, "I insist" Oh great.

I leave the room with Samantha in tow, take the long way around the formal living room, the entrance of which is clogged with all and sundry making their way to the dining area, and turn back out into the hall, heading towards the front door. I am a fast walker and hear Samantha's stilettoed sandals clicking on the parquetry as she tries to keep up but even with those long legs, it's a task. This makes me smile inwardly. I'm not sure where the serving ware is so I stand before the cabinet surveying the shelves through the glass. Samantha arrives puffing but trying not to sound breathless... it isn't working. I catch her expression and it is thunderous; here we go.

"You do not call me Sam. My name is Samantha."

Of course, it is. I turn my head to the side and smile, "Oh, I'm sorry. I didn't mean to offend." I'm so over this bitch throwing her weight around.

Samantha is having none of it, "Stop the crap, *Katrina*. Listen to me you inbred fucking whore. You think you have won... but mark my words, William is mine."

What the hell? Shocked by the vehemence when she spits my name at me, I stutter. "Wha… what the hell are you talking about?"

"Don't play dumb with me. You think you have him? Well, you just wait and see. Once he gets a taste of me, he won't be able to resist."

I cannot believe what is coming out of her mouth, "Samantha, what are you talking about? Seriously, have you become unhinged?"

"Stop the innocent bullshit. I don't know what you've got between your legs, and you have somehow managed to bed him, but you are not worthy. You will not get to keep him."

What? "…get to keep who? Who are you talking about?"

She hisses close to my face, so I'm sprayed with fine spittle, "With William, William is mine. I want him, I've always wanted him, and I WILL NOT STOP until I get him. You need to understand that. I am willing to do anything…ANYTHING to get him." I recoil in horror and do not mask my shock.

My voice shaky, "but… but you're with Greg. You love Greg."

Her face scrunches into a red angry mask and her cheeks are splotched with red spots. "I don't love *Greg*. Greg is a stepping-stone… William is the prize."

My eyes are so wide, I must look comical. Poor Greg, I can't believe she's using him. The poor man. I'm momentarily speechless and she fills the void with her sour reflection. "Imagine my disgust when you arrive on the scene and infiltrate the family, deceiving them all with your sweet smiles and winning personality and then, to my horror, you win William over when he is vulnerable."

"Are you nuts? You cannot mean that. Greg doesn't deserve this awful treatment. He thinks you love him. How could you?"

"You want him so bad? You can have him."

"No, I'm with William. You're with Greg."

"Oh, shut up about Greg. William will see through your charade, and he will see you for the common muck you are. William needs to be with someone of breeding; not some inbred whore who has backed out a littler of equally inbred whelps and couldn't even manage to keep the father."

Stung, anger rushes through me, "You are disgusting. You don't know me…"

"Oh, but I do… you're of poor lineage, with mongrel in your blood and you only get anywhere in life by relying on pure dumb luck because you lack the intelligence, skill, and drive to become anything other than *administration staff*. You're a nothing and a nobody and when William finally works it out, the poor dolt, he's going to run for the hills, all the while wondering how he became so besotted by your pedestrian nothingness in the first place."

"Breeding? Breeding only comes into the equation when discussing live cattle. I'm ok not being associated with bovine reproduction, thank you. You're a whack-job, *Sam*… You're a sandwich short of a picnic and you're dangerous. Stay away from me, you crazy bitch."

Her face is all up in my grill again, "Oh I'm dangerous all right. I'm your worst nightmare."

I almost lose an eye in an eye roll. "Oooh, I'm scared. We're not in a school yard, *Sammy*, so drop this tough act."

She clenches her jaw as I continue to use all the pet names she despises, but I will not be run off by this bullying psycho. I stand my ground, "I just feel sorry for Greg. How can you use a person like this? Have you no conscience? Add to that, you don't even know William. You think he's all about long legs and pretty blonde hair? You're a narcissistic idiot!"

There's a growling edge to her gravelly voice as she retorts "You need to shut your fucking filthy mouth. He can do so much better, and I know him *a hell of a lot better than you do*."

"Do you? What do you think he's going to say when he finds out you're using his cousin, Samantha?"

"Well listen up, *bitch*… you're not going to say a word. I know people who can make you disappear, *Kat!*" She folds her arms across her chest; her face a guise of cold loathing.

My face floods with heat and I am the epitome of an angry terrier facing off with a doberman, drawing myself to my full five-foot-two-inch height in the presence of her vile five-foot-eleven, "Are you threatening me? Don't you *dare* threaten me."

She's back in my face again, her voice laced in venom, "No, don't *you* dare! You don't know who you're dealing with. You're not going to mention any of this conversation to anyone. No one will believe you anyway. I have been in with this family since I was a little girl and I have loved him all these years…"

My bravado is unwavering, "…and yet you never managed to win him?"

She continues growling, "…my mother is Beverley's closest friend. I have known all of them for years… YEARS, so if you mention this conversation, not only will you look like a twisted jealous fuck, but you'll also lose them all." She straightens, satisfied that she has threatened me enough, "I trump you, Katrina, and I will win. Watch this space."

She spins and stalks like a runway model all the way down the hall and presumably back to the dining area. I feel cold, and sick to my stomach about what just transpired. What a psychotic, narcissistic crackpot. I have to settle down and get the bloody silverware.

Opening and closing the glass doors, I locate the silver serving utensils and platter. Beverley must be wondering where the hell we've gotten to. I make my way back to the dining area, trying desperately to rearrange my features to hide the shock and horror. My heart is pounding, my skin feels clammy and the whole situation feels quite surreal… like something straight out of a psychological thriller. She's a 'bunny boiler'. I hope she's prepared; Karma is a bitch!

* * * * *

Samantha

The satisfaction of seeing the shocked expression on her stupid face is delicious. The chase is just as arousing as the prize. I think I have made myself clear. She had better back the hell of, or I will have that bitch raped and hurled in a river, weighted down while still alive. I need her to disappear.

As I enter the dining room, everyone is seated except Beverley, she is standing beside William, and all eyes are on me. Of course, we took a long time. I reach, inward for my impeccable acting skills. "I'm so sorry we took so long, we couldn't find them, but we have them now and I think Katrina is just coming now." I make a great pretence of looking for the stupid bitch down the hall. Here she comes, the dumb arse, weighted down with the cumbersome ugly fussy silverware that only the classy elderly insist on utilising in this modern era. I pause and smile winningly while the idiot enters, carrying the tray and utensils. She looks shocked to the core but covers herself well as she manages a tentative smile. You'd better work on those acting skills and make yourself believable, Kat. It's very hard not to laugh hysterically at her pale complexion. I think my message has been received loud and clear. She looks a little worse for wear. I turn on my charm and add a cheery singsong lilt to my voice, "Oh there you are, Kat. I think Beverley has been waiting." I add a little giggle, like we're great friends.

The wench obediently travels over to Beverley, sounding all breathless when she finds her voice, "Here you go Beverley. I'm sorry we took so long. We couldn't find them." Good girl. Now play your part well and remember who you're dealing with. Beverley takes the silverware and puts it on the table but doesn't move to serve up.

I look around the table and they're all still looking at me. How odd. Greg looks hurt. What the fuck is wrong with him now? God he is hard work. Don't tell me I have to stroke his ego. I refuse to pander to this weak, pathetic man. I'm struck by a worrying thought.

What if our conversation was overheard. Then I relax, we were too far away to be heard. Maybe there have been some words exchanged here and we've just innocently walked into it. Silence still holds the table. I look to William, and he is glaring at me. His daughters are both wearing masks of surprise. Only the kid in the highchair continues making stupid baby noises. Greg's mother Barbara is also glaring at me. I must ask… the silence is too much. "What's going on?"

Nobody speaks. What the actual fuck? Beverley has a look of utter disappointment on her face. She addresses the whole table, "I think I will handle this." She turns to her sister, "Patricia, could you possibly come with me for a moment." Patricia obediently rises to do as the matriarch bids.

The silence continues. The echo of Patricia's sensible solid heels recedes down the hall as she follows Beverley, then the sound of her footfalls mysteriously grows louder again, the sound coming from somewhere on the buffet against the wall beside the windows. It must be the acoustics of the house. All eyes are still on me, except Katrina's. She is looking past me to the buffet. Greg stands and faces me, "Samantha, we should go."

"What are you talking about Greg? We haven't even eaten yet." No way am I leaving yet. I need some more time in William's company. Greg has seated me directly opposite him, what a win. I make my way behind Greg and seat myself. He is insistent, "Samantha, we need to leave now, please."

What is up his arse? "No Greg, I would like to have lunch first."

Beverley's voice is loud at the buffet, "I have arrived at the hall stand." Beverley sounds like she's in the room. I am perplexed and my bravado falters. Panic momentarily robs me of my confidence. What is going on here? For the first time in our relationship, Greg raises his voice to me, "Samantha! Stand up! We are leaving!"

"Gregory!" I retort, using his full name so he knows I am not having this shit, "I am *not* leaving until after lunch, so whatever the matter is, deal with it yourself and sit back down." My God, he's a pain in my arse.

"No!" he gestures to the entire table, "We all heard every single word you said to Katrina!"

I try to mask my shock and try for innocence, "What an earth are you talking about, Greg."

His face is red with ire; his expression infuriated. I've never seen him this upset. He yells at me, "There is a baby monitor near the front door and the receiver is over there." He points towards the buffet. "I am *not* your stepping-stone. Now grab your things because we are *leaving*!"

I don't know what to do other than muster my pride, rise, and gather my things. Greg doesn't touch me as I move past him… he doesn't even look at me. I look at William and he is still glaring at me with disgust. There's no softness in his eyes. She did that! That fucking bitch has made me *disgusting* to him. I hate her with a viscous blackness; I feel it flooding my veins like coal tar.

As I walk past that worthless bitch, I see a smirk tugging at the corners of her mouth. It takes every ounce of self-control not to grab the heavy silver candelabra from the buffet and smash her head in with it. I want to hit her head over and over with it. I want to split her head open and watch all the blood, brain, and bone shards scatter across this rich woollen rug. I want her to become nothing but the human stain she is. Then I want to finger paint obscenities all over the windows and walls with her thick coagulated fluids. The anger in me is so potent, that it has me shaking violently and I can barely keep hold of my handbag.

I obsequiously walk towards the front door before I act out my fantasies in front of all these witnesses and lose any chance with William. She will pay for this. Mark my words, she will rue the day she crossed Samantha Karisson. I will end her.

* * * * *

Katrina

I could not have predicted the rapid rate at which Samantha's maturation of karma would come into effect. Part of me is grateful; I could not have explained all the terrible things she said, but I am also very upset for Greg. He has done nothing wrong and yet he has been brutally hurt today. He has unwittingly played a component in Samantha's game, and everything he thought he knew was in fact, a lie.

Barbara and Robert look devastated for their son and Kevin looks disgusted. I half expected them to up and leave but they remain seated, looking shell-shocked. Everybody at the table is wearing a solemn expression. This is supposed to be a celebration lunch.

I stand impotently at the table, not sure what to do. Beverley gently touches my arm, "Katrina, could you help me bring the food from the kitchen?" I leap at the chance to be actively doing something. When we arrive in the kitchen, she suddenly turns and pulls me into an embrace, hugging me firmly. I'm not sure if this is for Beverley's or my benefit but I find I'm shaking and welcome the embrace. She mumbles into my hair, "I'm so sorry you were on the receiving end of that awful tirade." Tears prickle my eyes and try to keep a cap on my emotions. Beverley has not let me go and I think she needs this embrace more than I do so I increase the intensity of my hug. When she pulls away, I see her eyes are glassy with unshed tears. "I cannot believe what I heard. I cannot believe the things that came out of her vulgar mouth. She must be demented! All those awful things… and poor Greg. Oh Lord, how will we ever come back from this? Jane is my closest friend." Beverley looks miserable.

"It will all work out, Beverley. You'll see. Now let's get on with celebrating your Golden Anniversary, shall we?"

* * * * *

Kenneth is carving the roast as Beverley and I go about setting out the gravy and other condiments. The conversation is subdued but lifted with the excited babble of Emilee as she innocently giggles at her aunt's antics. We are all startled by the chiming of the doorbell. Beverley wears a 'what now?' expression. William tends to the visitor and returns with Greg in tow. "Sorry about that disturbance, everyone. That was quite unexpected."

"To say the least!" chimes Barbara, in a very high voice. "You weren't gone very long, where did you take her, love?"

Barbara can't even bring herself to say the name. "I drove her to Phillip & Jane's house and told her to get the hell out of my car. I didn't even wait to see if she had a key. It's probably not the right thing to do, but her parents can take her home. I'm a little unsettled. I don't relish the thought of being alone and would appreciate the distraction so if you don't mind indulging me, I'd like to finish lunch." Beverley draws him into her ample bosom for a motherly hug. Polite conversation ensues around the table, and we all make it through the lunch without reference to 'the incident', as nobody dares mention the elephant in the room.

* * * * *

Later in the afternoon as William and I lounge on the couch, replete, watching an episode of *The Office*, he turns to me and asks, "What the hell is going on with Samantha? Who says all that shit? She is really messed up."

Sighing, "I know. That was bizarre. She is seriously unhinged. It was like something straight out of a television series. Nobody talks like that. So weird!"

"...and poor Greg. Imagine that!" William looks genuinely unsettled.

He looks at me, "are you worried? Do you think her threats were something to take seriously?"

I ponder his question, "I want to say no, but she said she knows people who could make me disappear. That was frightening. She's so messed up in the head that I wouldn't be surprised if she was plotting my death right now."

"Hmmm, I wonder if we should chat to the police about it."

I have had enough interaction with the police lately with the whole Baby Abigail saga. "I think we should sit on it for a while. Everyone in that room heard what she said, and there were quite a few of us. I don't think she'll follow that through."

William contemplates this. "Either way, just take extra care when you're out and about. Promise me you won't put yourself in situations where you're vulnerable. Can you promise that?"

"Of course." Satisfied, he leans down and plants a kiss on my mouth. He deepens the kiss and I have to put my wine glass down. Abruptly, he stands and holds out his hand, pulling me up. He leads me into the bedroom to do all the delicious things that psycho Sammy can only dream about. A satisfying smile plays about my mouth.

34

Now I Can Dance

Felicity

I am sitting in the hospital room with Damien and his parents, Joanna & Chris. Although I have told everyone what has happened to Damien, I have kept my baby news mostly to myself. I barely have a bump yet and I don't want this joyous occasion overshadowed by Damien's situation.

I told Damien the happy news before his parents arrived; it was met with glacial hostility. The dream he has had of being a parent for so long has finally happened, but he will not have much control over anything since he can't even control his body or his bowels.

I am trying to be the loving wife, but his expression screams of violence, and I steer clear of his left side. He grunts, thrashes about, and moves his left arm, flailing it around in frustration, but I cannot understand him. He hit out in frustration at the nurse this morning and she tore strips off him afterwards. I hate that I took pleasure watching him receive the dressing down from the nurse, but it has been a long time coming.

After an hour, Joanna and Chris take their leave and I am left alone with him. I walk them out of the room and direct them towards the exit. Upon my return, I mistakenly walk too close to his left side, and he grabs the strap of my handbag and yanks me to him. Losing my balance, I stumble forward, barely catching myself on the edge of the bed. Damien releases the strap of my bag and grabs a healthy handful of my hair and yanks my head hard, smashing my face against the steel frame of the bed. A searing pain shoots through my cheek bone and my eyes smart.

"Mr Galbraith. STOP THAT AT ONCE!" The nurse he hit out at earlier has returned in time to see today's abuse. "There is absolutely no excuse for this behaviour, and it will not be tolerated on my ward or in this hospital. DO I MAKE MYSELF CLEAR?"

Damien glares at her with barely concealed contempt. She ushers me from the room, turning to glare at him one last time before she leads me to the nurse's station for some medical attention. I leave without saying goodbye. I am done with his shit.

＊ ＊ ＊ ＊ ＊

I wait three days before I come back to visit this time. I give him a wide berth and don't even attempt to make polite chatter. I sit on the other side of the bed and look at him, seething inside his broken body.

Last night, I reached the conclusion that I will not be transforming our house into a hospital suite – I'll make arrangements for him to go into a home. I refuse to spend the rest of my days avoiding his left side and God forbid one of our children should wander within arm's length. No, the slamming of my head against the bed frame was his last violent act against me. I'll never give him the opportunity to hurt me again.

I find my strength and confidence, "Damien, I will be making arrangements for you to go into a home where you can receive all the care you require. It's too much for me to nurse you at home, especially with the babies coming and quite frankly, I will not give you the opportunity to terrorise or abuse me ever again. You have caused me so much pain over the years, that I think you should be grateful that I come to visit you at all."

His face lights up with ire. I don't care, never again. I continue, "If you ever strike out at me again, or pull a stunt like the other day, I will not be visiting you *ever again*. You should also know that I have documented all the violence over the years; I have a box full of photographic proof, with all the abuse you inflicted on me written on the backs of the photos."

Damien's face is beetroot red. I look at him with what I hope is a deadpan expression.

The nurse enters, "Oh hello, Mrs Galbraith. How are you? Is your face healing, ok?"

"Yes, thank you, and thank you for your help, patching me up. It's Felicity, by the way. Mrs Galbraith is my mother-in-law."

"Oh, well you can call me Fiona."

She looks at Damien, takes in his irate countenance and advises, "you need to steer clear of your husband, Felicity, he looks to be in a mood again."

After Fiona leaves, I look at him with a realisation that Damien will never physically abuse me again. He will never inflict any form of pain on me or our children. I have woken from the terrifying nightmare, and I have survived.

* * * * *

After leaving the hospital, I have a coffee with the girls, which I had scheduled yesterday for this afternoon. They gather around me, unsure how to behave. They are all so sad for me, except Katrina. Katrina knows that I have been released from a life of control and torture.

"So, ladies, apart from the awful state that Damien is in, I just wanted to let you know my good news."

Silence descends at our table as they eagerly look at me to see if the news is good or bad. The café assistant interrupts as he arrives with our coffee and muffins. After he leaves, I smile gently, "I happen to be pregnant... with twins!"

The squeals of delight turn heads in the café. I need this happy joy, this delightful news. I look to Katrina, and she has tears coursing down her cheeks. Louise' face falls, "Oh, but poor Damien. This will just about kill him."

"Yes well, there's not a lot I can do there. I am planning for him to go into a home where he can receive the full time care he requires."

Sonja solemnly nods because, what options are there? One day soon I will tell them the terrible story about the Tyrant I married.

35

Bundles of Joy

Katrina

I stand on the lit street, the streetlights haloed in the early morning mist. I look at the track; it disappears into the darkness beyond. My heart thuds in my chest. I haven't been able to run here since Abbey. It's too dark to even contemplate entering right now but still I stand here, anchored to the light, longing to run her but anxious with the dread the recollection of her tragedy cultivates.

It's too early even for the birds to have begun their pre-dawn avian warble. The absolute silence is eerie, like the world is on mute and I am standing alone in a void. My breathing is loud by contrast.

I look to the bushes where her body was ruthlessly discarded; haphazardly interred beneath a light dusting of leaf litter. A deep sadness momentarily dwarfs the fear and anxiety. A pitiful mewling breaks the silence, barely audible. I wait in the silence, unsure if the sound was real or aurally manufactured. Again, tiny whimpering in the bushes. I switch on my phone torch and dubiously walk towards the shrubbery, senses on high alert, suspicious of everything.

As I approach the edge, I squat and shine the torch under the low bushes. A tiny little form stumbles out and squints in the light. I slowly approach on all fours and the little kitten comes closer, frightened but desperate. As I get closer, it cowers and hisses, then cries again. Removing my hoodie and wrapping it around my arm, I swoop on the little guy and wrap the ball of hissing, spitting wire up, gently stroking him through the fabric. I tuck him under my arm, take a deep breath to steady myself and crawl in under the bushes.

There I find another squirming kitten, too weak to put up a fight, and two lifeless kittens, laying against their deceased mother; she is huge by comparison. How long the mother and two kittens have been dead and the other two have been alone in here is anybody's guess but there is no strong smell of decomposition yet so I think it may only be hours. I swoop on the other one and bundle the two in my hoodie, stroking their squirming little bodies gently to keep them warm and give them a sense of security as I briskly walk home.

I phone Lucy and tell her of my booty, and she offers to duck to the pet supplies store to grab some kitten milk. When I return, we manage to find a medicine syringe in the medical chest, left over from a time when the kid were small, and we use the syringe to gently administer warmed milk into our tiny guests. The quieter one perks up considerably after the second feed.

Lucy and I return to the track with a bag and shovel to collect the dead mother and babies. We bury them in our garden beneath the lemon tree. After that solemn affair, we take the two little treasures to the vet for a check-up and to gauge their age. This turns out to be an obscenely costly venture, but well worth it. We return with a litter tray, a scratching post, a cosy bed for them to cuddle up in and other paraphernalia required for the new additions, and bottles with specialised formula to feed them with the advice the solids can commence next week.

We have a boy and a girl, both long hair and around four weeks old. The smaller of the two, a female, is all black and her brother, the larger and most definitely feistier of the two, is grey. Their faces look almost wild, which was explained by the vet to be a remarkable feature of their breed, Maine Coon, more than likely mixed. When we return from our Vet trip, we look up the breed – these cats can grow to be giants!

The boys are delighted with our new family members. We have decided to keep them both and agree to watch their behaviour over the next couple of days to decide their names. We settle on Raven for the girl and Loki for the boy.

* * * * *

Li Xiu

I press the doorbell and a distant chime echoes through the house. After several beats, the door swings open to reveal Lucy, Mason's sister. I haven't formally met her yet, but Mason has pointed her out to me. "Hi," she says.

"Hi, I'm Li Xiu. I don't think we've met before."

Lucy cocks her head to the side then the penny drops, "Oh, you're Mason's friend? Hi, I'm Lucy. Come on in. I think he's playing in the living room."

Playing? What the heck is he playing? PlayStation? He doesn't play an instrument… I don't think. As we enter the living room I see Mason on all fours with his backside up in the air, and his head under a couch, He reaches under and then jerks and yanks his hand back out, "Ouch, you little shit! That's not fair… I don't have needles in my fingers."

I have no idea what the heck is going on. After a moment Lucy clears her throat, "Ahem." Mason belts his head on the underside of the couch in surprise and quickly backs out. A moment later a small black ball of fur darts out from under the couch and legs it out of the room. Well, that explains that behaviour. I look at Mason and see he is sucking on one of his digits.

"You get clawed?" I grin at him. His eyebrows dart up when he notices me standing behind Lucy.

"Oh Hey, Li Xiu. Sorry, that little fiend you just saw run out of the room just attacked me – her claws are sharp."

"When did you get a new kitten? You didn't tell me."

"I haven't had time, we only just got them. Mum found them under a bush on the trail she runs... their Mum was gone and so were two of the kittens but there were two that were alive, so Mum grabbed them and took them to the vet. A boy and a girl... that was the girl, who we've called Raven, and her brother is Loki."

"God of Mischief? That's a big name for a little ball of fur."

"Oh, don't you worry, he definitely lives up to it."

As if on cue, the little black ball of fur bolts back into the room followed by a bigger grey ball of fur. Loki tackles Raven on the rug and they play fight before darting out of the room again. I am almost palpitating from an overload of cuteness.

Mason makes us both a hot milo and we return to the living room to chat. We talk school, work, and assignments. Katrina, Mason's Mum pops in and brings a plate of cookies with her. My eyes light up.

Katrina asks how things are at home. I tell them about dad returning. The kittens return and we hold them on our laps then Mason says they've been sleeping in his room and takes me upstairs. His room is neat but distinctly male. There's a framed picture of an NBA basketballer, The New York Knicks is written on top, so I assume he's a fan. We sit on the bed after putting the kittens down to sleep and we kiss. I can taste the milo on his mouth and my heart beats very loudly behind my rips.

36

Revenge is a Dish
Best Served Cold

Samantha

That fucking bitch is going to pay! I am so livid I could tear a puppy in two. Her demise is all I have been able to think about. It consumes every waking moment. My neck and shoulders are all sore from the constant tension as I squeeze my stress ball. I feel like I could crush a skull if I channelled this anger… her skull.

I'm sitting in my study, swanning around in the dark web. For months I have been coming down here, checking stuff out. It's not a place you can get to by using the usual browsers, not accessible by the common search engines. My Tor Browser ensures I can't be seen or identified - it encrypts my data together with the destination IP address and sends the requests through a virtual circuit of successive randomly selected onion routing relays – scrambling and unscrambling my IP address so I remain anonymous.

I need to vent before I do something out of anger that I will spend the rest of my life paying for. I need to be smart about this. At first, I just went around browsing down here. It's full of crack-pot conspiracy theorists and people who 'leak' government information they think everybody has a right to know. I couldn't give a shit about that stuff. There's also plenty of questionable stuff like sexual sadism and people who like to do some really weird shit for sexual gratification… like dressing up in adult diapers and smearing shit all over each other. Ugh. My stomach heaves at the thought of that. No wonder they're down here talking about it – it's pretty fucked up. There's nothing like kiddie porn or snuff movies down here… that stuff is much deeper on the dark web, and it is not at all easy to find. When people say, "Oh I accidentally stumbled onto a kiddie porn website", it really boils my blood! DO NOT INSULT MY IN-TELLIGENCE! You can't *accidently* stumble onto the really dark stuff down here, it is extremely hard to access – even highly trained hackers, including government IT experts, cannot access certain parts of the dark web. It requires knowledge of the URL and very complicated passwords. You really have to know someone to give you access to the really bad stuff. That's ok, I'm not interested in the weird shit anyway. I like to visit the chat rooms.

After surfing around down here for a while, I went onto a chat room where people were discussing stuff, they'd like to do to an ex. Someone was talking about revenge porn, someone else wanted to get someone to key the ex's car, another wanted his ex-wife raped with a baseball bat (ugh, tres extreme). So, I started contributing to the chat rooms. I gave myself the name HOMM83. It's my acronym for *Hands Off My Man*. That's for her. The site is a sexual fantasy site, where people talk about 'pretending' to hurt someone, so I play my role as a jilted lover who wants to 'punish' the bitch who cheated with my ex' – it's not too far off the mark. There are some weird nutters down here. Whilst venting, I made a friend. We created our own chat room, so we don't have to field the weird kinky shit these other weirdos post. He asked me my postcode; he said he is not far from me. This is the space where I vent about the fucking bitch and all the things, I want done to her. He talks about different things he can do to her for me; some of it is sexually kinky involving whips, paddles, and nipple clamps, and some of it is quite violent. It makes me breathless with anticipation as I imagine her suffering and it fuels my rage but satiates my appetite for revenge. It's all just fantasy shit, I know, but it feels good to type it and have it read without sending up red flags in every direction.

* * * * *

Things took a turn. My downstairs friend, DPRay2, which took me a good two days to figure out that his username was an acronym of sorts of David Parker Ray. David Parker Ray, also known as the Toy-Box Killer because he soundproofed his truck and made it his torture chamber, was an American kidnapper, torturer, rapist, and suspected serial killer, however, none of his victim's bodies were found. This guy did some pretty hinky shit. After discovering that little bit of juice, I wondered what my new friend was fantasising about. DPRay2 was talking about some room down here. He started to get specific, but in a general way. He asked if I'd ever heard of a red room. I had not, so he went on to explain it 'hypothetically' as a fantasy.

@HOMM83, imagine this fantasy, if you will. This will get your rocks off. Your little whore who stole your ex is drugged and kidnapped. When she comes to, she is tied to a chair, splayed, naked and all alone in a red room. When she focuses, the blinking light of a video camera is in front of her. She is on live feed. Now she is going to pay for what she did to you. People who have paid a hefty sum to be watching this live feed start a bidding war to have their torture played out on her. The final bid will be for the coupe de grace, and usually ends with a machete. I'll bet you're aroused!

My heart is thudding in my chest. I want very much for this to happen to the bitch. Imagine if I could get rid of her but make her pay on the way out. Yes!

@DPRay2, now you're speaking my language. how do you get rid of the bodies? I mean, it's hard to get away with it, isn't it?

@HOMM83, do you really want to know?

@DPRay2, oh, ok. You don't have to tell me.

@HOMM83, let's just say I have a tree lopping business and my industrial woodchipper is very useful and the fish love the burley when I go deep sea fishing. I saw it in a movie once.

@DPRay2, Now THAT is clever.

Part of me wonders if I seriously want to set this up. I guess I have twenty-four hours to decide if this is the way I want to go. My heart reminds me of the toll this bitch has taken on my life, and I decide with conviction that she absolutely must pay. I take a photo of the conversation on my phone. I need to protect myself at all costs.

* * * * *

DPRay2 is waiting for me when I get online.

@HOMM83, meet me in an hour at the crossroads. You can sell me your soul and the price is revenge.

@DPRay2, Soul trading, I like it.

Sitting back, I ponder at the place he has cryptically asked me to meet him. The crossroads would have to be the six-ways junction, but there are tens of shops there. I slide on my sandals and jump in the car. After securing a car park, I walk up to the third level of the car park, which affords me a view of the entire criss-crossed junction. As I survey the different shops, a lot of them large chains, I use my phone to zoom in on the shop fronts and find it… a café on the far side, on the pointy corner of the junction; "*Soulless Sister Café*". I marvel at how uncomplicated the meeting place is – he's clever.

Catching the lift down to the ground floor, I admire myself in the mirrored back wall of the elevator. I look confident and sexy in my white silk top, dusty pink Capri pants and white heeled sandals. Pouting, I strut my stuff all the way to the café. I don't want to look lost, so I take a seat by the window like I'm meeting someone there.

A young waitperson with a phone trapped in the crook of her neck, approaches with a tray. She places before me a small pot of tea, a teacup, saucer and teaspoon, a small sugar and creamer and a plate sporting a cookie. I accept it all like I ordered it. She disconnects her call, smiles, and leaves me. I pour the tea and add the milk. As I lift the cookie, I see a small envelope on the plate underneath. I ignore the envelope and devour the cookie, palming the envelope and surreptitiously slip it into my handbag.

Returning to my car, it takes all my self-control not to open the envelope. Instead, I drive home and go directly into the study before opening it and reading the contents. It is a URL and on the flip side, directions to collect the password. Within minutes I am back in my car and driving to a nearby park. I walk down the path to the third park seat, which is currently occupied by a young couple cuddled up on the end, making vomit inducing cow eyes at each other. I sit on the other end of the seat and pull out my phone, pretending to be looking on social media. The couple on the end of the seat look at me constantly because I've chosen this occupied seat in a park full of empty seats. I ignore them. Eventually, they rise and move to another seat. I consider following them, just for shits and giggles, but decide to stick to the instructions. Underneath the seat, dead centre, is another small envelope. I almost break a nail trying to remove it and slip it into my bag without drawing attention to myself. The couple keep looking over at me, like I'm weird. I give them my biggest smile and they look away, embarrassed at being caught ogling me. I return to my car again and drive home. Once in the office, I open the envelope. Printed in red ink is a code of sorts consisting of many letters, numbers and symbols, and a date is printed on the other side. Shit just got real.

* * * * *

After a coffee break to calm my nerves, I flip the keyboard to get the information taped there. I seat myself before my laptop and enter the URL and password. The screen is all red. After a moment, the screen 'bleeds' and the red drips down the screen like blood to reveal black letters that spell 'welcome to the red room'. The camera pans out to reveal the brick wall of the supposed 'red room'. As it draws out further, a graphic animation of a naked woman tied to a chair, her arms shackled to the brick wall behind her. As the camera pans out further, I appear to have been inside the lens of a camera. The scene continues to pan out and we see the back of the camera, then an audience... but the audience is all computer screens with an animation of the red room, silhouetted heads of the viewers watching. The whole thing draws backwards like the opposite of zooming in through a window and onto an object. The words 'chat' blink in the bottom corner. I'm not sure who types in the chat window, but I don't think it is DPRay2. This person is all business. Transactions down here use Bitcoin currency. I already have the necessary funds, thanks to a tip from my financial advisor a couple of years ago, and I'm advised how to transfer it. If I don't hold up my end of the bargain, not only will the deal not proceed, but I will more than likely have a target on my back, because I've seen too much. You cannot wrong someone down here; once you've accessed something like this 'red room', you cannot ever erase yourself to the people who have seen you – your identity is permanently in there and if something goes awry or you speak to someone about something you shouldn't, you will disappear. These people who create the dark websites want to know everything about those who access them and so you will be on their 'watch list' forever. I don't mind, I won't be saying anything to anyone – they will be doing the job *for* me.

I am now advised that I have to provide the name and details of the person I want to send to the red room. I experience a moment of panic that I might be found out. The back of my brain throws my earlier research into the dark web to the fore, and I recall that my Tor Browser is designed to encrypt everything. The dark web is where you go if you don't want to leave a footprint. I need to stop panicking about this shit and just get it done. The sooner she is gone, the sooner I can get my hands on William, the prize. I won't be watching what happens to her in the red room – I don't care. I just want her removed from the equation and dealt with and if others get off on it in the interim, that's their prerogative.

I tell them the name and advise I'll get back to them with the 'where' when I know more.

37

The Crescendo of the Dark Tale

Felicity

I have arrived at the hospital with a full suit for Damien. Today is Joanna and Chris' 50th Wedding Anniversary and I want Damien to look good for them, whether he likes it or not. I very carefully lay the suit across his bed, avoiding his left hand. I wander off to find a nurse on shift to explain that I'd like them to change him for his parents' visit later this afternoon. When I return to the room, the suit seems to be a little skew-whiff. I take it to hang on the back of the door as advised by the nurse at the nurse's desk as I tell Damien that the nurse will dress him for his parents this afternoon for the occasion of their Anniversary. I smile at him and see that he looks quietly lost today. There is no anger on his face, and he looks almost sad.

I turn abruptly away to hide my inner turmoil and adjust the thin plastic dry-cleaning bag that covers the suit. I notice that the tie is missing. Bugger! I must have dropped it. I dart back out of the room and retrace my steps but cannot find the tie either in the hospital hall, the elevator, the parking lot, or the car. I return to the room and tell Damien that I've forgotten the tie. He looks at me and half of his mouth smiles.

At the nurse's desk I tell them that I've forgotten the tie and will return in about half an hour with it. Damien's disposition is foreign to me. Has he finally accepted his fate? Perhaps he is exhausted, and the anger has finally left him. Perhaps he has missed me as my visits have become shorter in duration.

* * * * *

I return with a different tie as the previous one is completely lost. I even checked under the car seat, but it is a mystery where it has gone. I can only assume I have dropped it outside somewhere. Damien is already dressed in his suit but I'm not sure if I trust him not to harm me if I try to put the tie on. I lay the tie on the bed and begin to tie it, leave a large loop to go over his head. I have forgotten myself and have moved too close to his left side and his hand reaches mine. I whip it away in panic before I realise that he didn't grab at me, he touched me. I look behind me out the door and see Fiona is nearby. I am very scared to go too close but with the nurse just outside, I feel safe enough to tentatively reach for his hand.

Damien looks deep into my eyes as his fingers stroke mine. I don't know what to make of this as years of fear and abuse have made me wary. Such a dichotomy. I gently lower myself to sit on the bed beside him. I look at him and see his eyes are flooded with tears; one breaks free and cascades over his lashes to roll down his cheek.

Nurse Fiona is still outside so I steady myself and loop the tie over his head to settle around his neck. I lean close to adjust the knot at his throat and look up into his lopsided face. "Is that too tight?"

He shakes his head and grunts softly. His eyes are intensely looking into mine and my breath quickens. I miss this man; this handsome man full of love and lust that I married long before he became a jealous tyrant. I am still leaning over him, my face inches from his, breathing in the smell of him. Joanna and Chris enter, and the spell is broken.

Chris booms, "Oh, sorry to interrupt!" He grins mischievously and Damien gives him a lopsided grin.

"Oh darling, don't you look handsome. Gosh you look lovely in a suit." He grunts and motions writing with his left hand. I only now notice the large white board and marker beside his bed. Joanna reaches over and picks up the cumbersome board. In a large childish scrawl, he has written awkwardly, clearly with his non-dominant left hand, 'Happy Anniversary" on the board. Joanna gushes and cries and Chris stiffens with pride. Even I feel a little teary. I choose this time to tell them the wonderful news that Damien and I are expecting twins. Damien looks at me fondly while his parents cry in joy, hugging him and fussing, and all the while, his eyes are on me. Joanna embraces me and asks to feel my belly. My bump is small, but it is there.

The afternoon proceeds and we have a lovely time. Fiona brings in the sponge cake I brought in earlier, and we manage to get Damien to have some of the cream and a little of the soft cake. His face colours as I spoon it into his mouth but the look in his eyes is adoration. Perhaps it has taken this horrific tragedy to bring him back to me. I do not know what has changed or why it has changed, but for the first time in a long time, I am happy to be in his presence. This is a foreign emotion for me where Damien is concerned.

I kiss his lips gently before I leave; only half his mouth kisses me back, the other half sags. He slides his left hand behind my head and pulls me in for another kiss before pulling me into an awkward embrace. I leave the hospital feeling completely perplexed but pleasantly tingling all over.

* * * * *

I am jerked awake from my pleasant slumber by the shrill ringing of my mobile phone. As I detach it from the charging cord and put it to my ear, lying back on the bed, I note that it is 2.56am.

"Hello?"

"Mrs Galbraith?"

"Yes,"

"Hello Mrs Galbraith. I'm afraid that I am calling with some terrible news. There has been a horrible accident during the night. I'm so sorry, but Mr Galbraith, Damien is brain dead."

I sit up with such speed that I hit my forehead on the bookcase above the bed.

"What? How? How has this happened?" adrenalin has woken me completely.

"Could you please come into the hospital? I can call a taxi for you if you are too distressed to drive."

My heart is beating erratically in my chest and my sleep addled brain cannot process what the nurse is telling me.

"No, I'll be there shortly."

I leap out of bed and drag on a pair of yoga pants and a hoodie and don my sneakers before I run for the door with my bag. As it is the middle of the night, I encounter no traffic on my trip to the hospital. Fiona is waiting for me at reception, anxiously wringing her hands.

She pulls me into a room off the hospital reception area and presses me gently into a chair.

"I'm so sorry Felicity. This is such an awful situation. Damien managed to take his own life during the night. The last check Daisy, the nurse on shift, did was at about 10:30pm. She said he looked restful. She felt his wrist and took his pulse, checked him over and left him to his slumber. She would not return for her rounds again until 2:30am so this happened in between those hours."

"... but how did he kill himself? He's had a bloody stroke, for God's sake."

"I know, he managed to hang himself with a necktie."

"A necktie? How did he manage that?"

"He must have somehow hidden it… it wasn't the tie he was wearing this afternoon, so I wonder if it was the tie, you thought you had forgotten or lost?"

"Oh God, but I don't understand how he got the tie… or how the tie went unnoticed?" I have a sickening memory of the suit being moved… I had draped it over the left side of the bed.

"Well considering that Daisy gave him a sponge bath, the only possible place for him to hide it would have been inside his cast. He has lost weight since he had it put on and there must have been enough room for him to poke it in there at some point between you noticing it being lost and returning with the replacement. I'm not sure how he got the tie though."

"OK, but how did he hang himself?" I'm still trying to process all of this.

"When Daisy came in to check his vitals and found him… um, hanged, she said his pyjamas were soaked with sweat from what must have been exertion. He was still warm, so she thought we'd gotten to him soon enough and that there was still hope. He somehow managed to loop and knot the tie through the back of the bed frame, not an easy task with only one side of your body working, and then he looped it around his neck. He got himself to the edge of the bed and then just, allowed himself to fall off, I guess. The tie was short so he didn't hit the floor with a thud that would have alerted the nurse. Only his left leg had made it to the floor; he was asphyxiated very swiftly. We tried everything we could to resuscitate him, but we were unsuccessful. There is no way we could have seen this coming."

"Can I see him?"

"The doctor wants to talk to you first. There will of course be an inquisition into how this happened in the hospital, and I am so very sorry. He is currently on life support."

I am numb. I feel completely and utterly numb. I guess I am in shock. How could he have done this?

Fiona darts out to the reception desk and returns holding the white board from Damien's room. On it, in that barely legible childish scrawl that was hard to decipher, is his last message to me.

My Lissy. I had to go. I can't live in this broken body. I'm sorry for all the hurt. You deserved better. I loved you too much. Love our kids for both of us. Dance now, Lissy.

He had attempted to draw a love heart, but it looked more like a misshapen circle. Now the tears came flooding in. I used to love to dance but my sadness at what my life had become made dancing impossible. The doctor enters, introduces himself and talks to me about Damien's situation. He explains that the life support machine is keeping the air in his lungs and the blood pumping through his veins, but he has gone. "Due to the lack of oxygen to his brain, we could detect no brain activity, so your husband is unfortunately brain dead."

Well, I guess the right side of his brain now matches the left. I still can't come to terms with this.

"He didn't fall violently enough to break his neck, however, the ligature marks on his throat are quite glaring and I wanted to prepare you. There is also swelling in his face and tongue that may alarm you. I assure you he can feel no pain."

"No, of course."

He then asks a difficult question, "Mrs Galbraith, is your husband listed as an organ donor?"

I consider this, "No, I don't think so. At least not that I am aware of."

"Would you consider donating any viable organs? I know this is a difficult time bu…"

"Yes, I would like to donate his organs, to save lives if we can."

"OK. I will get you the forms to sign. Would you like to see him now or would you like some more time to prepare?"

I take a shuddering breath, "Yes, I'll see him now".

* * * * *

Even though the doctor told me what to expect, I am still shocked by his appearance. He looks so peaceful except for the tubes everywhere. The room is silent bar the rhythmic sound of the machine keeping his organs alive. I reach for his hand, which is warm. It doesn't feel right that he is dead, but his body is alive. Tears fall unchecked down my face. I press my lips to his hand. I want to kiss his mouth one more time but there are tubes down his throat and in his nose, intravenous lines going everywhere. I remind myself that this is vital to keep his organs alive.

I stand and try unsuccessfully to hold him one last time. There are too many tubes and lines, and I don't want to erroneously upset the machine or draw the nursing staff in.

I lean in close to his ear and whisper, "Damien, my first love. I don't want to say goodbye, but I must. Yesterday you came back to me but now I've lost you all over again, forever this time. Despite everything, I loved you. I love still you. I will always love you. You will live on through our children. Goodbye my darling."

I sit back down in the chair heavily and gather his hand back in mine. I kiss the back of his hand, kiss each of his knuckles and press it to my cheek. I sob over his limp hand in mine. Finally, spent, I stand and look at his face one last time, then turn to leave.

After signing the papers, I leave the hospital with a promise to organise his collection by a funeral home after I have been advised that he is ready for transport. The sky is beginning to lighten, and the birds have already started their morning conversations. My first priority is to call Joanna and Chris and break their hearts. This will be a terribly hard conversation to have, and I decide that I will drive to their home and tell them in person. I cannot tell them about this awful tragedy over the phone.

38

The Cold Dish

Samantha

I've stopped at the supermarket to grab a few things when I spy William. My heart beats erratically and I have to mentally calm myself. He is so handsome that he makes me swoon. Then I remember the whole shit-show with bitch face and my stomach plunges. Maybe I can use this moment to apologise.

I call to him, "William!" He doesn't hear me. I call louder, "William, hey William!" Still nothing. Gosh, he must be in his own little world. I try to be cool, but my awkward rushing gait unravels me. I practically scream his name, "WILLIAM!"

Finally, he looks up. Annoyance crosses his face before he rear-ranges his features, but I saw it. I press on, "William hello, how are you?"

He is cold, and emotionless "Hi Sam."

"Look, William, I just want to apologise for the whole thing that happened at your mother's house. I feel awful. I don't know what came over me. I was upset with Greg about something, and I took it out on Katrina." I give him my most winning smile, all teeth and concern.

"Well, Sam, it's not me you need to apologise to."

I arrange my entire face to show concern for poor Katrina, "Yes, I know. I'm wondering if you're seeing Katrina tonight, perhaps I could swing by with a bottle of *Moët* by way of apology. Do you think I could do that?"

He shakes his head, "Well, I'm not seeing Katrina tonight. She's going to the cinema with her daughter tonight."

"Oh, really? Which cinema?"

He frowns at me, "The one up the road. Why?"

"Oh, I didn't mean to pry. I'm just making conversation."

"I'll be seeing her tomorrow, so I'll run it by her and see if she'd be up for a drink at a bar, ok?"

"Ok, sure. Thank you. I owe you one."

I need to race home and tell DPRay2 where the bitch will be tonight so we can get her set up. I cannot believe how perfect this is all working out. By the time I wake tomorrow, she'll be as good as dead.

There is an obvious spring in my step as I make my way to the car. Everything is coming up daisies... and she'll be pushing up daisies before we know it. I chuckle to myself at my funny joke. I should be a comedian.

* * * * *

William

I have arrived at Katrina's house a little early and sit at the island bench downing a beer and making small talk with Jacob, while she finishes putting herself together. She was a little late getting started as she spent the day with her friend, whose recently stroke-paralysed husband somehow managed to off himself in his hospital bed. She looked bummed when she greeted me at the door and held on a little longer than usual when I hugged her, so I offered to postpone our date if she's not up for it. We weren't even supposed to be on a date at all tonight, she was supposed to be catching a movie with Lucy, but Lucy's boyfriend won a night at the *Crown Promenade* in a raffle and took her to the city for the night, so Kat asked if I'd come to the movies with her instead. She insisted we still go out because she really needs the distraction. I won't be surprised if she falls asleep during the movie if we end up going, but we're catching an early dinner first, so she can download, and we can decide on whether to see the movie at dinner. Either way, I'm stoked to be catching up with my girl.

I saw Samantha yesterday and tried to pretend I hadn't seen her. Unfortunately, she waved and hollered like a lunatic in the supermarket car park and called my name so loudly, everybody in the vicinity turned to look. I had no choice but to politely greet her. I was stiff and barely polite at all. She apologised for the whole fiasco at the anniversary lunch and begged my forgiveness. I told her it wasn't my forgiveness she needed; it was Kat's. I can't imagine Kat will want to be anywhere near Sam again and that's fine by me.

Dinner is an easy choice of dumplings at the local dumpling house, which happens to be opposite the cinema. She is quiet during dinner, and I don't know what I can do for her except hold her hand and let her download. It seems to be enough. By the time we are due to leave the restaurant, she is teary, so we ditch the movie and walk to a wine bar.

* * * * *

Katrina

We sit at the back of the bar in a quiet corner. William's friend, Jared, saunters over and quietly places our drinks on the table before us but doesn't linger; he has read the room and picked up on my sorrow. The seats are comfortable, and we can relax with our drinks. I snuggle into William and enjoy the warmth and familiar smell of him. I don't think I could have enjoyed a movie tonight. I'm still so shocked from the turn of events with Felicity and Damien. I am sure that she will find peace after the funeral. Damien was possessive and abusive, and she is most definitely better off without him, especially with the babies coming, but the whole situation feels surreal. I have been trying to wrap my head around the fact that he managed to kill himself while in hospital after a stroke. That is some determined stuff. Part of me is glad that he did this – the rest of her life would be a mess, but I feel for my friend.

William jerks me back from my contemplation, "Mum asked me about Christmas."

"What about Christmas?"

He looks uncomfortable, "She's wondering if we could have Christmas lunch at our house. She'd love for your kids to come… and partners, of course. Kaitlyn and Zoe will be there."

"You know, I haven't even thought about it."

"Well, it's less than a month away."

"Shit, is it? I'm NEVER this disorganised. I think that would be lovely, but I should ask the kids just in case. Can I get back to you on that?"

"Sure, now how about another gin and tonic?"

"My eager grin is answer enough.

After an hour or so, we decide to call it a night. We wave to Jared and the bar staff and make our way out towards the open car park. It is a beautiful clear night, but the wind goes right through me, and I shiver involuntarily. William offers to stay the night tonight and I accept eagerly. Waking up tomorrow morning with him beside me is just what I need.

When we emerge from the narrow path between buildings into the car park, my hackles rise. The car park is almost empty and is eerily quiet. Something feels off. It's unusually dark. My hand is in Williams, and he gives it a squeeze. I look up into his face as he drops a kiss on my mouth. I want more, I want to get him home and naked, and I want to take advantage of him. William settles my nerves.

I see movement out of the corner of my eye on the other side of the long brick wall bordering the car park. I try to make out the silhouette in the darkness, but it's too dark to clearly see. The silhouette stills and I sense the impending doom. William looks toward the silhouette but there is a rustle of material behind us, and he suddenly jerks beside me. My arm jolts at the shoulder as he drops to his knees. It feels like everything is unfolding in slow-motion. Several dark silhouettes spill out into the car park and surround us. Something hard hits me over the head and I lose my balance and stumble forward. Strong hands circle my throat and squeeze; I can't breathe. Another kerfuffle and the pressure is released from my throat; I gasp a lungful of air in panic. I look over to see William trying to fend off multiple silhouettes, punching and kicking him; one of them holds a cricket bat. I watch in horror as a silhouette raises a leg, bent at the knee and stomps on William's head. William becomes still. I try to scream but it comes out as a hoarse whisper. I feel a blow to my ribs and another blow to the back of my knees and drop to the ground. I try to move but I can't. I can't move my arms or legs; I can't sit up. I want to go to William, but I can't move. I try to commando crawl to William, but two silhouettes close in on me and I am lifted by my upper arms and dragged to a car with the rear door open. I groan and try to wriggle free, but I have no strength. I always imagined that if something like this happened, I would become super strong and fight but that's not the reality – that is the imaginings of someone who has never been in this situation before. The silhouettes either side of me try to shove me into the back seat but they stumble with my dead weight and as they shove me in, I bounce off the seat and slide back out onto the asphalt. I head hits with a loud thwack that makes the landscape before me swim. I watch in a daze as a car squeals to a halt and someone screams "I told you not to touch her... you were instructed not to touch her! Oh God, he's not supposed to be here... WILLIAM!!" Who is that? I know that voice.

The screaming someone is crouched over William, but William is not moving. This cannot be happening; this is a dream. I try to pull myself out of the dream. Loud male voices start yelling aggressively. A very hard blow lands on the back of my head and I see stars. Feet scuffle around me and Jared's face looms before me...

39

Emerging from the Fog

Katrina

My eyes feel gritty. I'm so tired. I try to open my eyes but only manage to creak them open to slits. Brilliant light momentarily blinds me, so I close them again. Voices and faces crowd me. Something beeps near me. Someone lifts my arm. My index finger is gently pinched. Immense pressure squeezes my arm. A feeling of dread fills my chest. Something is wrong. My arm is getting strangled by something. I try to call out. My brain misfires something about William. I feel the panic rise inside me and scream out in terror. Only breath wheezes out of me. I try to focus. Darkness descends and I welcome it.

* * * * *

Low voices murmur in quiet conversation somewhere nearby. I crack and eye, but the light is still blinding. I close my eyes again and lie still.

"…no, the doctor came in earlier and said all vitals are good – he said we just need her to wake up to see if there's any cerebral damage. It's been days. She has a serious concussion, so she probably won't remember shit."

"Darling, she's in the best place she can be. Try to focus on something else."

"…like what? Who did this? I have no fucking clue who would do this. Sorry about the language." A deep sign, "I'm worried about her."

"Of course you are sweetheart. Don't worry about it."

"I just don't understand. We're nobodies… why were there five guys in the car park waiting for us? Was it me or Kat they were after… or mistaken identity? Jared said they were trying to get Kat into a car when he and the others turned up."

"How did Jared, he even know you were getting attacked?"

"He said a woman came running into the bar, practically frothing at the mouth, blubbering that a couple was getting beaten in the car park, so he and some other staff came out to help."

"Do the police have anything?"

"They're not telling us much. There's nothing in the car park, nothing was left behind. It was so dark that Jared and the other guys couldn't even see them clearly enough to give good descriptions. Apparently, the lighting in the car park was switched off and they're looking into how that could be. It's a bit suss."

"Katrina told me about the little girl's body on the running track… could it be something to do with that?"

"Oh shit! I didn't even think of that. I'll call the station, although I reckon they'd have already worked that out. Her name would have come up."

My companions fall into a comfortable silence. I open my eyes. The first thing I see is an unfamiliar room with fluorescent strip lights on the ceiling. The constant beep of a machine and the muted sounds outside the room make me think of a hospital. I turn my head to the side and see William beside my bed. His elbows are on his knees and his head is in his hands; his fingers poke through spiked hair that look like echidna quills. I try to move, to reach out a hand but my whole-body aches. I call his name but all that comes out is a dry croak. It's like lightening strikes. William sits up immediately and looks at me. "Oh, hey sleepy head!" His voice is soft and gentle like he's talking to a frightened child. He has a black eye and a split lip and various bruises on his handsome face. I don't know what has happened.

My throat aches and feels bruised. It hurts to talk but I force my vocal cords to comply, "Hey yourself. Are we in a hospital?" the effort makes me cough and my ribs complain.

"Yeah, you've been out for a few days."

I try to sit up, but the room spins and I'm immediately nauseous. I stomach heaves and I humiliate myself by puking a disgusting yellow questionable substance on the front of my hospital nightgown. A blur of movement and the door opens to my right. A nurse enters, followed by Beverley. The nurse helps me to puke into an ugly green kidney shaped dish. This is mortifying. It gets worse… as I puke, I feel a thin stream of hot diarrhoea squirt out of my backside – great, I've shit the bed. The nurse looks up and asks William and Beverley to give us a moment. I hope they leave before the smell hits them. My body starts to shake violently and to my horror, a sob escapes me. The nurse rubs my back and helps me lay back down. He leaves the room and returns shortly after with another nurse and a tub of warm water and a cloth. They remove the catheter, and it burns. I hiss in breath between my teeth and the effort makes my bottom lip sting. The male nurse apologises. They proceed to give me a sponge bath. I cry through the whole ordeal and the female softly coos while the male gently bathes me. I don't want William to come back in and see my scrunched red face like the monkey's arse. I don't even know why I'm crying.

They help me stand and change my gown and allow me the

dignity of wearing some knickers, albeit paper ones. The male nurse quickly changes the bedding while the female steadies me. They both help me back into bed and I'm pleased to note that the room smells of soap and not shit.

William and Beverley are allowed back in. I mumble an apology but tears flood again. This is so embarrassing. William rushes and hugs me. When he pulls away, his eyes are full of tears. The white part of his black eye has a dark red patch. I don't know what happened to him.

"William, what happened?"

"You don't remember anything?"

"We were at the bar and now I'm here, but I don't know anything that happened in between, or how I got here."

"We were attacked on the way back to the car."

"Attacked? By who?"

"We don't know. The police are looking into it. A bunch of guys.

"Wait, the police are involved?"

"Yes. We both got knocked out and arrived here in an ambulance. The police were called."

"Shit! What did they want? Did they steal my purse?" I look around the hospital room and I don't see either my bag or my purse.

Beverley volunteers, "They put your personal items in that drawer beside you, honey."

"Oh, hello Beverley. This all feels quite surreal. You say I've been out for a couple of days?"

William answers, "Four days, actually. They put you in a medically induced coma for two days because your concussion was severe, and your brain swelled. You have a cracked skull.

"Oh my God. Really?"

"Yeah. They were worried, so they put you under to minimise the swelling or help it settle down. Apparently, it lets the brain rest or something. I don't know, but it was a big deal. You were in ICU for three days. Your head was hit really hard. You only moved to the ward this morning. You woke briefly twice but kept going back under. Either way, they knew you'd be out soon, and all your vitals were good so here we are."

"I can't tell you how weird it is to find out you've missed a few days. Like I've just skipped over them."

"Lucy was here all night, but Jacob took Mason home because he has a test today. Lucy went home to freshen up at around nine this morning, but I've just called her and told her you're awake so they're all on their way back here now."

"Thank you. My whole body hurts."

"I'm not surprised. You copped a bad hiding. You've got concussion, a fractured cheek bone and a couple of black eyes."

The burning in my nether regions eases and I realise I need to empty my bladder. "William, can you help me to the bathroom."

William picks me up in his arms and carries me like a sleepy child to the bathroom. He looks away as I pull down my knickers to pee. Afterwards, I walk slowly to the basin to wash my hands. William opens the door ready to go back into the room. I look up; the reflection in the mirror does not belong to me. My face is swollen, misshapen, hideously mottled, and almost completely purple. My bottom lip shows signs of some kind of trauma and is swollen on one side and my cheek looks like a botched implant job. There is dark bruising around my throat. My left ear is bruised and scabbed over. I gingerly lift my gown and see bruising on my ribs and legs, my knees and left elbow are crusted with scab. I look like I've literally been through the wringer. I meet Wil's gaze and my bottom lip quivers.

"Oh sweetheart, come here." He lifts me off my feet and carries me back into the room; folding himself onto the visitor's chair, curling me up on his lap and rocking gently while I sob into his neck. Beverley exits the room and gives us some privacy.

* * * * *

William

Kat is dozing again. The doc popped in and checked her over. I'm so happy to see she's emerged from her coma. Kat's kids have just left, and my girls are going to pop in this evening if Kat is up to the visit. All our kids met in the waiting room a few days ago.

The damage to Kat seems to be minimal other than her short-term memory loss, but the doc said that is normal with concussion. I've been wracking my brain, but I can't think who would do this to us. They didn't even take Kat's purse, my wallet or either of our phones. It's weird.

It was weird to wake up on Saturday morning in hospital. When they gave me all clear, Mum and Dad collected me and took me home to get a change of clothes. Before I could go back to the hospital, the police came over to interview me. I couldn't tell them much but promised I'd call them if I remembered anything. They will be coming in this afternoon to chat with Kat. I'm not sure she's going to be able to offer anything concrete. She can't remember anything after sitting at the bar.

40

Damage Control

Samantha

I've been in damage control, trying to fix the shitstorm since that stupid bitch thwarted the kidnap attempt. The stupid men who cocked it all up got away before the police came, or before anyone could get a good look at them, thank God. I don't know how they managed to get rid of the lights but that certainly helped.

I've even had to make a trip to the hospital to check on the stupid cow and feign concern. She was still out to it in ICU, so I hope she dies in her sleep and then she won't be an issue for me anymore. I saw William there. His face was so battered and bruised, I wanted to cry. I'm so angry with those dickheads for attacking him too but DPRay2 said they had no choice because he started to fight them. They were expecting two women… William wasn't even supposed to be there. I can't believe I put his life in danger.

The whole thing is over now and they're not giving me another chance to have the stupid bitch tortured. They nabbed some other random woman who was drunk and alone, stumbling along a dark lit street near the train station. They waited for her to be past the CCT cameras and smacked her on the back of the head. They had to have someone in the red room by Sunday night as promised to the bidders, so they improvised. Now I'm never going to get rid of the cow.

Now that my chance has gone, I'm going to get rid of the Tor Browser, although I don't think I can make it completely disappear. As long as nothing can be traced back to me, I'm out and not going down into the dark web again. It's best if I stay out of it now, at least until the dust settles.

* * * * *

William

The police are interviewing Kat. I'm out in the waiting room with Lucy, Jacob, Mason and his friend, Li Xui. I think she's Mason's girlfriend because they're holding hands. Lucy's boyfriend Nate arrives and joins her on the seats after shaking the hands of all the men. He smiles and nods at Li Xui. Jacob's face is sullen, so I strike up a conversation with him, "How are you all going at home?"

Jacob looks up surprised, "We're ok. A bit worried about mum. I'm bloody glad she woke up; I can tell you. We've been stressed out of our heads!"

"Me too. She took a hard hit to the back of the head. She can't remember much."

"I kind of hope it stays like that. I reckon she'll have nightmares if she remembers that shit."

"You're probably right, but she needs to remember so they can catch them. I'm not sure how much she'll be able to tell the police. Apart from the fact that it came out of nowhere, there was no lighting, none. So, we couldn't even see who was attacking us or where they were coming from."

"Do the cops know anything?"

"Nope, or not that they're sharing with me anyway."

The police exit her room and we're allowed back in. I hang back to ask if they got any details from her. They have nothing and they're still investigating who turned out the lights in the car park. That had to come from someone in the know.

I watch the backs of the retreating police as they exit the hospital. Mum smiles and nods at the officers as she enters, Dad follows behind her. I stay in the waiting area. Mum pecks me on the cheek but Dad walks up and gives me a full man-hug. "How are you going, mate? You, ok?"

"Yeah, I'm ok. We're still none the wiser though. Kat can't remember anything."

"Shall we go in?"

"She has a full room at the moment, so let's give her and the family a bit of space."

Thomas and Chloe enter, holding hands. Thomas shakes my hand and Chloe gives me a big hug. I hug her back, not realising how much I needed it.

"We're taking up all the seating in this room. There's a café on this floor, lets go down there and grab a coffee." I volunteer.

I dart into Kat's room and announce that we're all going to the café. Kat smiles at me, she looks tired.

* * * * *

Katrina

"Dad called. He and Anne send their love." I look at Jacob, but I don't see any of the animosity that usually follows any mention of his father and Anne. The trauma of recent events puts everything into perspective, I guess.

I notice that Mason and Li Xiu are holding hands. I wonder when that happened. That makes me happy. Lucy and Mason are bantering, exchanging insults in their usual playful way. Jacob joins in and both Li Xiu and Nate look on in amusement. I roll my eyes at them, but I am immediately plunged into acute pain.

"How are the furry little monsters?"

Lucy excitedly regales us with tales of their early evening zoomies around the living room, tiny claws getting no purchase on the floorboards, so they skate all over the place when they round corners. This delightful story makes my heart soar. I can't wait to get back home to some fur therapy.

I wish I could remember more about that night. I can't give the police anything. I asked them if they think there is any connection with the attack and me giving the police information about the man I saw on the tracks. They said they are looking into it but doubt it because there is no way anyone knows that it was me who went to the police or where I live, for that matter. The police believe the attack is completely unrelated but are not dismissing it entirely.

I feel exhausted. I close my eyes for a moment to rest them and see shadows behind my closed lids. The shadows are sliding along the brick wall to my right. One of the shadows leaps out at me and I jolt awake to an empty room. I look around me as my heart thuds in my chest. I am alone and the room is relatively silent but for the beeping monitor. A nurse enters and checks the monitor then takes my blood pressure.

"How are you feeling, Katrina?"

"Hi, I'm ok. I think I just dozed and had a bad dream."

"Well, your heart rate certainly went up, that's for sure. Everything seems to be ok though. Your family stopped by the reception desk and told us they're all going to the café, should you wake."

"Oh geez, I fell asleep while they were here."

"Considering your recent ordeal, I don't think anybody will hold that against you."

Hers eyes crimp at the corners. A grey-haired older woman in a blue apron pops her head in, "Are you ready for your lunch, love?"

I realise I'm ravenous and nod enthusiastically.

The nurse rolls the tray around and exits. The food services woman deliver my lunch of lukewarm soup and a dry bread roll. After a little while I find I'm full, so I push the tray away and lay back on the pillows again. My tray is collected shortly after.

It's nice to be alone for a bit. I try to pull at the threads of the dream that woke me earlier. The shadows scare me and send my heart rate skyrocketing again so I leave it alone. Someone has kindly put my phone on charge. I open it and find a colourful display of missed calls and messages from friends and family. I'm too tired to deal with them all now so I put the phone back down and lay back on the pillows. I'm drowsy and close my eyes again.

The shadows return and they are menacing. A crescendo of loud noise builds around me; indistinct shouting, jostling, and scrapping then silence. Tyres squeal and I'm laying on the hard asphalt. I can see William laying near me, but he is not moving. A woman is yelling at the shadows and crouches over William's inert body. The shadows all suddenly disappear. I am ripped from the scene into a room full of concerned faces. William is hovering over me.

"You were on the ground and a woman was leaning over you" I blurt.

"What?"

Realisation that I was asleep dawns on me. "Oh, I had a dream. Sorry."

"Where were you in the dream?"

"I think I was in the car park; you know the one near the cinema?"

"Yes, that's where it happened. Who was this woman?"

"I don't know, but she was familiar to me. I couldn't see her properly because it was so dark. It was so, so dark. But you were on the ground, and you weren't moving."

"I wonder if that was a memory."

"I think it was just a dream. It was weird, and things were happening that sort of defy explanation, like they do in dreams."

"I think only men were there. Jared said he only saw men so maybe it was a dream."

My heart is still thudding. I look beyond William and see Thomas as well as Wil's daughters and Beverley and Ken. We have a full house.

"Hi there." A chorus of polite greetings bounce around the room. William helps me sit up just as Chloe enters carrying a takeaway cup of coffee, which she hands to me.

Compared to the awful insipid tea I had with lunch earlier, the coffee is delicious. I thank Chloe and close my eyes to savour the coffee. Everyone engages in polite conversation. William takes my hand in his and gently squeezes it. He winks at me with his unblemished eye and butterflies take flight in my stomach.

* * * * *

With the white coat of the doctor retreating, I swing my legs off the bed and start to pack the small bag Lucy brought in. I've finally been given the all-clear to go home. I am definitely missing my bed and the quiet of home.

William fusses over me like I'm going to break at any moment. I gently still him with my hand over his. "I'm fine. I'm going to be fine."

"I'd like to stay with you at home for a few days if that's ok. Just humour me. I promise I won't get under your feet."

The hope of some quiet time dissipates into thin air, "sure, you can stay with me, but you have to promise not to fuss over me."

He stands erect with his feet together and executes a salute, "Yes, ma'am!" He gathers my bag as I check the drawer and bathroom for forgotten items. I sign a bundle of forms and I am finally set free.

On the drive home, William tells me he has endured ongoing headaches since the fight in the car park. He has a fractured occipital bone, which explains the residual swelling under his black eye.

The familiar smell of home assails my senses as the door swings open. William grunts as he lifts my bags and takes them into my room. As I make my way down the hall, the smell of freshly baked scones makes me salivate. I enter the kitchen to find my children fussing about; Mason is setting out the placemats, jam and cream on the table, Jacob is rifling through the cutlery draw and Lucy is standing in the middle of the kitchen holding a wicker basket lined with a red and white checked towel, filled with the delicious bounty. William smacks his lips behind me, "that smells divine, Lucy!" Lucy beams at the complement. I feel so blessed to have these three beautiful children taking care of me.

Stuffed full of fluffy scones, I dose fitfully on the couch. I wake with a start as the shadows disappear. "Are you OK, Kat?"

William is sitting in the armchair behind me, "Are you watching me sleep? That's not creepy at all."

Hand on chest in mock umbrage, William pouts, "How very dare you! I am reading the paper. It just so happens that the most comfortable room in the house is the one you fell asleep in." His hoity-toity postulation makes me laugh.

When William strips down to his trunks for bed, I see all the bruises on his ribs and back that he hasn't mentioned. He looks up at me and sees my horror, "I'm ok. They don't hurt much." He grimaces involuntarily as he climbs into bed. I have an overwhelming desire to cry like a child. He takes in my expression and leaps out of bed to envelope me in his embrace.

"Hey, I'm ok. They're just bruises."

My voice is muffled by his chest and unusually high, "but you got really hurt. Why did this happen, William? I can't understand. They didn't take our wallets or any of our possessions. Why us?"

William's sits on the bed. His face drops, "I really don't know,

Kat. What I do know is that the most frightening thing was to see the doctors and nurses all around you and you were unconscious and in a very bad way and they were very worried that you wouldn't make it. I've never been so close to losing someone I love before, and it was terrifying." His voice cracks and he let out a sob, he looks at his lap, "so please don't get upset with me if I fuss over you. I nearly lost you because I couldn't protect you."

I step to him and press his face into my stomach, "Oh Wil, you said yourself there were five of them… the odds were stacked against us. If I hadn't made it, it wouldn't have been on you… it was on them. They did this awful thing!"

We cling together, quietly letting our tears roll unchecked. I've been so absorbed with my own mess that I didn't stop to think of how if was for him. Not only hours of not knowing if I would survive, but days of not knowing how severe the damage was going to be.

"William, I'm so sorry you had to go through this. I can't believe I didn't even think about it all from your perspective."

"I didn't even really think about the gravity of it all until just now. I've been so worried that I guess now that you're out of hospital, I can finally take a breath, you know?"

"Yeah, I know."

We climb into bed and snuggle. I drift off in his arms but wake with a start in the small hours. William whispers beside me, "You, ok?"

"Yeah, just a dream." My heart thuds in my chest but I don't recall the details of the dream. Closing my eyes, I try a relaxation technique where I allow colours to flood, usually reds and pinks, sometimes oranges and yellows. Only this time, onyx black swirls like ink in water.

I open my eyes in the dark and try to reset my brain, but only the black ink floods in and I wonder if this is some part of my subconscious trying to tell me something. I wish I could remember who the woman was. As I finally drift off, her voice is loud in my head.

My eyes fly open, and I sit up. William sits up too.

"Sorry, I just had a memory of the night… the woman. I recognised her voice, but I can't make it match. I just heard it again. I'm sorry William. You get some sleep; I'm going to get up and make a cup of camomile tea to help me sleep.

As I sit in the living room sipping the tea, I try to pick at the memory. I don't know why I can't put a face or name to the voice. Whoever she is, I think I know her somehow.

41

The Voice of Evil

Katrina

William parks the car and runs around to open my door. He is still treating me with kid gloves but after hearing him lay himself bare the other night, I take it in my stride and let him protect me.

The heavy front door swings open before we even climb the stairs and Beverley welcomes me with open arms. She gushes, "I'm so glad to see you out of that hospital room."

"I'm glad to be out of there myself. As Dorothy says, 'there's no place like home'".

Beverley leads us to the sunny conservatory room. I sink into one of the yellow window seats lining the glass windows and feel the welcome warmth of the sun on my back. This room instantly relaxes me and I almost swoon with drowsy contentment.

I haven't slept well in days as the nights are peppered with dreams of frightening shadows and that awful woman's voice. No matter how hard I try to retrieve the lost memory, I cannot bring the owner of that voice to the fore.

The memories of the night have started to come back in fits and starts. In that small space between consciousness and sleep, a memory will flood, and I'll be ripped from sleep into a sitting position, shaking with fear. The sliding shadows were the men. The darkness of the car park made them look like shadows, but they were large hulking men. I remember being hit on the back of the head on at least one occasion because the sound inside my head was like an explosion and my sinuses burned like they'd been flooded with water.

The memory of lying on the asphalt and seeing the still body of Wil still haunts me. I think in that moment I thought he was dead. I also hear the screeching of tyres and that voice that I can't place. Whoever she was, she was concerned about William, but not about me. It was like she was expecting to find me there but was horrified to see William. The lack of conviction in the subliminal memory is driving me bonkers.

Beverley enters the conservatory with a tea tray. She checks that I am comfortable before she pours the tea. William follows with a plate of butter cookies. The doorbell rings and William hisses an expletive under his breath. Beverley looks at him pointedly and the tips of his ears pink.

"Sorry… I'll get it." He makes his way to the entrance.

⁎ ⁎ ⁎ ⁎ ⁎

William

I place the plate of cookies on the conservatory coffee table as Mum pours the tea. She makes a mean brew and I'm looking forward to a cup. No sooner does my backside hit the seat that the doorbell ring. Shit! Mum looks up, annoyed. "I'll get it."

I stride to the door and open it, only to see Samantha standing on the porch; her face flushes when her eyes fall on my face. I'm annoyed, because I don't want her to be here and I certainly don't want Katrina to have to deal with her, but try to mask it, "Hi Sam."

She gushes coyly, "Hi William, how are you?"

"I'm fine, Sam. What's up?"

"Aren't you going to invite me in?"

"Samantha, the last time you were here all hell broke loose. I don't think anyone has forgotten that."

Her face reddens and ire flits across her Scandinavian countenance "I've already apologised to your parents for that! I came to the hospital to try to apologise to Katrina."

The ire returns followed by a coldness devoid of emotion. As usual, she turns the conversation to revolve around to herself... quite the narcissist, "I've also lost my fiancé, so I think I've paid the price already."

"Well Katrina is in there and she's still quite delicate after being attacked." Samantha's face flushes red with what looks like embarrassment, but it's gone before I can properly register it.

Mum calls from the Conservatory, "Who is it, Wil?"

I unsuccessfully stifle my sigh. "It's Samantha." I imagine Katrina won't be too pleased.

"Well invite her in then!" Shit! That's all we need.

I gesture with my head for Samantha to come in. She enters then stands aside to allow me to show her the way. I walk over to Katrina and sit beside her, taking her hand in mine. She looks at me and rolls her eyes but like the trooper she is, she bucks up and says hello.

"Hi, Samantha."

Samantha gushes all fake pleasantry, "Katrina hello! I hear you've had a bit of an incident."

Katrina stiffens beside me and her grip on my hand almost crushes my fingers. Her breath is coming in short bursts, and I can feel her shaking.

Samantha looks at us, waiting for Kat to reply. Kat is looking at her with wide eyes, clearly frightened, her grip unrelenting and her shaking visible. Mum picks up on it, "Katrina, what's happening? Are you ok love?"

A fine film of sweat appears on her face and beads on her top lip.

"Hey Sam, as I said at the door, Kat's not been well so perhaps another time, hey?"

Samantha will not be swayed and says through clenched teeth, "What's going on?"

"As I said, she's not been well. Another time, perhaps?"

I stand and usher her to the front door, to hell with etiquette. She tries to turn but I stand too close and force her to keep walking. "Uh, sure. Will you call me?"

I keep walking forward towards the front door and practically push her out of it without answering, before closing the door on her surprised face. I can see her mottled silhouette through the glass pane beside the door, bewildered. Get the hint, Sam, and piss off.

* * * * *

Samantha

I watch the retreating silhouette of William. My heart thuds in my chest and I think I can feel it split, like a physical tear. My bottom lip quivers and it takes all my self-control not to sit on the step like a worthless hobo and sob. I dash to my car with as much decorum as I can muster. The interior is so warm it is almost hot, so I start the engine and ramp up the cooling, so I don't start to *smell* like a hobo. I'm so heartbroken that he doesn't love me back. I lose the battle with my tears and sob inconsolably, my face in my hands above the steering wheel.

I love him so much and he treats me like I'm an annoying pest. I can't stop the tears and allow myself to cry with abandon until my chest stops heaving. Pulling the rear-view mirror around, my ruined makeup and swollen nose and lips makes me look like a poorly made-up Drag Queen. No Samantha, don't you do that to yourself. You're beautiful even when you cry.

Meanwhile, that fucking feline bitch with nine lives continues to hold his heart when she is clearly not worthy. He belongs with me. It was all planned, she wasn't supposed to be in the picture anymore, I'd dealt with her... but she managed not only to live through the ordeal, she also dragged my beloved into the fray with her. She was supposed to be chained to a wall right now, being punished like she deserves, and I'm supposed to be consoling William after he reports her missing, joining in the search for her and ingratiating myself in his heart. Instead, she has William running after her like a little puppy. I have known him for decades, but I'm suddenly dismissed because *she* is feeling 'quite delicate'. Not delicate when it counts, though. Stupid bitch.

My heart rate escalates as I imagine her dead. I scrunch my eyes and gnash my teeth together so hard I see stars and there is a roaring in my ears. I hate her. She fuels my rage. I hope she dies in a car crash and gets decapitated. I hope her decapitated head flies out the window and smashes against a giant tree, bursting open and spilling her brains everywhere. I would visit that tree every anniversary and lay flowers in celebration of the day William was finally free to choose me.

I dab at my tears and manage to pull myself together before driving home to an empty unit. I will draw a hot bath and spend time mending my shattered heart.

* * * * *

William

I sprint back to the conservatory to see Mum on her knees before a quaking Kat.

Mum's face is etched with concern, "What is it, love?"

I join mum on the floor and look up into Kat's terrified face. Her jaws are chattering like she's freezing. Her face completely pales, and Mum and I scatter as Kat rushes for the powder room. I run after her but halt near the door when I hear her retching. Darting to the kitchen, I fetch a glass of water and wait beside the door. I can hear her breathing heavily in there. She is sobbing, "It's her! It's her!" repeatedly, like an incantation.

Mum joins me at the door and anxiously wrings her hands. After a good twenty minutes, the powder room door opens. Katrina's face looks stricken.

"What happened, Kat?" I gently query.

She draws a deep breath and her voice quivers, "can I sit down, please?"

We escort her back into the conservatory. I gently encourage her to sit while Mum presses a cup of hot sweet tea into her hands. The cup rattles in the saucer but she manages to take a sip of the beverage.

She takes a shaky breath, "William, that woman… her voice!"

"You mean Samantha?"

"Yes, it was her!"

Mum is confused, "What about Samantha? She just left."

Kat looks between Mum and I, fear etched into her delicate face, "Yes, it's her voice, Wil. I heard her voice that night."

"What on earth would Samantha have to do with anything? Could you have just misremembered?" Mum is not understanding at all.

"No mum, look at her reaction. She's terrified." I look deep into Katrina's eyes, "Honey, are you sure the voice you heard that night was Samantha's?"

"Yes, I am positive. She was there, leaning over you. I was lying on the ground, and I could see you there, not moving. She was yelling at them that they were not supposed to hurt you. It was her car, her tyres squealing. Her voice. She has something to do with it,

Wil." Her face crumples and she begins to cry. I take the cup and saucer from her and pull her into my arms.

"OK, I think we should take a trip down to the police station and tell them what happened. Just settle your nerves, OK?"

I take Mum by the elbow and steer her into the kitchen.

"William, what does she mean?"

"She remembered that there was a woman's voice on the night. She said she recognised it, but she couldn't place it. It's been driving her nuts. When she just heard Samantha speak, the memory locked in, and she finally remembered that it was Samantha's voice she heard that night."

"William, I just can't imagine that Samantha had anything to do with that night. It's preposterous."

I quirk an eyebrow at her, "Really, after what happened here, you think she's not capable of anything sinister? I tell you, that was an eye opener for us."

"Oh gosh, I completely forgot about that. Oh, Geez!'

"Mum, I don't want you to tell anybody about this. I'm going to take Katrina down to the police station and we're going to let them handle it. It would be best if Samantha doesn't get a heads up that Katrina has remembered hearing and seeing her. Can you promise to do that?"

"What, not even your father?"

"Well, of course you can tell Dad but nobody else, ok? And Dad can't say anything to anyone either. Let's just keep it to ourselves and let the police at least check some things."

42

Seeking Justice

Katrina

My body is still shivering on this warm afternoon from the shock of this revelation. I knew Samantha had a dislike for me... but organising an abduction? An abduction for what? It is terrifying to ponder.

I don't like how familiar I have become with the inside of this police station. The constable on duty leads us to an interview room. Only moments later we are joined by the sergeant I had met on previous occasions... he introduces himself and I finally catch his name, "Good afternoon, Ms Johns."

"Hi, this is William Milburne, my partner."

"Sergeant Roach," he thrusts a hand at William.

"Hi, nice to meet you."

Sergeant Roach doesn't waste time wading in, "So Ms Johns, I understand you have remembered something pertaining to the assault on your person on..." he consults his notes, "...December twelfth, is that correct?"

"Yes. I've worked out who the woman was that I heard that night. I was lying on the ground, and I could see the figure of a woman leaning of William and she was yelling, "it's William, he's not supposed to be here." I can't remember the words exactly, but I do remember that I knew the voice, but I couldn't place it."

"And you have since remembered the owner of the voice?"

"Yes, Samantha Karisson. She just came to my partner's house and as soon as she spoke, I knew it was her."

"Does she know that you have worked that out?"

"I don't think so. William got her to leave quickly before I could tell him and Beverley, William's mother, that I'd placed the voice."

William butts in, "Why do you think she was surprised I was there?"

I don't know. She originally said, "I told you not to touch her" until she realised it was William and she said, "it's not the daughter." It's like she was expecting me and Lucy, which was our original plan before Lucy was asked out by a friend."

Sergeant Roach frowns, "Do you have any idea how this woman would have known you were going to be there at that time?"

I shake my head – this is a mystery to me that I can't figure out.

William jerks himself rigid beside me, "I saw her that day, in the afternoon... in the supermarket car park. She asked what we were up to... some pretence about wanting to apologise to Katrina because she had made an awful scene and was threatening to Katrina the last time we saw her, and I said I wasn't seeing Katrina that night as she was going to the cinema with her daughter. I think she even asked which cinema, which I thought was odd at the time, but I did tell her. Oh shit, this is my fault, Kat!"

Sergeant Roach holds up his hand to still whatever dramatic guilty declaration was coming next from William.

"You mentioned that there was an altercation. Could you please tell me about that?"

I provide details from my recollection of the *altercation* and

William provides the other side heard by those at the table."

The sergeant asks a few more questions then advises that he will be in touch.

* * * * *

Samantha

I am disgusted. Flipping through a high-end fashion magazine used to be my favourite pastime. Now I am confronted with the morbidly obese, downs syndrome and the ultimate insult, a man in a dress. He's not even a gay or a Drag Queen – he's just a pop star who has forgotten his place. When did this all-inclusive bullshit happen? We've gone from beautiful photography of immaculate men and women who work extremely hard for their perfect bodies, often starving themselves and undertaking extreme measures for fitness and physicality to seeing a gross fat woman sprawled on the sand seductively; huge heaving tits oozing out of her hammock-like bikini top and rolls of lard with a fat mound of a pussy on display, smiling up at me from the glossy pages like she thinks she's a super-model *Angel* about to strut down the runway. The only wings this fat bitch is getting will be the ones that take her off this earth when her heart gives way from trying to pump blood around her gross, fat, huge body. Then these retards and cross-dressing wankers... give me *strength!* They call this diversity... I call it bloody revolting and an insult to the fashion industry.

The doorbell sounds loudly. I slam the magazine closed in disgust, walking to the front of the unit like the model I *am*, and open the door to find a couple of cops on the doorstep; a young male who is so white he's almost blue and a middle-aged woman who looks like a lesbian with all that masculinity. The blood drains from my face but I remember that they know nothing and smile winningly.

"Hello, can I help you?"

The woman takes the lead, "Good morning, Ms Karrinson, is it?"

"Yes, that's me."

"We were wondering if we could we come in and ask you a few questions?"

"What is this about?"

"We understand that a friend of yours was recently involved in an incident and we're trying to piece together what happened."

My heart pounds in my chest and I try to keep my voice even, "What has that got to do with me?"

"Ma'am, could we please come inside?"

I hesitate for a moment but if I'm going for no guilt, then I need to act like I haven't got anything to hide I stand aside and allow them in, steering them into the living room. The kid pulls out a small notepad, "Could you please advise the last time you saw Ms Katrina Johns?"

Her surname is Johns. How very boring. My voice is perfectly even as I answer, "I saw her yesterday".

"Could you advise your relationship with Ms Johns?"

Relationship? She's my arch fucking enemy if you must know, "I don't really have a relationship with Katrina. She is dating my very best childhood friend, William." My heart flutters at the mere mention of his name.

"Did you see Katrina before yesterday?"

"Yes, I went in to visit her when she was in hospital, but she was still in the ICU." I should have been attending her funeral if those dickheads could do what they were supposed to do instead of running around in the dark like a bunch of boneheads. If stupid could fly, those fuckwits would be a squadron of jets.

"Did you see either William or Katrina on Friday?"

"Yes, as a matter of fact I saw William at the supermarket. Why?"

"Did you talk about anything in particular?"

Where the fuck is this going? "No, just small talk."

Both officers look at me like they're expecting more. I shrug. They continue to look pointedly at me. What do they know I wonder.

Silence is deafening.

"Are you sure you didn't talk about anything in particular?"

"No, we just made small talk… I asked what they were up to that night, just in conversation."

"What did William tell you?"

"He said that he wasn't seeing Katrina that night that she was going out with her daughter."

"Ms Karisson, where were you on Friday night?

I swallow hard and it is not at all unnoticed, "Am I a suspect?"

"Ma'am, we're just asking some questions."

"I was at home."

"Can anyone verify that?"

"Well, no, I live alone. I did call my mother that evening and we chatted for hours."

"Approximately what time did you call your mother?"

"I think it was around 8.30…pm".

Both officers stand, "Thank you for your help, Ms Karisson."

"Well, I hope you find those awful men who did this to her. Thugs!"

I close the door on the Keystone Cops and pop the kettle on.

43

The Scent of a Rat

Samantha

The mirror squeals as I wipe away the fog and condensation after my shower. Releasing my wet hair from the towelling turban, I let it fall on my bare shoulders. The doorbell chimes. I hastily throw a robe on to answer the door. The two cops are back. The younger guy blushes beetroot red and looks away. I stifle my smile.

"You're back." I say as a way of greeting – nothing to see here.

"Ms Karisson, we need you to accompany us to the station, please."

What the fff… "Why?"

"We just have some follow up questions."

"Can't you ask me here?" annoyance is clearly in my voice.

"No Ms Karisson, we need to ask these further questions at the station."

"Well, I'm just getting dressed."

"We will wait for you out here."

Shit! I hastily throw on a tiny jumpsuit that barely covers my arse and couple it with a cute pair of wedge sandals. Taking my time to apply make-up, I finish with my hair tied in a high ponytail. I saunter back and grab my keys and handbag on the way.

I wish this shit would just go away.

* * * * *

The kid blushes as he leads me into an interview room, the red stain of it travelling down his neck and into his uniform shirt. I sit at the table and try not to fidget. I need to look confident. I already surrendered my mobile phone. Good luck getting into that without my face. Dumb arses.

When the door opens, it's not the kid or the dyke, it's a hot sergeant. He barely glances at me before introducing himself and sits down. He hasn't noticed me at all – I am just a common criminal to him. He hits record and states names, the date, and the time.

I want to appear assertive, so I ask, "Am I under arrest or something?"

"No, not currently. But I will ask you before we go any further if you would like to arrange for a lawyer or solicitor to be present?"

Jesus. What the fuck does that mean?

"What? No! I haven't done anything."

"So, you waive your right to a lawyer?"

"Yes, as I said, I haven't bloody done anything. What am I being accused of?"

"Ms Karisson, you're not being accused of anything at this point. Now, we spoke to your mother, and she confirmed that you did have a phone call on Friday evening."

I answer sharply, "I know, I was there."

"Your mother said the phone call was only around fifteen minutes in duration."

"So?"

He picks up a small note pad and reads from it, "Ms Karisson, you said your phone call with your mother, and I quote, "lasted for a couple of hours."

"Well, it certainly felt like a couple of hours, she *can* go on, my mother."

"You said you ran into William on Friday. What specifically did you talk about?"

"I already told the other officers what was said. Will & I are very good friends, so lots of things."

"William said the conversation was short."

"Well, I guess it was because he was in some kind of a hurry." Struggling to hide my fluster. They spoke to William.

"Could you please tell me the nature of your conversation?"

"Well, I just wanted to know if he was seeing Katrina."

"Why did you want to know that?"

"What does that matter to you?"

"Could you please answer the question, Ms Karisson?"

"… well, if you *must* know, there had been a little incident where I was in a mood and perhaps a little rude and wanted to drop by with a bottle of bubbles to apologise."

"To apologise to whom?"

"To her," The stupid fucking whore with nine lives.

"Ms Karisson, who is 'her?' Do you mean Ms Johns?"

"Yes, fucking Katrina, why does it bloody matter?"

"Do you have a problem with Katrina Johns?"

"She's a SNAKE IN THE GRASS!" I almost hiss this like I am the snake, which is ironic. The irony makes me grin and I look up to see the sergeant frowning at me.

"So, you don't particularly like Katrina Johns?"

"Well, I don't have a fucking choice, do I? Because she's got *him*."

"Who does Ms Johns have?"

"William. She has William and so I have to be nice to her because he's too stupid to see what is right in front of his *goddamned eyes!*"

"Ms Karisson, I'm going to ask you to please calm down."

"FINE!" I know I'm not doing myself any favours but this whore keeps popping up and ruining my life!

"During your conversation with Mr Milburn, did he tell you where either he or Katrina would be that evening?"

"He just told me that Katrina was going to the movies with her daughter, why?"

"Did you ask which cinema?"

"Well, yes, just, you know, conversationally."

"And did Mr Milburn tell you which cinema Ms Johns and her daughter would visit?"

"Yes. So?"

"So, you knew where Ms Johns would be that evening?"

"Well, yes, but it's not like I went and attacked her myself, is it?"

Silence

"What? There were multiple men that attacked her."

"And how, Ms Karisson, do you know that there were multiple men?"

"I don't know. Maybe I heard it on the news? Maybe William told me? I don't know how I know but I heard it somewhere."

"Ms Karisson, this assault has not been covered on the news and Mr Milburne has advised that he did not mention either the gender or number of offenders to you."

"What are you saying?"

"Ms Karisson, could you please explain how you knew it was multiple men who assaulted Ms Johns?"

"Look, this is not about me."

"Ms Karisson, could you please answer the question."

I give him two full minutes of silence and the fucker just stares right back at me for the entire duration. I notice my knee jiggling and curse it for making me look guilty. He asks the question again... like I haven't heard him.

"Ms Karisson, could you please explain how you knew multiple men assaulted Ms Johns?"

"Are you seriously thinking I had something to do with this? I've got better things to do with my time than follow *her* around."

My face feels hot. This prick is not going to railroad me into anything. Fuck him.

"Ms Karisson, could you answer the question."

"No! No more questions. I need to speak with my lawyer because you're trying to trick me into saying I did something that I had nothing to do with".

"Ms Karisson, I am not trying to coerce you or *trick* you into anything. We are asking questions, and we require an answer."

"NOT WITHOUT MY LAWYER!" I shout.

"Ms Karisson, we will be detaining you for a period of time until your legal representative can join us, and we can continue this interview." He looks at his watch, "Interview suspended at…" and he rattles off the time and date. My heart is going nuts in my chest. I think I've dug myself into a hole and now I need to claw my way back out of it.

I don't think this sergeant is so hot anymore. He's a dick.

* * * * *

Three fucking hours later, I'm sitting in the filthy, cold lockup like a common criminal before Luca Spalding finally waltzes in. His suit is impeccable and expensive, his tan is golden and Mediterranean, his shoes are polished to high shine and tap softly as he walks to the cell door. I can smell the red wine on him. He flashes his perfect teeth at me as the guard opens the cell door to allow his entry.

"Hello Samantha, how are you?" Luca looks around for a clean place to sit. Finding none, he withdraws a handkerchief from his pocket, flaps it open and neatly places it on the seat beside me before tentatively sitting down

How do you think I am, arsehole? Glaring icicle daggers at him,

"Gee Luca, I'm just dandy. What took you so bloody long?"

He glances at the sergeant, then back at me, the epitome of patience and entitlement "I was actually at lunch with a client when your mother called. I came as fast as I could, Samantha". Calm as you like. Oh, don't mind me, freezing my tits off in this stinking cell while you swan around partaking in a luncheon. My God this smug arsehole frustrates me.

My eye sockets ache with the drama I put into my eyeroll. "I'm so sorry to have *disturbed* your little tête-à-tête with someone more important, Luca!' This rich arsehole couldn't give a flying fuck about me – he just wants the dollars. Well, he'd better earn his bucks and get me the hell out of this cold cell before I lose it.

The sergeant leads us to the interview room, and we all sit down.

Luca's attention returns to the sergeant, "I will need to consult with my client alone. No recording equipment, please."

"I know the rules, Mr Spalding. The tape was turned off when Ms Karisson requested your presence."

He watches the sergeant leave the room and waits until the door is closed before finally turning his attention to me.

"What is going on, Samantha?"

I detail the police visit to the house.

"Why do the police think you had something to do with this?"

"How do I know? I'm innocent."

"Well, you need to say nothing and admit to nothing. If they had any tangible evidence, they'd have made an arrest by now."

The sergeant gently raps on the door and comes back in. "Can we proceed with the interview?" Luca nods his permission.

The sergeant hits record again and repeats the question for the third time.

"Ms Karisson, could you please explain how you knew multiple men assaulted Ms Johns?"

I sigh loudly to let him know I'm not having fun. "I made an assumption. I don't *actually* know

"That's an odd assumption to make, Ms Karisson."

"Well, it's not really. One guy wouldn't have been enough. It was a simple enough deduction to make."

Silence

"I know nothing about this – why do you keep asking the same questions. I've told you; I don't know why I said it. It made sense that it would be more than one!"

I am pissed off and my voice is getting louder.

Spalding finally finds his voice, "My client has answered the question."

'Mr Spalding, Ms Karisson has not answered the question to my satisfaction." He looks at me, "Previously you said you heard it somewhere. Now you're saying you made an assumption. Which is it?"

"You're confusing me. I don't know."

"So, you had nothing to do with the attack on Ms Johns?"

"That's what I've been telling you. Why the fuck do you keep asking me the same goddamned question?"

"Because you answered differently on two occasions which makes me suspicious."

He stares straight at me. Doesn't say a thing.

"What?" I yell, "I had nothing to do with it. How many ways can I say this? I don't know what you're talking about, I don't know who did it or why. I didn't have anything to do with her attack in the carpark!"

"Ms Karisson, nobody said the attack took place in a carpark?"

"You did"

"No, I did not. Why do you think Ms Johns was attacked in a car park."

Luca barks "I need more time with my client alone please!"

* * * * *

He turns to me, suspicious, "Samantha, do you know anything about this?"

"Oh, come ON! Not you too."

"Well, then you need to stop talking. Just say no. No, no, no. Don't elaborate because you're putting yourself in it. No. Not one word other than NO."

The sergeant doesn't return for a good while. The tension in the interview room is thick.

Ninety minutes later, the good sergeant graces us with his presence. God knows how much this wasted hour and a half will cost me while Luca has been manicuring his perfect nails. The sergeant hits record again like no time has passed.

"Ms Karisson, we have just been granted a search warrant to search your unit. Is there anything you wish to discuss before this search takes place?"

"No." My voice is uncertain. I think of what is in my unit. Shit.

Sergeant Roach stops the interview and leads me back to my cell. Luca follows but I tell him to piss off – I'm not paying him any more money to do absolutely nothing.

44

Closing In

Sergeant Roach takes a moment to celebrate the small victory of obtaining a search warrant for Samantha Karisson's unit, based on her interview.

In her office nook, officers found a small strip of yellow paper taped to the underside of her keyboard. Written on the paper was the URL and password for a chat room, according to the IT guys.

This is a brilliant breakthrough that set his heart thudding. Web experts have already scoped the URL and found a 'red room'. Officers also discovered a crumpled note balled up in the waste bin.

DBRay2 – David Parker Ray No 2 – ToyBox Killer. AKA Sick fuck.

Roach stood in the corner and watched the search. When the discarded paper with DPR2 was found, Roach delved into David Parker Ray or the Toy Box Killer. He had an idea of his fame, an American kidnapper, torturer, rapist, and suspected serial killer. Reading through the details of his depravity and those who helped him execute these crimes made him feel sick in the pit of his stomach. For someone to call themselves DPR2 raised the hairs on the back of the sergeant's neck. He wondered if he had a serial killer on his hands.

Clearly Samantha Karisson had absolutely no idea about cyber security apart from the illegality of the room in question, or she was unaware of the target on her back as an individual who had accessed the URL in question. While she is in custody, she will be safe, but the technicians and web experts need to keep a step ahead of the site and red room creator, if they want to catch him, he thought.

A technician, who had been working on accessing her confiscated phone, called him over.

"Look at this serg."

Scrolling through recent images, the technician had found an image of a screen chat, incriminating someone calling themselves "DPRay2", matching the description on the crumpled note recovered from the waste bin.

Now begins the process of trying to find the sick bastard who has orchestrated this whole disturbing venture and stop him before he commits any further ventures in the Red Room.

Roach climbs in his car ready to return to the station for another chat with Samantha Karisson.

* * * * *

Samantha

The sergeant is back at my cell, ready to lead me to the interview room but we're stuck waiting for Luca to join us.

When Luca arrives, impeccably dressed as always, we are led to the interview room. What the hell have they found?

He hits record and after his preamble, looks at me and asks, "Ms Karisson, have you ever communicated with someone calling themselves 'DPRay2'?"

The blood drains from my face. Oh no, how could he know that.

Did that piece of shit rat me out? I swallow hard, "Why are you asking me that?"

"I'd appreciate an answer please Ms Karisson."

So much for the anonymity of the deep web. How the bloody hell could they know that? I was assured they couldn't find me.

"Look, I want to go home please. Either arrest me or let me go home. I'm done talking."

After a pause, the sergeant stands and says, "Ms Karisson, we are placing you under arrest for suspicion of conspiracy to kidnap Ms Katrina Johns." He asks me to stand and slaps hand cuffs on my wrists behind my back. What the actual fuck?

The sergeant reads me my rights. This cannot be happening. This shit happens to someone else. Not me.

While all this is happening, Luca is just sitting there watching on, silent and letting it happen. I look at him, and yell, "What are you doing? Why are you letting him arrest me?"

Luca shakes his head, "Samantha, I can't stop the police for arresting you. I'll see what I can gather now for your defence." Why am I paying this idiot?

"Ms Karisson, I will return you to the holding cell."

Alarmed, I blurt, "Ok, ok, I want to talk!"

My heart races… I just want to go home. I take a deep breath and sigh it out before starting, "Look, I met some guy down there."

"You met a 'guy' down where?" he uses finger quotes when he says 'guy', like he's never heard the word before.

"Down in the web, you know?"

"Down in the web?"

"Yes, in the bloody deep web. Last time I checked that wasn't illegal to go on the deep web!"

Silence.

Luca slowly turns in his chair to glare at me. I ignore him.

"…and we just got to chatting and he said something about a room."

"A room?"

"Yes, a red room or something."

Sergeant Roach's eyebrows move ever so slightly. He knows something.

"Could you please elaborate on what this red room is?"

"Look, I didn't do anything. I just told them where she would be, and they organised it. I had nothing to do with it. They just needed someone for some entertainment, and I didn't ask questions."

"Why would you tell them of the whereabouts of Ms Johns?"

I feel the heat rise from my neck to my face and flare, like struck match. Spittle flies out of my mouth as I vehemently scream, "because I *hate* her! I wanted her *gone!*"

Suddenly I'm sobbing, and I can't even cover my face because my hands are cuffed behind my back.

45

Justice

Katrina

Beverly has just called with the extraordinary news that the Ice Queen has been arrested for trying to orchestrate my kidnapping and murder. She is pleading not guilty, but the evidence is apparently stacked up against her.

Beverly has had her sobbing friend Jane, Samantha's mother, at her house devastated by the news that her daughter is not only arrested for an insidious crime but refusing to see her or talk to her. She cannot come to terms with it. Phillip was a mess and could not believe that his little princess has an evil bone in her body, maintaining that the truth will come out and it will all be a misunderstanding, although the damage to Sam's reputation will be forever.

I utter in disbelief, "I can't believe she tried to kill me."

"Well, *she* wasn't going to kill you," reminded William, "she hasn't got the guts. She was getting someone else to do it."

"But… why? Because I'm with you? That's just crazy."

"Yep, she's crazy."

Such a cold blooded, evil thing to do. I can't wrap my mind around how close I came to being a statistic. And now there will be a trial and a court case and it's just going to be a nightmare. Add to that, whenever the court case for baby Abby comes up, I'll probably be called as a witness to that too. This is just too much.

William senses my despair and pulls me into his embrace.

* * * * *

Nathan

After hearing about the sick shit that blonde chick was planning for Lucy's Mum, I had a chat to Lucy about what I'd walked in on with my flat mate and what was on his screen that he was beating off to.

Lucy came home with me, and we thought we'd have a bit of a snoop with the other being guard. The weird unit was at uni, and I was supposed to be at work, but I called in sick this morning after waking up feeling a little chesty.

We entered the unit and checked for certain that he wasn't here. His car was missing the unit was quiet. I checked his bedroom anyway.

I opened the door using a cloth Lucy had in her bag to clean glasses with, which made me feel stupid, but Lucy said it's better to be safe than sorry. I looked all around his computer desk and saw a sticky note with a website and a bunch of letters and numbers.

Lucy stated, "that's a URL and what looks like a password."

Feeling kind of dumb because I'm not at all tech savvy, I shrugged at her. Surely if it's something for one of those websites down in the dark web, this dickhead should be taking better care of his shit… but I guess he wasn't expecting me to be home.

Lucy took a photo of the sticky note, and we took off to the police station to have a chat with the cops.

When we explained who I was and why we were there they took us to an interview room and the sergeant joined us. Lucy showed him the photo of the sticky note. The sergeant left the room with Lucy's phone to verify something. He came back and asked Lucy to forward the photo via email, which she did, and asked us to give a statement about what we said and signed it.

I told the sergeant that we would keep it to ourselves and not give the flatmate a heads up, to which the sergeant nodded. Knowing that Katrina is Lucy's Mum, it didn't really need to be said but we were just giving him some confirmation that we wanted to be helpful.

* * * * *

Three days later I opened the door to police with a warrant to check the house. I let them in and waited outside while they did their thing.

I heard Matt inside, very vocal in his surprise. His voice sounded so high I thought he was going to pop a testicle. A little while later I heard him crying. I felt a little sick in my stomach and didn't want him to see me, so I walked a few meters down the road to the bus stop, where I still had a clear view of the yard and sat there to wait.

They came out with brown paper bags containing all kinds of shit, including Matt's laptop. Then they led Matt out and put him in the car, and he was restrained. They were taking him to the station for questioning.

I walked up to one of the police and asked if it was ok for me to leave? The police had no qualms and said they would call my mobile phone when they had finished so I could come back and lock up.

I called Lucy and told her what was going. We met for a coffee in a café near the flat so I could pop home when I got the call.

46

Release

Brian

I don't feel safe. There is an impending doom that keeps raising the hairs on my arms. I've felt it for the last two days. If David knows I'm caught, and I'm sure he does, he will want to keep me quiet, even if it means taking my life. He can not let me be. David knows people… people who will do whatever he wants because he pays them well, and he won't stop… he can't stop. He likes to see people suffer. He is not well.

The guard on tonight keeps checking on me, sneaking a peak. I pretend not to notice but it scares me. I think he means to do me harm. I think he will kill me tonight. I hope it is quick – I don't want to feel pain… pain is not my friend. I imagine what it will be like after I'm dead. I can't wait to see Mum and Dad again. We will have a cup of tea together and a scone in the golden place above the clouds.

When Mr Teabag visited yesterday, I asked for a piece of paper and a pen. I wrote a note to Sergeant Roach. He's a nice man, I like him. He is only doing his job and I need to help him.

After I'd written my note, I took the paper and put it in my pocket and handed back the pen. He is trying to help me, but I can't give him anything. The first hearing is tomorrow. I'll say I'm pleading not guilty.

I have the paper folded very small, wrapped in my cotton pocket that I tore off my pants and I have it wedged in my underpants between my bum and my balls. Apart from being a little gross, I don't want the person David sent to find it, I want the Sergent to get it when they try to find out who killed me.

The lights outside the cell go out – those lights never go out and I can hear some noises that sound like somebody is unscrewing them or something.

I am lying on my side, facing the wall. Out of the corner of my eye, I see a dark silhouette of a man creeping. A small gentle sound makes my spine go rigid. I think it was the key slowly turning in the cell lock. The time has come. I close my eyes and picture my parents. "I'll be seeing you," I whisper to them. The approaching shadow stills and waits, probably unsure if he has been detected… then moves towards me.

I picture the farm how it used to be; the breeze gently moving the grass to and fro in front of us as we take long, slow strides. My dad, my best mate, is whistling beside me, Marty Robbins, of course. I join him, humming because I can't whistle very well. The sun is warm on our backs as we make our way to the chickens to pen them in for the day.

The reek of his sweat fills my nostrils; this is his first kill. I ignore his breath, smelling of coffee and cigarettes, warm on my neck. I try to relax. I will embrace my release. In my head, I whisper to mum and dad 'I'm coming now…'

* * * * *

Sergeant Roach is awakened by his phone, shrilly ringing beside his ear. He grabs it and silences it, whispers an apology to his wife. He tiptoes out of the room to take the call. He recognises the number belonging to the station.

Brian Porter has been found dead in his cell. He allegedly managed to cut his own throat, which Roach finds bloody hard to believe but doesn't say so to the night desk constable. After the cell has been processed by crime scene, he will be transported to the Coroners Court for autopsy; and Roach will reserve his opinion until after that process.

Porter was quiet when Roach last checked in on him before leaving for home last night. He doesn't… *didn't* seem to be the suicidal type, but stranger things have happened, and Roach doesn't purport to know the inner workings of the man.

A remanded prisoner dying while in police custody will bring a whole host of headaches he doesn't need, and internal affairs will be crawling all over the place by the time he gets in. Hopefully CCT footage will shed some light.

Wide awake now, Roach makes his way to the adjoining ensuite to hurriedly shower before starting his day at the brutal hour of four am.

* * * * *

As Roach makes his way to the holding cell, his progress is halted by Larry, the maintenance guy, up on a ladder replacing the fluorescent strip light in the hall. Oddly, he is wearing disposable gloves.

"Hey Larry, did we blow a light?"

Larry looks down at Roach, "Oh hey, serg, no. Both lights have been removed. They've asked me to wear gloves to 'preserve evidence;" he makes finger quotes with his latex covered fingers as he says this. Roach looks up again at the light fixture and sees the smudges; it has been dusted for fingerprints.

Roach feels his stomach clench. "Shit!"

"You can't go down there yet anyway – the crime scene techies are still in there processing, and they've only now taken his body to the Coroner's Court for the autopsy."

Roach turns on his heel and ascends the stairs to the station room, calling over his shoulder, "thanks for the heads up, Larry."

Roach approaches his office to wait for the Internal Affairs Unit to commence his interview. He doesn't have to wait long. His recorded interview commences around thirty minutes after his arrival at the station.

* * * * *

After the interview, Roach ducks out to grab a coffee. Upon his return, he is advised that a call came in from the Coroner's Court.

When Roach returns the call, he learns that a small note was found on Brian's person, discovered during the autopsy, and addressed to the sergeant. As the note is evidence, Roach drives to the coroner's court to see the note.

When he asks where the note was discovered, the coroner looks at him over his glasses and flatly returns, "wedged between the cheeks of his buttocks."

'Creative', Roach thinks.

He takes the neatly penned note and reads through the clear plastic evidence bag:

> To Sargent Roch,
>
> I think sum one is going to kill me becoz I no things. I dont wont to take this to heven.I am sorry were I poot the not. I wontd yoo to get it and not my kiler.
> My bruther is David. He is very sic and duz very bad things. I havent seen him do the things but I seen the rapt things he

brort out of the undergrownd howse after. Wuns when I went clows to the bak dor, I herd a lady screem and it scard me. I ast David abowt it, and he sed that sum chiks luv a ruff root. I think he meens sexy tim. Then he sed to stop spiing on him or hell do me in. That meens to kill me. He sed I am a dirty perv but Im not I promis. I didnt ask eny more qestians.

The farm were yoo came to find me and poot the metol things on my hands wos the farm we grew up on. When my dad dide, David killd all the chooks and the crops. That made me very upset and I cryd a bit. He dug up the grownd and bilt a undergrownd howse that yoo cant see from on the grass unles yoo no wear to look. I have never been in it becoz David wont let me see. There is a door on the sid near the piep stikking out of the grownd. It is a door that gos ova the steps that go down. I have never been alowd in that howse, but I did see the steps onse when David wos down there in the spayce soot with the hoses.

What he brings out of the under howse goes into the wood-chiper and then he taks it away in bukets and poots it in the see. I dont no how meny rapt up things have cum out. I try very hard not to look.

One tim I snuk up wen David wos insid the under howse with the hoses. I fownd the smol, raptup thing that had sum blud on it. That wos when I new his seekrats. It wos the baby. He hert her very bad. I had to tayk the baby. She coldnt go thru the chiper and her famely needs to bery her. I wos so sad after seeing her litle body. I stil cry for her. Children are preshus. I pray for her befor I go to sleep.

I cant tayk Davids bad things to heven becoz he will keep herting pepal, and I hav to let yoo no so yoo can stop him. I am very sory that I wosnt brav enuf to tell yoo while I wos alive. David scars me and I didnt wont him to no it wos me who told the polis. But he nos I took the baby.

Dont wury abowt me, I wont to go. Then the scary nite dreems will stop, I dont wont to spend eny more tim being scard of David. I go to my grave without the secrets now. I am looking forward to seeing my mum and my dad again.

Thank yoo or being nise to me, Mr Roch.
From Brian

This revelation brings a flurry of activity as Roach takes a photo of the evidence and returns to the station to organise his search warrant.

EPILOGUE

Roach wastes no time in organising a search warrant for both the farm premises and the alleged underground bunker.

Tactical Response arrive en-masse to the property and stealthily circle the building. Roach hangs back down the street until he is given the ok to attend via the radio communication in his earpiece. He can hear the proceedings as they occur in real time through the earpiece as he waits patiently for the result. The farmhouse is clear and there is no sign of the suspect David.

The TR team moves out of the house and into the vast back garden, looking for the entrance to the underground bunker. The entrance is located as described by Brian, and what appears to be a body wrapped in a tarp rests beside it. The heavy smell of bleach rises from the bunker and can be detected meters away where Roach stood. TR walks past the wrapped object and the team moves into the bunker.

Urgent shouts bark in the earpiece "get down on the ground and put your hands on your head. GET DOWN, NOW!!!!"

A short while later, the suspect, David, is frogmarched out of the bunker, his wrists zip-tied behind his back, his white hazmat suit billowing around him as he walks. He is loaded into the back of a waiting van and transported to the station for questioning.

TR reports that he was discovered inside the bunker in the white hazmat suit, holding a broom, hosing the bleach from the walls and floor down the drain. The room he was hosing was only partially cleaned due to the interruption, so there is still plenty of evidence left behind however, forensics will pull the drains apart if necessary to find any evidence they suspect has been washed away.

After Technical Response exits the bunker, forensics move in to start processing the bunker. After photographing the outside of the bunker and the wrapped remains, forensics carefully unwrap the object to reveal a body that is so grievously beaten that it is unrecognisable. The face is mashed to pulp and only the one remaining breast and the remnants of what had once been female genitalia identify the gender of this victim as female.

Roach's stomach sinks. He had not seen anything like this in all his years on the force and he hopes to never see anything like this again. His stomach roils suddenly, and he abruptly leaves the residence before the contents of his stomach pollutes the crime scene. He makes his way back to the station to sit in on the interview with the alleged perpetrator of the atrocities that have occurred there.

* * * * *

Clothes, jewellery, shoes, keys, and other personal items were all discovered in a room beside the 'red room', locked in cupboards. All belongings will hopefully shed light on the victims, the poor souls who lost their lives at the hands of these sick individuals. He imagines a few missing person cases will be solved after they sift through the collection but rather than triumph, the thought leaves him numb. They still have the arduous task of informing the loved ones of the deceased.

Inside the locked cupboards, hundreds of tapes were discovered.

The camera gear and computers were seized along with the woodchipper, the boat and the vehicle at the residence, all owned by David Porter. Forensics found bone fragments, teeth, hair, a nipple, the pinkie finger of a child and other small remnants of the once living in the expanse of grass surrounding the woodchipper. Every day reveals another find that adds to the horror of this serial killer and the sick people who eagerly participated in the viewing of the mutilation of the victims.

Numerous participants were connected and revealed, their computers were seized, and their houses searched in a coordinated sting that caught them unawares. The entire operation was kept out of the media until arrests had been made.

* * * * *

David Porter was silent during his entire interview and refused to answer any questions. This behaviour was moot anyway because he was caught red-handed trying to clean up the scene and he had filmed himself front and centre committing the atrocities. The evidence is stacked against him, and he will eventually be charged with seventeen life sentences, one for every victim identified by either recovered possessions, DNA, or dental records.

All officers who viewed the tapes required counselling to cope with the horrors they witnessed, the most horrific involving children and a baby... baby Abby.

Matt Freeburgh was charged with possession of child pornography and a raft of charges for his participation in viewing the acts of rape, extreme violence, and the murder of numerous victims. He is still awaiting his trial.

Samantha Karisson made bail, not deemed a flight risk, and awaited her court appearance for her participation in the attempted abduction of Katrina Johns. Whilst awaiting her initial court appearance, Samantha was discovered by her mother, naked and lying in a pool of her own blood on her bathroom floor. Her cause of death was clear; a large kitchen knife was imbedded in her skull, protruding from her right eye.

Although an investigation was undertaken, there have been no updates as to who is responsible for Samantha Karisson's murder. It is suspected that David Porter silenced Samantha Karisson before she could incriminate him further, but this suspicion has not been substantiated with clear evidence.

For a highly intelligent man, David Porter is a little stupid. Everything found in the bunker and on his computer directly links him to the crimes. While nobody has been charged with Samantha Karisson's murder, Roach is hopeful that someday this will change.

* * * * *

There are days when Roach despairs for the depravity of man, and the gravity of the information that has been revealed in this whole nightmare has taken a toll on his health. But on the darkest of days, he finds comfort and solace in the warm affection, love and support of his wife and is pulled from the inky black of evil by the innocence and joy provided by his baby daughter. He took himself to therapy after the case closed, to ensure his state of mental health wasn't compromised by the evil he bore witness to.

Roach has booked a vacation with his family to the Sunshine Coast in Queensland to experience the everyday joys of life taken for granted and afforded to those not involved with seeking justice and dealing with monsters. He continues to serve his city and protect the innocent. Roach and his wife are expecting their second child in Spring.

* * * * *

Katrina

I lay back and rest against William's broad chest as we snuggle on the couch before a fire. The small branches pop and hiss and the room flickers in warm tones of red and orange. The familiar smell of Wil makes me sigh. I'm exhausted by the rush of events that has happened in the last few months.

The Ice Queen is dead. I should feel relief that she can't cause me any further grief but it's a hollow victory. My guess is she was silenced by the man she was organising my abduction and murder with. This shit happens in movies… it doesn't happen in real life and yet it almost did.

Through these connections, a man has been arrested with multiple charges including conspiracy to murder… to murder me. The realisation of what was planned for me plunged me into a state of deep despair that I struggled to rise from. Wil has been a pillar of strength and calm during this turbulence and so have my kids.

How Samantha could hate me with such ferocity is beyond me, all because she wanted William for herself. And just look at the consequences of this hatred. Now Greg is grieving. Despite all she did to him, he was in love with her, and she broke his heart. Even William has struggled with her murder.

The sick bastard who was responsible for the deaths of so many people in that underground bunker should not be given the privilege of a prison sentence. Like cancer, he should be removed from existence and discarded but I'm not sure I'd be happy with that swift justice either. I'm not sure how I feel about any of it. This awful human shit-stain's brother, who I thought was the murderer of baby Abby, was in fact the brother of the murderer. It turns out he was a good man who shared the same fate as Samantha – a bitter end to silence him.

So, life goes on and we try to keep it as normal as we can. We will endure the trial, when it finally happens - there is a lot to for the authorities to unpack and a lot of work to be done before a trial can begin because this man left a big mess.

But until then, I'll continue to find the good in most things and enjoy the people around me because tomorrow isn't promised, and we should live today for today.

About the Author

Donna Newlands is a married mother of two grown children and lives in Camberwell, a suburb of Melbourne, Australia. She is passionate about writing and looks forward to the day when she can devote herself to it full-time.

"My Year 12 English teacher told me I had a talent for writing and encouraged me to nurture this gift. It took a couple of decades for me to take that advice seriously. With each new book I publish, I harness this gift and embrace it with passion. There's no ceiling to creativity, so I shoot for the stars and hope my work is received warmly and appreciated by readers."

This is Donna's second novel and third book, the first being a memoir.

Also by Donna Newlands
Shit Happens
Threads

You can purchase these previous books via Donna's website,
www.doonamoolands.com